DEVLIN
THE ANCIENT FUTURE

DEVLIN
THE ANCIENT FUTURE

RAY ROONEY

Copyright © 2024 Ray Rooney

The moral right of the author has been asserted.

Apart from any fair dealing for the purposes of research or private study, or criticism or review, as permitted under the Copyright, Designs and Patents Act 1988, this publication may only be reproduced, stored or transmitted, in any form or by any means, with the prior permission in writing of the publishers, or in the case of reprographic reproduction in accordance with the terms of licences issued by the Copyright Licensing Agency. Enquiries concerning reproduction outside those terms should be sent to the publishers.

This is a work of fiction. Names, characters, businesses, places, events and incidents are either the products of the author's imagination or used in a fictitious manner. Any resemblance to actual persons, living or dead, or actual events is purely coincidental.

Troubador Publishing Ltd
Unit E2 Airfield Business Park,
Harrison Road, Market Harborough,
Leicestershire LE16 7UL
Tel: 0116 279 2299
Email: books@troubador.co.uk
Web: www.troubador.co.uk

ISBN 978 1 80514 414 4

British Library Cataloguing in Publication Data.
A catalogue record for this book is available from the British Library.

Printed and bound in Great Britain by CMP UK
Typeset in 11pt Adobe Garamond Pro by Troubador Publishing Ltd, Leicester, UK

A heartfelt thanks to Máire, for everything.

Thank you Caroline Barden, for your fine proofreading. I would like to recognise Matty McKeown's imaginative editing input in the early stages of the book. Brid McElvaney's Irish language translations were essential and much appreciated. I am very grateful to Sue Murphy, for being a willing reader and plot checker. And finally thanks to Kevin Littlewood for his support throughout the project.

CHAPTER ONE

Dawn was breaking and from his flat on the thirteenth floor, Devlin had a fine vantage point for looking out over the sprawling patchwork of allotments, housing estates, trees, industrial parks, high-rises and vacant lots that stretched with little discernible order until the more imposing buildings of the city's centre came into view. The mighty river was alive, flowing and surging through these outlying districts and while he had been engrossed in observing the effects of the increasing daylight sparkling on the old waterway, his attention was starting to waver and other, more pressing thoughts were coming to the forefront of his mind.

Watching the tall and agile-looking Devlin in the half-light, James cleared his throat before he spoke. 'You look like you're master of all you survey.'

'Of course, I could be if I wanted to be,' he said, turning round with a mischievous smile, 'but haven't I other fish to fry? Well, I have to say, I'm amazed to see you at this time of the day.'

'It's early for me, for sure. We're going to see my mother who has been ill. As you know, I am travelling with Ceridwen, but I did not know if you knew that she was actually my half-sister…'

'Now that I didn't know.'

'Yes, we share the same father, who passed on a long time ago. He was a cleric who liked to travel.' James smiled self-consciously, the thinning in his sandy hair showing as he leant his head forward.

'He obviously liked to do more than travel.'

'I asked for that. Anyway, Ceridwen grew up in Wales and I was not aware of her existence when she was younger. I never actually met her mother – my Auntie Gwen. When Ceridwen and I did eventually talk for the first time a few years ago it was great, as we found we had a lot in common. It was a meeting of minds, you could say, particularly when it came to politics. Since then we've kept in touch and been travelling companions on a good few occasions. And by the way, thanks for putting up these weary travellers for the night.'

'Think nothing of it, James. Aren't I one of the few hotels still operating in this part of the city? Mind you, the rates are very pricey. Wait till you get the bill.'

James smiled unevenly, saying, 'Oh, you've got me worried now. I see that Presto the mysterious cat is here. I am assuming that his owner Amir is around too.'

Devlin stroked the cat that had been standing beside him and she immediately responded, curling herself around his legs. He looked up with an amused look in his deep blue eyes, saying, 'They were also blown in, windswept and in transit, somewhere between A and B, looking for rough lodgings. They have been on the camp bed in the work room and I believe they will be leaving tomorrow.'

Looking down and noticing that his host was wearing shorts and trainers, James remarked, 'You look like you are going for a run; I thought you had given that up years ago. Have you got your Recreation Pass?'

'I have and as we are experiencing short supplies again at work and I've been allocated a month off, I'm taking the opportunity to start pounding the streets again. There's a strange mood on me and the jog will do some good.'

'Why the strange mood?' James asked, his wiry figure moving quickly across the room to take a seat by the table, which still contained some dishes from the previous evening.

'Don't be getting so interested,' Devlin said, running a hand through his dark wavy hair, 'though knowing you, you probably will. I dreamed about my mother last night and it was odd, in that it didn't feel like a dream at all – it was like it really happened.'

'You know, there are some strange goings on when it comes to recall. The Regime have developed powers that are not clearly understood and many feel that memory will be the final frontier – once they have got total control of our recollections, they will control us completely. God knows they have manipulated our history already to suit themselves.'

'You are some priest, James. You have a conspiracy theory for everything,' He hesitated a moment before adding, 'The simple truth is I've been cooped up in this flat too much lately and I just need to blow away some cobwebs.'

'Listen to me, Devlin, you stubborn Celt – what I'm saying is you need to be looking after yourself. You know from your involvement years ago how the Regime has long tentacles and doesn't like to let go.'

'OK, the sermon is heard loud and clear. You could say we're singing from the same Celtic hymn sheet.'

'Talking of Celtic matters… There's another reason they are interested in you and that is your nationalistic connections. I've heard there is unrest building again and I wonder what you know of what's going on?'

Devlin looked directly at James and countered with a playful edge to his voice, 'Why, if I did not know you better, I'd think that you were fishing for information. And there is none to be had. Those old sleeping dogs laid down a long time ago.'

'No, of course. I didn't mean to pry,' he replied with a thoughtful expression on his face.

'Good morning, Devlin,' Ceridwen said in a rich Welsh

accent, her blonde hair moving rhythmically as she walked into the room.

'Good morning,' he replied. 'You're looking well. I hope the sleeping arrangements worked out OK for you.'

'Oh, I am fine with a put-me-up,' she responded, a bright expression lifting her fine features. 'You have to let the old-timers have the comfort of the feathered bed, what with all their ailments and everything.'

James looked from one to the other and blurted out in mock outrage, 'I hope ye are enjoying yourselves.'

Devlin moved towards the door, nodding his head and saying, 'Well, it's good to see you both and last night was grand indeed. I'm off for this run before I change my mind. In case you're not here when I come back, I hope your mum's OK, James. Don't do the dishes and pull the door to when you leave... Oh, and feel free to call on your way back.'

'As you insist, I'll leave the dishes, but we might well call,' James called after Devlin as he was leaving the flat.

Striding down the stairs two at a time, Devlin took the old fire exit to leave the building. He had taken to using this largely neglected stairwell of late because the extra exercise appealed to him; he'd just turned fifty and being of a positive nature, he was convinced that challenges lay ahead and therefore it was important to stay in shape.

Leaving the block of flats and jogging easily down the familiar road, he felt a sense of release, the coolness of the early morning air invigorating him. There were different routes that he took, depending on his mood and energy levels; that morning he was going to take the longer one that passed beside the river before moving through the Business Region of the old city. Devlin felt his limbs moving easily from the outset and the rhythm of his breathing fell quickly into place.

Passing the allotments that stretched over a hundred yards from the front of his apartment block, Devlin regarded his plot, which was one of the furthest from the road, being marked out by a particularly high and irregular sequence of canes. He knew that his neighbour Rachel would soon be out diligently working and tending her cultivated stock; as would his other neighbour Denis, who loved to engage them both in conversation. There were already people out there working, but as he was not looking for social engagement he pulled his hood down and ran on. The allotments had become an important feature of the neighbourhood and its local economy, with so many people now having their own holdings. Across the city, the plots had become more numerous following the depopulation caused by the Strickland pandemic, so called because of its perceived mishandling by the politician Lord Strickland.

The Greenall shops and galleries were at the end of the road and, rounding the corner, Devlin noticed a stationary Transkill transporter. He tried to make eye contact with a couple of individuals on board but they did not seem to notice him, gazing blankly out of the darkened windows. He often wondered where they came from and how they were trained, for he knew they had very specialist skills. The unresponsiveness of the Transkill workers was in stark contrast to the migrant farm labourers, who waved readily on their way to the outlying fields.

He was finding his stride and running comfortably as he came to the Village, the political and commercial hub of the area, with the Town Hall, which was the nerve centre of these activities, dominating the main square. Facing the Town Hall was the Market Hall which had a bustling atmosphere, being fronted by many stalls and further along the plaza, were the prominent frontages of the Theatre and the Colosseum sports venue. Surrounding the square was a network of close-knit streets, consisting of shops, offices, work premises and residential housing.

Entering the Inner Suburbs, he was feeling good and breathing regularly. Devlin was moving into an area where a more intense surveillance programme was in operation. Authorised joggers and cyclists were allowed to pass through the Inner Suburbs to get to the river, but he always felt exposed passing the grand detached houses of notable and favoured people. It was the part of the run he least liked and he tended to pick up the pace at this point to enable him to move through as quickly as possible.

Devlin passed the imposing high-rise buildings of the Ascension Party, the political arm of the Regime, and then felt a lovely cool breeze nearing the river. Crossing the bridge, he looked down at the inner dockland area to the west, with its many marinas and apartments, before turning east. To his surprise, a man was begging on the bridge, tucked away behind a buttress with a broad-brimmed hat covering his features.

Devlin smiled and, shaking his head apologetically, said, 'Sorry, Pilgrim, you're out of luck.'

It was unusual to see a beggar in the city centre; it was a throwback to another time. He was thinking about the harsh way the authorities treated people who begged when his attention was drawn to the yachts moored down in the river. The tide was coming in strongly now and the pure white hulls of the yachts were bucking against the current. The noise of the tackle and rigging was ringing out, as if alarmed by the incoming tide, and he thought as he pounded on, *It's too good a day for all those old dark thoughts. Let's just enjoy the morning and let the run do its work.*

He crossed back over the river, passing the old Parliament buildings that would soon be open to visitors. He found the ornate architecture ridiculous and pompous and as he had been brought up on stories of the old clashes between the Celtic nations and the British Parliament, he had always felt a certain hostility towards the place. Leaving those historical buildings behind, Devlin was still feeling a good rhythm to his running and a definite optimism in his spirits.

After the Parliament buildings came the Recreation area, or Reckie, whose only impressive structures were the Ferris wheel and rides of the old fairground. Behind them were numerous stalls and buildings, offering a wide range of interactive and physiological experiences. The most advanced of these offered to take people to "the edge and beyond", but these innovations were viewed very suspiciously by many, as they gave people experiences that were so individually responsive that they could only really be operated by a higher form of AI. Devlin did not even glance down the narrow lanes of Reckie, which were still dormant and would be for many hours to come.

The city was starting to come to life as he ran on into the old Business District. Some of the skyscrapers had been converted to residential accommodation but many retained business and commerce as their primary purpose; the vacant plots that had appeared during the commercial downturn had been converted to parks, complete with transport access areas. He took a detour from his route to go past the Rawlins Building, an older skyscraper built in concrete and darkened glass. Curiosity had drawn him to premises that he had once regularly visited himself and he noticed two women dressed in smart-casual attire and a man in a suit going in through the main entrance. The man in particular caught Devlin's eye; there was something familiar about him, although he could not bring his name to mind. Aspects of the building differed from his recollections and he was certain that the Ground Floor Gallery was a more recent addition. Devlin stopped at an advertising poster as he was attracted to the powerful abstract image, even though it was not a style of painting that he usually liked. He checked the opening times, thinking it was an exhibition he might visit in the coming days, before setting off again at a steady pace.

Leaving the Business District, he headed down the Inner Highway that bordered the Stockdale Estate, known locally as the Stocks. Densely populated and with streets of shanty buildings and old terraced properties, it had a reputation for being the most difficult area for the Regime to maintain its authority in. People who were wanted had successfully gone to ground there for many months and in some cases disappeared altogether. Devlin was starting to feel the effects of the run now and he looked resolutely ahead, concentrating on keeping the momentum going. He was breathing heavily when he turned off the Inner Highway, but he felt a sense of relief upon reaching the outskirts of the Village. The long run through the city and its many districts felt like a psychological journey and even though the Village was not his home, he was relieved to be back in known territory. He chose to avoid the main square this time by going through a maze of backstreets that brought him back out at the allotments.

He was nearing the apartments when his attention was drawn to the unmistakeable figure of Denis, with his dreadlocks and long cardigan, calling from over the road, 'Wow, look at you go, man. You're like a man who's been caught stealing radishes!'

He turned his head and between gasps replied, 'You got me, Denis. I own up – I am the Radish Runner!'

After showering, Devlin was having breakfast in the living area when Amir came in and poured three quarters of a glass of water, as he did every morning. Very slender with short dark hair, he took very considered steps, carrying his drink to a chair by the large window as if he was crossing a stage. He then sat down with great care and after taking two mouthfuls of water, placed the glass on the small table.

Having taken a moment to look out at the city as he usually did, Amir gazed earnestly at Devlin and said, 'Well, my friend, we shall be gone tomorrow, so this is the last morning we have – until the next time comes round.'

'You're right there – though I am not sure time can come round; it's more of a linear thing for me.' Devlin smiled. 'I'm going to miss these philosophical jousts.'

The cat, who had been curled up on a chair, leapt down and walked over with languid steps to Amir, who reached down and slowly stroked her three times. Presto, realising that this was the extent of the physical affection she was going to get, wandered off again to sit in front of the window.

Still watching the cat, Devlin said, 'There is one thing that I have always meant to ask you. How did she get that name?'

Amir was looking at Presto with a proud expression on his well-defined features as she stretched out in the bright morning sunlight, her tortoiseshell fur impressive against the dark floor. She gazed at the two men in turn with a look that was more reminiscent of a dog than a cat, before settling into a comfortable position.

Amir turned to Devlin, saying, 'We are all creatures of habit and she has certainly settled here. In answer to your question, my friend, about the strange name and its origin: it was quite a few years ago now and I had been to the Northlands. Having stayed with some good people there who had had their problems with the Regime, I was travelling back and keeping a low profile. It was summer, a warm night, and being out in the country, I settled down for the night beneath a spreading oak tree, which was a giant of great age. I was very tired from the long day's travelling and slept deeply for many hours until I was awakened by the sound of rain on the tree's leaves. However, you will be glad to hear that the foliage was so dense that I didn't get wet at all and as my blanket was warm, I drifted off back to sleep.

'I woke the next day to a bright sunny morning. I had slept longer than I would do normally and my first instinct was to look down the lane to check that all was well. The air was full of a wonderful chorus of birdsong and, from beyond the dry-stone wall, the baaing of Herdwick sheep. I experienced a great feeling of wellbeing and became aware of another presence very close by. I was pleasantly surprised to see a tortoiseshell kitten curled on the top of my bag, sleeping peacefully. And as she had appeared as if by magic, I said instinctively, "Hey Presto! And here you are."

'There were no houses in the immediate vicinity and as I had some milk with me, I fed her. She settled very contentedly in the top of my bag as I walked along and when I enquired at the nearest house, they knew nothing about the kitten. I didn't ask again and then we travelled south together. And that's how the tortoiseshell kitten became known as Presto.'

'It's lovely and it sounds like a parable or a children's story, Amir,' Devlin said. 'I thought Presto would have a mysterious past. And there's another thing I'd always meant to ask you. Where are you from originally yourself?'

Amir hesitated a moment before answering. 'I was brought up by relatives on the other side of the river. My parents travelled over here from Syria years ago, on one of the old routes. I have been told conflicting stories about what happened to them and where I came into the picture. It's a mystery that in truth has been playing on my mind recently and one I am determined to explore in the near future.'

'I am not surprised there is mystery in your past and it's a search I wish you good luck with. As you are leaving tomorrow, I have planned to have a dinner this evening to send you on your way. Is that OK with you?'

'That would be most welcome. You know all my dietary requirements by this stage, so I know my system is safe in your hands.' Amir smiled shyly at his own remark and he got up to his feet, saying, 'I have a few things to do in the Village today, so I will leave you and Presto to it.'

Amir left and Devlin went and sat in his favourite chair by the window. Laying on the nearby table was an open book; the love of literature that had been so strong in his teenage years had returned of late and he was enjoying reading again. Books were discouraged by the Regime as they obviously contained many ideas that ran contrary to their own, leading to them being considered dangerous. But it was also true that most people had become so used to receiving information in soundbites that the reading of a book represented a daunting challenge; so therefore, through a combination of suppression and apathy, the reading of literature had largely died out.

Devlin was reading a very ancient book, Dante's *Divine Comedy*, which he had "borrowed" from a friend many years previously; he had been attracted to the cover depicting a surreal figure assuming the foetal position. Settling back in the chair, Devlin had to tilt the book towards the window in order to read the faded print on yellowing paper. He was reading in a very slow, systematic way as the book had a very demanding structure; each chapter had a prose introduction, with the action following in poetic form, followed by reference notes about the people, places and historical significances. It was one of the most bizarre things he had ever read, but after struggling with it initially, he was starting to enjoy it in a strange way.

He enjoyed having a leisurely day at home for a change and the planned meal came together quite easily; by the time Amir returned, the table was laid, fine culinary odours filled the air and a feeling of bonhomie pervaded the flat.

Devlin gestured with his hand to the furthest chair by the table and announced, 'Sit down. I hope you have an appetite.'

Amir settled by the table, saying, 'I have and it looks like you have everything under control,' he said. 'Is there nothing I can do?'

Devlin turned towards the window where Presto was sat, saying with an incredulous expression, 'Can you believe this? He comes in when everything is done and offers help.'

The cat opened her eyes slightly and re-adjusted her reclining position. Amir was delighted by the scene and smiled brightly at his host, who proceeded to open a bottle of wine.

'I know you're not a man who is known for drinking,' Devlin said, 'but I felt a bottle was called for. You could say it's a Last Supper.'

'Hopefully not a Last Supper, my friend. Things became very distressful for your Lord afterwards, I seem to recall. I will break bread with you and partake in some wine, as long as it isn't your blood we're drinking.'

Laughing, Devlin poured the wine into the two glasses on the table. 'I'll drink to that,' he said, 'and fair play to you. You know your religions, I'll give you that.'

Amir talked easily as the meal was served up before him. 'I took a great interest in the old religions when I was younger. It's interesting, isn't it – we seem to be looking backward for answers, whereas there was a time when people were looking more to the future.'

'You're so right there,' Devlin agreed, taking his place at the table.

Amir thanked him for the meal and started to eat in his slow, methodical manner. He spoke in the intervals between chewing his food and Devlin was content just to listen.

'Yes, it made perfect sense to look into the classical beliefs. I was a young man looking for answers in difficult days, but the thing that started to resonate with me was the great similarities in the core beliefs of the great religions, particularly when you go back to their origins. There was also the realisation that many of the practices shared a great deal of similarity. It was only the interference of mankind in these great theories, rituals and practices that caused so much division. This was something that made a big impression on me.'

'And tell me, what conclusions did you come to after all this intense thought and research? Did you commit yourself to any one way, Amir?'

'The simple answer is no, but as you might imagine, it is not quite that simple, my friend. Of all the great teachers I read, Guru Nanak, who was credited with founding Sikhism, probably had the greatest effect on me. He emerged from three days' immersed in a river and his first words were, "There is no Hindu and no Muslim." This simple statement was saying there is only one God. If you are asking what I believe in, it would be close to those Sikhist lines of, "To train the mind and senses to recognise the divine light within oneself and within all of creation and to be of service to others."'

'Well, I was with you there, Amir, until you got to that last phrase.' Devlin smiled easily, raising his glass.

'If one is allowed to contradict one's host, you have been of a great service to myself and Presto in providing shelter for us. Also, it was truly a great meal tonight and nothing like a Last Supper, my friend. Very tasty and an occasion I shall remember.'

Amir raised his drink to Devlin, who drained his glass and, refilling it, moved over to the window. He then turned up the volume of the music that had been playing in the background and stood gazing down at the streets bathed in a warm sunset glow. Amir moved over from the table and settled into an armchair, and for many minutes there was no conversation in the room as they listened to a haunting song accompanied by the uilleann pipes. Devlin looked out of the window, totally immersed in the mournful notes that seemed to be playing a lament for the sun setting over the city; a mood that had hitherto been easy and playful had become infused with gravitas. Amir had heard this very old Irish music before in the background or from an adjoining room, but on this occasion, when he could clearly hear its melancholic beauty, he too was deeply impressed. When the song finished, Devlin seemed to come out of a trance and his friend said, 'There is a great power and sadness in that music, just as there is a power and sometimes a sadness in you, my friend. What is the story behind that haunting song?'

Devlin took a few moments to compose himself before answering. 'The song is *Na Connerys*, a very ancient air indeed. It's sung in Irish and tells of three brothers who have been transported to New South Wales, Australia. The song curses the miseries heaped upon the brothers and damns the powers that transported them.'

The next set of tunes to play were reels and though they were much livelier than *Na Connerys*, the heightened mood still permeated the room.

Amir leaned over to stroke the cat, saying, 'I don't understand the language the song was sung in, but when you say it's about transportation, that makes perfect sense. The whole sound fits such an emotional theme so well.'

Devlin's mood, which had been one of preoccupation, now lifted quite suddenly and he laughed, saying, 'Well, Amir, as a nation, the Irish have had plenty of practice singing about transportation and emigration over the centuries. You could say we have perfected the art. The music and the language combine perfectly to convey that essence of loss. You could say they were made for the job.'

'Often I have seen you gazing out of that window and wondered what you were thinking about, but then you have turned around and joked with me. One moment deep in thought and then a few seconds later, the life and soul of the occasion. You have some unusual gifts, my friend.'

'I'm not sure I would call being moody a gift, Amir, but the fact of my being Irish has certainly become more prominent in my thinking of late.'

'Devlin, you know that I am interested in the ancient religions of the world and I know your ancient Celts believed that objects, places and creatures all possess their own spirit. I have met people who have a great Celtic spirituality who have some quite lovely beliefs, such as recognising the huge importance of landscapes, seasonal cycles and thresholds between one space and the next. They believe in acknowledging the gifts and graces we receive, seeing the wonder of everyday things and knowing the importance of close friendships.'

Devlin had a knowing smile on his face when he said, 'You have done your research well, my friend. You could also add to this list the importance of dreams and the seeking out of solitude and silence at times. Oh, and also a tendency to wander.'

'I might have known that you were aware of all such Celtic beliefs, my friend. When I have watched you at the window at dawn and sunset, I have often wondered.'

'I was brought up many years ago a long way from here and lately I've begun to feel the pull of that landscape again, even though I have not been back there in so many years. Your talk of Celtic spirituality I did not expect, Amir. These are beliefs that go back to the ancient times, which still have their place in Ireland today.'

Devlin picked up the wine bottle and offered Amir a refill.

'You know that I can't take the drink, my friend,' Amir politely declined, placing the palm of his hand over the top of his three-quarters-full glass.

'It's a wise man who knows his limits, Amir, so fair play to you. But this talk of Ireland has intensified my mood for sure. So much has happened since I left my home place and as for the future – those ancient Celtic beliefs that I had not thought about for years might well have their place. For so long I have been looking forward, trying to visualise the future, but now it seems that I was looking in the wrong direction. But we shall see, my friend; hopefully both of our journeys have a distance left in them and we can retain the ability to be surprised.'

'That sounds like one of your Irish blessings.'

'If it is, I think it's a contemporary one. But who knows?' Devlin shrugged his shoulders and continued, 'I am going to miss Presto for sure and even our meandering conversations, which have often led to surprising places.'

'If you don't mind me saying, Devlin, I don't think it is us you will be missing really. There are other things clearly playing on your mind and maybe other things you are missing. You are known to have done important things in the past and I'm wondering if there are important things you have yet to do.'

'There's maybe truth in what you are saying, but I am not aware of anything at this time. So let's not get morose – it's been a grand farewell meal. I wish you luck as you're moving on.'

Amir rose from his chair and, placing his half-finished glass of wine on the table, said, 'Some people will always look to you, Devlin. It's the way of it. Some people, like yourself, are capable of doing weighty things and are sure to be called upon. But it is *your* choice, why should you not enjoy your life? I am sorry about the lecture, my friend. Thanks again and hopefully we shall see you soon.'

Devlin ran his hand through his hair and there was a gentleness in his voice. 'Goodnight Amir, and I won't take it as a lecture. Given our shared perspective on Celtic spirituality that's appeared tonight, I will take it as the advice of a friend who I respect. So, all's good and travel well tomorrow.'

Amir's expression was one of contentment going to bed. Presto got up and jumped into the warm seat, moulding herself into the heat of the cushion, purring loudly.

'Purr on, my friend,' Devlin spoke with a reflective tone in his voice. 'Enjoy the night, for there are different days ahead.'

Amir had never asked him what he thought about the politics of the time, recent history or the Regime, and for that reason Devlin never saw him as a threat. Some people found his ways strange, but he found them oddly engaging, so he had always been willing to offer him accommodation.

Devlin looked out of the window again and if you had walked in at that moment, you would have seen how absorbed he was in the view. If you watched for longer, you might have sensed a growing restlessness as he intently examined the cityscape. Looking at different areas, he eventually focused his attention on the Business District, where some of the structures seemed to be illuminated too brightly given their diminished influence and the fact that much of the city lay in a semi-darkness due to power-conservation measures. He was trying to recall the exact street layout of the Business District, both from his memories and the details of his run earlier in the day, when he noticed the silhouette of a building that's most defining feature was that it was virtually unlit. At first glance it looked unfamiliar, but the more he looked at this vague dark shape in the distance, the more he became certain that it was the Rawlins Building. He exhaled slowly and then whispered, 'That's it. That's how you would be, shrouded in a shadowy darkness. I must have deliberately blanked you out of my skyline for these years. Are you still withholding those secrets and pursuing your intense agenda?'

He brought his focus back to the local area where the usual muted lights emanated from the Village, giving the familiar outline of the civic buildings a grand appearance, but he also noticed beside the Town Hall that there seemed to be a pulsing multi-coloured glow. He was puzzled and blinked a few times, clearing his bleary eyes, and when he looked again the light had returned to its familiar amber shade. Devlin put it to the back of his mind, rose wearily from his chair and went to bed.

The following day, he was out early on his plot digging up a batch of carrots, onions and parsnips. Denis appeared in his dishevelled overalls, which made for an amazing sight as they had been patched so many times over the years that Devlin maintained that they could stand up on their own. Even though they dressed very differently, with Devlin wearing working trousers and a worn tweed jacket, you could tell by their body language that they got along very well. The talk between them was always jovial and the banter constant.

On this particular morning, Denis said in his lilting accent, 'Well now, the kettle's going on now in my old shed, so would the early bird who's been catching worms fancy a brew?'

'What sort of brew would that be? As long as it's not laced with any of your fiery water, it will be grand.'

'Well, it's a bit early for that. Even for me,' Denis grinned.

'Watch out you don't get lost in that shed. There are many who reckon it's not a shed but a time machine – you disappear for so long in there.'

Walking away he responded over his shoulder, 'There could be truth in that, so before I retire to the Bronze Age for the day, I'll make that brew.'

Devlin had an even larger batch of produce dug up when

Denis returned with the tea and said, 'You going to the Produce Market in the Village today?'

He put down the spade and reached over, accepting the drink, saying, 'I am. Have you got any surplus veg yourself at the moment?'

'No, not today,' Denis chuckled contentedly. 'You know my family – they see off most everything I grow.'

'They've got a wondrous appetite alright, and isn't that a good thing?'

'It is, Devlin. The growing, the eating and then the resting. That's the old way of it and long may it stay that way.'

Devlin raised his mug. 'Long may it stay that way,' he said. 'Oh, are you OK for baccy?'

'Now that could be handy,' Denis replied, raising his thumb.

Devlin had found himself spending more and more time at the allotment of late, as he enjoyed the easy rhythm of the digging and weeding and he had also felt that working the land was a connection with his past in rural Ireland. Finishing his work, Devlin gathered his produce together, filled the large holding bag and slung it over his shoulder. The way to the gate took him past his friend's holding and Devlin called out, 'I shall see you later – and don't you be working too hard, now.'

Denis responded in a leisurely way, 'This isn't work. No, no, not in this sunny weather. It's a pure pleasure, man.'

'Well, if it's pure pleasure – feel free to enjoy yourself on my plot any time.'

'And deny you the pleasure?' he said, smiling widely as he spoke. 'I just couldn't do that to you.'

Nodding his head slowly to acknowledge that Denis had won this particular verbal exchange, Devlin turned and headed down the path. When he reached the gate, he dropped his heavy bag to the floor near the railings and went on to his flat. He would collect the bag again after lunch, on his way to the Village.

CHAPTER TWO

Devlin strode jauntily along the street as if he hadn't a care in the world, wearing a worn tweed suit of good quality, a casual shirt and a pair of old brogue shoes. Slung over his shoulder was a very large and full holding bag made out of a red netting material, with carrot leaves sprouting out of the top in a bright green plume. If you were to look at him, you could be in no doubt about what business he had in the Village.

The outlying streets of the Village he passed through contained some semi-detached houses but as he neared the centre they were predominantly terraced, with occasional purpose-built modern developments. The tightly packed streets near the centre had a particular charm as they were original Victorian buildings, whose style and character had been enthusiastically maintained by the local residents, many of who had holdings on the allotment. Devlin had a great familiarity with the area, passing the time of day with many people as he went about his business.

Entering the main square, Devlin's mood changed as he had the feeling that he was an actor walking onto a film set, just as the action was about to start. To his left, in front of the impressive Town Hall, was a selection of small stalls selling confectionery and souvenirs, which, even on a warm day, seemed to attract little attention. The smaller Market Hall that stood opposite was constructed during the same era in a complementary style of brickwork and attracted a range of local traders, who sold their goods in a lively manner on the front. The Theatre was adjacent to the Market and its style seemed to jar with the adjacent buildings, being constructed in searing lines of steel, purple glass and concrete. At the far end of the square stood the Colosseum Stadium, the events space with a retractable roof, its entrance imitating the classical lines of Roman architecture. Devlin walked across the square and, looking upwards, smiled in a leisurely way, as if appreciating the clear sky and the fine day. He saluted a stall holder with a wave of his hand and then walked into the Market Hall.

Jenkins stood very erectly at the counter of the Produce Exchange and hailed Devlin in his strong Welsh accent. 'Well, if it isn't one of the leaders of the rebel-rousing Allotments Association. You are welcome with your humble veg.'

Being used to such greetings from Jenkins, Devlin countered, 'We will see how welcome I am, when we see what prices you are offering.'

'The organisation is offering a fair price as always. A fair price to all.'

Hoisting the bag off his shoulder, Devlin placed the carrots onto the scales while Jenkins watched the screen closely. The same process was repeated with the onions and parsnips. When the weighing was done and the overall sum presented, Devlin inserted his card, which was duly credited.

After the transaction was completed, Jenkins leaned over the scales, his ruddy features very prominent, as he said quietly, 'Does it never strike you as strange that at this time, we are still weighing carrots and onions? There's nutrition that is produced in a much more convenient format, which we could be consuming instead.'

'Strange it is indeed, Jenkins, but as a fellow Celt, I thought you'd understand the benefits of us still working the land. Anyway, aren't the allotments feeding half the city now? And besides that – wouldn't you be talking yourself out of a job?'

'There you are – those are the words of the Allotments Association, if I ever heard them. I'm glad you're still in good spirits and fighting the cause.'

Devlin picked up his bag. 'Oh, there's no cause to be fought nowadays, just good veg to be grown,' he said, touching his forelock and bowing slightly. 'Good day to you, Jenkins, until the next time.'

After exiting the Produce Exchange, Devlin stopped to fold his bag on the steps of the Market Hall, taking a few moments to glance around the square before moving off towards the Colosseum. There was a poster advertising an event in a few days' time, which he considered for a few moments before turning to his left down a side street off the square. He walked more urgently now and, turning down a narrower lane, he moved into a district that was called the Leanings – so called because the buildings were of a greater age and for the most part not upright. Devlin passed the Café Jordan where the tall, sandy-haired proprietor Marcel was cleaning down tables and they exchanged cordial waves.

Further along this lane, after a row of houses, was a sprawling licensed premises called the Rainbow. The sign was weather-beaten and if you were to look closely at it, which no one ever did, it actually read "Finnegan's Rainbow". Walking in through the main door, Devlin passed by the grocery shop on the right-hand side and carried on into the bar area, sitting down in an alcove. Quinn, the landlord, a commanding figure with a shock of black hair, came over to collect some empty glasses that had been left on the table.

'There's a few in,' Devlin said. 'Is there something on that I don't know about?'

'There's not as many as I'd like,' Quinn replied with a lazy smile. 'I'm not sure if I can tell you what you don't know, Devlin, but I can tell you we have some mighty traditional musicians who'll be playing soon.'

'That's great,' Devlin responded with a lift in his voice, then enquired casually, 'Have you seen Niall lately?'

'Not for a week or so, but he could be in later.'

'I'll have a tea and a large whiskey, while you're here.'

The Rainbow had not changed since he'd started going there. With the shop in the front and the bar at the back, it was like a rural Irish establishment from the early twentieth century. If you were to walk through its doors, the rambling layout would give the impression of stepping back in time and that was undoubtedly part of its charm.

Quinn returned with the drinks and Devlin said quietly, 'I'm glad you're still going strong. I heard they were looking to close you down – that they weren't impressed with your bookkeeping.'

'Ah, don't you worry yourself, it was only a slight misunderstanding. They just didn't have a grasp of the business model being used here.'

'Well, they're not on their own there!' Devlin replied.

Raising his eyebrow in an amused way, Quinn said, 'Enjoy your drink,' and took himself back to the bar.

Devlin had been thinking about his cousin Niall recently and, knowing that the Rainbow was a regular haunt of his, knew there was a good chance of meeting him there. He also found it easy to relax in the Irish-themed bar, with its Celtic designs on the walls, aged brass light fittings and faded images of ancient, sacred sites. In fact, he found it *too* easy to relax there and so he always made a conscious effort to be alert to what he was saying and to take careful notice of what was going on around him.

As he was drinking his whiskey, he thought about his conversations with Quinn and also with Jenkins at the Produce Exchange. Many people that he knew spoke in an elaborate, even circumspect way and this had become more prevalent in recent times. It was something that had developed in response to, or you could say as an act of defiance against, the very functional language of the Regime. At first Devlin hadn't noticed the trend, which was perhaps understandable, given that he came from a part of the world where a more poetic use of language was commonplace. When this had come up in conversation with Niall, he had said in a spirited way: *'In a society where surveillance is accepted, or even expected, why make it too easy for those who are listening to understand your meaning? Make them work for it.'*

Devlin finished his whiskey and told Quinn that he was going to get some tobacco for a friend, walking out like a man who had an errand to run; out into the tight-knit lanes, where the late afternoon sunlight contrasted with the growing shadows. There was a lull in the activity around the Village as trading had for the most part been completed and many of the retail premises were closing for the day. By the time Devlin returned some twenty minutes later the music had started, the Rainbow was filling up and there was a healthy burble of conversation around the bar.

The alcove where the four musicians were seated had a wooden floor and ceiling, which undoubtedly helped to amplify the music; the rhythm pulsed through the Rainbow and people were keeping time either by tapping their feet or drumming easily on the tables. Devlin got his drink at the bar and as he was on his own, he found a table with two chairs close to the players. Although he had not seen this group before, he really appreciated their very traditional style of playing jigs and reels. After a few sets of tunes, the fiddler brought down the mood by playing a slow air that captivated Devlin and it was near the end of this rendition that Niall approached stealthily, sitting down beside him at the table.

When they were applauding, his cousin inclined his head, saying, 'Does the old music take you back?'

'It takes me back for sure,' Devlin responded brightly, but his tone became mellower as he continued. 'We could be in that little bar out west by the Atlantic, where I had sessions years ago with your Liam. That wouldn't have been long before I left the home place.'

'Oh, I would have only been a cub back then,' Niall commented and, running his hand through his light brown hair, he added, 'It has that power alright, but maybe we are always waiting to be taken back.'

'How are your people doing?' Devlin asked. 'I've not heard much of them for a while.'

'My folks are fine. I'd be more concerned by an old tale about the man from around your home place, who had the head turned by thoughts of fame and fortune and lost touch with the family that had reared him. You could even say, from what I heard, he was a voice lost to the cause.'

Devlin smiled, but there was a sharpness to his gaze as he said, 'Lost to the cause? You would think we were conspirators in a Dublin pub during the old nineteen-twenties War of Independence. Anyway, Niall, maybe that man of yours isn't as lost as you're thinking he is.'

'Well, at least you haven't forgotten your history and I'll take your word about your man.' He paused, fixing his sharp blue eyes on Devlin, before adding in a whisper, 'By my reckoning though, to be conspirators, we would have to be on the same side.'

The set of tunes finished and the cousins applauded loudly together. They conversed in light, gentle tones and if you were to observe the two men, you might think that they were commenting on the music. Devlin continued in that vein, looking directly at the musicians as he spoke slowly in a voice that was just about audible.

'Like the mighty Shannon River, there has been too much water gone under all those bridges to even start on that course of conversation. There are many young men set out from those lands over the centuries. There was always going to be mistakes along the way.'

'Indeed there was. Indeed there was,' Niall repeated and, pointing at Devlin's glass, asked, 'Are you sticking with the Devil's fiery water?'

'Well, as I'm halfway to hell, I may as well stick with the Devil.'

Niall went to the bar, but before he could order the drinks he became involved in conversation with two men who seemed vaguely familiar to Devlin. It was obvious that he knew them well as they fell immediately into a deep discussion and Devlin reflected for a moment on how well his cousin blended into the crowd, dressed in a dark coat, shirt and jeans, before turning his attention back to the music. His was thinking that the drinking sessions with Liam in the west of Ireland were so long ago and he was interested by how vivid the memory of them was, particularly in comparison to some more recent events that seemed to be slipping completely out of his mind. This unpredictability in his memory was something that he'd been monitoring, not least because he had always prided himself in having accurate powers of recall.

Three more sets of tunes were played before Niall eventually returned. 'Sorry about that,' he said, putting the drinks on the table. 'I just got caught up with two old acquaintances at the bar.'

'It's no problem at all. The music's great.'

'It is,' Niall said, sitting down. 'Do you know those fellas?'

After a cursory glance over to the bar, Devlin replied, 'I don't believe I was ever in their company.'

Leaning in close, Niall said quietly, 'I'm going to have to go shortly, but I am wondering, do you still have any links with the Business District? I know you used to be a regular visitor.'

'Oh, no. You're talking a long time ago there, Niall. I lost contact with that side of things years ago.'

'Oh, I just wondered. Anyway, no matter. If by chance you did, you could always let me know.'

Devlin did not respond and they continued to listen to the music for a few more minutes. Then, drinking most of his pint, Niall put the glass down on the table, saying, 'Well, I'll be seeing you soon, cousin. No doubt. It seems that you are closer to us than you have been for a good while.'

The two men shook hands and Devlin slowly said, 'Oh, I have

never been that far away and our paths are sure to be crossing again soon.'

'I'm sure you're right and I hope all is well at the home place.'

Niall moved away and after a quick word with the two men at the bar, he walked energetically out of the Rainbow, talking on his phone.

Deirdre came over to Devlin's table, saying cheerily, 'Well, it's good to see you, stranger. I suppose you could be looking worse.'

'I'm glad to hear that,' he said smartly before asking, 'have you only just started work?'

'They'll not let me out during the day,' Deirdre smiled, her brown, bobbed hair shining as she leant down to pick up the empty glasses. 'Are you on your way?'

'I am indeed. It's been a lovely afternoon, but I wouldn't want to outstay my welcome,' Devlin said, standing up and inclining his head before he walked away.

'Little chance of that,' she replied under her breath, wiping down the table and watching him cross the floor.

Leaving the Rainbow, Devlin was surprised to see that it was early evening; the day seemed to have passed very quickly. The streets that he walked down were running northwards and as they were predominantly terraced houses, they were already largely in shadow. He was in good form as he'd enjoyed having a drink and now he was looking forward to the stroll back to his apartment.

He had been walking for less than five minutes when his device rang and he knew by the unregistered number that it was Amir's old device.

'Sorry we missed you this morning,' he said in his precise, unhurried manner, 'but Presto and I needed to be travelling.'

'Don't worry about that, my friend. As I was out early, I thought I might miss you. Is all going well?'

'We are well on our way now. I would like to thank you again for your great hospitality.'

'It's a pleasure.'

'Goodbye, Devlin, and I hope to see you again in the future.'

'Goodbye, Amir, and safe travelling.'

Devlin was soon at the outskirts of the Village and he was thinking about Amir, as well as other friends of his who were regular travellers. While it was not something that was totally outlawed, it was actively discouraged by the Regime and a valid reason was required for any travel outside of the local area. These restrictions, along with the fact that organised travel had become excessively expensive, were enough to discourage most people, but Devlin knew some very resourceful individuals who were not easily deterred, even though they could face a heavy fine or even incarceration.

He had been walking at a leisurely pace and, reaching the allotments, he stopped and leaned against the railings. The great range of produce and vegetables being grown was highlighted by the setting sun, which shone low across the holdings. There were still some gardeners working late, no doubt reluctant to go indoors on such a lovely evening. His neighbour Rachel had gathered her tools together in a wheelbarrow and was taking one last appreciative look at her plot. The sound of children from the playground on the other side of the allotments could be plainly heard, but it was another sound that caught Devlin's attention. Rooks nested in the tall ash trees that grew alongside the playground and the sound of them returning to their nests was something that he always listened out for. On this evening, a memory came back to him of his mother explaining that when the rooks cawed raucously, they were telling one another stories of the great day they'd had, roving round the countryside. He'd been told at school that the collective nouns for them included a parliament, a building, a clamour and a storytelling, which gave them additional activities and seemed to confirm the mysterious status of these crows. The idea of them being in a parliament, making the laws of the land, really appealed to him and the rooks became special birds in the mind of the young Devlin.

If you were to see him at that moment, you would think that he was appreciating the clamour of the rookery, which he was, but the crows he was seeing were in skies four hundred miles west and forty years beforehand.

'Good evening, Devlin,' Rachel called out from down the path in her bright trilling way, bringing him back to the here and now.

'I am sorry, I was miles away then,' he said, shaking his head. 'I have to say, your patch is looking great as always. Putting me and Denis to shame.'

'Not at all. We're all growing well,' she said, laughing in a self-conscious way in response to the compliment. Her curly white hair caught the light as she walked off down the street.

After watching her go, he looked up at the trees for a few more moments before heading in the other direction. Devlin felt a weariness getting back to the apartment but he was also very hungry, so he laid some bread, cheese and pickle out on the table and began to eat. The day had been enjoyable and the music had been great, but his mood had become more introspective and dark since leaving the Village. Niall's tale of the man leaving his family was a clear warning that all might not be well at the home place and he resolved to make contact with his mother tomorrow. He also wondered about the enquiry about his links with the Business District, as it was clearly a thinly-veiled reference to his past involvement with the Regime. The enquiry was not hostile in any way, which was strange, as Niall had made his opposition to Devlin's involvement clear at the time – believing that he was selling out. The raw emotion of those days came back to him and, pouring a drink, he sat down by the window. He was not normally a person given to reflection, but that night he thought about a decision that was to have such a defining impact on his life.

Devlin had been a very bright student at college and was approached by the Regime to work on the Celtic Regional Programme. The idea was sold to him as a chance to help shape a better future for the Celtic areas and although he had initially been unsure – as he believed in greater autonomy and even independence for those regions – the CRP offered him the chance to improve his people's infrastructure and trade and so he enlisted. He found the work interesting at first and he received excellent feedback about his input into the project. Devlin's ability to think outside the box and challenge the norm was seen as a real asset and the message he got during individual contact sessions was that his work was valued and therefore projections for his future were positive. The thought of moving up the ladder and having more influence appealed to him, as he thought that he would be able to stimulate ideas that would lead to greater autonomy.

It was in the period just before his father's death that he started to have real doubts about his involvement with the CRP. Concerned about the direction the work was taking and questioning certain decisions, he realised that there were limitations to his influence. He understood that being openly critical of the Regime could have implications for his future and so, knowing that he would have to give plausible reasons for resigning, the ones he chose were stress and the level of instability in his life at the time. This seemed to be accepted, with a break to recharge his batteries being suggested, and despite his envisaging all sorts of scenarios when it came to leaving the CRP, in the end it was surprisingly undramatic. He remembered his final individual guidance session before he left; it was facilitated by Don, as they all had been, via a link onto the large screen. Devlin had always found sessions conducted through this technology to be very stilted affairs, so he was surprised at feeling genuinely emotional on that occasion. Don rounded up the session by saying that Devlin's flamboyance could take him far in the organisation, as they needed that sort of flair in order to bring new ideas into the Regime. He even pointed to a possible future role in politics with the Ascension Party and then, in his summing up, it was stated that they realised the conflict that existed between Devlin's aspirations regarding independence and the progress of the CRP. The level of empathy displayed came as a surprise to Devlin and as he walked out, Don's final words surprised him even more: *'You can come back. You don't need to become a stranger.'*

The odd thing about Don's choice of phrase was that it was one Devlin was known for using, but not normally in the work setting. That had troubled him at the time, as had the lengths they seemed to be prepared to go to to convince him to stay. It felt like the Regime had addressed him as an errant teenager, confident in the belief that he would eventually change his mind and return. Devlin was not without ego and prepared to accept that he'd made an impression, but on the other hand, he did not feel he was important enough to be treated as a special case. They had immense powers that they could use, but he was being shown a benevolent side of the organisation – there appeared to be no repercussions from him resigning.

Finishing his drink, he stood up and was about to go to bed when out of the blue the identity of the man he had seen entering the Rawlins came to him. His name was Carr; Devlin had been appointed as his mentor when he'd joined the CRP due to their shared links with the west of Ireland. Devlin remembered some positive conversations with Carr at the time, as he was very enthusiastic and they did indeed have many things in common – in particular Gaelic games.

As he was going to bed, an idea was forming in Devlin's mind that seemed to make perfect sense; he wanted to talk to Carr, to find out what work the CRP was currently doing and what their political agenda was in relation to the west of Ireland. He soon dropped into a deep, troubled sleep, dreaming that Carr and his mother were acting out a scene in the Ground Floor Gallery at the Rawlins. The script was very emotional and his mother's future seemed to depend on the audience's response to her performance. She ended up on her knees, proclaiming that Devlin was a man of great importance and if they followed him, he could change everything. His mother's gestures were very expansive and seemed to be alluding to events far beyond the gallery, but the audience were getting restless and losing interest…

The next morning Devlin did not wake up refreshed, as the residue of unsettling thoughts and feelings from the previous few days were still with him. He stood in the shower for longer than usual to revive himself and in those ten minutes he resolved to contact his mother and to visit the Rawlins. The thought of going to the exhibition in the Ground Floor Gallery appealed to him and, knowing that a call to the home place was well overdue, Devlin decided to take decisive action on both counts. He stepped out of the shower in a positive frame of mind.

He dressed and then after breakfast stood beside the open window, looking down at the streets below and plotting the route he was going to take that day. Devlin used his device to request a visit to the Rawlins and surrounding areas, which was immediately granted. The clouds were high and moving slowly across the sky; it was a good day for a bike ride and he planned to take the most obvious route.

Leaving the flats, he wheeled his bike beside the railings and, noticing that the door to Denis's shed was open, Devlin turned into the allotments. His friend stopped working when he saw him coming.

'Well, you're the action man,' Denis said, pointing to the bike. 'One day running, one day cycling – always on the go.'

Devlin's only reply was to proffer the golden tobacco pouch in his palm.

'God bless the delivery man with essential supplies,' Denis's voice purred with appreciation.

'Oh, I couldn't see the workers going short.'

'I'll see you straight next time, my friend.'

Devlin cycled at a leisurely pace to the Business Region and if you were to see him riding along in his casual attire, you would take him to be a local person enjoying the exercise. He slipped easily into the role, finding that the skill of projecting a different persona came back effortlessly to him. He also found an exhilaration from knowing that there was an element of risk to what he was doing and that he had no idea of the possible consequences of his actions.

He had thought it would be risky to approach Carr when he was arriving for work in the morning, as Devlin was unsure how he would react after all these years and also it would be hard to pass off as a coincidence. Therefore, he decided that since he had a genuine interest in the art exhibition, an afternoon visit to the Ground Floor Gallery would be a much better option. This would give him an opportunity to explore that part of the building and if he did bump into any former colleagues, the narrative that he was interested in his old work department would come easily, as that was certainly true.

Cycling through the Business District, it surprised him to see that there were more people around than he would have expected at that time of day. When he arrived at the Rawlins, he secured his bike to a stand in the large gardened area opposite, where a canvas refreshment parlour was doing a brisk trade selling ice creams. He was warm after the bike ride, so it seemed a very natural thing to join the others in the queue. Waiting, he noticed how well the gardens were maintained. The Rawlins stood directly opposite and it occurred to Devlin that he had never studied it closely in the past, as he had either been in a hurry coming to or going from work. He was struck by its sheer size, matching any of the other skyscrapers nearby, though because of its dull cladding and darkened glass windows, it gave the impression of not being as big. He was convinced that the building had been purposely designed in such an understated way to ensure that it did not attract too much attention.

As he was being served, a couple who had been ahead of him in the queue were standing nearby eating their ice creams. They obviously had an interest in the Business District, as she was pointing out buildings and he was saying what businesses operated in each premises. She had gone through all of the buildings they could see, when as an afterthought she looked at the Rawlins and said, 'What's the story with this dark monster, Pete?'

Pete, who had managed to give some information on all the other buildings, looked it up and down and said in a disgruntled voice, 'Don't know anything about that place. No idea what goes on there – God knows!'

Devlin was amused by the effect that the Rawlins had on this couple. Smiling, he ambled through the gardens, finishing his ice cream, and as he approached the Ground Floor Gallery he had the demeanour and appearance of a sightseer out to enjoy the day. He went into the foyer, passing by a double doorway that was set back to the left, with a *No Public Access* sign above the entrance.

When he entered the gallery, he accepted an exhibition sheet from the invigilator, who was dressed in a formal dark blue suit. 'Do you know Gráinne's work?' she asked.

'I'm afraid I don't,' he replied, glancing around the room, 'but it certainly looks interesting.'

'It's proving very popular. I hope you enjoy your visit.'

Devlin bowed in response, before walking away to view the exhibition.

The large canvasses were very impressive in their sheer scale and he was immediately drawn to them. There was one initially that held his attention, with sections of colour and brushwork that he found particularly appealing. Looking at the leaflet he was startled to read that the title of this work was *Ainspiorad Glór na Maidine* (*The Devil's Morning Glory*). Devlin was surprised as it was the strange name of a cliff-top view that was just down the coast from his home place. Standing back from the painting, there was no doubt in Devlin's mind that this landscape had been painted there, even allowing for his unfamiliarity with its abstract style. He also felt a glow of pride at seeing the title being written in the native Irish language.

He had not meant to become so engrossed in the exhibition and when he checked his surroundings, many people were now viewing the paintings. The public toilets sign caught Devlin's attention in the farthest corner of the room and walking that way, he entered a short corridor that led towards the main part of the building. Without hesitation he entered the gentlemen's and while using the urinal he found he was making a rough calculation of the floor area of the gallery in relation to that of the Rawlins overall. Washing his hands very thoroughly, he made a spur of the moment decision that when he left the toilets, he would turn in the opposite direction and find out where that corridor went.

Devlin turned right when he came out of the toilets and while looking down at the exhibition leaflet in his hand, walked past a *No Public Access* sign. After another twenty yards, the corridor turned to the right and a large set of doors confronted him. He came to a standstill, knowing any attempt to push them open would be futile. The security lights that were set in a box besides the door casing had been on constant red when he'd approached, but they changed to amber, flashing repeatedly for over twenty seconds. Devlin was aware that to stand any longer would be confrontational and was about to turn away when the lights suddenly changed to green and the doors opened. He peered down the anonymous-looking corridor beyond and after a moment's hesitation, he walked through.

CHAPTER THREE

The décor of the corridor was a very subdued light grey colour with dark green skirting, like the one leading from the gallery, and it curved to the left, bringing him to another set of doors, which opened as he neared them. Devlin entered a large hall that was in total contrast to the corridors he'd passed through, as the walls were a fluorescent sky blue and the metal skirting and picture rails were a light ochre shade; large landscape paintings hung on the walls at regular intervals and the space gave the impression of being a gallery.

Exhilarated by the sequence of events that had led him to this point, he breathed in deeply before walking the length of the room. Devlin noticed that the pulse of light in the picture rail moved alongside him and when he retraced his steps, it stayed with him until he came to the fifth doorway on the right, where it stopped. The architrave around the doorway glowed and there was a quizzical expression on his face as he moved his hand towards the handle saying, 'Open sesame.'

The door opened before he had so much as touched it and walking through, he got the distinct feeling that he was crossing over a threshold – which of course he was. The room itself was unremarkable and very much like one of the offices he had worked in all those years ago, with people sitting in front of individual screens. Devlin's entrance had gone unnoticed, so he cleared his throat with a strong theatrical cough and a fair-haired man close by turned around, saying, 'OK, OK, what do you want? A drum roll. Can't you see we're otherwise engaged?'

Devlin smiled. 'Why, if it isn't Chilton. I'm amazed to find you still here.'

'Well, be amazed, because I obviously am,' Chilton said, the lines in his thin face hardening into a fixed smile. 'I suggest you sit down and look into things. You could learn so much here.'

'"Look into things. I could learn so much?" You make it all sound so mysterious.'

'The same old Devlin. You were always a bit of a rebel, but you've come back all the same.'

He was stung by the rebuke and was about to respond, but as Chilton had already turned his back and become engrossed in his screen once more, there seemed no point. Intrigued now, Devlin wanted to know what was holding their attention so completely, so he found an unoccupied desk and sat down. When he viewed the screen it assumed far greater proportions than the external dimensions of the monitor and this gave the sensation that he was entering another world altogether. Initially, he had seen just a blur of swirling colours, but then Devlin could make out what looked like a house. The more he focused on the image, the more the house became familiar to him and then it came to him in a flash of recognition: *That's where I was brought up. It's the home place.*

Devlin's eyes were wide with amazement, not least as he hadn't thought about the actual house in years and would have struggled to remember it in any detail; yet there it was, right down to the crack in the brickwork beneath his old bedroom window and the mark on the fascia boards underneath the gutter that leaked. Everything was so familiar to him that it felt uncanny and sent a shiver down his spine. The sensation of joy was mixed with slight unease, as he noticed that even the front garden was exactly as it should be, right down to the minutest of details: the many native plants and shrubs and the swing in the old oak tree. It was almost too perfect a likeness.

The more he examined the picture, the nearer he seemed to get to his point of focus; the screen was obviously responding to his visual and mental stimulus. Eventually, it was as if he was actually in the garden himself and he saw the unmistakable figure of his mother on her knees, weeding in the corner flowerbed. A wave of pure emotion came over him at the sight of her working away in that thorough manner that was so familiar. The movements of her vigorous body were slightly slower, but besides that, she was exactly how he remembered her.

She stopped her work and turned to look back at the house. Strands of greying brown hair fell across her well-formed face and she smiled warmly in Devlin's direction. He did not know if it was his imagination or not, but something told him that she was reflecting on what was most important in her life: her family, her home and the garden she loved. He was quite certain that she could not see him, but he did get a feeling of being included in her thoughts. It was at this point that Devlin's concentration wavered and the image before him started to blur.

For the first time in what seemed like ages, he took his eyes off the screen and looked around. Nothing had changed. The people around him were still engrossed, causing him to wonder about all the different stories and narratives that were being played out in the room at that very moment in time. A woman nearby with short blonde hair and green eyes looked at him intently for a few moments and even though there was no attempt to communicate through language or gesture, Devlin felt a great strength in her gaze and that they had made a definite connection. Turning away, she blended once more into the company and he detected a different form of activity on his screen, which he knew instinctively was someone trying to communicate. Blurred images of an office environment came into focus, where the woman with whom he'd just made eye contact was facilitating a meeting, dressed in a formal dark green trouser suit.

'I am Elenora,' she said, turning from her work colleagues, who remained inanimate, 'and this is where I used to work. I hope that everything is working out in your scenario and that your mother is OK.'

This is a strange and powerful system, Devlin thought, staring at the screen. *Can she view the images I see, or is she picking up my thoughts? And what does she mean by "hope that everything is working out in your scenario"?*

The remark about his mother immediately raised his concerns and he instinctively thought about her again. The image of Elenora's office disappeared and his home place came into view once more, only this time, two men were approaching the house from down the lane. One was of a very tall stature with short dark hair while the other was of a smaller height and his curly, red locks were much longer. The strange way these men were dressed really caught the eye, with each wearing a long frock coat that would have been fashionable in another age all together; they would not have looked out of place in a Dickens novel. Without hesitation they walked through the creaking gate and while his mother looked up from her weeding, she did not stand up or offer a greeting. It was obvious that she was not in the least surprised to see them at all.

'A good evening to you, Mrs Devlin. It's your friendly representatives from the Foundation, your husband's former employer. Hard at work as always, we see. I hope you are happy – well, not *too* happy, actually… Wouldn't you say, Blake, that a person can be too happy?'

'I'd say she looks as happy as could be expected, given the changing circumstances in the world, Mr Coulthard,' Blake replied, gazing down on his colleague with a concerned expression.

'Yes, what with all the downturns and turbulence.'

Comments flowed between the two men as if they were an

old comic duo, until finally Mrs Devlin spoke. 'Good evening,' she said. 'I don't know about all those high-power things, but I'm happy at this time of year, when the weather is fine and I'm in my garden.'

The two men shared a glance and then they both started laughing as if this was the funniest thing they'd ever heard. 'That's what we love about you,' they sang in unison. 'That's what we love about you.'

Blake was still laughing as Coulthard continued. 'Yes, it's your humour. Mostly unintended, but nonetheless funny, wouldn't you say, Blake?'

Mrs Devlin did not respond in any way to the theatrical performance, but simply looked down and spoke as if addressing the flowers. 'You know I can't pay more. My son's condition is getting worse, my husband's long gone and the meagre savings we had are gone as well. Gone like the seasons of years gone past.'

The two men erupted into laughter once more and then sang again in unison, 'Like the seasons of years gone past. Like the seasons of years gone past.'

Looking up at the two men, she said with an extreme tiredness in her voice, 'You know I can't pay any more. This is my home and I've nowhere else to go. This won't be news to you. You already know everything about me, I'm sure. Everything and more.'

'Well, she was right about one thing in that touching little speech. We do know virtually everything about her.'

'I know even more than has been mentioned so far, Coulthard. Her husband was an accountant for the Foundation for all those years and some of his accounting was a little too creative, if you know what I mean. Yes, a little too creative by half.' Blake stopped at this point, laughing at his own remark. Then, running his hand along his lapels, he added, 'The other thing is Mrs Devlin's eldest son, who has long flown this nest, was a real wrong 'un – let me tell you. He and another lad vandalised the Dexter monument.'

'These are great days, when nothing is truly forgotten. And all these irregularities. More fines to pay, or worse? Why, we do love a good irregularity to get our teeth sunk into, don't we, Blake?'

'Yes, much as this family would like to forget things, nothing is truly forgotten nowadays – much less forgiven. Plenty of work for us indeed.'

He was so focused on what was happening with his mother that he had not noticed that someone else was also observing the scene in the garden. It was only when he readjusted his focus that he realised that a channel of communication had opened up on the outer reaches of the screen, which he knew was Elenora.

'I sensed your anxiety,' she said. 'It was reaching me clearly. We have obviously made a good connection.'

'Anxiety is a good way to put it,' Devlin replied. 'My mother seems to be under threat, but it's so surreal a situation. Did you know about this? I mean, you did say that you hoped my mother was OK, so you must have known something was wrong?'

'I may have picked up concerns that you were projecting, as that can sometimes happen. I can tell that you don't really know what you have walked into here, so I will explain my understanding of the situation. The Regime obviously knew so much about us already and then they developed these screen intelligences that can harness our thoughts and emotions, through which the experiences of our lives can be played out or even extended. We can experience scenarios from our real lives, as well as other aspects of existence that interest us.'

'This is crazy, Elenora. It doesn't make sense. On the one hand my mother is being threatened by these characters from Dickens, which is totally bizarre, but on the other hand the bit about me vandalising the monument is true. That tells me this isn't just a fantasy and that they obviously want her out of her house. It feels so unreal and yet so real.'

'Maybe it is both those things. It is obvious that you feel a strong emotional pull and want to intervene. We can intervene sometimes to alter what is happening and I do know it's possible to ask for help from colleagues in order to avert a total disaster in your life scenario.'

'Is everyone in this room locked into versions of their own lives?'

'Many are, but not all of them. There is someone here called Calder, who is replaying the Football League season of many years ago. He is a Leeds United supporter and he's visiting crucial matches to improve outcomes. He wants to make sure they win the league that year.'

'Now that is crazy. I'm going to have to think about this, Elenora. I realise now that I have the means to reconnect with you. I will be in touch.'

'You do, Devlin. You have very quickly zoned into the peripheral part of the screen and found its functions.'

Leaning away from the screen, Devlin felt a great emotional pull towards his mother and her desperate situation. His younger brother had always suffered bouts of ill health and he knew that there were some doubts about the security of the house, but to hear his mother talk of their plight in those terms took it to an altogether different level. Niall's words in the Rainbow had already put him on alert regarding the home situation and Devlin was planning to ring home later, but he was starting to wonder if he could directly affect the outcome through this world on screen. There was no doubt he was feeling very emotional, but overriding these feelings was another thought.

What I'm seeing here, is it true? Is it actually happening?

Regardless of the truth of the matter, Devlin was feeling the need to respond to the drama that he was seeing played out before his eyes. He briefly considered the possibility that the whole story had been concocted as a way of drawing him back into the Regime, but the thought that kept returning to him was this: *If this situation is real then I can intervene and try to secure the home place and if it is not, then what harm can be done? But I could do with finding out a little more before I act.*

He focused on the screen again and the home place quickly came into view. The two men from the Dexter Foundation were just leaving the garden and his mother watched them go, kneeling in an upright position.

Pausing at the gate, the men turned back around to face her.

'Don't worry, Mrs Devlin,' Blake said, 'we'll see you right. Won't we, Coulthard?'

'Indeed we will. Nothing surer, A little flat in the town for the two of you. Nice and handy.'

'Yes, we'll even sort out your finances. All those long days gardening will be a thing of the past. You won't have to worry about this big old place anymore.'

Standing outside the gate, they saluted informally and said in unison, 'You won't have to worry about this big old place anymore,' before bowing to Mrs Devlin and then to each other, as if they had just delivered a great stage performance. With that, they turned and walked off down the lane, leaving Mrs Devlin knelt in the flowerbed that she'd just weeded.

Devlin zoned back out from the screen and, settling into his chair, made a concerted effort to pull together what he could remember of the difficult years at the home place. As a teenager, he'd questioned why the family didn't own the house when for all those years his father had been the Foundation's senior accountant – a very prestigious positon. It was Devlin's understanding that the bosses at Dexter's had required more 'positive' figures than his father was prepared to submit and that became a major point of contention. The house being visited by representatives from the organisation caused great anxiety for the whole family and he clearly recalled the sense of foreboding that hung over the place at the time. He had always felt he had good reason to feel animosity towards the Dexter Foundation, as in addition to them forcing his father to retire, they also seemed to control everything in the area. The police and the courts had been privatised and their powers eroded to such an extent that they were no more than an administrative body for low-level disputes; while the Foundation had taken over the key functions of the disbanded local council, leaving their representatives free to pursue Dexter's agenda with impunity.

Thinking again about the vandalising of the monument, they were drunk teenagers who didn't care to hide their faces, but despite there being numerous security cameras around, nothing had happened. Why? He had often wondered about it, especially as he, like many people, saw the police as little more than a security arm of the Dexter Foundation. There would have been plenty of footage to serve as evidence, making the lack of a follow-up a complete mystery to him. Shortly after this incident he went away to college and further measures to restrict travel were brought in by the Regime, so trips home became very infrequent.

Devlin then thought about so many things that he had not thought about for years, things that made him feel extremely uncomfortable. When receiving a communication about his dad's death, he could have got permission to travel but he just did not want to go home at that time; he was seriously doubting his involvement with the CRP and did not want to be exposed to hostile questioning from his cousins and neighbours in Ireland. Devlin was not given to harbouring regrets, but if he could go back in time, this was one decision he would definitely overturn.

More thoughts were crowding in on him when he noticed a low pulse on the periphery of the screen. He welcomed the distraction.

'Devlin, its Elenora here. How are you getting on?'

'Was I putting out such a strong vibe? Will other people pick up on it?'

'No, don't worry, it won't reach others. It's because we made such a good connection – and just for your information, these links can be closed off at any time of the host's choosing.'

'Oh I see, that make sense. There is something about this whole thing that I had not thought about before. Have you been following the dilemma I'm having?'

'Couldn't stop myself, Devlin. I'm on the inquisitive side. Also, I worked for a large corporation and I had heard of the Dexter Foundation, even though they weren't in our area. They were not good reports, I have to say.'

'That does not come as a surprise. I've been pondering on something – let me run this past you. What if Dad had something on the Foundation? Something that could incriminate them. Something that he could have talked about while he was alive, but not when dead. It would explain why there was no action taken about the vandalism at the time.'

'Yes, Devlin, it would. Also, it might explain them moving in now to get your mother moved out of the house. It's in such a lovely location. Do they actually own it?'

'I think they do now, though there was a story that it was owned by some local people years ago – the Murrays, I believe, before they left the area altogether. It's all very murky how it changed hands. I don't think we ever owned it, but I'm pretty sure that it was contracted to come with Dad's job.'

'Would your mother know anything about that or the specific dispute your father had with Dexter's?'

'She may, but she wouldn't do anything, as I'm sure she fears for Ben's welfare and losing what they have. You said that I could intervene, Elenora. Is that right?'

'Yes, you can visit your scenario for a few hours, but it is my understanding that if you stay too long – I think it's over four hours – you can't return.'

'I have decided to visit and see if she knows anything that could help change this situation. What exactly do I need to do?'

'You need to get up the image of your home place. Concentrate on the left-hand edge of the screen at the halfway point. You will know you have found it when you experience a pulling sensation, like the draw of a magnet. It will happen suddenly. The sensitivity of the screen intelligence is such that you will materialise out of other people's line of vision. To return, take yourself away from view and gaze left of centre again and you will be drawn back. I must warn you, Devlin, not to become emotionally involved when there – and be prepared as it may be a shock to your mother, as you could appear ghost-like to her. The image transfers are not always perfect. Are you sure about this?'

'It seems totally incredible but yes, I'm sure. I'll contact you when I return.'

Devlin had decided to act decisively, so he immediately re-engaged with his scenario and Mrs Devlin appeared, finishing the weeding in the far flowerbed. Gazing at the left side of his screen, which was in line with the laburnum tree, he felt himself being drawn by a pulling sensation. Devlin did not resist, but just let it carry him until he found himself materialising in the woods on the far side of the lane. It took a few seconds for gravity to take hold, but he was soon standing on *terra firma* and feeling fine.

Walking towards the house, Elenora's warning about not becoming overly emotional came back to him and he stopped to take five deep breaths before entering the gate. Turning her head as he walked down the path, his mother did not react for several seconds, then she extended her two hands towards him in a greeting and they briefly embraced. He got the sense that she was worried they could be overheard or observed, as she said very quietly, 'We had nearly given you up for dead, Michael. Mind, you don't look particularly of this world, I must say.'

His mother still had a questioning look on her face when he said, 'It's a situation that I don't think I can explain at this moment, Mam. I am sure I don't look good to you now – but I'm fine.'

'For years, I always thought of you returning and walking through that gate. In truth, I think I'd nearly given up hope, and then you make this appearance.'

Devlin gazed into his mother's deep blue eyes as her voice faltered, experiencing a deep emotional surge, but he quickly recovered his poise as he knew he had an important task to accomplish. 'There is too much for me to attempt to explain now. The main thing is, I am aware of your situation with the Foundation and them wanting you out of the house.'

'Ah,' she said, almost as a sigh. This expression seemed to convey an understanding and acceptance of the whole situation.

'I need to know some things. When all that trouble started with the Foundation and Dad, do you know what it was specifically about? Whose accounts was he working on? Did he ever talk about it to you?'

Taking a few seconds to gather herself and looking away from him, she spoke in whispered tones, 'They were very strange times and your dad was under a lot of pressure from the Foundation. I guess he wanted to protect us all, so he didn't talk about his work. They started to come around to the house. They tried to make out it was just colleagues visiting, but it was more than that; it was their way of keeping an eye on him. I was there for him, but it was difficult as there was no doubt things had got to him and there were days when we struggled. I know the accounts with the Crossley Corporation were a major concern as he brought a lot of work home at that time. They were involved in some important joint work with Crossley's for the government and there were some areas of contention regarding grants and funding between the two organisations. My understanding was that the Foundation was not showing all of its profits and I suppose there were tax implications that affected the Crossley partnership. Your dad wasn't happy, as he had good contacts with Crossley's – particularly a man named Lockhead, I seem to remember. The whole situation became very tense and Foundation representatives came and cleared out your dad's study. They said they wanted to make sure that important material wasn't lost. They were nervous for sure.'

'Was there anything that they missed when they cleared stuff out, Mam?'

'No, not really, Michael. Your dad was so shaken up by all the trouble that he just seemed to go along with everything they said and in the end accepted the early retirement. I know that we should have got the house with his job, but there was nothing in writing.' She stopped at this point and looked at the house again. She said in a quiet but precise voice, 'If you go into the front room, there are three old art books of the French Collection. In the middle one, there are some sheets of paper stuck down between the dust cover and the book. I have no idea what they are about – probably nothing at all. You know how much he loved art. Anyway, I'm just an old woman mithering away.' She then looked directly at him, saying, 'Are you going to stay?'

'No, I have to be away. I am sorry it's so brief, Mam.'

And it was as if she had known that this would be his answer, for a slow and certain smile crossed her features.

'How is Ben?' he asked. 'I would love to go and see him, but I really need to, you know…' His voice trailed off, but then, looking downwards, he added, 'Could I use the toilet before I go? It's above the front room, as I remember.'

Crossing the lawn, he entered the house and Mrs Devlin cleared away her gardening tools as if she had just been interrupted by a neighbour who needed to use the bathroom.

Leaving the house, he did not see his mother again as she was storing tools away in the garden shed. Devlin walked briskly down the path and across the lane, as he was keen not to encounter anybody else during this visit to the home place. After standing for a few moments in the woods looking at the house and the expansive surrounding countryside, he rested his eye on the left-hand side of the horizon and it was with a great sense of relief that he felt the magnetic pull.

Sitting in front of his dormant screen, Devlin was feeling very emotional having seen his mother and he came to the conclusion that he could not ignore her predicament.

There was a low pulse on the edge of the screen, which he accepted.

'Well, how did it go?' Elenora asked.

'It was a weird experience but of course, you knew it would be.'

'The first time is always momentous, especially when returning home. Are you OK?'

'Oh, I'm fine, Elenora, but I must admit this situation has got to me. These scenarios of our lives projected with the aid of this higher screen intelligence are an addictive thing, I can see that. I am fascinated to know, are they watching our progress, virtual or otherwise?'

'For the most part, there is no need to, unless people stray into the area of being destructive to the Regime, or they are overtly political. All the people here have had, or still have, careers in the organisation. I believe this activity is seen as a leisure stimulus that keeps people on their toes and up to speed with the technology.'

There were many things that he could have asked Elenora about the screen intelligence system, but his mother's pressing scenario was uppermost in his mind and he said, 'Well, your help is much appreciated and the importance of these hours are not lost on me. You said about political things being watched. What if I go after the Dexter Foundation, would they intervene in that?'

'It depends on what level. I looked into their present profile in your absence. They are relatively small now and if you were righting an obvious wrong, such as this, I can't see it being viewed unfavourably. I would imagine, given the representatives who went to see your mother, that it would not take much to frighten them off.'

'I know a man here called Chilton, who was a financier. He moved in these circles, so he may well know something. The papers my dad left hidden in the library seem to show some strange transactions, but it would take a sharper financial mind than mine to make complete sense of them. I'll zone in on him.'

'It sounds like a good plan, Devlin.'

Elenora zoned out and Devlin was about to contact Chilton when he thought, *Everything has happened so quickly. From knowing nothing about this world of screen intelligence, I am now communicating effortlessly in it. It's addictive stuff indeed.* He knew to look to the far right of the screen to make a new contact, but what was strange was that Elenora had not told him how to do this. The sophistication of the system started to dawn on him and the thought occurred to him that his actions were sometimes being prompted by the screen.

Chilton responded straightaway to his communication. 'Why, if it isn't Devlin the rebel.'

'Hello to you, Chilton. I hope life is good on your side of the room.'

'Very good. Have you some sort of a problem? People only seem to make contact when they have a problem,' he said in his harsh, clipped way.

'Well, it's funny you should say that,' Devlin answered knowingly, before proceeding to outline the situation with his mother and the home place.

There was a momentary pause and then Chilton asked, 'Have you got the papers that your father left in the library? If the figures and budgets are laid out in them, it could be very interesting. Lockhead must have been a young man when your father left Dexter's, because I believe he is still at Crossley's.'

Devlin took out the sheets of paper that he'd taken from the library and held them up to the screen. Chilton scanned them through using the holographic copier facility that retained images for thirty-six hours and then communicated, 'Give me a while to look at these calculations. I will be in touch shortly.'

In the time he spent waiting for Chilton to assess the figures, he considered the events that had led him up to this point, double checking that he still wanted to go ahead with this course of action. He then glanced over at Elenora, who was looking at an individual on the far side of the room.

It looks like they have connected as well, he thought.

As she turned her head towards Devlin, he noticed a slight

smile on her face and he gave her a nod. A low pulse had appeared on his screen – it was Chilton.

'Well, Devlin, this is a can of worms you are opening up here. I knew Dexter's could be a little sharp in their practice, but this is very underhanded. They were making profits that they were not declaring to either their partners at Crossley or the authorities. Even though it is a few years ago now, this information would still be of interest, so you probably wouldn't need to involve Lockhead or Crossley's in this matter.'

'You mean, the threat of revealing this would be enough to frighten them off?'

'Oh, I should say so. There is a good market for information like this. I suppose it all depends if you really want to damage them as an organisation.'

'No, that isn't my aim here. All I'm interested in at this point is my mother's security and the house. The unwritten agreement was that she and my dad would own the house, but then Dexter's backtracked. My understanding is that the house was part of the offer they made when they approached him to work for them.'

'Well, that could be easily accomplished I would think, given the information here. Still, you need to get those original figures securely stored away. I could act as your representative, if you want?'

'That would be great. To be honest, I don't really understand the figures in detail.'

It was obvious from the way Chilton responded that he was relishing the situation. 'Dexter's have an information officer, like most of these organisations,' he explained, 'though theirs is actually more like an intelligence officer. They handle the shadier parts of the operation. In a case like this, you would offer a little information, just to show that you have something of value. Then, you make your demand. They will want the original papers in exchange.'

'As long as it's final, that would be OK. I've been thinking about this and Dexter's could even make it public if they want. That way, they could say they have gifted the house to the family of their valued former employee, who did so much for them, etcetera, etcetera. That would also mean they couldn't go back on it.'

'That's good thinking. I didn't know you were capable of such deviousness. I thought you were more of an idealist in the old days, Devlin.'

'Maybe I was then, but this is now. Will you go ahead and contact Dexter's? It's really appreciated, Chilton.'

'That's fine. I'm going to enjoy this. It was the sort of work I spent many years doing, so leave it with me. I am assuming you want this all confirmed and public before we release the originals?'

'Yes, that'd be great. Who would have thought we would be working together like this before this day was over?'

The screen went dormant and Devlin relaxed, thinking about everything that had happened in such a short space of time. Thoughts of the home place led to him reflecting on his childhood and memories of the games of chess that he used to play with his father came back to him. His dad would check the board when he returned home from work and then respond to a move that the young Devlin had spent most of the day working out.

The screen cleared before him and suddenly a chess board was set up, with a game in progress. Devlin looked at the position of the pieces and realised that there was something very familiar about this contest; the aggressive move by the black rook was one that his father would often make. Proceeding to play, he was soon in a deep state of concentration, oblivious to his surroundings. Devlin had no idea how much time had passed when he received an incoming communication from Chilton.

'Well, Devlin, I did enjoy that. The information officer listened to what I had to say about the house and your mother being forced out. Then, when I spoke about the information of past dealings, or should I say non-dealings, with Crossley, he went very quiet. I got the impression that he had some idea of what had gone on. He asked what I was proposing, whereupon I told him that the expectation was that your mother would now own the house as agreed, in exchange for the relevant paperwork. He said he would re-contact me shortly and in no time at all the reply came and, I have to say, his manner was very bright. He said that the representatives of the Foundation involved must have misinterpreted things in the confusion of the times and that it was a lovely idea that your mother should become the owner of the house, as well as any relevant land. The publicity was seen as a great idea and he also said he would inform your mother of the decision this afternoon, as long as you are in agreement.'

'That's great. Well done, Chilton. Give him my agreement to letting Mam know, but stress she shouldn't know that I have been involved in any way.'

'That's great, Devlin. I'll let him know and send you a transcript of this.'

'Thanks again. When they publicise this, I will send over the information they've requested. I won't be needing it then.'

Bringing the chess match back onto the screen, Devlin examined the permutations on the board and figuring that he was only two moves from checkmating his dad, he stood up. Elenora was looking in his direction with a strangely distant expression until he caught her eye and then a bright smile lit up her face. Devlin would have liked to have gone over to shake her hand or even embrace her, but he sensed that such actions were not appropriate in this formal setting. He did, however, speak out loud to her for the first time, saying, 'Chilton's done the deed and my mother won't be going anywhere. Thanks, Elenora.'

'You're welcome. Now you take it easy,' she said, with a slight waving motion of her hand.

Approaching the table where Chilton was sitting, Devlin lifted his thumb in an affirmative gesture and, smiling broadly, said, 'Well, you can definitely say that I owe you one.'

'Oh, don't you worry. I won't let you forget it. My old rebel colleague,' Chilton replied with relish.

'Now, why am I not surprised by that?'

Walking towards the exit, Devlin hesitated before reaching the door, struck by the thought that he'd entered the room with no expectations and now he was leaving feeling a strange sense of satisfaction, after a truly bizarre chain of events. He was also reflecting on how the screen intelligence was far more sophisticated than anything he had come across during his time working for the CRP – and he couldn't help but wonder what other developments there had been since his days working for the organisation.

CHAPTER FOUR

Devlin returned to the gallery and was about to start viewing the paintings again when he noticed the invigilator was stood in conversation with a man. He was surprised to see that it was Carr. Devlin walked decisively forward to engage with his former colleague, who lifted his hand in greeting and smiled uncertainly, saying, 'Devlin, fancy meeting you here after all this time. What a strange coincidence.'

The invigilator bowed slightly and then stood back, allowing the two men to move out through the doors of the gallery and into the street.

'It's good to see you,' Carr said as they stopped at the corner in the warm sunlight. 'Strangely enough, I was thinking about you the other day. I did wonder what you were doing with yourself.'

He responded somewhat mysteriously, 'You could say it's a long story.'

'That does not surprise me,' Carr said, having regained his composure. 'It would be really good to talk, but there is somewhere I really need to be right now. Could we meet again, perhaps even here? Are you free tomorrow at the same time, say, three o'clock?'

'I'm off at the moment, so that should be fine. We could go for a walk.'

As Carr departed, Devlin noticed that there was a youthfulness to his movements; he looked like a man in his early thirties, which he knew was not the case. Walking back across the park to his bicycle, Devlin was unsure how long he had been in the Rawlins, but observing the sun's position, he knew it was now late afternoon and the time he'd spent there amounted to many hours.

The return journey was unremarkable and Devlin took the time to enjoy the exercise, the warm weather and the bustle of the streets. The allotments were still a hive of activity when he got back, but without stopping he rode to his apartment block and, using the lift, took his bicycle up to the flat. He was going to call his mother that evening and the thought of it was causing a bizarre range of emotions to stir within him. It had been a long time since Devlin had spoken to her on the phone and yet he had seen her earlier that day. But had he? The thought of his mother at last owning the home place hung tantalisingly in his mind, but he dared not believe it and now he was more inclined to think the whole drama was just a fantasy concocted by AI. Either way, many questions would be answered by the call.

Later, when the sun was starting to drop in the sky, he heard the rooks coming home to roost and decided it was the right time to talk to his mother. He settled in the chair by the window and with a cup of tea on the table he inserted the number of the home place in his device. There was a delay of a few seconds before the call was activated and it started to ring repeatedly until it was eventually answered by a familiar voice.

'Hello, it's Mrs Devlin here. I'm sorry, I couldn't find the phone.'

There was an echo on the line when he replied, 'It's Michael here.'

'Oh, Michael! This is a wonderful surprise. How are you doing?'

The delight in her voice washed away any awkwardness he might have felt when making the call.

'I'm doing really well, Mam. Though I should have been in touch long before now.'

'Oh, don't you worry yourself about such things, Michael. You're in touch now and that's the main thing.'

'Are you and Ben keeping well?' Devlin's voice went lower as he asked this question.

'I'll be honest, Michael, your brother has not been the best. His health hasn't been good of late. You know he had to give up his job and that was a real blow to him. He does get down at times. I'm fine myself and Miriam is great, she visits us regularly.' Her tone became more upbeat as she talked about his sister. 'Well, this is an amazing day, Michael. I have some great news for you.'

'And what's the news, Mam?'

'It is really amazing. After all the years of worry – would we be able to stay here? – Dexter's have turned around today and said that in recognition of the work your father did for the Foundation, the house is to be signed over to the family. Can you believe it?'

She sounded incredulous and Devlin was stunned by this revelation himself. While preparing for the call he had convinced himself that the scenario played out in the Rawlins was some sort of virtual or illusionary game. Therefore he was not prepared for this news and his mother had to prompt him into responding.

'Michael, are you still there? Did you hear what I just said?'

'Oh, Mam,' he said, gathering himself, 'that is such amazing news indeed. Did you have no notion that this was going to happen?'

'No notion at all, Michael,' she said, clearly still marvelling at the news. 'To be honest, I was expecting the very opposite. They've been putting pressure on us to leave the house by putting up the rent and I was starting to think that Ben and I would have to move into a cramped flat in the town.'

'It is truly amazing.'

'A great day indeed, what with this news and you contacting

at the same time.' She paused a moment, before adding in a more questioning tone, 'It is a great coincidence indeed, or is it more than a coincidence? Do you know anything about this, Michael?'

'Oh, Mam, what could I know about it?' he said with a note of incredulity in his voice, having recovered his composure. 'I'm only doing a bit of casual work over here now. I wouldn't have any influence over such things.'

A period of silence went by before she replied, 'Of course, as you say, dear. Anyway, we are all looking forward to your cousin Thomas's wedding in the coming weeks, he's getting married to the youngest of the Gleason's, Bernadette. It's a great shame you can't be here. There's great excitement about it. There hasn't been a wedding in the neighbourhood for years.'

She spent the next ten minutes relaying all the local news as he relaxed, enjoying the soft inflections in her lovely accent, until finally she said, 'Will you listen to me, talking the hind legs off a donkey. Are you sure you are well, Michael?'

'I'm great, Mam, and all the better for hearing you. I'll be in touch again soon.'

'It's great to hear you say that. I was worried that you were going to become a stranger.'

'Oh, don't worry yourself. You'll become used to hearing from me again, I promise.'

The conversation ended and he settled back in his chair with plenty of food for thought. Life had been drifting recently, but the events of the past couple of days had energised him and he was looking forward to meeting up with Carr tomorrow, fascinated to find out what direction the work of the CRP had taken. Was it one that could lead to greater autonomy in the west of Ireland? Many thoughts and questions crowded in on him, not least concerning the recent events at the Rawlins, and he was beginning to think that some intriguing possibilities could lay ahead. Devlin spent the rest of the evening fully engaged, listening to Irish traditional music and reading, before going to bed early that night.

Waking the next morning after the most restful night's sleep he'd had in weeks, Devlin decided not to go to the allotment that morning. He felt in great form and after breakfast took on a job he'd been meaning to do for months: the mending of a wooden chair. It was a fiddly job requiring both wood glue and pins as the cross piece that held the legs together had cracked and come loose. Many people would have just thrown the old chair out, but Devlin enjoyed working with his hands and had become a keen believer in the idea of making do and mending. When this task was complete, he put the piece of repaired furniture in his workroom to dry and settled down by the window to read more of Dante's *Devine Comedy*.

It was late morning when he realised that his concentration was wavering, as his thoughts were turning to his meeting with Carr that afternoon. He went to look at what was in the fridge for lunch and since he had a busy day ahead of him, he laid out and consumed a substantial meal.

The weather was good and so he left early, thinking that this would give him the opportunity to have another look around the Business District and view the exhibition. As with his previous trip, the journey was uneventful and he reached the Rawlins forty minutes prior to meeting Carr. Having decided to follow the same routine as last time, he stopped in the gardens to secure his bike to a stand near the refreshment parlour and as there was no one queuing he did not have to wait to get served, but this time he strolled with his ice cream along a path that led him to the far side of the Rawlins. He then spent the next twenty minutes exploring the streets on the east side of the building, before returning to the gallery with plenty of time to spare.

Walking into the gallery, he was not greeted by the invigilator as he had been the previous day and he immediately started to look at the paintings. Devlin was drawn to a large canvas that had not initially attracted him, entitled *Tindhreach Aislingí Ársa* (*Landscape of Ancient Dreams*). Standing back from the image that had seemed totally abstract, a sense of the landscape started to dawn on him and although he was not able to place its exact location, he felt he knew this place. He was also intrigued by the title, as it suggested somewhere that was firmly rooted in ancient times and the world of dreams; the connection with Celtic spiritualism was not lost on him. Devlin had become so engrossed in the painting that he did not notice the invigilator, who had appeared by his side, saying, 'These paintings do have the power to fascinate, don't they?'

Devlin turned, saying, 'They do indeed. It's a part of the world I know well.'

'I could see that you have a connection with them, Mr Devlin. Oh, I have a message for you from Mr Carr. He has been unavoidably delayed and won't be able to meet you today. I believe it's due to a family sickness.'

He looked quizzically at the invigilator, who continued, 'His message said you were the gentleman who left the gallery with him yesterday and that's how I knew who you were. He also suggested that you should go on into the Rawlins Building – that it would be beneficial to you. My name is Smith, by the way.'

'I see. That's fine, Smith,' he smiled. 'Thank you.'

Turning away, not showing any emotional response to the change in arrangements, Devlin ambled across the gallery to the toilets. After using the urinal, he washed his hands for over a minute, all the while staring intently at his own reflection in the mirror. He did not know what Carr's motives were for suggesting that he should go on into the building and Devlin was aware it could well be the Regime who were setting the agenda – these were factors that would normally make him cautious about going forward – but his natural curiosity and a desire to find out more about the organisation overrode these concerns and he decided to go ahead. He turned right when leaving the toilets and walked away from the gallery.

Reaching the double doors at the end of the corridor, he waited for the security lights to move from amber to green, which they duly did. Devlin passed through the next corridor and came to the large hall, where people moved about their business between the various rooms. Following the pulse of ochre light in the picture rail he got to the far end, before crossing to the other side and walking back. A man came towards him and the light on the picture rail stopped. Smiling in amusement at this procedure, Devlin noted that it was the opposite doorway to the one he had entered the day before.

The man stopped alongside him, saying in a very genial way, 'Well, it looks like you have found your way, my friend.'

There was a glint in the man's eye and Devlin regarded him carefully for a few moments. He looked vaguely familiar, as if he might have been someone he'd seen around the building years before, though not necessarily a work colleague. He smiled, replying, 'It does indeed. And a very good day to you.'

The man watched him walking into the semi-darkness of a viewing room that was like a small-scale version of a cinema, with plush seating and a large screen. There was also the distinctive smell of popcorn in the air, which Devlin recognised straightaway even though he had not encountered it for a long, long time. He was trying to recall the last time he had smelled that distinctive odour when a voice announced over the sound system.

'Please sit down for a screening of the story of the Celtic Regional Programme.'

Walking down the aisle of the empty viewing room, Devlin chose a seat near the front and as soon as he sat down the film commenced. The story started with the historic years of unrest in the west of Ireland, going back to the armed struggle, which was portrayed as futile. It also showed unrest during the time when the systems of democracy had become dysfunctional in the middle of the twenty-first century, with social media and the internet becoming totally unworkable. The Regime then rose as the organising power, denying access to world-wide platforms to the masses, establishing order out of political and social chaos by dividing society into smaller, functioning components. The areas of space exploration and scientific advancement, which had been faltering badly, were taken on solely by the Regime to ensure their continued progress. He recognised many of the historical figures shown as the story alluded to the political divide between the Regime and the nationalistic leaders. Moving on, the film showed how the CRP had managed to offer the Celtic regions a level of independence appropriate to their financial development. Footage was shown of some CRP officials visiting a crofting community in the Hebrides; they were talking to the fishermen, who demonstrated how they mended their nets, and a younger Devlin was asking them if their catch was sold to the local community or on the mainland.

The film came to an end and he wondered what audience it had been made for, as it had documentary content but the epic scale of a movie. The credits were rolling on the screen when Devlin declared out loud, 'Well, fame at last. I never thought that I would make it onto the silver screen.'

To his surprise, the unseen announcer responded, 'The Celtic Regional Programme has done some very good work and is highly regarded.'

There was a pause after the credits had ended and the lights remained off. Devlin got the distinct impression that the announcer was waiting for him to respond, which he eventually did.

'Indeed, the development of roads, agriculture and fisheries kept the more remote regional economies going through difficult times.'

The lights came back on and the announcer said, 'There has been some very good work done, Mr Devlin.'

Rising up out of his chair, he smiled at the use of "Mr".

'Go through the door to the left of the screen,' the announcer said more formally, 'and we will continue.'

Devlin walked through the door without any hesitation and if you were to observe him at that moment, you would say he looked relaxed, like an employee who was involved in a regular training programme. On the other side was a very large open-plan area, which did not appear to have any outer walls; instead, it had beams of different-coloured light forming the exterior of the space, which gave it the appearance of being a large cubist hologram. In the centre of it was a group of people gathered around a table with a large screen at the front and surrounding portals showing different images.

Devlin approached the group but they did not seem to see him. The conversation among them was very intense and was apparently focused on the matter of fishing rights in the west of Scotland. The announcer's voice from the cinema spoke again. 'This is the current CRP Team. You can ask them about the work they do. There is also an old computer that will relay information to you.'

Sitting down at the computer terminal, Devlin asked, 'What proportion of the taxes paid by the communities of the Hebrides is paid back in fishing grants?'

There was a piping of notes on the portals and the beams of light around the hologram pulsed strongly. The question was relayed to the group in a version of his voice that was slower with a slight mechanical edge to it and the group of people gathered around the screen, immediately starting to discuss the question he'd raised.

'Different rates are set for fishing grants,' a woman dressed in a cream all-in-one suit, who was obviously facilitating the group, opened the discussion, 'depending on the amount of activity in that area.'

'The overall taxation rate has remained at twenty-one percent for the last twenty-four years,' a small man sat beside her added, 'though there were some variations in the years when the catch was particularly bad.'

As he was speaking, information was coming through on the screen next to Devlin, who was impressed by the energy of the group in answering his enquiry. Pictures from the portals were relayed back onto the screen and he found himself enjoying the experience of being involved with the group, with the responsive outer hologram lights making it appear like a large interactive game. He asked many questions of a largely logistical nature before venturing the one that was at the forefront of his mind.

'Are you still holding the regional conventions? What are the issues that local communities are bringing up with regard to a greater level of autonomy?'

When that question was relayed to the group, the light beams sustained slightly longer and there was undoubtedly a delay. The facilitator, who had short brown hair, seemed to consider the request for at least ten seconds and then responded without making recourse to her colleagues.

'We have been asked to provide you with information about the work we're doing. I would say that you have been involved in this work and that is made obvious by the precise nature of your questions.'

'That would indeed be fair to say. I was involved in the early years of the CRP.'

This time, the woman looked around at the rest of the group before answering. 'The relationship with the members of the regional conventions is one of the most delicate areas of our work. This you will obviously know, given your experience. I will answer your question to the best of my ability and as for my colleagues here, I invite them to input at any point they see fit. There is also the possibility that there may be a screen intervention from our colleagues in the Regime.'

At this point, the beams of light pulsed a bright yellow and a jovial voice emerged from the screen.

'You may be sure that we will intervene if clarification is needed at any point. But I doubt it will be. Our fine CRP team has a great understanding of all these things.'

The ambience had changed considerably after he'd asked the

last question, with the lights becoming more subdued, and he had the feeling that he was now in the same space as the group even though they still could not see him.

Without receiving any obvious direction, the members of the CRP all sat down and the woman with short brown hair occupying the head of the table commenced speaking. 'You know the history of this maybe even better than we do ourselves. I am judging from the way you asked your question that you want to know about the political response within the Celtic regions to the current programmes and the Regime.'

The man seated next to the woman said to her, 'There is one point that clearly needs to be made, Kerry, and that is that the response is not uniform. It depends on which area you are looking at.'

She looked away from the group and smiled in Devlin's direction, as if she could in fact see him, and said, 'Yes, it would be good if you specified a region, so that we can comment on how the programme has been received and how the regional conventions have gone.'

'Oh, shall we say the Connaught region of the west of Ireland?' Devlin responded casually.

Kerry turned to speak to a dark-haired man seated at the far end of the table. 'Sienna, that's your area, I would say.'

Sienna, who had not spoken up to this point, answered, 'That is the area I have been heading up, yes.' He paused a moment before continuing. 'The history of this region and particularly its conflicts are well known, so I will not go over old ground. In more recent times, the work of the CRP has been particularly interesting. The convention, and therefore the parties involved in the political process, are very varied in their aims, which makes it a forum that can be contentious. There are representatives from the business foundations, the food producers, community groups and local political parties. As you will no doubt be aware, we have to evaluate the members before they take part, to make sure that it is a workable assembly. At the end of the day, we need to be able to do business.'

Here, the jovial voice of the Regime blared out from the screen again. 'All very true – the right balance must be struck. You will hear the full story from the CRP.'

Sienna started to talk again and it occurred to Devlin that his accent was from the Cornish region. 'You will be well aware of times in the past when there were food shortages in the west of Ireland. The role of the CRP is to create the conditions to enable people to live well, within set parameters that are sustainable. We have coordinated a programme that has stimulated very good outcomes in food, clothes and goods production and this has led to a healthier population. The budget we are working within is set by the Regime and that reflects the tax income and the proportion available to any given area. As you may well be aware, the four monthly convention meetings can be lively affairs, as passionate people make the case for their own particular organisation or industry. We are always at pains to be objective and it is important that we are seen to be fair. The majority of policy decisions are made before the meeting, based on the previous discussions, taking in the input from the Regime, of course. In reality, we gather much information at the convention and then set the policies and finances for the coming period. It is a system that seems to work well. Now, judging by your question, I presume that you are interested in the wider political picture to some extent?'

Waiting a few seconds and taking Devlin's silence as an affirmative, he continued. 'There are parties who pursue a nationalistic agenda, such as the Celtic Movement for Autonomy, who want a greater level of independence for the region, and I think it goes without saying that there are also some who don't agree with them. The past failure of democratic institutions has highlighted the shortfalls in the argument for greater autonomy, in what is a very old debate indeed. I would say that the majority of the people of the West are wary of such talk. The culture of the region has flourished greatly over recent years – the music, the Gaelic Athletic Association and even the language have re-emerged stronger than before, all with the blessing of the Regime. So, while there has always been a call for greater independence, I would say it is a distant one and it comes from a vocal minority.'

Sienna's voice had been gathering momentum as he spoke, to the extent that when he stopped, there was a profound silence, which was eventually broken by the voice from the screen.

'You have spoken with truth and passion. Well done, the CRP.'

Kerry stood up, nodding in agreement, and said, 'Thank you, Sienna. It's good for us to be reminded of the wider agenda and why we're doing what we are doing.'

Another silence descended and realising that it was down to him to bring this encounter to a suitable conclusion, Devlin said magnanimously, 'Thank you for your time and for all the information you have given me. You have a great understanding and passion for the work you are doing.'

Standing, Devlin made his way towards the door, but before leaving the room he paused to look back at the scene once more; the CRP workers were still in their workplace, within the supporting beams of coloured light. *A fascinating sight indeed,* he thought as the cubist hologram was dimming. He knew that if he stayed there long enough, the image would disappear altogether.

He returned to the viewing room; the screen was showing a pattern of various muted colours. He was leaving when the announcer said, 'We hope your visit has been useful.'

The casual smile on Devlin's face did not change in any way in response to the comment from the screen, nor did he alter his steady pace as he made his exit.

CHAPTER FIVE

After leaving the viewing room, Devlin returned to the large hall and walked briskly towards the exit as he did not want to be seen lingering around unnecessarily, even though he felt that he had been given permission to enter the building. Reaching the gallery, he made his way over to Smith, who was sat at the desk, and asked, 'Have there been any more messages?'

'I'm afraid not, no more messages. But I have some good news – Gráinne's exhibition was due to finish this week, but it's now been extended for another three weeks. I'm delighted as it has proved to be very popular.'

'That's great,' he said, turning to face the exit, 'I will no doubt find an excuse for visiting again.'

'I'm sure we'll be seeing you again,' the invigilator called as he left.

Devlin smiled faintly, thinking, *A lot of people seem to be keen that my links to this place are maintained. One way or another.*

Collecting his bicycle, he set off along the sunlit streets of the Business District, looking forward to the gentle exercise on the journey back. He was feeling very alive. The fact that the future was suddenly far less certain was not a concern as he was intrigued to see how current events would work out and if they might open up opportunities he had not foreseen previously.

After riding into the allotments through the main gate, he got off the bicycle and leant it against his shed. Devlin always looked forward to the time that he spent on his plot and this was undoubtedly the place in the city where he felt most at home. He had just changed into his working clothes when he heard the unmistakeable sound of Denis approaching; his neighbour had a weakness in his right foot, causing him to drag it slightly when he walked.

Devlin emerged from the shed, holding his spade in his left hand, saying, 'You nearly caught me working.'

Denis rolled his eyes and laughed. 'What time of day is this to be starting? The early bird's not getting the worms today, especially after he's had some time off as well!'

'True enough, my friend. How have things been in my absence?'

'Well, it's funny you should ask. There's a gathering at the hall this evening – the AA's quarterly meeting. Had you forgotten?'

'I had indeed. What are the hot topics in the veg world these days?'

'I hear that the big talking points will be veg tariffs, our relationship with the traders in the Village and the link with the Anglers' Partnership. Oh, and our links with the Regional Traders Convention.'

Devlin looked at his friend slightly quizzically, before replying, 'Fair play to you, Denis. You really do know what's going on around here. You must be going along yourself, then?'

'I certainly am and it would do no harm for you to come, too. It's been a few years since you last showed your face and we miss that political nous of yours.'

'Now, there's no point resorting to flattery – it just doesn't become you. I'll tell you what, though, I will come down and listen in. Is it still a six-thirty start?'

'It still is, for sure.'

Denis had clearly approached Devlin with the intention of

convincing him to attend the AA meeting and he looked very pleased with himself as he wandered back to his plot. As for Devlin, he had agreed to go initially out of a sense of loyalty to his friend, but when he thought about it, he did have a real interest in how the organisation was getting on.

He dug over the area he had recently taken vegetables from, enjoying the warm sensation of the afternoon sun on his face and the smell of the rich earth in his nostrils. Straightening up from his work, he looked beyond the allotments to the old church hall, which stood under the ash trees; originally groups of Girl Guides and Boy Scouts met there but it had been vacant for years before the AA took it over, and although no formal agreement was ever signed, the local church was happy to give their blessing to the arrangement. Devlin had stood back from the politics of the AA in recent years, figuring that his profile had become too prominent and that it was time for others to do their bit. It was now late in the afternoon and having completed the tasks that he'd set for himself, he gathered his tools together. Devlin was feeling hungry and looking forward to getting back to the flat for something to eat.

He was sitting enjoying his meal at the table when a message came through on his device:

Hi Devlin, we are in the area again, on our way home. Is it OK to call? Ceridwen.

Devlin replied: *I'm out until 8.30, but any time after good. You're fine to stay over.*

That's great, see you later.

He left for the AA meeting feeling in good form. The raucous calls of the rooks rang out in the early evening sunlight. Walking towards the hall, he noted that the exterior was beginning to look rundown, with some missing slates on the roof and the cracked fascia boards in need of painting. A group of people were gathered outside the front entrance, enjoying the last of the sunshine before the meeting commenced, and Devlin exchanged greetings with many of them on his way in. He did not recognise everyone as some were representatives from other areas that had only recently established links with the AA. What was immediately familiar to him was the damp, musty smell of the old building.

The majority of the people seated themselves on an assortment of haphazardly arranged chairs and pews, while others preferred to stand in the aisles. Devlin sat on a rickety old stool situated near the back wall, where he would be fairly inconspicuous but still had a good view of the whole room. The meeting was to be recorded in accordance with the requirements set out by the Regime and the AA also took minutes of their own.

The meeting was run impressively as the agenda was followed closely and those wishing to speak were given an attentive hearing. He listened intently as the points that Denis had mentioned earlier were raised and discussed in depth. The need for the hall to be renovated was also brought up, but people questioned the wisdom of using their limited funds on a building that they did not own and this triggered a lengthy discussion, during which Devlin raised his voice to direct a remark towards Denis, sitting two rows in front of him.

'The organisation has grown so much in the last few years, Denis. Maybe the expectations should change—'

He hadn't even finished the last sentence when the room became quiet and the majority of those in attendance turned to look at him expectantly. Devlin glanced around and, realising that the floor was his, continued.

'Could I just say that the meeting has been well chaired and it's a mighty turnout. I have not attended in years and, viewing things with a certain objectivity, it occurs to me that things have changed quite a bit. The amount of vegetables and flowers going to the Product Exchange has gone up significantly and trade with local merchants is well up too. Looking around the room, there are also many more representatives from other associations now, which is great to see. This hall is only ever used by us gardeners and as the church has long since ceased its involvement, it seems to make sense for the AA to take responsibility for the upkeep. Otherwise, it will eventually fall down and there will be nowhere to meet.'

It was at this point that there could be heard a general murmur of approval, prompting him to add, 'I really wasn't meaning to speak today but,' he paused for a moment, during which there was an expectant silence, and then continued, 'it occurs to me that many of the difficulties brought up about tariffs and links with other organisations are a result of the piecemeal nature of the arrangements that we have. This is no one's fault, it's simply that the AA only had to organise a small number of allotments back when the original charter was agreed. Now, however, most of the veg sold in the Village comes from our local allotments and some even goes out further afield, so why not expand the AA to formally coordinate all local growers?'

This sent another, even stronger, ripple of enthusiasm through the crowd.

'If the AA was to be organised in such a way, it may then be considered for representation on the Regional Traders Convention, which would provide a means of resolving many of the issues raised here this evening. It's something that could be put to the Regime, as it would make life easier for everyone involved.'

Once he'd finished speaking, a discussion ensued that raged around the room for several minutes.

Denis turned to Devlin and, rolling his eyes theatrically, said, 'Well, you've gone and done it now, haven't you!'

Eventually, the chairperson, Kirsty, who was wearing overalls and a chequered shirt, managed to restore order by banging loudly on the table. 'There seems to be widespread approval for the points well made by my predecessor,' she said with authority. 'It is unusual that a contribution like this comes so near to the end of the meeting, but I have had a quick discussion with my colleagues on the board and we have agreed a course of action, pending a unanimous agreement, of course.' She looked over at Devlin before continuing. 'We are proposing that we take a vote on the merging of the different allotments under the AA banner, to improve consistency and communication. If that is successful, we also propose an application to join the Regional Traders Convention.'

Such was the groundswell of agreement, she had to bang the table once again before saying, 'Let's have a show of hands, then. All those in favour?' she asked. Immediately getting an affirmative response, she continued, 'Well, that is clearly carried here, so I will speak to the representatives from other areas after this meeting has been concluded. If they are able to gain the approval of their members, we will proceed to action.'

The mood in the room became jubilant, with many loud cries of "hear, hear!", and when the formal meeting was brought to a close, virtually everyone stayed to discuss what had been agreed.

Kirsty joined Denis outside for a smoke and Devlin followed. They quickly fell into an easy conversation about jobs that needed to be done on the hall and which of those were a higher priority than others, until Kirsty looked directly at Devlin, saying, 'We'll get the agreement of the other areas, of that I've no doubt, but do you really think that the Regime will go for it?'

'I do,' Devlin said with conviction. 'As long as there is no loss of power for them and they know exactly what's going on, they'll see it as a positive. It just needs to be presented the right way.'

'I told him we've missed his political nous,' Denis piped up.

'There is no doubt that you know your way around this stuff, Devlin,' Kirsty nodded, her greying brown hair moving as she asked. 'Are you willing to get more involved again?'

Devlin regarded her with a considered expression before responding. 'I'd rather not at this time – there are other things coming up. You've a good board and you're well fit to handle it.' He laughed and, running his hand through his dark hair, added,

'If you want a chat, you can always come down to the rough end of the allotments and we can convene between the turnips, cabbages and runner beans.'

His speech had been so effective that if you had been in attendance, you might well have wondered if it was really a carefully planned performance, rather than something that had come off the cuff. The truth was that as he walked away from the chatter of the excited hall, he was wondering the same thing himself, as he had not gone to the meeting with the intention of contributing, never mind intervening in such a conclusive manner.

The meeting had lasted longer than he'd anticipated and as a result James and Ceridwen were waiting for him outside the apartment block when he returned. James raised up his hand, from which a bag was hanging, and proclaimed, 'We come bearing gifts.'

'Not some kind of Trojan Horse, I hope,' Devlin said, fumbling around in his pockets for his entry pass.

'Oh, you never know,' James replied with a mischievous glint in his brown eyes. 'There could be anything in this bag.'

'We have been so fortunate with this weather,' Ceridwen said, changing the subject, as they went through the front door and headed for the lift.

'Have you had a good trip?' Devlin asked.

'Oh, fine,' she said.

No one spoke in the lift and Devlin found he was attentive to the mechanism that seemed to be producing a slightly different tone that day. Looking at him, James opened his eyes wide in an exaggerated way, signifying that he was also listening, before smiling in a conspiratorial manner. Devlin gave his friend an amiable expression, then looked blankly ahead.

They entered the flat and Devlin swept his arm round in a grand gesture, saying, 'Make yourselves at home. Feel free to have a shower if you want. It's actually working at the moment and I have power.'

'We will do just that. You're always a great host, it has to be said,' James said, placing his bag carefully on the table.

Ceridwen said, 'I will have a shower, Devlin, if that's OK?'

Devlin was examining the contents of James's bag when he answered, 'Of course – you don't have to ask, Ceridwen. Believe it or not, I already had a meal planned for tonight, but with these additions we will be dining in luxury.' He set to work preparing the lettuce, tomatoes and radishes by the sink, turning his head to ask, 'How is your mum doing, James?'

'She's good really – her powers of recovery are great, especially at such an age. I do get worried about her, but then I'll see her bouncing back again.' He added with a laugh, 'She'll probably see me off at this rate.'

'I would say there's a good chance she will.' Ceridwen was laughing as she added, 'Do you need a hand at all, Devlin?'

'No hand needed here – it's all under control. You can just give me a round of applause afterwards, if it meets with your approval.'

'I'm sure it will,' she said. 'I will go for that shower now.'

'There are towels in your room.'

James took a seat by the window and looked appreciatively out at the view. A few minutes passed in comfortable silence, broken only by the sound of vegetables being prepared, and it was James who eventually said, 'It really is an incredible sight to see from this perspective. You can see all the different districts clearly if you take the time to look. But I'll tell you one thing – it's changed for sure. When I first came south, there was a lot more residential accommodation. And do you remember the old high streets?'

'I do,' he responded, continuing to prepare the food, and the two men fell into an easy conversation about the city and places they had known in their past. It was amazing to Devlin how many locations that had a significance for him that his guest also knew, and he eventually commented, 'It's a small world, alright.'

'It is for sure. Here's me reminiscing away. Are you sure you don't need a hand over there?' James asked.

'Ah now, James,' Devlin exclaimed jokingly, 'at least Ceridwen offered when there was actually some work to be done. I've nearly finished now and I think I heard her coming out of the bathroom, so I'll go freshen up myself.'

As the three friends finished their meal, the wine that James had brought was opened and Ceridwen placed scones on the table. Devlin admired their full shape, with mixed fruit bursting up through the surface, and remarked, 'Well, there weren't any shortages where these were baked. They look a real treat.'

'There doesn't need to be a political discourse on the origins of the scones, Devlin,' Ceridwen said, shaking her head easily. 'Just enjoy them.'

Devlin smiled and refilled their glasses.

'Oh, Ceridwen's a wonder,' James said, leaning back from the table, placing his hands behind his head. 'She baked them at my mum's – God knows where all the ingredients came from. Oh, and I meant to ask you, Devlin, are you still involved with the Allotments Association?'

'It's strange you should ask that. I haven't been for years now, but I went along to a meeting earlier this evening,' Devlin said, before recounting what had happened at the hall.

He finished by outlining the outcomes of the meeting and James just gazed at him for a few moments before commenting, 'It appears you haven't lost the touch then.'

'Oh, I'm not so sure about that,' Devlin said, obviously wanting to change the subject. 'Anyway, what of your latest travels, James? You normally come back with some great stories and conspiracy theories for me.'

'And this time is no different,' James answered, settling deeper into his seat. 'We met a woman named Rowan – she was on the old pilgrim's path to Canterbury with her partner Maggs. We spent a few intriguing hours with them.'

'When you are lucky enough to be travelling, you must always be on the lookout for like-minded souls,' Ceridwen said quietly. 'Folk who take another view on what's happening.'

'Indeed,' James nodded in agreement. 'Rowan told tales of a distant world comprised of three empires, which is something I have heard about before. According to her, there was significant interaction between them, ensuring that they were not in competition with one another, as they realised years ago that if they did not compete in commerce and accepted established territorial borders, there would be no need for conflict. Her belief is that artificial intelligence was central to the running of all three empires, effectively pulling them together into one. Clever stuff, eh?'

'It sounds very interesting,' Devlin said, running his hand along his chin. 'Tell me this, though. Where do the scientific and space exploration agendas fit into this imaginary world?'

'The three empires were persuaded to operate these ventures jointly, on the basis that it made financial sense,' James answered. 'That kind of work is so expensive and they had already come to accept the notion that competition was futile.' Like a barrister, he paused before delivering his closing statement. 'Now, there was little mention of those developments in their media. But the projects and advancements, if you do indeed view them as such, never stopped – in fact, they gathered pace.'

'It wasn't as though the poor of these empires were going to see the benefits of such achievements,' Ceridwen added, 'so no point worrying their simple little heads.'

'You have such a delightfully succinct way of rounding things up, Ceridwen. And James, as always, your hypothetical cases are fascinating. Tell me, did all of that come directly from the lady Rowan?'

'Not entirely,' James acknowledged sheepishly. 'Some parts might have come from other sources and I suppose I must claim some ownership myself – you know I'm a bit of a dreamer.'

'Ah, but dreams can never truly belong to anyone. We just

have to piece together what we can from them,' Ceridwen said, seizing upon the theme before adding thoughtfully, 'They seem to have as great a significance now as they did in the ancient times.'

'You could be right there, Ceridwen,' Devlin agreed.

'Another thing I've heard is there are still some places that are not ruled by any of the three empires,' James recommended. 'Places that, because of their remoteness or harshness of climate, are not an attractive proposition and so, to a large extent, they have been left to their own devices.'

'Aren't they the lucky ones?' Ceridwen whispered.

'I always thought those ideas of small independent lands were just urban myths,' Devlin ventured.

'I thought the same,' James said, 'but then there have always been these distant places where resources are scarce and the populations are too small or insular to ever be considered a threat. I've long been intrigued by the ancient colony islands, like Trista da Cunha, the Sandwich Islands and Diego Garcia.'

'Now you're just showing off,' Devlin protested, opening his deep blue eyes very wide before continuing, 'and you've totally lost me. You'd have to be an explorer or an ancient mariner to find such places.'

'Talking of figures from history, how are you getting on with Dante's *Divine Comedy*?' James asked, having noticed the book that lay under the table.

'Oh, it's some comedy alright,' Ceridwen said wryly. 'It's very much like the farce we are all living through today.'

The conversation meandered on until eventually James got to his feet, saying, 'I'm going to turn in – I'm bushed. Thanks for a lovely meal, Devlin. Goodnight.'

'I thank both you and Ceridwen for your contributions. It was a grand occasion. Sleep well, James.'

Devlin refilled Ceridwen's glass and his own and they were chatting away when his device started ringing. The number was his mother's and he immediately accepted the call.

'Hello Michael,' she greeted him. 'I hope I'm not keeping you from your bed.'

'No, not at all,' he said, as lightly as he could manage. 'It's great to hear from you.'

'I'm ringing to let you know that Ben's not well again. I'm hoping he will be alright, but—'

'Has something changed, Mam?'

'There seems to be significant heart failure, the doctor says, along with the respiratory problems he has always had. Miriam is coming down from Donegal…' Her voice seemed to falter for a moment, but she regained her composure and continued. 'He still gets the seizures and they don't get any easier.' She paused again before adding, 'But you know Ben. We all think things are at their worst and then he rallies once more.'

'Let's hope so. I'm really glad Miriam is coming down and that will be a help. I don't suppose there is anything I can do?'

'Oh, don't worry, Michael. I just wanted to let you know… but here's me talking away. How are you?'

'I'm great, Mam, and I'm really glad you rang. I will call in the next few days to make sure the recovery is underway. Meanwhile, you can tell Miriam to contact me. Are you OK yourself?'

'Yes, don't worry about me. I'm fine.'

'Oh, these are such hard times,' Ceridwen said, looking with concern as Devlin put down his device, 'being parted from loved ones.'

'It's my young brother in Ireland.' Devlin's voice was low, with an air of resignation. 'He's very ill again. He's suffered so much but he's pulled through so many times, let's hope he can do it again. Here's to Ben.'

They each raised their glass and said in unison, 'To Ben.'

Ceridwen stood and placed her glass down on the table. Devlin did the same and there was a moment when they just looked at each other. There was a strangeness to the situation as the hour was late and he had never spent time alone with her before.

'I'm sorry that the good humour didn't last the night,' he said.

'You have been a great host as always and the humour has been as it should be,' she said warmly. 'The most important thing is Ben, isn't it?'

Later, he would try to remember how the embrace came about, as Ceridwen didn't seem to make a forward movement and he certainly hadn't envisioned it beforehand. The hug was prolonged and Devlin put this down to a shared concern for the welfare of his brother on the night. If you were to observe them at the moment, you would assume it was a natural action; something that they had done many times before.

They parted and Ceridwen smiled. 'Goodnight, Devlin,' she said, before adding playfully, 'and sleep tight.'

They had always had good fun together and there was a definite symmetry to their political beliefs, but he had never thought of Ceridwen in any sort of romantic way. But watching her deep blonde hair bouncing loosely as she walked out of the room, he could not help but admire her natural elegance.

Taking himself off to bed, Devlin's thoughts inevitably returned to Ben's latest health scare. The fact that his mother had called made him think that it was serious this time as she had never done this on previous occasions, but there was also a part of him that was pleased she had felt comfortable enough to get in touch.

Devlin didn't have long to mull these things over because he was tired and soon slipped into unconsciousness. In no time at all he was dreaming that he was standing on a large sand hill overlooking the beach, wearing only swimming trunks. He waved to his family, who were camped on a red chequered blanket at the shore's edge. His father waved back and then he saw Miriam paddling in the water, holding Ben's hand as he kicked out wildly at the waves. Bright sunlight was sparkling off the breakers and everyone was smiling.

His mother called out to him, 'It's Michael the explorer, returning again from his adventures to foreign lands.'

Beating his chest, he gave a bloodcurdling cry then, taking giant steps, galloped down to the beach and charging as fast as he could across the soft, warm sand he plunged into the cool, glistening sea.

His father called out in a great sing-song voice, 'There's lunch ready here for all you mariners who have an appetite. Let's have you here, before your sandwiches get cold.'

Tempted by the offer of food, Devlin emerged from the water, close to where his sister and brother were playing. Miriam was smiling brightly, Ben gave him a lopsided grin and the three of them walked out of the sea together.

Kneeling on the edge of the blanket, Devlin looked out at the horizon as he ate. He pointed to a small boat that was bobbing up and down in the distance, appearing and then disappearing with the rise and fall of the swell. 'Dad, it's a mackerel boat,' he shouted triumphantly, knowing that only his father would have noticed it.

Smiling, his father leaned over and gently ruffled his hair. His mother, in a green swimsuit, cuddled Ben, who was nibbling on a chunk of cheese, relaxed in her arms. Picking up a harmonica that had been lying on the blanket, his father played a tune with some very sweet notes. There was no one else on the beach and Devlin was aware of there being a great happiness that seemed to radiate out from the family like sunshine.

CHAPTER SIX

Devlin had breakfast with his guests and arranged to meet them for a late brunch when he got back from the Village; he had agreed to pick up a delving spade and some seeds from the Produce Exchange that morning. Cycling towards the allotments, he whistled a tune that he could not place at first, but then realised it was the one that his father had played on the harmonica.

As he neared the entrance to his plot, he noticed that Rachel was already at work and went over to speak to her.

'Hi Rachel,' he said. 'I'm going down to the Produce Exchange. Do you want anything?'

Straightening herself up into a kneeling position and peering through strands of her curly white hair, she answered, 'Well, there's always the gloves – small for me. Oh, and see if there are any beetroot seedlings and maybe something interesting, like the French running beans, courgettes or kale. I do enjoy growing some different things.'

'I will see what they've got in, Rachel, and get gloves for you and Denis. He's not about yet, but he's always after them.'

'Yes, a couple of types of any interesting seedlings would be good. They'd fit in that basket on your bike.' She paused for a moment before adding, 'Although, with this arrangement of getting things for one another, I'm not sure of who owes what to who.'

'And that's after all the bartering with the Regime, so who knows?' he laughed. 'I do think Denis is keeping a running total. We could check with him next time.'

She smiled very widely. 'Oh, Devlin, I wasn't accusing anyone. It's a lovely arrangement and I am sure the figures will tally. Thanks – and do take it easy in the Village.'

Rachel's parting words caught his attention as he could not remember her advising concern in such a way before; she only usually commented on the growing of vegetables and the weather.

Parked on the outskirts of the Village was a transporter for Transkill workers and judging by the equipment that was being unloaded, Devlin figured that they were communications workers. Looking up at the tinted windows as he dismounted from his bicycle, he noticed a worker who he'd seen before and, catching her eye, he smiled at her. Her response was curious; she met his gaze blankly at first, but then her dark eyes opened wider as if wanting to make contact, before turning her head sharply away. Intrigued by this strange interaction, Devlin gazed for a few moments at the spiky silver hair covering the collar of her overall, but knowing that he could not reasonably expect to engage her further, he remounted and carried on his way.

Jenny, who he knew from the AA, was pulling a cart along one of the streets just off the Square, wearing brown dungarees and a dark blue shirt. Devlin called out to her in passing.

'That's a great load you've got there. I always suspected that those plots in the south end produced more veg.'

Smiling with relish, Jenny's thick brown hair bounced in time with her stride as she replied, 'It's nothing to do with the position of the plot, Devlin. It's just that we're better growers.'

'Oh well, I'm going to the Exchange now, so I'll see if I can get some green-fingered gloves!'

'With you being an Irishman, shouldn't you already have the green fingers?'

Devlin was still smiling when he rode into the Square, but his mood soon changed. His attention was drawn to an area in front of the Colosseum that was clear of people, where a slow-pulsing light was glowing in the mid-morning brightness. He thought that he could make out interlocking lines within the glow, but it was hard to be sure as they were very vague and fading.

The few people who were in and around the Square were very focused on going about their own business and Devlin didn't linger himself when crossing briskly to the Produce Exchange.

'Hello Jenkins,' he said, entering. 'I've no produce for you today. I'm just here for supplies.'

'Oh, that's fine,' he replied. 'I'll see you, then.'

He stopped to give Jenkins a quizzical look, as normally a lively conversation would ensue whenever the two men met. Instead, Jenkins offered nothing but a stony face.

'There aren't many about today,' Devlin remarked. 'Things aren't exactly flourishing.'

'You could say that someone has been weeding the garden,' Jenkins answered, smiling sadly.

'You'll be telling me next there are seasons for these things.'

'There are indeed. There are indeed.'

Devlin carried on to the Supplies Outlet, where the robust figure of John the manager stood commandingly behind the counter.

'You'll be glad to hear that your delving spade has finally arrived,' John said, producing the item, which he laid down on the counter with a resounding thud.

Devlin picked up the spade and, as if he was handling a gun, felt the weight and balance of it.

'It's been a long quest to find it,' John said with a satisfied smile. 'I must admit, I derive a certain pleasure from being able to lay my hands on such an implement. It's for digging turf, isn't it?'

'It is, especially in the old country, but with its long, tapered blade, it's handy for lots of things. It's great for getting out deep roots and you could dig yourself a great narrow trench with it.' Devlin was still admiring the spade when he asked, 'Have you got any interesting seedlings ready for planting?'

There followed a long exchange, with many trays being inspected and commented upon. Eventually Devlin walked away with a full holding bag on his shoulder, two trays of seeds balanced on one forearm and his new spade clasped firmly in the other hand. Glenys and Jenkins were in deep negotiations when he passed them on the way out and the bustling commerce of the Village was back in full swing as he left the building. The fancy goods stallholder, who Devlin had never bought anything from, once again hailed him like a long-lost friend.

He took his time arranging the seed trays in the basket with the gloves and twine and then tied the spade to the crossbar. The late-morning sun shone brightly upon the stallholders and the civic buildings as Devlin walked his bike across the Square towards the Town Hall, from where a familiar-looking man emerged, dressed in a dark grey suit.

'Good morning.'

'Good morning,' the man replied. 'You have a full load there.'

'Oh, don't I know it.'

'You look well for it,' he said and then, glancing over towards the Colosseum, added, 'have a good day.'

'And the same to you,' Devlin said, mounting his bike and riding slowly away. Going through the narrow streets off the Square, he carried on until he came to the Rainbow, where Quinn was sweeping the pavement.

The proprietor stopped working and, leaning on the brush, said, 'It's early to see you.'

'I've been doing big business,' Devlin said brightly, bringing his bike to a halt.

'I can see that,' Quinn replied and then, noticing the spade, he raised an eyebrow, saying, 'Good God, Devlin, I've not seen a delving spade in years, except in the old photos inside the pub.'

'Ah well, someone's got to keep the old traditions alive.'

'Talking of traditions, we have musicians in later, if you're around.'

'A good session is always welcome,' Devlin said, starting on his way again. 'Hopefully I'll see you later. Good luck.'

Cycling away, he swayed from side to side, his heavily laden bike creaking on the old cobbles. He heard Quinn call out after him.

'Good luck to you too, Devlin. You look like you may need it.'

Denis and Rachel were working when he got back to the allotments. Devlin didn't delay when dropping off the seedlings and supplies with them, although Denis did have time to comment on the new delving spade.

'I hear the Transkill workers are coming to install a security screen around that old shed of yours,' he grinned, 'to protect that new spade of yours.'

Devlin made his way back to the flat, where the sweet smell of a meal met him in the hall, along with a babble of conversation. When he entered the living room, James turned around, saying, 'Here he is now, and isn't that perfect timing?'

Ceridwen was putting the finishing touches to the table, the centre piece of which was a brown pot vase containing cornflowers, poppies and fuchsias. The colours of the arrangement had a transformative effect on the whole room.

'That's fantastic,' Devlin said. 'Where did you get the flowers from?'

'Oh, I went out for a walk,' Ceridwen answered, coyly placing a finger on her lip.

'You are wasting your time. She won't reveal her sources,' James commented.

Not taking his appreciative gaze off the table, Devlin said,

'Now that is a spread. New spuds, veg, salad and even some chicken there – and where did you get the pickle from? That's a real treat.'

Ceridwen smiled in a self-assured way before adding decisively, 'I suggest you sit down and eat, instead of analysing how it got here.'

'Then that's what we will do,' Devlin grinned, taking his seat.

'I am sure you are aware that Ceridwen is a Welsh name,' James said, joining him at the table, 'but did you know she was a goddess who had the power to transform herself? A goddess of literature and inspiration – the white, fair or holy one, they call her.'

'I am not surprised.' Devlin looked around, saying, 'She has certainly transformed this humble table, so why would she not be able to transform herself?'

Placing the teapot down, Ceridwen ducked her head slightly and whispered earnestly, as if letting them into a great secret, 'Well, I may have a bite to eat with you mortals – before I fly off out the window.'

They ate in silence for a few minutes, before James said quietly, 'Isn't it something we all have to be able to do – transform ourselves? I mean, to survive these times, holding body and soul together.'

'Don't you sometimes feel that the whole world is acting?' Ceridwen spoke, developing the theme further. 'What's that old line of Shakespeare's again? "The world's a stage and all the men and women merely actors."'

'I heard of a village and if it staged a drama, it would be a tragic one,' James reflected softly, in between slow mouthfuls. 'On the face of it everything was normal, but the unexplained and unexpected happened just out of earshot – maybe not quite visible, but always there. But the strange thing was that the people who lived there retained their animal instincts for survival and knew that they were under threat. Deep down, like animals laying low, they sensed that a predator was about – they knew it.'

'Talking of Shakespeare, isn't drama an amazing thing,' Devlin said brightly, looking to raise the mood. 'Even though things can be all doom and gloom sometimes, fine oratory can uplift people and often the subtlety of it can be lost on those who are not aware of what is really being said. Many fine speeches are delivered and not fully understood.' He lowered his voice before adding, 'If I were talking to the gods, I would thank them for such small mercies.'

Ceridwen raised her teacup, saying, 'Here's to small mercies.'

James gazed at Devlin and said, 'I have not had that discussion about the gods with you yet, Devlin. Maybe sometime soon… But anyway, how have you been sleeping? Have you been having any unusual dreams?'

'Last night I had a lovely dream about my childhood and slept well enough,' Devlin answered. 'This fine spell of weather would lift anyone's spirits, wouldn't it? So, what are your plans from here?'

'We were just talking about that before,' Ceridwen said, 'and we wondered if we could take you up on your offer to stay another night.'

'Of course,' Devlin replied wholeheartedly. 'I am planning to go to the Rainbow later for some traditional Irish music – Quinn has only the best musicians – if ye fancy joining me?'

'It sounds good, but I'll have to decline. There are two people I have been meaning to look up in the area – old Jacobites like myself. I said I'd see them later.' James spoke quietly when giving this information.

'It's all very mysterious, Devlin,' Ceridwen responded, 'but you know he knows people everywhere.'

'It must be all that priestly work that makes him so popular,' Devlin said. 'People love to hear him preach, you know. I believe you would call them disciples.'

'Oh, you're very funny, my friends.' James feigned offence, while clearly enjoying the moment.

As they began to clear the table, Ceridwen said to Devlin, 'I will join you for the music, if that's alright? It sounds like it could be fun.'

'That's great. It'll be late afternoon when they're on.'

'Enjoy yourselves.' The older man nodded approvingly. 'I'll be back this evening.'

James took his leave shortly after they had done the dishes, carrying a small rucksack on his shoulder. He had continued to be mysterious about the people that he was meeting and although Devlin was not surprised that he did not give an exact location, he found it odd how he continued to be evasive about where he knew the Jacobites from. The only answer he gave when pressed further was, 'Oh, you don't want to know about these reprobates. I'm going back to the old days here. Don't you know how ancient I am?'

'I've got a few things to do myself,' Ceridwen said after James had left, 'and then I'll get changed for this little jaunt to the Village.'

With time on his hands, Devlin sat down in the chair by the window, picked up Dante's *Devine Comedy* and once again became immersed in all the historical and religious references. He was still deeply engaged in the book when Ceridwen appeared in the doorway, wearing a black calf-length dress with silver and green motifs that fitted her perfectly. Looking up, he just smiled at her. If you were to view the scene, you would think it was simply a man admiring his partner.

She lifted the Aran cardigan on her arm, saying, 'With this run of settled weather, I'm hoping a coat won't be needed.'

'I think we'll be fine,' he said. 'I'll just go and get ready myself.'

'Oh, don't worry, there's no rush. I know the way of these Irish occasions; they always start late and run later.'

Taking his time to get ready, Devlin checked his device intermittently, but there was still no further news on Ben. He was looking forward to the afternoon's music and when it came to his brother, he was fairly relaxed as he reasoned that no news was good news. With Ceridwen having dressed stylishly, he decided to dress accordingly, picking out his good tweed jacket, trousers and brogue shoes.

When he walked back into the living room Ceridwen gave him an approving smile, saying, 'Will you look at us. You'd think we were the King and Queen of Sheba.'

'It will do no harm to have a bit of style in the Rainbow for once.'

They went down in the lift and Devlin noticed Ceridwen's scent.

'Now, that's a fine smell,' he said, lifting his head and sniffing in admiration.

'I'm glad you like it. I'm well practised in the art of making oils and perfumes. Everything is homemade.'

'Isn't it just.'

Passing the allotments, they were engaged in an animated discussion about horticulture, with Ceridwen being very interested in the range of vegetables that were grown, how the produce was bartered and the politics of the AA. The conversation continued as they strolled through the outskirts of the Village, until finally they reached the pub.

'So, this is the legendary Rainbow,' she said.

'I'm not so sure about legendary,' he laughed. 'It's humble enough.'

'Aren't all the best places?'

On their way into the building, walking past the grocery shop, Ceridwen said enthusiastically, 'It has such an old-style feel and even the photos look ancient. They give it a real mysterious air.'

'Isn't the place itself a mystery? So they're definitely appropriate.'

Quinn was in the middle of serving someone when they approached the bar. 'I'll be with ye now, shortly,' he called over to them.

There was a good crowd in, with a reassuring chatter filling the room, and the musicians in the alcove were engaged in a leisurely conversation, having already got their instruments out to play. Quinn came over to take their order and his gaze was immediately drawn to Ceridwen.

'And what would you like?' asked the barman.

'Do you have any wine in?' she answered.

'That's quite a coincidence,' Quinn said jauntily. 'I have a little West Country red that's just come in today.'

'That will do fine,' she said.

'I'll have a pint this time,' Devlin added.

The proprietor said that he would bring the drinks over and they sat at a table close to the musicians.

'That's Quinn. He runs the place and he knows the whereabouts of most of the people who pass through the Village. Do you want me to introduce you?'

'Oh, why spoil the mystery?' she said playfully.

Quinn came over and put the drinks down, stealing another quick glance at Ceridwen and saying, 'There you go. Enjoy.'

'We will,' Devlin said, smiling at his companion. 'Cheers.'

The group started off with a moody jig, which immediately got the attention of the clientele. Devlin picked up the rhythm, drumming his fingers easily on the table, and Ceridwen did not look away from the musicians during the entire first set of tunes.

As the set came to an end, she applauded loudly. 'That was great,' she said. 'They really can play.'

He replied warmly, 'That they can.'

The musicians played on through the late afternoon, with the occasional song being very warmly received by the crowd. The room became very full of customers, making table service difficult; consequently Devlin went to the bar to order their drinks. He had a few pints before switching to whiskey, but Ceridwen continued to drink wine.

After a particularly pulsating set of reels, the musicians took a break and Ceridwen turned to Devlin, saying, 'Leaving aside the feeling that we have gone back in time, there is a timelessness about this place, if that makes sense?'

'It has that effect, alright,' he replied distractedly, his attention having been drawn to the far side of the bar, where his cousin Niall had just come in and was talking with two men, one of whom had attended the recent AA meeting.

'Oh, don't worry about me if you need to talk to anyone,' Ceridwen said, following his gaze. 'I'm happy enough here.'

'It's just my cousin, Niall,' he explained. 'No doubt he'll come over to speak to us later.'

She asked for directions to the ladies' and as he watched her cross the room, he was aware that he was not the only person taking an interest in her progress. She disappeared from view and Carr strode purposefully towards the table.

'I am sorry I couldn't meet you,' he said, sitting down briskly. 'My father has not been well and sometimes has off days.'

For a few moments Devlin regarded his companion's soft features and alert gaze, before saying, 'Well, well, well, in all the years, I've never seen you in this establishment before.'

'You're right in your thinking – it isn't totally a coincidence.'

'I'm sure it isn't,' Devlin said with an edge in his voice and a glint in his eye.

'The thing is, Devlin, I suggested you went on into the Rawlins as there is an interest in you; they recognise that you did some good work in the early days. You could even say that you have some collateral in the bank, in that department.'

'What an interesting way of putting it.'

'That is why the door has been left open, but I suppose you might have worked that out for yourself. There is no real point in us meeting now, as your subsequent encounters in the Rawlins will have answered your questions.'

'You are right about the encounters answering my questions for the most part, Carr. The one thing I did wonder was, are you still in the same line of business?'

'Oh no, I've moved on since then. There are many things to do in the organisation.' Carr smiled knowingly. 'You could say "my father's house has many rooms", and maybe you should consider that. For future reference, I mean, if a comeback was on the cards.'

'You are not trying to convert me to Christianity, are you, Carr?' Devlin laughed. 'It's certainly been an interesting talk and don't worry, I always consider things… Though I haven't played cards for years.'

Ceridwen returned from the ladies' and Carr stood up and bowed towards her as she sat down.

'Don't leave on my account,' she said brightly.

'I only came over to say hello; I must be off.'

'He's a man in a hurry,' she said, watching Carr disappearing into the crowd.

'He is indeed,' Devlin nodded. 'By the way, I've been meaning to ask you about your name. It sounds like it could have interesting origins.'

'You are right there and I have to say, it isn't only the Irish who have their mythology and story cycles.' Smiling brightly, she continued. 'I'll tell you about the goddess Ceridwen and how she was married to Tegid Foel, the giant. They had a beautiful daughter, Creirwy, and a son, Morfran, who was ugly. Ceridwen was concerned for her son and she decided to make a potion that would make him both wise and handsome. It would take a year and a day to make, so she gave a servant boy, Gwion Bach, the job of stirring the cauldron. The first three drops were the ones that contained the magic potion, but unfortunately, Gwion Bach became slapdash and spilled three drops on his thumb. Because they were hot, he put his thumb in his mouth and instantly became wise and handsome.

'Fearing Ceridwen's anger, Gwion ran away. To hasten his escape, he used his new powers to transform himself into a rabbit, but Ceridwen became a dog and followed. The boy then turned himself into a fish and jumped into the river, so she took the form of an otter and swam after him. The fish changed into a bird and flew away and she pursued him as a hawk. Finally, the bird fell to the earth, becoming a grain of corn and the goddess, now a hen, ate him whole.'

Devlin smiled approvingly, saying, 'Amazing. Is that the end of the story?'

'Why no, it's only part of it. Maybe I'll tell you more another time.'

'I hope so,' he said. Spotting Niall approaching, looking intently in their direction, he added, 'It looks like we have another visitor.'

'Well, Devlin, how's the craic?' Niall said, his eyes not leaving Ceridwen, pulling up a stool and sitting down between them.

'It's grand,' Devlin answered, 'and seeing as you're here, I'll introduce you to Ceridwen.'

'My name is Niall,' he smiled, 'and I'm a cousin of Devlin's here.'

'Great to meet you,' she replied easily.

The group started up again with a fast-paced set of reels and she immersed herself in the music once again.

Lowering his voice, Niall asked Devlin, 'Is everything OK over yonder?'

There followed a conversation about Ben and the home place, until Niall changed the subject.

'I heard that there could be changes afoot at the allotments,' he began, but then stopped and looked at Ceridwen in a questioning way.

'Oh, don't worry.' Devlin waved away his cousin's concerns. 'She's far more interested in the tunes – and anyway, she already knows what's going on in the world of veg and politics.'

At this, Ceridwen turned, affirming Devlin's comment with a smile, and then looked away from them.

Leaning in closer to Devlin, Niall said. 'Listen, I don't know if you know, but there could be widespread unrest about. You know the way of it when precious things go missing and for the life of them, folk just can't find any trace of them. It's as if they have dropped off the face of the earth.'

'I had a sense that we are going into one of those phases again.

Sorry for smiling, Niall, but an acquaintance from the world of horticulture amused me earlier by suggesting that someone had decided to weed the garden again.'

'Well, I've never heard that expression before,' Niall said, returning Devlin's smile, 'but as long as you know. Take care and if that man you know decides he wants to join a more traditional movement after he's finished stirring up revolutions in the radishes – something that stretches back even further than these jigs and reels…'

'I'll let him know, if I see him. The thing is, I hear it's the traditional nature of it all that troubles the Radish Revolutionary.'

'Oh, but things are different nowadays. He wouldn't have to be part of an old armed struggle, Devlin. It's another time and another way. He might consider that. I'll see you no doubt soon.'

Ceridwen turned to face them at that moment, with a timely, amused expression.

'Well, it was good to meet you,' Niall said, suddenly smiling very warmly, 'and maybe we'll meet again.'

'You never know,' she replied casually.

'Look after yourselves,' Niall said, heading back towards the bar.

'Did you hear what we were talking about?' Devlin asked.

'I wasn't really listening, but when you hear a phrase like "Radish Revolutionary", it catches your attention,' she said, not able to conceal her amusement.

The group finished their final set shortly after Niall had left them and as the applause faded, Ceridwen simply stated, 'That was brilliant.'

'I'm glad you liked it,' Devlin said. 'While I'm willing to concede that you Cambrians have some fine stories, you'd struggle to match our music.'

'There are many different forms of music, Devlin, and I would contest that we have superior choirs – any day.'

By the time they'd drunk up and were ready to leave, the

Rainbow was starting to empty out. A group of people were congregated on the pavement outside and looking down the street, where Devlin noticed a glow of bluey green light outside the Café Jordan. Ceridwen had turned to put her Aran cardigan on and he was not sure if she had noticed the strange occurrence, so it was without comment they turned and walked in the opposite direction.

There was a definite change in the weather and for the first time in days, the air was decidedly cooler. They fell into a natural step walking back, talking sporadically like a couple who'd spent many years together, and when they reached the allotments, Ceridwen stopped by the railings to look up at the rookery. He recognised the fineness of her Welsh features as her blonde hair tumbled down over her shoulders.

'The rooks are amazing, aren't they?' she said, her eyes shining bright with excitement. 'Listen to the cacophony they are making. You'd think you were deep in mid-Wales.'

'Wouldn't you just,' he agreed. They were nearing the apartments when a sharp shower commenced.

In the lift, Devlin kept the conversation going by saying, 'It was a grand afternoon, wasn't it? I hope it met with Cambrian approval.'

'It did indeed,' she nodded. 'I think there is some bread and cheese left over.'

Back in the flat, a meal was put together and they chatted about the day while they ate. They both knew that this light-hearted mood could not continue with the spectre of James's absence hanging over them, and it suddenly changed when Ceridwen said in a low, serious voice, 'I did notice the disturbance earlier and that doesn't bode well for travellers. Am I right in thinking that this change in weather indicates a rough spell across the region?'

'Yes, I'm sure you've read it right,' he said, his voice reflecting her concern. 'Anyway, James is smart enough. I'm sure he will have taken shelter.'

'Let's hope so,' she said, standing up. 'I'm going to lie down for a while, as I seem to have a headache coming on.'

It was getting dark and Devlin was attracted over to the window to watch the torrential showers and lightning sweeping across the city. The skyline had changed dramatically and there was a radiance in his gaze as he became engrossed in watching the storm, occasionally looking down to check his device. He had expected Miriam to contact before now and he'd made the decision to instigate the call himself if she didn't call in the next half hour.

Ceridwen came back into the room and it was at this point that his device rang. He sat down to answer and after a pause for the connection to be established, Miriam's voice came through.

'Michael, is that you?'

'It is, Miriam.'

'Sorry for not getting in touch earlier, but… when I got here, Ben was very ill and there didn't seem to be time.' There was a pause before she gently said, 'Michael, I'm really sorry. Ben's passed away.'

'Oh no.' His features froze into a look of disbelief for a few moments, before he said solemnly, 'I only wish I was there with you and Mam.'

'Michael, we all know that you can't be.'

'I was worried when Mam rang,' he recovered himself, 'and I knew things weren't good, but I guess I was thinking that Ben would stage another of his amazing recoveries. What a fighter… I'll take comfort from the fact that you were there. How is Mam?'

Miriam talked about their mother's reaction and then speculated about possible funeral arrangements before eventually saying, 'I suppose it's virtually impossible for you to get over?'

'I am going to do everything in my power to be there. I'll be in touch tomorrow.'

After putting his device down, Devlin did not move, allowing himself a few minutes to dwell on the significance of his only brother's death. He also reflected bitterly on the twisted politics of the time and the subsequent travel restrictions that had meant he had never really got to know him as an adult. He smiled ruefully at this fact and then turned to face Ceridwen.

'I'm so very sorry about Ben,' she said. 'I really am.'

'Thank you, Ceridwen. It is much appreciated.' He paused before adding, 'I need to be making some arrangements.'

'Of course.'

Going into his workroom next door, he sat down at the old machine with its large screen. He was determined to lodge the travel request immediately with a strong case on the initial form, which would hopefully negate the need for a face-to-face interview. Devlin completed the request, asking for eight days to enable him to sort out the legal details of the home place with his family. Funerals were usually held within a couple of days of death in the west of Ireland, so he requested permission to travel the following day, or failing that, the morning after. He re-read the request a few times to make sure it struck the right note and then sent it.

He returned to the living room to find Ceridwen looking out of the window, which was now covered with a fluid film of water. Turning round to face him, she said with a slow deliberation, 'It's a night when you wouldn't want to be caught out and you've lost your only brother today.'

'James knows of more safe harbours than anyone I know,' he said with conviction. After a few moments, he continued with obvious pride, 'And as for my wonderful brother Ben, both he and my mam did brilliantly. When he was younger, she was told that he would probably not live to twenty-one, so fair play to him, he more than doubled that.'

Opening the bottom door of the cabinet, Devlin rummaged around momentarily before pulling out a bottle of whiskey and after picking up two glasses, he sat down opposite Ceridwen.

She turned away from the window and in a voice that was not much more than a whisper said, 'To think, we had such a lovely afternoon and all the while…'

'In the midst of life, there's death,' he said, opening the bottle and pouring the drinks. Devlin handed one golden glass of spirit over to Ceridwen, saying resolutely, 'We drank to Ben's recovery only last night. But that wasn't to be. Tonight we shall drink to his life.'

They raised their glasses.

'Sláinte,' he said and they toasted his brother.

The storm continued to swirl around the tower block and they both knew that James would not be returning that night. Ceridwen asked Devlin about his upbringing and he relaxed and talked about his early years in the west of Ireland. Fascinated, she listened intently, at one point remarking, 'You always talk in terms of the home place, yet you never say where it is.'

'It's just habit,' he shrugged. 'There is no reason not to, I don't suppose.' He thought for a moment before adding, 'I was brought up in the townland of Knockbrack; the word means the hill of the badger. It's not far from Mullnamorran (Meall Uí Mhóráin), a town that's in the ancient kingdom of Connaught, facing out towards the wild Atlantic.'

'There is the restlessness of that ocean in you, Devlin. I always imagined that you came from such a place.'

She refused the offer of another whiskey, but he continued to drink, until eventually he said to her, 'It's a strange night in strange times. It's hard to know what lays ahead, but your company has been truly appreciated. You seem to have been watching over me.'

'Oh, Devlin, didn't you know?' she said with an air of mystery. 'It's what Welsh goddesses do.'

Standing up, they briefly embraced and she looked at him, saying, 'I'm going to turn in now.'

'You're the wise one. If James does return during the night, the bell is loud. So rest assured, you will hear.'

'Thanks, Devlin, and goodnight.'

CHAPTER SEVEN

Devlin eventually went to bed. It had been a truly momentous night, but even with his great fatigue and the whiskey, sleep didn't come easily. For a while, he had the feeling that he was falling slowly, but never quite landing, until eventually he did lose consciousness… He found he was back inside the Rawlins, in the space where he had recently engaged with the current Celtic Regions Programme team. Everything was as he remembered, except he was on his own this time and the portals were all blank.

One of the screens suddenly came alive, showing James walking down a dark street with the small rucksack on his shoulder. The footage was very cinematic, with a sepia tinge and a soundtrack of slow pipe music. He headed in the direction of the docks, passing under the old Victorian streetlamps on his way with a look of determination etched into his features. An intensifying sea mist was coming in from the river and it was especially dense on the corner where two men waited. They looked earnestly at James, who opened up his rucksack and took out a small package, and then all three of them turned to face the screen as if they had suddenly become aware that they were being observed.

The men froze and the image was transferred onto the large screen. A neon tent-like frame of steadily pulsing red and yellow beams descended slowly on the silhouetted trio and enveloped them. Devlin did not take his eyes off the scene, until gradually the light beams changed to a bluey green and began to fade, along with the outlines of the figures within. All that was left behind was a vague residue of coloured light that gave the now-vacant corner the mysterious look of a stage, on which a perfect illusion had been performed.

Glancing around the room to check that he was still on his own, Devlin's attention was drawn to vibrating patterns that appeared on the closest screen, interspersed with moments of stillness. It was a curious display and somehow knowing that a response was being sought, he simply nodded his head towards the screen, saying, 'Well, well, well.'

On one of the other portals, the Café Jordan came into view. Marcel, the proprietor, and his partner Scott were wiping down the outside tables when they were enveloped in the same way as James and his comrades. The two men stayed frozen in the beams of light for a significantly shorter period. Devlin watched as the lights turned bluey green before starting to fade, only to be surprised to see the figures of the two men remaining. The lights then faded altogether and Marcel and Scott were back in motion, folding chairs and collecting candles on the forecourt.

Marcel was about to go into the café when he turned and said to Scott, 'Some fresh flowers would look nice on the tables tomorrow.'

Scott looked puzzled for a moment before replying. 'You are right. They would freshen the place up.'

The shot panned out from the café and the screen went blank. Devlin had no idea how much time had elapsed, but after a short period, when he seemed to be falling, he was grateful to be back on the edge of consciousness. He was aware of a bright moonlight, which seemed strange, as the weather had been very stormy when he'd gone to bed. When he fully came to, the halo of a moon appeared to be in his line of vision, but upon closer inspection, it was actually Ceridwen's blonde head resting against the side of the bed – she was kneeling on the floor.

'Strange nights in strange times.' She turned her head and looked up at him, adding, 'There are some very disturbing dreams about tonight.'

She shuddered as she uttered the last few words.

'There are indeed,' Devlin replied, 'although I guess not for the first time. We will have to wait and see.'

'Indeed and all might be well, but, but, but…'

He found the way she emphasised the Ts at the end of 'but' to be mesmerising.

Standing up, Ceridwen walked over to the hanging rail in the corner and he watched the outline of her figure through her nightshirt. She returned to the bed with his heavy topcoat draped across her shoulders and after a deep, deliberate breath said, 'I will stay here tonight.' Lying down on top of the bed clothes, she pulled the coat up to her chin and, turning away from him, said, 'We will need all our strength in the days to come. Sleep tight.'

Settling her head into the pillow, Ceridwen gazed out through the window. Devlin looked at her hair again eclipsing the moon outside and after a few moments fell into a deep sleep.

The next morning, Devlin woke in a thoughtful mood and slipped quietly into the living room to make a pot of tea, lilting a slow air. He was stirring his drink when Ceridwen entered.

'Do you fancy some tea? There's plenty in the pot.'

She smiled faintly, saying, 'That would be good.'

Her expression was one of quiet resignation. She clasped her two hands around the mug. They looked at each other briefly before Devlin said, 'I'm just going to see if I've had a response to my travel request.'

Going into his work room, he logged on to the old machine and immediately saw an envelope icon looming large on the screen, which he opened. Devlin was struck by the simplicity of the communication, which read:

Request granted. See travel details attached for tomorrow – funeral the day after.

You are expected to visit the Rawlins Building on your return. Contact to arrange.

A huge surge of relief went through him and even when he looked again at the last two points regarding the Rawlins, it provoked no emotional response in him at all. They were matters that could be dealt with when he returned.

He clicked onto a news bulletin from the Regime that advertised a feature about the CRP. The item highlighted work being done to develop the shepherd communities in the Welsh Hills. Devlin smiled ironically as it had been a long time since the CRP had featured on the news and it seemed an interesting coincidence indeed.

Entering the living room having changed into his running gear, Devlin told Ceridwen that he'd been given permission to travel. She was visibly lifted by the news.

'That's great,' she said enthusiastically. 'I know how much getting there means to you.'

'Yes, at this moment in time, I'm just grateful to be going. Any news on James yet?'

'No, nothing so far. To be honest, it's doubtful if he'll make it back here now.'

'I think you're probably right. I kept going over things and how they happened. We will have to stay positive for him,' Devlin replied, smiling resolutely.

'We will have to stay positive. He's been in scrapes before and we don't know the outcome yet,' she said, running a hand through her dishevelled hair. 'Anyway, you are all geared up for your jog. You go and we can talk later.'

'I've got a few bits to do at the allotment, but I'll be back by lunch time.'

He left the flat, bounding down the old fire escape before exiting and then maintaining a quick pace all the way to the outskirts of the Village. He chose a route around the suburbs, avoiding the centre that took him along largely unfamiliar streets.

On the way back, curiosity took him past the Café Jordan. He waved to Marcel, who was wearing glasses with brighter coloured frames than usual, placing cutlery precisely on the outside tables.

'You're setting the pace today,' the owner called out approvingly.

'Don't worry, I'll be flagging soon,' he replied.

At the allotments, Devlin went straight into his shed to get changed and he was still sweating when he emerged ready to start work. He spent an hour generally tidying up around his holding and then went to tell Denis that he was going home for his brother's funeral. His friend commiserated with him and said he'd keep an eye on the plot in his absence.

Devlin was on his way back when Kirsty appeared, walking briskly down the path.

'I thought I saw you, Devlin,' she said eagerly. 'Is there any chance of a quick chat about that AA stuff?'

'That's fine, Kirsty,' Devlin replied. 'Should we take a walk?'

They walked through the allotments and out through the gate by the old Hall. They talked about the proposal that was going to be put to the Regime and any possible pitfalls it could face. Devlin liked the fact that Kirsty was so thorough; she wanted to be ready for any eventuality in the coming negotiations.

'Hopefully there'll be no great dramas,' he said as they were on their way back towards his plot. 'Try not to overthink it. We all might have our thoughts and misgivings in a wider political sense, but leave those out of it. A good proposal presented in good faith has the best chance of success. So it's just a matter of me saying good luck.'

'That's great, Devlin. I hope the next few weeks go well for you.'

He watched Kirsty walk away and reflected on the fact that the outcome of the proposal was of great interest to him, and while part of him would have liked to have been the one putting it forward, Devlin felt that it was another political cause that was destined to be demanding his attention. After one last glance at his holding, he turned decisively and locked up his shed. He headed for the apartment block.

Devlin walked slowly up the fire escape stairs to his flat, where he and Ceridwen sat down to a lunch that she had prepared. He again remarked on her resourcefulness in creating such a fine meal from the little food available and then they proceeded to eat in silence, each very much lost in their own thoughts. Knowing that this was an extremely difficult time for her, he had great admiration for how dignified she remained.

When they had finished eating, he said very calmly, 'I am just going to check everything ahead of tomorrow and then I'll let them know at home that I'll be travelling. Could we go for a walk after that?'

She simply nodded her assent, her face set in a resigned smile.

Devlin went into the work room and, checking his old machine, he was relieved to see that there were no further communications from the Regime. He rang Miriam to let her know that he would be home for Ben's funeral, outlining the travel plans. She was overjoyed, as was his mother, to whom the conversation was being relayed. At the end of the call, Miriam told him that she had already spoken to Liam, who had said he would meet Devlin at the Ben Bulben stop; all he needed to do was message an ETA when he got to Ireland. This arrangement suited him as it would be an opportunity to discuss the political situation with his cousin and also to catch up on the news locally.

After the call was finished, he sat for a few minutes reflecting on the events of the last few days. He had been deeply saddened by Ben's passing, but he could not deny that he was genuinely excited by the prospect of going home and his spirits were high as he went to have a quick shower and change.

'Do you fancy going for that walk now?' he asked gently, returning to the living room. 'We could go to Boundary Park, which is over in the docklands' direction. There's great views of the open country and I've not been out that way for ages.'

His words seemed to pull her back from deeper thoughts and she said quietly, 'That would be good. Just give me a few minutes to change.'

Devlin started to wash the dishes, noticing their bland cream colour and the lack of any discernible pattern. As he was drying them, his mind drifted back to the china plates that his mother had at the home place, with their green, blue and yellow nature scenes and rounded ruffled edges, which only ever came out when they had special visitors. A large dresser that carried rows of these plates dominated the living room and as children, they had been well aware of the importance of its contents. Normally they would stay well clear of it, but he remembered vividly the day that he broke a dinner plate with a misdirected ball and especially the shocked expression on his mother's face when she saw the damage done. He could not recall what his punishment was, but the efforts that went into replacing the piece of china stayed with him. There were contacts made all over Ireland and he felt a stab of guilt every time he went into the living room until many months later, when an exact replacement was found.

He had just finished putting the dishes away when Ceridwen came back into the room. She was wearing a red anorak over a casual top and trousers.

'You look like you're ready to walk,' he observed.

'I am, indeed.'

They left the flat, taking the lift down to the ground floor, and although he detected that she had a different scent on, he refrained from passing comment. During the descent she appeared to be listening to the sounds emanating from the lift, though on the one occasion where their eyes met, neither conveyed any meaningful expression. At the reception desk, they stopped to leave a recorded message at the door, saying that they would be back in a couple of hours.

Outside, they set off in the opposite direction from the allotments and heading towards the docklands they fell into an easy stride pattern, with Ceridwen seeming content to walk along without engaging in conversation. The route they took passed through a complex maze of suburban streets, predominantly of large terraced houses.

The further they went, the more Devlin could sense a tension building in her, but Ceridwen did not look to him for reassurance. She allowed him to lead the way and without any verbal agreement, the pace of their walking increased until they reached the place he'd had in mind. They turned into a street lined with large Victorian lampposts, which stretched for fifty yards before turning down towards the docks.

That was when Ceridwen came to a dead stop, freezing on the spot. The suddenness of her action took him by surprise and he was already a couple of yards in front of her when he realised and stopped himself. He turned to face her and the expression that he saw looking back at him was one of pure consternation.

'I'm really sorry,' he said. 'It wasn't a good idea. Let's go to the park.'

Turning and retracing their steps, they came eventually to a lengthy, descending street of brightly painted houses. He pointed out the park entrance that was prominent below, being marked out by tall red sandstone columns that stood at its entrance, which were in turn dwarfed by the towering and gnarled trees beyond. The scene was very Gothic, prompting Ceridwen to break her silence as they passed through the gates.

'It's a very dramatic entrance.'

'It's seen better days, like many things down here,' he replied, before adding, 'but once we're through the trees, the view is worth it.'

The wind was fresh and large clouds moved quickly across the sky as they strolled through the woods with the old park opening out in front of them. There were several ways they could have gone, but he chose the crazed, undulating asphalt path, leading them through overgrown lawns to a disused bandstand. From there, they took another path that brought them to a large sandstone boulder secluded within a copse of trees, offering a vantage point of the entire landscape; a broad scene of rolling countryside beneath dark mountains that rose impressively in the distance.

They spent a few minutes absorbing the view, before Devlin sat down and said, 'I thought this would be a good place.'

'I am assuming that we can talk openly here,' Ceridwen said, sitting beside him on the worn sandstone. He nodded and she continued with a level of hostility in her voice, 'That felt like a trial, Devlin, as if you were testing me out.'

'I'm sorry, it wasn't meant to be. I suppose I just wanted to know what you knew and how you knew it.'

'I suppose I could say exactly the same thing to you. And anyway, you could just have asked,' she said with great deliberation.

'You are right and I apologise again. So can we put this behind us? I have come to this place to talk openly and I trust we are both of independent mind and speaking from the heart.'

'It does come down to trust, independence and the heart,' she agreed. 'My response is uncomplicated. If we were playing cards, I would look at my hand and simply say, "I'm in."'

'That's very courageous of you, Ceridwen, particularly given the circumstances. I will tell you the truth. Last night, I dreamed that James was lifted on that street and I wondered how you would react if we went to that spot today. It was a strange experience. Obviously you knew the significance of the place, but beyond that there are other things I don't know.'

'Fancy that, Devlin,' she said with a slightly caustic tone, 'you not knowing everything that's going on. Well, I have to report that things were not that straightforward. When James didn't come back yesterday, I feared the worst. Before I went to bed, I had what seemed like a premonition of what was going to happen and I couldn't sleep. I sensed all was not well with you, so I went to your room and saw that you were obviously having a nightmare. Sitting by your bedside, the images and thoughts you were experiencing were so strong that I picked up on them and so when we walked that route earlier, I recognised the street with the old lamps. I knew where I was and what had happened there.' Ceridwen had been gazing at the scenery while talking, but she turned to look at him directly, saying, 'He knew there were risks to that meeting, Devlin, especially with a purge being underway. And that's the bit I don't understand.'

'Yes, it seems to have been a very rash act. And of course, if he has been lifted, it's a real concern how he comes out of it, for sure.'

'How and if…' Her voice trailed off. She looked back out at the countryside before carrying on. 'We joked about him being an old timer, even a dinosaur, but he was one of the last of a very old breed. He could not cope with being tampered with in any way – the internal conflict it causes would be too great. We will just have to wait and see what the situation is. You know what I'm saying.'

'I know and I really appreciate your openness with me, as I could be seen as being tainted by my former employment by the Regime.'

'Ah, back to that old trust thing. Listen, you are the mercurial Devlin, who seems to be able to float between worlds. Someone who has been in there in the Devil's kitchen, drank the broth and not been poisoned – so we are to believe. But maybe it's that that makes you trustworthy. Have you ever considered that the reason your old Regime colleagues still find you fascinating is that they have a purpose in mind for you?'

'I am coming round to that way of thinking myself.'

'And there seems to be others, too. Your popularity is on the rise again.' She tilted her head before adding in an overly concerned voice, 'Poor Devlin.'

'I'm not sure it's popularity, but you're right, there is a pull to this whole thing, for sure.' They sat in silence, gazing for a few minutes before he spoke again. 'The old powers and stories really do interest me and I have found I have been becoming ever more engaged with Celtic spiritualism of late. Some people believe that the ways of the ancients may be the best way to navigate through these days ahead.'

'They do shine a light where there has been darkness and dogged overreliance on logic, which has left us at the mercy of other intelligences. We move too slowly that way – instinct and emotion have always been our stronger suits. The old story cycles and powers operate on a more visceral level and I do believe that these are the tools that will be needed.'

She stopped and Devlin, who was looking at her approvingly, said, 'I think I have been coming round to the same conclusion myself.'

'Travelling to the home place is going to be an interesting journey for you on all levels, I'm sure.'

They instinctively moved closer together on the ancient sandstone seat as a cooler wind began to blow. She linked his arm and they pointed out landmarks, chatting about the countryside, and if you were to come across this couple by chance, it would be difficult to say if they were siblings, colleagues or lovers; they just looked natural in each other's company. The landscape seemed alive, putting Devlin in mind of one of Gráinne's large impasto paintings at the exhibition in the Corner Gallery.

The pair waved cheerily at two anglers returning from the canal with their tackle and fishing baskets and the timeless noise of children playing in the nearby woods provided a heart-warming soundtrack to the afternoon.

'Listen to them,' Devlin spoke reflectively. 'They could be echoes of children playing two hundred years ago.'

'They could indeed. Some things haven't changed at all.'

'You're right there. The other thing that never changes is the unpredictability of the weather. Those showers could catch us out yet.' He eyed darker clouds coming in from the border hills. He had also noticed drones sweeping along the river's course, no doubt checking out blind spots. 'Shall we head back?'

'It's probably time,' she said, zipping up her anorak and taking one last look at the scene before getting to her feet.

They took their time ambling to the park's entrance, but once back on the streets they walked briskly in the direction of the apartment block. Devlin called at the desk to check with the receptionist if anyone had called in or posted anything and as there were no messages, they took the lift up to the flat in silence.

Going into his work room, he logged on to find further details of his arrangements for the next morning; he could either be picked up at the flat or catch the shuttle from the Village to the ferry port. He chose the latter. Travelling home by boat was a pleasant surprise as it was the more traditional way of making the journey and the thought of the open sea brought a natural smile to Devlin's face as he closed down the old machine. Returning to the living room, he found Ceridwen studying her device.

'I've received a formal message saying that he won't be coming back here,' she said. 'It says he has travelled on and will contact me soon.'

'Are you OK?' His forehead was furrowed as he spoke.

'Deep down, it's what I'd expected.' She lifted her face from the screen and while there was a residue of tears in her eyes, there was a fortitude in her tone as she spoke. 'Though I do think he will be in touch soon.'

'You can stay on here if you want. I'll be away…' He gestured vaguely with his hand.

'I will just stay till morning. If that's alright?'

'Of course, you know you are always welcome here. Now, I'll clear out whatever's in that fridge and the veg basket. I must admit I'm hungry.'

Devlin prepared a meal from the remains of a chicken and

vegetables that were left over and after thanking him for his efforts, Ceridwen joined him at the table and they ate. After they had finished, she opened her bag and produced some oat biscuits, nuts and a bottle of red wine, which she duly opened.

'Still producing food from that bottomless bag of yours, and vino as well.' Pouring out two glasses of the red, he added, 'That's certainly a welcome addition.'

'It's been the strangest day and look, it's evening already. The time has certainly flown by,' she sighed, cupping the glass in both her hands. 'If it wasn't for what happened last night, it would have been a lovely few days.'

'It's a time of sunlight and shadows, but we are Celts – who have had to learn to live with such profound uncertainties.'

Ceridwen took another drink of wine and said, 'And I suppose there has been a coming together in a deeper sense – despite, or even because of, the loss and uncertainty.'

Devlin spent the evening packing his luggage and preparing for the trip, while Ceridwen spent time meditating in the bedroom and reading. Later on they came together again round the table.

'I hope your trip goes well,' Ceridwen said, pouring out the remaining wine. 'It's bound to be very emotional.'

'It will be, I'm sure, but that is to be expected. There is a good tradition of neighbours and family coming together to mourn and remember on the night before the funeral. The Wake. It is part of the process of letting go.' He paused, then asked, 'What are you going to do now?'

'Strangely, my arrangements haven't changed,' she said, tilting her head to one side. 'James and I would have been going our separate ways from here anyway. I'll be going back to the flat I share with Glenys, to touch base. But beyond that, I have been thinking about returning home to Wales many times lately – I'd like to plan for that.'

'Wales is a beautiful land for sure and there are different days coming, Ceridwen.'

'There are for sure and may we live to see them.' She rose up out of her chair, saying, 'I think I will go to bed now.'

'Good night.' He stood and bowed his head slightly. 'Hopefully, this night will be more peaceful than the last one.'

'Hopefully.'

Standing in the middle of the room, they shared a short embrace and then kissed each other's cheeks in the style of friends. He would later feel that these moments were like a ceremony, a confirmation of what they had said and a commitment to support each other in the days to come.

'Take care in Ireland,' she said quietly, 'and sleep tight, Devlin.'

'Good night,' he responded, watching her walk slowly across the floor.

Putting on some traditional Irish music, Devlin reclined into his chair by the window. The reels evoked scenes of the landscapes around his home place and it wasn't long before he was feeling quite drowsy. When the recordings had finished, he listened to the sound of the wind blowing outside, nowhere near as strong as the night before, which reassured him that tomorrow would be a calm day for the sailing. He made some tea and went to bed thinking about tomorrow's ferry crossing and soon fell asleep.

He dreamed he was in the CRP area again that night. The room was crowded, with people shouting and swearing at the events that were being shown on the various screens. Slips of paper were strewn across the table with mathematical calculations written on them and Devlin realised that they were gambling. Looking at the portals, he saw that betting odds for different outcomes were displayed prominently in two columns on either side of the screen, one headed *Interloper* and the other *Subversive*.

His attention was drawn to the main screen, which showed a still shot of the interior of the Rainbow. Quinn could be seen behind the bar, Deirdre was cleaning tables and he recognised the back of Niall's head, along with the faces of those in his company. A group of musicians were in the act of playing; the fiddler's bow was on the strings, the flute player's fingers were on the notes, the melodeon was extended out and the uilleann piper was gazing straight ahead at the camera. Behind the musicians, deep in conversation, were sat Ceridwen and himself.

The screen started to flash and a large overlaid caption appeared that read "Rainbow Starting 2.30", then there was a great roar of approval as the announcement came: 'And now we're off!'

Devlin could not keep up with events as all the portals were showing different footage from the action and there were commentaries in many different languages. The energy in the place was amazing and he was swept along with it, especially when the participants were revealed to be either an *Interloper* or a *Subversive*, drawing loud cheers from the crowd. Those who'd backed the correct outcome celebrated most enthusiastically, but everyone seemed to be enjoying themselves regardless. The last thing he remembered was Quinn being interviewed as part of the post-event analysis. His eye rested easily on the camera and he was saying, 'I always suspected that he was from out of the area and was up to serious no good. Ah, you develop a nose for these things.'

The dream of the gambling in the CRP area started to fade, with the crowd all leaning towards the main screen, intrigued to hear how Quinn had made his deductions.

Coming round slowly, Devlin checked the time and was surprised to find that he had been asleep less than an hour. A mug of tepid tea sat on the bedside cabinet, and, supporting himself on one elbow, he took slow deliberate mouthfuls while watching the changing skyline outside. His eyes soon became heavy and lowering himself down, he drifted off to sleep again.

He slept in later than intended, but he wasn't unduly concerned, as there was still plenty of time to get the shuttle. Devlin dressed for the trip and walking down the hallway, he noticed the wide-open door to the room where Ceridwen had been sleeping. He stopped and walked back, already sensing that she was not there. Devlin stood for a few moments in the doorway looking at the made bed and a single sheet of paper lying on the pillow. He went over and picked it up, then read: *Devlin. Hopefully there will be different days ahead, Ceridwen x.*

On the bottom of the short note was a drawing of a smiling moon and flying towards it on her broomstick was a smiley witch.

CHAPTER EIGHT

Devlin walked in a jaunty way along the road, dressed in a tweed suit and with a leather holdall slung across his shoulder. A Transkill transporter was parked just off the Village Square, in the exact same spot it had been the other day, which surprised him as they did not normally work in one area for more than a few hours at a time. He noticed that the worker with the spiky silver hair who he had engaged with before was again looking out through the darkened window of the vehicle, so when he got alongside he smiled and waved at her. Seemingly caught off guard, she gave a startled smile before offering an uncertain wave in response. Devlin did not try to prolong the encounter but carried on his way.

The Village Square was a hive of activity, with traders erecting stalls and some of the earlier risers stocking out; it made for a very busy scene indeed; merchandise was stacked on the pavement and vehicles were parked in locations convenient for dropping off, and a general hubbub of conversation flowed in the background. Walking briskly to the far side of the Square, Devlin encountered Jenkins stood in front of the haberdashery stall, regarding the scene.

Glancing at the holdall, Jenkins said, 'I see you're travelling today.'

Devlin briefly outlined the reason for his journey home and

a deep look of sadness came over the Welshman's ruddy features. 'You have my sincere condolences. I hope it goes well.'

He smiled faintly in response and walked on towards the pick-up point outside the Colosseum, where he presented himself at a travel screen, which flickered a couple of times before saying, 'Welcome, Mr Devlin. The shuttle will arrive in approximately seven minutes.'

'Thank you,' he smiled wryly.

Sure enough, the shuttle arrived on time and he followed the pulsing light strips to his designated seat. Once he was seated, the clamps came into place and his screen was activated. From the options given he chose the Regime's history channel and settled back as a programme about the development of the Ascension Party began.

The journey seemed very short and it occurred to him that they had arrived at the ferry terminal without passing through the old docklands area that he knew. He followed the other passengers disembarking from the shuttle as they filed into a bustling reception area bedecked with bunting. Uplifting music was playing and he was struck by the life of the scene; there were couples in lingering embraces, travellers consulting their devices for information, families saying their farewells and groups of people who were plainly in the mood to party. He moved through the crowd until he found the correct boarding gate and he was waiting to confirm his attendance when a porter said enthusiastically, 'There will be no need for that. Don't we know who you are and aren't you very welcome.'

Devlin smiled in response and his gaze was automatically drawn to the ship that towered above them, which was predominantly white with green trimmings and a large red funnel.

The porter who had a round jovial face and red curly hair, clearly enjoyed talking, as he continued in a pronounced Irish brogue. 'Hasn't everything has been arranged to the minutest detail,' he said. 'Your cabin is awaiting, should you need a rest. All you have to do now is have a pleasant crossing.'

The passengers started moving along the dockside towards the gangways. Another porter, who was very tall in stature, joined his colleague, engaging the travellers in a very loud English voice.

'Good day, you fine folk. We would like to wholeheartedly welcome you all to this ancient crossing of the Connaught Princess – and isn't she beautiful?'

The passengers looked up and in response, the deck lighting flashed and the ship's horn sounded; people around Devlin cheered boisterously. The tall porter walked with precise steps along the dockside edge, before leaping athletically onto a capstan and spreading his arms wide, to ensure he had everyone's full attention. He then pointed to his colleague and said, 'This is my fine Irish friend Dermot. Not quite as fine as me, you understand.' The crowd murmured their approval and after a pause he added, 'He and I are like the old nations of England and Ireland. Once, we were in conflict, but now we have been brought together by the great healer of division, those great bringers of peace, the Regime!'

More cheering followed this remark, at which point Dermot raised his not inconsiderable voice. 'Barleycorn and I will be speaking as one unified voice, wishing you all a safe journey as we hand you over to our colleagues aboard the Princess. Though they are not in any way as splendid specimens as we are, they are still very good, bless them!'

The ship's horn sounded hurriedly, as if displeased by Dermot's jibe, and Barleycorn stepped off the capstan and started to walk up the hawser, splaying his arms to keep his balance. The broad rope swayed from side to side as he progressed slowly upwards, seemingly in total control until he faltered near the top. Flailing his arms, he appeared to swim in mid-air and then Barleycorn fell. There was a gasp from the passengers, who instinctively moved forward as if to try to catch him. Suddenly letting out a mighty cry, he grabbed a rope that was dangling from the hawser and swung towards the ship. The movement was expertly executed and the passengers cheered along while he made his spinning descent, dismounting with a flourish onto the capstan, where he stood to receive his applause.

Dermot joined him and the two men called out in unison, 'Bon voyage… bon voyage…'

Devlin walked past the performing porters and Barleycorn rolled his eyes and fixed him with a mischievous look, as if the pair of them were party to a great secret. Following the movement of the other passengers, he moved further along the dockside to where a group of people were gathered round a stout man in a long raincoat, who was viewing the gangway with trepidation.

'Look, I told you that it is moving,' the stout man was saying.

'Have you not seen that the ship is also moving?' a woman beside him asked.

'I can't see the ship moving at all.'

'The ship has to move because the sea's moving,' she said in exasperation.

The couple were being heckled by others in their party and a loud voice from behind called out, 'Well, the ship *will* be moving and pretty damn well soon.'

There was an outbreak of laughter and derisive comments and Devlin took the opportunity to squeeze through the crowd, repeating, 'Excuse me,' as he went, even though nobody acknowledged his passing them by.

Once aboard the ship, he looked back down at the terminal and he could not help but smile at the sight of Dermot coaching the stout man through his slow ascent up the gangway.

He headed for the reception area, where a large information screen advertised events that would be taking place during the crossing. Noticing an exit at the far side of the room, Devlin went over and pushed the door open, walking along a short corridor that took him out onto the deck, where he breathed in the deeply salty air infused with the many sharp dockside odours, while the noisy gulls cried plaintively, circling round the ship.

Leaning against the railings, he observed that the dockside had become surprisingly quiet, with the gangways being hauled in and Dermot and Barleycorn walking slowly in the direction of the ferry terminal building. There was something both tragic and comical about their progress; the two seasoned performers reluctantly leaving the dockside, where stevedores were getting into position to release the hawsers of the Connaught Princess. Devlin's attention was drawn to the stern of the ship, where the last of the freight was being loaded from a warehouse area he had not noticed before. The ship's speakers announced that they would shortly be setting sail and Devlin turned to find a crew member standing behind him.

'It's funny really,' the sailor said a little morosely. 'Even though I've done this crossing so many times, I still get a tug of emotion whenever we set sail.'

'I can understand that,' Devlin smiled. 'There is a great excitement about this old voyage.'

'Oh, there is. A great excitement, as you have observed. People travel for many different reasons – some very joyous and others very sad.' The sailor nodded courteously.

'You are right there. Let's just hope it's a smooth crossing,' Devlin said, walking past the crewman on his way back to the reception area.

After viewing the berth allocations, he took the holdall to his cabin and then made his way to the bar area. The level of excitement and noise in the lounge surprised him, as the voyage was yet to commence. He crossed the floor and had no trouble catching the barman's responsive eye. 'I'll have a pint. Good God, they're in great form.'

'Aren't they always in great form,' the barman responded, 'and many of them never even trouble me for a drink. They generate a great atmosphere on the Princess, alright.'

Devlin returned the barman's smile, trying unsuccessfully to place his strong Irish accent to a specific area of the country. A group of passengers, including the stout man from the gangway, were close by and in high spirits; the only time they broke off from their animated conversation was to sing along with songs that a lively four-piece band were playing in the corner. Devlin, who was starting to feel in a reflective mood, took his drink and found an unoccupied table by the far wall.

The Band began to play a very emotional ballad and the crowd in the lounge, which seemed to have grown even larger, joined in lustily. Devlin waited for the high note at the end, as he'd often heard it catch out poor singers, but he was surprised when the group at the bar all hit it perfectly. He was still listening when the barman who'd served him appeared by his side saying, 'They are in very good voice and why wouldn't they be?'

Another barman joined them at the table, commenting brightly, 'Indeed, why wouldn't they be, Mr Kelly? After all, they're off on their jolly days.'

'Yes, you are right there, Mr Scanlon. "Off on their jolly days" – you have such a way with words.'

Both men laughed enthusiastically at the remark and then Scanlon said to Devlin, 'You need not stir. Bide your time and I'll bring you another pint over.'

The two men laughed again in unison, before moving away across the floor in synchronised steps that were clearly choreographed.

A couple approached and the man pointed to the empty seats beside Devlin's table, asking, 'Are we OK to sit here?'

'Of course,' Devlin smiled, 'be my guests.'

'I'm Conor and this is Catherine.'

'Nice to meet you. I'm Devlin.'

They settled into their seats and proceeded to talk quietly between themselves. This suited Devlin as he was comfortable with his own thoughts and passing the time watching people in the lounge.

Before long, Scanlon appeared with another pint. 'Here you are, sir,' he said cheerily. 'A pint of the old black stuff. Enjoy.'

As the barman walked away, Conor placed his elbow on the table and, leaning over, said, 'I would say you are a man who has a certain political insight.'

Devlin just smiled, waiting to see where this was leading, while many of the revellers in the lounge began singing along to a jaunty political song with particular vigour.

'Have you ever considered the lyrics of this song, my friend?' Conor spoke fervently. '*"I sang with pride of my nation's life – Then crown troops, struck with all their might."* That's where they had it wrong in the old days, but things are different now. They have a wonderful culture and aren't we right to let it flourish? That way, we can all benefit.'

'There is plenty of truth in what you are saying,' Devlin agreed, now regarding the older man with greying hair and dark-rimmed glasses more closely.

'I worked for the Regime from leaving college,' Conor moved in closer again, 'and then I joined the Ascension Party.' He paused for a moment and Devlin looked over at Catherine, who was gazing approvingly at the two men. 'Anyway, as I was saying, I joined the AP and I have never really regretted it. Oh, there have been times where I've had moral dilemmas, but that would always be the case. If you had a brain at all, you would have moments when you'd question, but…' He paused again and once more Devlin did not feel the need to comment. 'Yes, things have moved forward. There is a greater tolerance now and the future can be a different animal.'

Devlin smiled at the last phrase, saying, 'I'm sure you're right,' before raising his pint and taking a mouthful.

'Nice talking to you, Devlin, and sorry for the emotional outpouring. It's just this is our dream trip… We have been looking forward to it since—'

He stopped to exchange a glance with Catherine, who smiled benignly and, standing up, said, 'Shall we go and have that rest, Conor? We have some very exciting days ahead and we want to be at our best, don't we?'

Devlin shook hands with them both and watched them leave. He was struck by the way the tall man and his very erect wife linked arms, despite neither of them appearing to need any physical support. As the lounge was becoming even more boisterous, he made his way towards the snug bar in the corner. Devlin was trying to navigate his way through another high-spirited group who were singing along to the music, when a woman with a piercing gaze and long earrings turned to him, saying, 'Isn't it terrific? Can't you just feel that Celtic spirit?'

'Isn't it just,' Devlin agreed somewhat wearily.

'We've heard so much about the Irish and Ireland. Why, a business colleague told me we're bound to have a fantabulous time,' she said eagerly, then looked more closely at him. 'Have you been over before?'

'I have indeed,' he smiled. 'I'm sure you'll have a grand time.'

'Oh, that is splendid in itself. As I can tell, you're Irish and will know what to expect. So thank you.'

He went into the snug and found a seat in the corner beside the hologram of a turf fire. There were only a few people in this smaller bar and it was a welcome relief from the exuberance of the music and hubbub next door. He had just ordered another drink when a man in a dark suit and trilby hat approached.

'Do you mind if I join you?' he asked sombrely.

'Not at all.'

The man sat down and gazed into the fire and Devlin soon became lost in his own thoughts, forgetting that he had company. It was not until he had nearly finished another pint that the man spoke again.

'I'm thinking that you have folks back in the old country. What part would that be?'

Devlin considered a moment before answering. 'I have family out west,' he said, 'near Ben Bulben.'

'I've heard that's a lovely spot. I did have a cousin who was further north; he fished out of Killybegs.' The man paused to take a drink then said, 'I'm from Glengarriff myself and I am on the worst of all business. I am going home to bury my mother.'

'You have my sincere condolences.' Devlin paused and, observing the sadness etched in the man's face, he added. 'Unfortunately, our journeys have much in common. I am going to my only brother's funeral.'

'An awful thing.' The man shook his head. 'You have my sincere condolences as well. I suppose we are both lucky to be getting there, though fortune has little to do with anything – there is probably a great conversation that we will never have.'

'There is indeed,' Devlin reached over and placed his hand on the man's forearm, giving it a reassuring squeeze. 'Glengarriff is a beautiful part of Cork, I hear. Safe travelling.'

The man in the dark suit looked deep into Devlin's eyes before replying, 'and you. Good luck.'

'I'm going to rest up for a bit,' Devlin said, after finishing the last of his pint. 'Good luck.'

He left the snug to find that the group outside were still in the mood to party. The woman with long earrings was singing with particular passion. Seeing him, she moved forward, intent on picking up the conversation again. 'They had such a devil-may-care attitude all those years ago.'

Her face distorted as she shouted over the commotion. 'It's fantastic really. They were living right on the edge. We're so looking forward to it.'

'Oh, I'm sure that you'll be grand,' Devlin said, smiling politely, then he moved decisively away, waving to Scanlon as he left the bar.

Walking steadily along the corridors to his cabin, he became aware of the very consistent movement of the ship; the roll and pitch seemed to have been exactly the same since they set sail. Devlin reached the cabin and lay down, letting his head sink into the pillows, and as he was dropping off to sleep he thought how quiet the ships engines were.

He woke up with a start, as the purser knocked on the cabin door, announcing that they had arrived in Dublin. Devlin got ready for the onward journey and when he entered the reception area, it was alive with people requesting information and disembarking. In the middle of the floor, Kelly and Scanlon were in full flow, interacting with the travellers as well as with each other. He stopped for a few moments to observe their jovial interactions.

He lifted his holdall and was making his way to the gangway when Kelly turned to him, saying earnestly, 'I hope your journey goes well.'

'Yes, we hope your journey goes well,' Scanlon chimed in. 'May the prevailing breeze guide your fate.'

They then said in unison, 'May the prevailing breeze guide your fate.'

He smiled at them and, walking to the gangway, Devlin joined the descending passengers and was struck by the colour and vibrancy of the busy dockside, as the gulls' searching cries echoed incessantly in the late afternoon sunshine. There was a palpable air of expectation amongst his fellow travellers and, knowing how many times he had dreamed of making this journey, he allowed himself to be swept along in the moment.

Nearing the ferry terminal building, he saw Conor in a long coat with Catherine, who was wearing a smart Connemara tweed suit, and he said, 'I hope your trip goes well.'

The couple turned to face him and Catherine said, 'I'm sure it will. We are so looking forward to it. I'm sorry, we were so preoccupied with our own lives and never even thought to ask why you were travelling.'

'Oh, just some family business,' Devlin replied lightly.

'Well, I hope it goes well,' Conor said, 'and I really am sorry – mithering on about my working life. It's just I thought you'd understand and it seemed the right time.'

'Of course it was the right time,' Devlin said emphatically, then smiled. 'Now, enjoy yourselves.'

He walked briskly through the terminal building to the shuttle area. There was a slight smile on his face as he looked around at the various modes of transport arriving and leaving, as if everything was precisely as he had expected. If you were to observe him at that moment, you would see a person at ease with his surroundings, seemingly unbothered and certainly unthreatened. When he presented himself at the North West shuttle point, a precise voice greeted him.

'Good to see you, Mr Devlin. Welcome to the Glens Lakeland service.'

After viewing the timetable, he messaged his ETA to Miriam, who replied almost immediately saying all was well and she'd let Liam know. The shuttle arrived as expected and Devlin followed the guiding lights to his seat. After consulting the on-screen menu he chose a potato and egg dish. For his viewing option he chose the Regime's history channel and as he did not pick any particular programme, the auto-play function selected a feature that included footage he'd seen recently in the Rawlins.

The shuttle had external viewing points, reminiscent of small port holes, and he divided his time between the on-screen presentation and the landscape speeding past. The vehicle stopped during the journey on four occasions to allow passengers to get off and when it eventually slowed down in countryside that was very familiar to Devlin, a notification appeared on the screen to inform him he had reached his destination. Looking out to see the unmistakeable mountain form of Ben Bulben towering above, a wave of emotion came over him that he would later identify as sheer pleasure.

He gathered his luggage and on alighting the vehicle he stood transfixed on the ancient road, looking at the panoramic views and enjoying the sensation of the fragrant west wind blowing gently on his face. The noise of the shuttle faded in the distance and only when it had fully disappeared over the horizon did his cousin Liam appear from behind a large oak tree, extending his hand and saying, 'Welcome home. It's been a long, long time.'

'It has indeed.' Devlin nodded and as they shook hands slowly in the middle of the road, he reflected on how his cousin's pleasing rugged features, unruly brown hair and old tweed jacket blended perfectly with this mighty landscape – you could not doubt he was of this land.

'I've brought an old banger to get you back to the home place,' Liam said, pointing to a vehicle covered in mud and dust parked down a side-track.

Walking over to the far side of the road they gazed over a dense hedgerow to where the rippling surface of Glencar Lake lay far beneath their feet. A bright bevy of swans caught Devlin's eye and he felt reassured seeing the sparkling outline of the waterfall cascading down to the river, which in turn fed the briskly lapping lake; this was exactly the scene that he remembered. Above them reared the sharp escarpments of the cliffs of Ben Bulben, making for a truly awe-inspiring sight.

'You know, I have never forgotten the beauty of this place and there were many times when I dreamed of it,' he uttered breathlessly, 'but the sheer scale of it would truly stun you... when you've been away as long as I have.'

Liam did not say anything. He just smiled as Devlin continued to match the familiar landscape with his recollections. He looked across the plains that commenced at the foot of the mountain, effortlessly covering the few miles that led down to the ocean, where the sun was setting over Sligo Bay and a burnished path of sparkling light lay across the Atlantic waves.

'It's a rare evening,' Liam said, 'and that is some sky, I have to admit. What's it like to be back after all these years?'

'You have no idea,' Devlin replied. But then his mood changed quite suddenly and he said, 'It's not the occasion that I would have chosen for my return, that's for sure. How are Mam and Miriam doing?'

'Your mam is very upset – as you know, she and Ben were so close – but she still has that great resilience. He was a remarkable man in his own right, you know. He managed to work against all the odds, until this latest illness… Oh, I'm sorry. I don't need to tell you of all people.'

'Don't worry, Liam,' Devlin smiled ruefully. 'It *is* me of all people that you should be telling.'

'Miriam has been an absolute star,' Liam went on, 'getting everything sorted out. No fuss – just getting on with it. She's arranged everything with your mam since she came back. My partner Tony, who you'll remember from years ago, no doubt, has been down helping her out as he's in between jobs at the moment. They get on like a house on fire.'

'I do indeed, he was always a great fella. Well done cousin,' Devlin said and reinforced his approval by hugging Liam's shoulder strongly with his left arm.

The sense of camaraderie had resurfaced between the two men and if you were to see them stood together, you would assume they were regular companions rather than relatives who had not seen each other for over twenty-five years.

'Different days to when we were growing up, for sure,' Liam reflected. 'Do you remember all those long political discourses and the drinking?'

'I do,' Devlin nodded slowly. 'They always went well together, the discourse and the drinking – but the talking must have led somewhere because shortly after that, the Celtic Movement for Autonomy was formed and you were in the thick of that, I heard.'

'Yes, you are right. The CMA started just after that and of course, the direction you took with the CRP is well known.' He paused before adding in a more measured tone, 'There is a wake for Ben tonight and I'll tell you all about the arrangements in a moment. I just wanted to have a few words with you first, if that's OK?'

Devlin turned away from the dramatic Sligo landscape and

the gaze of his full blue eyes rested on his cousin. 'You have my full attention.'

'When I say the direction you took is well known, that is true, but no one knows what you think, where your heart lies.' He stopped and for a few moments the two men looked steadily at one another. 'Or what political direction you would take now.'

'I'm not sure I am going to take any political direction, to be honest. But you know as well as I do, Liam, political action doesn't happen in a vacuum and its success is dependent on many factors. It's all well and good wanting some ideal, but if it is doomed to failure – I've always struggled with that notion.' Devlin paused and, looking round at the landscape once more, added, 'Though I have to say that I believe in the people of this land as strongly as I ever did.'

'That's fair enough and I think I understand what you're saying to me, so let me say this and then we'll travel on. For many in the CMA, initially there was an outright hostility to the CRP, but now many have reappraised their position and there is a recognition that the organisation has delivered some good outcomes commercially and that it has, broadly speaking, benefitted people.'

'So, I am now viewed in a different light.' Devlin smiled and there was an unmistakeable glint in his eyes. 'Now that's interesting. Are you saying that the position of the CMA has changed then?'

'You are still as sharp as ever when it comes to reading the politics.' Liam's thick brown hair waved as he nodded appreciatively. 'And yes, you are probably right about the CMA changing. I believe because of the things you have chosen to be involved in, that your heart is in the right place; I have heard about your work with a local Allotments Association, and is that not creating a greater autonomy for a community?'

'Are you saying that the CMA has turned away from the notion of an armed uprising?'

'I am not sure I was ever totally sold on that course of action.

The majority of the organisation has moved on, I'm sure, though a few still hanker after the old bloody struggle. But what these people are ignoring is that the latent power of the Regime is so great that…' Liam left the rest unsaid, his dark blue eyes gazing solemnly at Devlin for a few seconds before continuing. 'Besides, there is a greater cultural freedom now and people are starting to prosper. The point being that if there was a place for political discourse, greater freedoms could be negotiated.'

'Is there a split within the CMA? It certainly sounds familiar, just like the politics of old – the nationalistic forces divided. This is all very interesting, but it doesn't explain why you have brought this up with me now.'

'All I am saying is that you are very welcome home and if you decided to take up a fuller political role again, it could benefit the people of these communities. I am opening this discussion with you now, so that we may talk again in the coming days.'

'And we will for sure, Liam,' Devlin said, glancing up and noticing that the stars were starting to appear. 'The heavens seem to be aligning in a certain way,' he smiled playfully, 'but I can't quite figure out what the future holds.'

'I'm sure you will, Michael,' he said, opening the door to the vehicle. 'I'm sure you will.'

Devlin settled in his seat and, looking straight ahead, the lines of his face dropped noticeably as he said, 'I was so sad to hear about your mam's sudden illness, it must have been so difficult for you and Niall, especially after the tragic death of your dad in that tractor accident. They were both so young. As you were to lose your parents… It was hard to believe and I would have loved to have come over.'

Liam looked directly at him and spoke gently. 'It is something that doesn't make sense, even now, but somehow we have had to learn to live with it. I do find some comfort in how much they loved the home place and as the seasons go by, with us tending it as well as we can…' He looked away and said resolutely, 'I know the travelling was virtually impossible at that time – why, even Niall struggled to get over.'

A silence descended in the car, disturbed only by the intermittent buffeting of the wind as the two men looked at the last rays of the sun, which was sinking below the horizon. There was so much that could be said in a regretful, angry or guilty way, but for Devlin there was a cathartic sense of healing in these minutes and he had the notion that this was also the case for his cousin.

Eventually his thoughts came back to his own mother and he said, 'I expected Mam to have a wake for Ben, but I didn't know if they were a common event nowadays?'

'Oh yes, they have become the norm again of late, like many of the old rituals – and another change is that local Celtic customs have been reborn to a great extent and superseded Catholicism for many. But you will find these changes easy enough in the coming days…' Liam considered before saying, 'The house will be open for family and neighbours to perhaps share a drink or two; it won't last the whole night – at least I don't think it will.'

'And the service is eleven tomorrow?'

'It is, and I'm sure you know that it is cousin Thomas's wedding on Saturday.'

Liam started up the engine and as they drove off into the growing darkness, he spoke about family matters and the neighbourhood news. Listening without comment, Devlin watched the headlights searching out the hedgerows, fields and gaps along the road; the effect was hypnotic. Many familiar landmarks appeared as they journeyed on and he had the feeling of being on a spiritual journey, one that he was determined to savour.

When they entered the lane by the home place, there was no room to park beside the house, so Liam pulled up outside the gates and as the two cousins walked down the driveway Devlin noticed the star constellations being particularly bright overhead. Nearing the house, he saw Miriam standing in the porch. With her shoulder-length coppery-coloured hair and lithe figure emphasised by the long dress she was wearing, she had barely changed since she was a teenager – the last time he'd seen her. Miriam ran out of the house and they hugged instinctively. When they parted, he looked at her, feeling an instinctive surge of emotion.

'You're so welcome home, Michael,' she said and as if reading his thoughts, added, 'don't worry, there will be plenty of time to talk.'

Looking past his sister, Devlin saw a slight man of athletic stature, who had short hair, standing in the doorway and after a moment's hesitation, he strode over and embraced him. 'It's good to meet you again, Tony.'

'It's good to see you, Michael,' he replied, a faint smile visible on his lips, 'and I'm so very sad about Ben.'

'Thank you for all you've done, Tony. I know your friendship meant so much to him.'

Devlin stepped into the hallway just as his mother was coming out of the kitchen with a large teapot that she put down on a chair. Her greying brown hair was slightly dishevelled, moisture glistened in her eyes, but her alertness was very apparent. He walked slowly towards her; she regarded him intently, as if double-checking it was really him before they embraced. When they parted she cupped her two hands around his face and gently stroked his chin, saying, 'Well I am so glad to see you. You are a sight for sore eyes and mine are a little sore now for sure… Are you alright, Michael?'

'I am fine, Mam. Just let me know what you want me to do.'

'We will mingle with family and neighbours in honour of Ben,' she said, looking at him carefully once more.

'That sounds like what we should be doing, for sure.' Saying this, Devlin bowed towards his mother.

Peering into the front room, he heard the deep murmur of many simultaneous conversations that hadn't really registered with him up to that point. His mother picked up the teapot again and, following her into the crowded room, Devlin got the distinct impression that everybody had observed his entrance, even though the noise levels did not alter.

The next hour passed with Devlin immersing himself in the occasion; there were many expressions of loss and affection in the heartfelt exchanges that he had with relations and people from the neighbourhood. Eventually, realising that he was in fact very hungry, he went to the table and after looking appreciatively at the wonderful spread of food he filled his plate, with a generous slice of his mother's pie taking pride of place. Devlin ate slowly, savouring the evocative taste of the home cooking. He was finishing when Miriam appeared at his side.

'Michael, don't be afraid to have a break,' she cupped his elbow in her hand and spoke gently in his ear, 'there will be people here for hours. Your room is all made up for you and Ben is in the living room when you want to go see him. It's quiet in there now.'

'I will go and see him now then.' He nodded and looked round. He was struck by the strong resemblance between her long elegant features and those of their mother's, one that he had never seen so clearly before.

Noticing his gaze, she looked knowingly with a twinkle in her eyes and then went over to talk to Auntie Anne and Uncle Ronan. Devlin was putting the plate down as Thomas walked towards him, tall, lean and smiling, with his arm loosely round his diminutive fiancé Bernadette.

'You must have been ready for that,' Thomas said heartily, observing the empty plate.

'I was indeed,' Devlin said, picking up a glass of whiskey, 'and I'm ready for this as well.' He took a sip. 'Ah, Bernadette, look at you. Weren't you a small child when I last saw you?'

'I'm sure I was,' she spoke hesitantly, her eyelids drooping over her shining dark eyes. 'I am so sorry for your loss. Ben was such a lovely person.'

'He was,' Devlin smiled openly, raising his glass, 'and he would have been the first to congratulate you on your big day coming up on Saturday. I am sure he's smiling down and I'm sure ye will be very happy.'

'Thank you, Michael,' Thomas replied magnanimously. 'We have a place at the wedding for you and we would love you to be there.'

'Just try to keep me away.'

They wandered off and he walked slowly into the living room, cradling his stemmed whiskey glass in his right hand. He nodded to a couple of neighbours who were readying to leave and then all of a sudden, he was completely alone with his brother. Looking slowly around the candle-lit room and in particular at the oak dresser with the familiar crockery, he eventually let his gaze come to rest on the open wicker coffin. Ben looked different, but no matter how much he studied his features, he could not work out in what way.

Maybe it's just the process of ageing, he thought, before a smile came to his lips and he whispered, 'I can imagine you saying to me, "No wonder I've aged. It's been a long time, you know. Where the hell have you been?" And you're right – where have I been, my brother?'

Pulling up a kitchen chair, he sat down beside Ben, who had been laid out in his favourite dark teal Aran jumper and tweed trousers, and reflected upon how at ease his features looked despite the unreal waxy glaze there was to his skin, contrasting his natural dark, wavy hair. Devlin had not thought about what he might say to his brother, but he found that the words came easily. 'You did so brilliantly with your work and you lived a great life out here in Connaught, there's no doubt about it. I never got the chance to say it, brother, but I'm very proud of you.'

The old clock ticked along very slowly and the solemnity of the passing minutes were imprinted on him; Devlin knew he could never have the time back that they had lost, but he savoured these special moments – ones that he would return to many times in the future. He had the unmistakeable sense that Ben was not far away and he would never totally leave this place. Devlin smiled sadly at his brother and whispered, 'Well, it looks like your big brother has been wasting a lot of time, Ben. Out there chasing and exploring, like when I was a boy, and missing the important things closer to home.'

He was breathing easily when Miriam came in and looking up at the clock, Devlin was surprised to see that twenty minutes had passed. No one had come in during that time, which he assumed had been out of respect, to allow him some time alone with his brother.

Standing behind him, Miriam put her arms around his shoulders and, looking at Ben, said, 'Well, big brother, you wouldn't believe how glad we are to have you here.'

Their mother entered the darkened room and her eyes glowed with a surprising brightness when she started to pray beside the coffin. Both Devlin and his sister instinctively bowed their heads. He could not make out all the words, but he was aware that it was a prayer he did not know and when she had finished, she walked slowly around to join her children, nestling herself between them in a warm hug.

After releasing her hold, she addressed Ben, saying, 'You gave us all such joy and pride – really and truly. You have all our love.'

They stood as a family for a few minutes, after which their mother shepherded them slowly out of the room. Devlin stood in the hallway listening to the volume of the conversation from the front room, which was even louder than before. Picking up his holdall that he'd left by the front door, he said, 'I'll go and drop this off and freshen myself up a bit.'

Walking up the stairs, he became aware of the temperature dropping considerably and he thought about how hard it must have been for his mother and Ben to maintain this old house. The floorboards creaked as he crossed the landing but on entering his bedroom, he was pleasantly surprised to find that it looked much like it had all those years ago. The small cottage armchair with the floral upholstery was still by the window and sitting down, he looked out at the garden in the moonlight. He continued to listen to the dull sound of conversation rising up from below, provoking the thought that there was so much he did not know about the place he had grown up in and even about his own family.

He returned downstairs and joined Miriam, Liam, Tony and his mother, making tea, serving guests and washing the crockery. Devlin mingled easily when he went back into the front room, replenishing cups and bringing out used dishes. He kept himself so busy that he did not notice the room thinning out as the night progressed. By the time Liam and Tony came over to say their farewells, it was the early hours of the morning and there were only a few neighbours left.

'We will be testing you on the names of all those people, Michael,' Liam spoke gently, tilting his head.

'I certainly hope not,' Devlin responded, widening his eyes. 'But seriously, I am so glad ye are carrying Ben with myself and Miriam tomorrow. Talking of which, it's not that far away now. Go on now. You'll need to get some rest yourselves.'

'It will come around soon enough, alright,' Tony said, a hint of resignation in his voice. 'Goodnight.'

After seeing off the last of the guests, Devlin and Miriam went to join their mother in the living room for one final vigil. She stood between her two remaining children, arms locked around them both, drawing comfort from their presence. All three stood in silence, looking down at Ben's still, silent body as the clock ticked away with great conviction in the candlelight.

Eventually, his mother said emotionally, 'Well, Ben, it's a big day tomorrow. But I know you will not be fearful. Goodnight, my courageous fighter.'

With that, she left the living room and, looking neither left nor right, went straight upstairs to bed. The two siblings lingered a while longer with their own thoughts and then finally walked slowly out into the kitchen, where Miriam instinctively started putting the last of the plates and glasses away.

'You must be shattered,' Devlin said, seeing the obvious lines of fatigue in her face.

'I am, but I don't feel like sleeping.'

'I'm the same. Will you tell me about Donegal and what you've been doing?'

Sighing, she put her arm around him casually. 'OK, Michael,' she said, 'it's not a long story to tell and it may well put you to sleep… So maybe it would be a good thing.'

Going out of the back door into the garden, they sat on the bench beside the lawn. The sky was clear, it was a beautiful moonlit night and a gentle breeze was blowing in off the sea. There was a slight rustling of leaves and with the outlines of all the trees and shrubs moving, it gave the garden a great feeling of abundance and life.

Devlin noticed the old rope swing that his father had attached to the largest bough of the oak tree and he was thinking about times they'd spent playing on it as children. The garden had been another world to him when they were younger; a place of games, magic and sanctuary. Miriam smiled intuitively at him and said, 'You know that Mam always felt the garden was a special place. I think it is her gift to us really, somewhere where we were free to play and grow in safety. She was never a fussy gardener or protective in any way, and she never scolded us if we broke a plant. Do you remember her saying, "Don't worry about the plants, children; if you break the limb of a plant by accident, it will grow back even stronger. But if you break it on purpose, then it will die."'

'I do remember her saying that.' He smiled and added, 'Talking of plants that have grown, tell me what happened to the bold Miriam in Donegal? She obviously flourished. I know you are a teacher that you married and have a son, Finn, but there's so much I don't know… You will have to tell me the whole story.'

'Devil the much I feel bold at the moment and in truth,

there is not a lot to tell. I went to college and developed a love of literature, but teaching that was not an option, as you know. So, I taught English to the young ones and some Gaelic on the quiet. I met Gerry when I was at college and we married too young, I guess. But the great thing is we had Finn, who's grown up now and a stone worker – he does everything from dry-stone walling to mad sculptures. He's brilliant.

'Gerry and I did not so much split up as never really got going. Anyway, I stayed on in Donegal with Finn and I have a great group of friends up there, so life has always been interesting. I love the songs and the old language and being a teacher has served me well, as I have been able to spend holidays here with Mam and Ben. I am down as a carer for Ben…' She stopped, her voice breaking slightly, 'Which is a joke really, since he's so independent. I mean, *was* so independent.' She paused and added, 'Oh, what the feck, Michael. Maybe he is truly independent now and looking down on us – amused at our deliberations and cogitations.'

'He may be doing that alright… but I do have to admit that I'm suddenly feeling the pace, sister,' he said, stifling a yawn.

'Oh, Michael, it will be your advanced years. I could never imagine living to such an old age.'

'I don't think you're that far behind me, sister… And I have to admit, you were right about putting me to sleep.'

'Now listen to you – you're only home five minutes and you're getting decidedly cheeky now,' she chimed back, plainly enjoying the sparring, before adding in a more subdued tone, 'And I was planning to get the full uncensored Michael Devlin story, but I have to admit, I'm running out of steam myself.'

'I'd sleep alright, Miriam. But don't worry, you will have the story alright. Just don't build up your hopes for too epic a tale.'

After they'd gone inside Miriam checked all the rooms downstairs, closing some of the windows. Then they stood at the door to the living room and said goodnight to Ben again, before going up the stairs to bed.

Once back in his room, Devlin walked instinctively over to the window. He could not resist sitting down in the old floral chair again and was asleep before he had time to feel his eyes closing.

CHAPTER NINE

Devlin woke up to a chorus of bird song that was startling in its volume and he spent several minutes listening intently, trying to identify the various calls. The sadness of the occasion was not lost on him, but he could not deny the deep sense of satisfaction he felt from being at home in his old room.

When he did get up and go downstairs, dressed in his best tweed jacket, shirt, trousers and brogue shoes, he found Miriam and his mother preparing food for the after-funeral gathering. He looked around the kitchen, marvelling at all the fine local fare that had appeared since they had gone to bed only hours before.

'I'm sorry,' he said, running both his hands through his hair, 'I seem to have slept in. Is there anything I can do, Mam?'

'Oh, you must have needed that sleep, Michael,' his mother said, as she stopped covering platters of food and walked over to embrace him. 'And don't worry, we have been getting things ready for days, haven't we, Miriam?'

'We certainly have,' Miriam nodded. 'There's fresh bread and scrambled eggs for breakfast and even some bacon if you fancy it.' She then gestured towards the table and, giving him a sharp stare of her very bright blue eyes, added, 'But you can't touch any of this until the guests come later, under pain of death!'

Devlin smiled as his mother said genially, 'Have plenty to eat now while you can. It will be a long old day. And just to let you know what is going to happen – Mr Doran, the registrar, and Erringal, who's conducting the service, will be here soon to sort everything out. If you could talk to them, that would be great. Pat O'Grady will be over soon too with the horse and trailer for Ben and the neighbours will bring over more flowers, no doubt.'

'I will do my best,' Devlin said, looking between his mother and sister, 'but to a large extent, these ways are unfamiliar to me now.'

'Oh, Michael,' his mother exclaimed, 'I want you as involved as possible. Just remember, there is no right or wrong way for this day to go. There are no rules and all that matters is doing what's best for Ben, so if you could talk with Erringal and Mr O'Grady about how Ben will ride on the trailer and also discuss the flower arrangements, that would be great.'

'Of course, Mam,' he responded confidently, 'I'll do it.'

'I didn't realise the time.' She wiped her hands on her apron. 'Miriam, we'd better start getting ourselves ready. And one more thing, Michael. If you want to say a few words in the hall later, that would be nice. Miriam will be singing, of course.'

A dog walked in through the kitchen door and glanced at each of them in turn.

'Oh, it's great to see you about again, Bran,' Miriam enthused. 'Are you coming in with Ben today?' She turned to her brother. 'He is very much Ben's dog and has been laying low in the shed for days now.'

As mother and daughter went off to prepare upstairs, Devlin filled a plate and sat down at the table, with Bran lying down at his feet. The dog looked up at him sometimes while he ate, not to beg for food but seemingly wanting reassurance, and he reached down occasionally to stroke the brindle-coloured sheep dog.

After breakfast, Devlin went into the living room to have a few final moments with his brother, but he had only been stood there a few minutes when two men entered the hallway. One of them, who he knew to be Mr Doran, strode confidently towards the coffin and shook his hand.

'It's good to see you back home, Michael,' Mr Doran said, his dark eyes regarding him slowly, 'and it's a fine morning indeed. You'll know Erringal here, a keeper of the ancient ways and customs. He will lead us through the ceremonial matters today.'

'Oh, doesn't Ben look so peaceful,' Erringal observed, stepping forward and giving Devlin's hand a prolonged shake. 'And rest assured, Michael, we shall send him off properly.'

Devlin could not help but stare at the two men; the tall and sartorial Mr Doran in his smart suit and Erringal, a large man with strongly weathered features and thick wavy hair, dressed in a long, threadbare tweed coat.

'Would you give me a hand please, Michael?' Erringal asked as he circled the wicker coffin. 'We will move with all the care we can. It is but a short journey today,' he said, addressing Ben, 'and you have longer to go, so don't think harshly of our humble efforts.'

He pointed Devlin towards the cover that was hinged to the side of the coffin and together they lifted it upright.

'The lands of eternal youth were always there,' Erringal bowed his head slightly, 'just beyond your mother's garden. A place of wonderment that I am sure you can see clearly now, Ben.'

With that, they lowered the lid down slowly and without needing to turn his head to look, Devlin knew that both Miriam and his mother were watching from the doorway. Erringal showed him how to knot the first in a series of leather strips that held the lid in place and then he worked his way round the coffin, fastening the rest himself.

'These bonds could never hold you in this place,' Erringal repeated with the tying of each one, 'or keep you from your eternal way.'

Looking down at his handiwork, Devlin could not help but

feel satisfied as the leather strips served to embroider the edge of the coffin in a very natural way.

'That's lovely, Michael,' his mother said, moving to stand beside him. 'Now, could you and Miriam start the floral display on Mr O'Grady's trailer? Liam and Tony will return with you when you're done, to help carry Ben. I think it is time.'

When he went outside, the murmuring of the people who had filled the driveway became audible to Devlin and looking around, he was pleased by both the size of the crowd and their multi-coloured attire. Ahead of him, two large black horses stood restlessly between the shafts of the funeral trailer, with contrasting purple and bright yellow ribbons threaded through their manes.

'Easy now,' Mr O'Grady said, his dark green velvet coachman's jacket catching the eye as he patted them reassuringly, 'it will be a while yet. There are a great number of flowers for Ben.'

The floral tributes that lined the front of the house contained stunning hues of all the local blooms and taking great care, Miriam and Devlin decorated the far side of the trailer, stepping back regularly to view the display and make adjustments. Liam and Tony waited patiently until the flowers were arranged and then the four of them walked back into the house and approached Ben, where Mr Doran and Erringal directed them as they lifted him up onto their shoulders.

Devlin and Liam were the bearers at the rear, with Miriam and Tony taking the front. They walked slowly out of the house and lowered the wicker coffin, which creaked as it was placed onto the trailer and slid into place. Devlin and Miriam then took some time to put the rest of the flowers in place, the crowd murmuring its approval while they worked, and Devlin found that the more he looked at what they had done, the surer he became of the arrangement. Once they had finished, brother and sister walked around the trailer together to perform one final inspection, drawing spontaneous applause from those assembled.

'Feel free to come with us on this slow walk with Ben,' Erringal addressed the crowd, after letting the applause die down, 'along this road, where all of an honest heart are welcome.'

Mrs Devlin, who was dressed in a long teal dress complimented by a cream knitted shawl, came alongside the trailer and Mr O'Grady supported her elbow as she took her place in the high passenger seat.

'Will you join me, Rosie?' she called out to her neighbour Mrs Gillespie, who was leaning heavily on a walking stick. 'There's room enough for a little one up here with me.'

After a moment's hesitation, Mrs Gillespie moved forward and, with some support from those standing nearest to the trailer, climbed up alongside Mrs Devlin. Meanwhile, Mr O'Grady checked the tackle again, before walking around the horses to take his place in the driver's seat, clasping the long whip that the people took as a signal to clear the way. Then, having surveyed the crowd to confirm that everything was in order, he brought the whip down with a single light crack.

'Giddy-yohaa!' he called out, spurring the horses to walk on as the trailer creaked along the first rickety steps of its slow journey, with Devlin, Miriam, Liam and Tony walking behind the coffin and the crowd following at a respectful distance.

The day had started very brightly, but now clouds were being driven forth by a fresh, bracing wind off the Atlantic and though it would have been hard to accurately predict the coming weather, it was obvious that there would be rain at some stage during the day. Below this increasingly animated sky, the procession moved at a pace set by the horses and a gentle murmur of prayers and conversation burbled among the people as they approached the brow of a hill, from which the road swept downwards to Mullnamorran. This view from Knockbrack, of the small town with its pier nestled beside the endlessly moving ocean, was an image set deep in Devlin's memory. He smiled when he looked down to see that Bran had since joined the mourners and was walking between himself and Miriam, who wore a floral embroidered suit of many autumn colours. More neighbours merged with them along the route; some were already inside the old church when they arrived. When Devlin, Miriam, Liam and Tony were in position to lift the coffin, an observer looking down on the scene would be struck by the great naturalness of the proceedings, with no single person taking charge. Directions were given through nods and gestures as Ben was carried from the carriage and, after a slow walk, laid down on two plain wooden trestles beside the old altar.

A song with a repeating refrain was sung while the congregation filed in and Devlin noted an earthiness to the tune that was rendered with emotion, which he found deeply moving. The church was soon full, with many unable to find a place inside, but this did not prevent those left in the yard from picking up the song, their slightly delayed notes creating a harmonic echoing effect that Devlin found pleasing, and once the singing had come to a natural end, the birdsong and wind came to the fore again. Erringal made his way unhurriedly to the front of the church, smiling benignly to both the left and right. Placing his hand upon the coffin, he turned around and started to pray in a gentle voice that carried surprisingly well.

'It is with ancient words that I now address you, Ben, as you start on your sweet journey – a journey that we all hope to make one day – onwards in the realisation that it is not so far. It can't be, as it is rooted in this landscape and our Gaelic spirituality, handed down to us throughout the centuries, all-enduring, so long as we have the mind to listen. Like the returning dew, your spirit will refresh our future mornings and our dreams.'

Listening to Erringal as he continued to pray in a manner that was clearly unscripted, Devlin was moved by the symmetry of his words, as well as the thought that perhaps he was experiencing a spiritual awakening of his own, inspired by this humble oratory in the land of his childhood. When the holy man had finished speaking, all eyes turned to Miriam, standing with head bowed between Devlin and her mother, as she lifted her gaze, took a single deep breath and started to sing. Her voice filled the high arches of the church, the effect amplified by the congregation's reverential silence, and though Devlin did not dare to look at his sister for fear that he would disturb her, he realised afterwards that this was a foolish notion on his part, such was the unerring certainty with which she delivered the song. Singing in the native Irish tongue, Miriam skilfully timed the lowering of her voice to coincide with the final notes, allowing it to softly mingle with the natural sounds from outside. The ritual continued with prayers, songs and passages of music played on fiddle and flute until, near the end of the ceremony, family members moved forward to take turns touching the coffin. When it was time to say a few words, Tony talked effusively about Ben's great love for the home place as well as his importance to the local community and Devlin recalled warmly his brother's great affinity with the sea, before stating his wish that they would know such times again. Miriam spoke of when she came home to help care for Ben – it was really he who supported and sustained her – and after several impromptu tributes from various other friends and family members, Erringal changed the mood completely by starting an upbeat song that was duly taken up by the whole congregation. The ceremony ended in a very uplifting manner, with people hugging and shaking hands.

Once the activity in the church had died down, Devlin, Miriam, Liam and Tony moved to the front and after some brief closing words from Erringal, they picked up the wicker coffin and walked slowly back outside, where Mr O'Grady stood with his horses, watching closely as they placed Ben back on the funeral carriage and the four bearers set about rearranging the flowers. Devlin was very heartened to hear so many of those assembled speaking in the native Irish tongue as they gathered around the family for the final send-off. Once Mrs Devlin and Mrs Gillespie had been helped up into the front passenger seat, the fiddle and flute players took their places on either side of the coffin.

Mr O'Grady looked over the horse tack again, causing some

wry amusement among a small section of the crowd who felt he was overemphasising his own importance to the occasion, and once satisfied that everything was in order, he mounted the trailer and, lifting his whip, turned to Mrs Devlin.

'Are we ready to go, Mam?' he asked solemnly.

'I believe that we are.' She tilted her head in answering.

'Giddy-yohaa!' He gave his distinctive call, bringing his whip down from a great height but barely touching the horses' hides, as the procession moved off through a side gate, taking a track that led directly to the graveyard while avoiding the town.

The musicians played hornpipes and marches in a lively manner as they went, with progress slowed by the crowd having to thin out to pass along the narrow lane, until Mr O'Grady brought the horses to a halt just inside the cemetery gates, this being the nearest point of access to Ben's burial place at the crest of a hill, underneath a large rowan tree. The quartet of bearers came together beside the wicker coffin, while friends and neighbours filed past with offerings of condolences and appreciation for having known Ben, most of them clutching wreathes that Mrs Devlin handed out at the entrance. Once all the flowers had been removed from the trailer, Erringal stopped the oncoming people with a wave of his hand. If you were to look down on the scene at that moment, it would be hard not to be impressed by the vibrant colour of the many floral tributes making their way up the hill, as the graveyard came alive with people gathered under the dominant rowan tree, while Devlin, Miriam, Liam and Tony slid the coffin to the edge of the trailer and lifted it onto their shoulders for the last time. The ascent was not too far in distance, but became very uneven in places, so the bearers talked to one another throughout, with Miriam and Tony forewarning of any particular hazards. Upon reaching the graveside, other relatives came forward and took the weight and the coffin was brought down to the ground with great care.

Erringal waited a few minutes to allow the last few mourners to join the assembly before gently addressing Ben, talking about a life well lived and reminding him of all the good wishes that went with him. The fiddler then stepped forward and played a slow air that featured a remarkable range of notes, finishing with a double stop, the two low notes moving with the swaying of the wind. As these notes were dying out, the sound of two hovering drones could be heard across the graveyard, but no one looked over in their direction or gave any acknowledgment that they were there. Erringal said a prayer in native Irish, some of which Devlin was able to discern – enough for him to infer a theme based on the changing of the seasons. He was pleased to notice that the drones left in time for Miriam to sing the final song as the coffin was lowered into the grave. Devlin's attention was drawn momentarily to a jaunting car on the road below and as the woman driver removed her shawl, revealing long, auburn hair, he wondered if she had paused to listen to Miriam's beautiful voice, or if she knew that the singer was lamenting the loss of her younger brother.

The first soil was thrown into the grave by the closest relatives and then other mourners came forward. As the crowd gradually began to disperse, Mrs Devlin led her family back down the hill, where they congregated next to the trailer.

'Ben loved the rowan tree,' she said softly, as she hugged the four pallbearers in turn, 'and Mr Doran had to pull some strings so that he could rest there. He loved it when the berries were rich with that deep red colour. Through the sadness, it's been a fine day and there will be a few coming back to the house no doubt, so I'll away to home with Mr O'Grady to prepare.' She looked to Devlin. 'Are you alright, Michael? I'll be amazed if you don't walk down to the sea.'

'You read my mind, Mam,' he replied, smiling faintly.

'Maybe I'll join you for the walk, Michael,' Miriam queried, 'if that's OK?'

'Of course it is.'

Walking through the graveyard, Devlin and his sister crossed the main road before taking a footpath marked by the remains of an upturned boat, stopping briefly to inspect the old red hull with its exposed keel and then going right at a fork in the track, starting their descent towards the ocean. The wind was becoming gusty as they passed two large pine trees and came to a set of jagged limestone boulders, known locally as the Sailor's Eye due to their use as a landmark by sailors and fishermen. It was a vantage point that they had visited regularly as children, playing pirates and the like and watching the boats that went in and out of Mullnamorran Harbour, and it had also taken on a different significance as they'd got older, being a popular spot for lovers in search of seclusion.

'Do you think Mam will be OK?' Devlin asked as they came to a standstill and he took his jacket off, throwing it over his shoulder. 'This must all be a massive shock to her.'

'She will be busy organising and doing now,' Miriam answered, her bright blue eyes remaining fixed on the rolling waves. 'She'll have Liam and Tony fully occupied, of that I've no doubt. She is an amazing woman, Michael, and I have often wondered at her certainty. She is like Erringal and many of that older generation. They seem to have a great spiritual belief, which I swear has only grown stronger over the years, not diminished. She loved Ben deeply, but she does not believe that she's lost him. She still sees him as being here to a great extent and I think she's right.'

'And I'm sure you're right,' Devlin agreed. 'I have to say, Ben's funeral has amazed me; so many in the community appear to be fervent about the ancient ways and beliefs. What puzzles me, though, is what you said about Mam's spirituality, as I don't remember it being so evident years ago.'

'You are right, Michael,' she turned to face him, 'but as you know, Dad was very sceptical about the ancient ways, so as a family we did not get involved back then. It changed soon after you left, though. Mam's beliefs seemed to come very much to the fore and there is no doubt that Dad became less resistant, perhaps because this way of thinking was also more prevalent in the community in the wake of the relaxing of restrictions around religion.'

'Of course, that makes sense.'

'You know, I haven't been out here for years. I've meant to come many times, but never quite got around to it. I'd forgotten how beautiful the views of the harbour are.'

'Yes, this place has always stayed with me,' he said, gazing seaward once more. 'It's amazing really.'

'You know, that reminded me of our childhood, Michael. Do you remember when you would go off exploring, with me, the little sister, trailing after – the one you couldn't get rid of?' she said, with a slight needling in her voice.

'Oh, I'm sorry, I wasn't thinking,' he said hurriedly. 'I just had it in my mind to come here.'

'I knew well you did, big brother. It's lovely and everything is as it should be.' She smiled widely and then continued, 'We will have to look at the Golden Strand while we're here.'

They went back the way they came and at the fork took a sandy track, before negotiating a network of paths that led through dense shrubbery until eventually they came to Roaches Dark Rock, which overlooked the Golden Strand.

'Well,' Miriam placed a hand on her brother's shoulder, 'you certainly remember the way.'

'I could always find my way around here,' he said, looking down at the coastline and realising that the recent dream of the family picnicking was connected to this place; the colour of the sand and the way the tide rolled in were exactly the same. Devlin was experiencing a strong sense of déjà vu when he said, 'I dreamed of us all on the beach when we were little. I had been exploring and you were paddling with Ben in the sea. Mam and Dad were settled on a blanket and we had sandwiches. It seemed so real… Miriam, do you remember Dad playing the harmonica?'

'No, I don't think so. Why?'

'Oh, nothing. It's just that in the dream he did. I've been

dreaming a lot lately and the reality of them has been very striking.'

'Ah, the dreams. There are strange things happening with dreams and memory, and maybe we'll talk about it in the coming days. Interestingly, some people believe it is happening – the rise in vivid dreaming, that is – because of Regime activity, whereas others point to the ancient Celtic powers being revitalised.'

Devlin took a moment to study his sister's long, comely features. Before making the trip he had hoped he would get on well with her, but he was in reality delighted by the way they were tuning into each other's thoughts and how much they had in common.

'And maybe both explanations are true,' he said, smiling broadly, and they turned to make their way home.

Strolling into town, Devlin and Miriam had the road to the harbour on their left, with the small fishermen's cottages visible on the outskirts. All the familiar landmarks that he remembered were still present in the main square: Sheehan's Stores, Grogan's Bar, the Bamboo Lounge, the Dexter Monument and the Patriots Memorial.

'Is it anything in particular that you're looking for, Michael?' Miriam asked, following his gaze. 'As you can see, little has changed.'

His attention had been drawn to the street lights, which had been updated significantly since his youth and now had a very modern appearance.

'No, there's nothing I'm looking for,' he said. 'Like you say, nothing much has changed.'

'It's funny, we never spent much time in the town really, except when going to Sheehan's for supplies with Mam, hoping we would get an ice cream. And then, when we were older, it was only for sessions at Grogan's and the Bamboo.'

'Yes, the sessions. Maybe we will return if we have time in the coming days,' he said, before pausing to observe the dark clouds that were starting to roll in off the Atlantic. 'We should make a move for home, for it looks like a good downpour's on the way. It's like the old days – me, you and Ben rushing to make it home between the showers.'

'It is indeed and I think he is definitely with us today.'

They walked briskly away from the town and had gone a few hundred yards in silence when Miriam said suddenly, 'Your returning has caused a great interest in some quarters, it would be fair to say.'

'So I believe,' Devlin replied. 'Liam has spoken to me already, though not in any great detail.'

'There is a thirst for greater autonomy, but to what extent and the methods to be employed to get it are issues that have become divisive ones within this community. There is no doubt that life has improved of late. There are no shortages of food, we are free to speak the native language and to live life in accordance with the ancient customs to a large extent, but for some it is not enough. As things have been relaxed and the community has grown stronger, some hanker for a state of total independence from the Regime and a minority appear prepared to go to the extremes of a violent rebellion to achieve it.'

'It's strange for me, Miriam. I feel a great nostalgia at being back, even on such a sad occasion, but I have indeed sensed a restlessness in some people.' He paused for a moment before continuing. 'I knew coming back that some people would be aware of my past involvement with the CRP and thus the Regime, so I was prepared for a mixed reception.'

'In my mind, there is no doubt that the work of the CRP benefitted us,' she said with conviction, 'and there is a growing understanding that it was the start of the movement towards greater freedom. However, you should be aware that some will see you as an enemy and particularly as you are here and the Regime remains so distant and powerful, they could see this visit as an opportunity to strike out at you.'

'I trust you, Miriam, and your words are welcome. I shall consider myself forewarned.' And with that, he hugged her.

'The reason I am bringing this up now is that there are some within the family who wish to pursue a more violent way. Cousin Pádraig and his wife Aoife are of such a mind and no doubt they will be back at the house when we return.'

'Thanks, sister. I will bear it in mind,' he said, his thoughtful blue eyes searching out hers.

A heavy shower started a hundred yards or so from the house, just as they reached the high part of the road. Bran came bounding out of the hedgerow, barking excitedly, and Miriam started to run.

'First to the gatepost ain't caught by the bad ghost!' she called back over her shoulder.

Devlin gave chase, but after stumbling over the dog initially, he needed a few moments to get into his stride. There was no doubting the intent of the two competing siblings, but Miriam maintained the more direct line and edged her brother out.

'First to the gatepost ain't caught by the bad ghost!' she shouted triumphantly, tapping the limestone pillar.

He complained theatrically about her tactics, saying how underhand she was.

'Don't all the best races include a bit of cunning?' she laughed derisively. 'You must be slowing down, Michael. If not in the legs, well, certainly in the head.'

They were still in dispute over the race, with Devlin demanding a rematch, when they walked past the many vehicles surrounding the house. Miriam went upstairs to get changed and he carried on into the kitchen, where Tony was laying out a tray full of sandwiches.

'Well, you look like you have caught some of our great westerly weather,' Tony said, looking up from the table. 'There's tea there, or drink in the living room.'

'The tea will do for now,' Devlin said. 'Is there anything you need me to be doing?'

'I think we're fine, though Mrs D might say differently.'

As if on cue, Mrs Devlin walked in and put an arm around her son's waist.

'I see you're back,' she said, 'and wet as well. I suppose Miriam's along with you?'

'She is, Mam. Just getting changed.'

'That's good.' She looked down at the dog, who was watching them from the doorway. 'Bran's been like a lost soul for days. He seems revived now and you appear to have found a companion.'

Moments later, Miriam reappeared to join her brother and two cousins as they waited on those who'd come to honour and mourn Ben's passing, while her mother kept a watchful eye on all aspects of the proceedings. Devlin was very content to move between people in his role, not getting embroiled in any in-depth conversations, and though he couldn't help but notice that some of the guests were slightly cooler towards him than others, he did not try to figure out if this was because they did not know him or the result of them having a certain political agenda. He did, however, engage in a lengthy discussion with his Uncle Ronan and Auntie Anne, along with their children Niamh and Fiona, which inevitably led to them talking about Thomas's upcoming wedding.

'Michael, it is a sad day,' John McSherry, the family's next-door neighbour, said sombrely, catching Devlin on his way back to the kitchen. 'But if you don't mind me saying, not necessarily a sad occasion.'

'I would agree with you, John,' Devlin replied.

'What I was wondering was,' John continued with an inquisitive look on his weather-beaten features, 'as Clancy the fiddler and Maloney the flute player are here, do you think some gentle music would be acceptable? Now, I may be mistaken here, but I'd say there is a considerable chance that Ben himself would be in favour of such a thing.'

Devlin just loved the way the request had been framed, the subtlety and gentleness in John's use of language.

'I'll go and ask Mam,' he said, leaning forward and clasping John by the forearm.

He found his mother in the kitchen adding a garnish of lettuce and tomato to a plate of sandwiches and when he told her about John's request, she smiled and said, 'He's right. Ben would have been in favour and so am I. Tell them to play away.'

Thus, throughout the afternoon, the gentle talk in the living room was interspersed with melodic tunes, while a constant babble of conversation was maintained in the front lounge. The weather, which had been unpredictable for most of the day, became more settled and by late afternoon shafts of sunshine were breaking through the clouds, drawing many of the guests out into the garden, where the native trees, shrubs and plants were now looking resplendent.

Devlin walked past a group of neighbours who were admiring his mother's exceptionally tall mallow and bushy fuchsias, on his way to the large oak tree that stood in the furthest corner of the garden, and noticed that the seat cover on the swing had changed. It had once been a dark green but was now a burgundy colour and turning back to look at the house, the realisation came to him that this was the exact perspective he had seen the home place from on the screen at the Rawlins Building.

He was peering up at the old oak tree, examining its trunk and branches, when Pádraig and Aoife approached from across the lawn.

'Have you taken to hiding in the woods, Michael?' Aoife asked playfully. 'You must be reliving your childhood.'

'Oh, such things can start to happen when you get to my age,' Devlin answered lightly.

'That fits,' Pádraig said, 'as I always had you down to be this Peter Pan figure, always staying young. The man who left these humble townlands and went away to do so much in politics.'

'There is nothing humble about these townlands,' Devlin smiled knowingly, detecting the edge to the last remark, 'and nor should there be. Not to mention, the things I have done could be viewed differently, depending on your point of view. Now, do ye fancy a walk?'

Leaving the garden by the side gate, following Bran, they ambled along the back lane that was bordered by banks of bright ox-eye daisies. There was no conversation between them as they headed up towards the rise of the hill, until eventually Aoife spoke.

'Ben was amazing,' she said, her face glowing in the evening sunlight, 'really and truly. How he kept going was something that would inspire anyone. And your mother has the spirit of Connaught in her.'

'He was,' Devlin agreed readily, 'and he will be sorely missed, while Mam remains a wonder to us all. The older she has got, the more impressive she has become.'

'Indeed, but this land has changed since your childhood days, Michael,' Pádraig talked as though he was adding to the point. 'Should we say, it has become more radical politically and more embracing of the old ways.'

There was a sense of inevitability about this turn in the conversation and while Devlin knew he had every right to avoid it on such a day, he decided to respond.

'It has certainly changed since my childhood days,' he conceded, 'but there is a big difference between the old political ways, in terms of the struggle for independence, and the ways of our ancient ancestors when it comes to Celtic spirituality. There are points where they converge, I agree, but they are not to be confused.'

'Look, we hadn't meant to approach you in this way, especially on the evening of your brother's funeral,' Pádraig said very matter-of-factly, 'but now the subject is broached…'

They stopped beside a deep hawthorn thicket with stunning white and rose blooms, where the deeply churning ocean came into view below them, and as Devlin expected, it was Aoife who spoke next.

'If you know your Irish history,' she said, 'which I'm sure you do, you will know about the years of violent struggle for independence. Well, aren't we in that position again, where we don't really have a voice? The only difference is that the enemy has changed, so now the only methods really available to us are the very old ways. For years, nothing has been happening here, but now, to use the words of an old song, "the West's awake, the West's awake". Indeed, more and more are beginning to believe that only through rising up can meaningful freedom happen.'

This woman would be an asset to any cause, Devlin thought. She was undoubtedly easy on the eye, with her bobbed blonde hair and hazel eyes, but it was her eloquence and passion when speaking that he found most impressive. He was also struck by the way Pádraig was content to look out to sea, an appreciative expression on his broad west coast features, while his wife continued to talk.

'It is meaningful independence that we want,' she said, 'not just a few concessions that we might get here, that you wouldn't have over the water. You must have noticed your fellow travellers from the Regime coming over on the boat, to sample the old country, the home of the *Oirish*. And why are they coming? Well I'll tell you why – because their own lives are so boring, they love the notion of the cousins over the water who know how to have the craic and who are wayward and even a little bit dangerous in their ways. We are in danger of becoming a theme park, Michael.'

'You have a point there, Aoife, for sure.' Devlin could not help laughing.

'Listen,' Pádraig interjected, suddenly coming alive, 'we know all about your involvement with the CRP years ago and we are assuming that you left because it wasn't really going anywhere in terms of real independence for the West. If that's the case, well, fair play to you.'

Devlin looked directly at him but did not respond.

'We are thinking you must have a great overview of the politics,' Aoife continued, placing even greater emphasis on her words. 'So, cutting to the chase, our guess is that you left the Regime because it wasn't delivering what you wanted for our people. Well, now you return to Mullnamorran and there is an opportunity to become involved in something that *will* deliver the desired outcomes. Believe you me, we are a culturally legitimate group, aligned to the long-term aspirations of this great nation, with the wherewithal to bring these things about.'

'Oh, be in no doubt, I take you seriously,' Devlin said with gravitas. 'I also notice that you don't mention Liam and others, for instance, who do not believe in such methods.'

'Come on now, Michael,' Pádraig said, his bluey grey eyes glinting sharply, 'you must recognise that they are going nowhere. They will not bring about change – just hold meetings and run debating societies.'

'I need to be clear about what you are saying,' Devlin said flatly. 'You are talking about an armed struggle against the Regime?'

'Perhaps not exclusively.' Aoife flashed him a mischievous smile. 'There is always a need for information and influence, too, from people moving in the right circles.'

'Unfortunately, I do not move in the right circles nowadays,' Devlin responded. 'My past involvement with the CRP is no secret, but the only membership I hold currently is in an Allotments Association over the water. If it comes down to influencing the price of radishes, though – I could be your man.'

The humorous remark did not lift the tension in any way; in fact, the couple were staring at him with even greater intensity.

'You are a resourceful man,' Aoife broke the awkward silence, 'and we hear you are well thought of. You could find a way to enter those arenas of influence again. Surely you must have had occasion to think about how such a move could be of real benefit to your people?'

'These aren't situations that you can opt in and out of easily,' Devlin said, noticing that Bran had moved closer to his side and his back was slightly hunched. 'They are not fools. Their surveillance systems are very advanced and their ability to strike is on another level altogether… So my people, as you call them, need to be safeguarded from such a reaction.'

He was on the verge of going further but quickly stopped himself, having realised where this line of conversation was likely to go.

'It is exactly this kind of knowledge and information that we need,' Aoife immediately seized upon his words, her eyes bright with curiosity, 'so take your time to think it through and remember, this is a serious offer.'

'Our forefathers faced great odds as well,' Pádraig spoke up, 'and were eventually victorious.'

'Fear not,' Devlin looked back towards the house, 'you are being taken very seriously. I have no doubt that we will talk again.'

'We will,' Aoife said, her voice noticeably warmer now. 'I recognise that we have sprung this on you out of the blue and this was probably the wrong time to approach you. I'm sorry that we have intruded on your grief and I understand your caution, but as I'm sure you yourself realise, the time is so short—'

'There is never a right or wrong time for a conversation such as this,' Devlin interjected, 'and as you know, the grief is shared between us all in this family.' He paused a moment before adding, 'Ben never avoided the issues that came his way.'

'You're right there, Michael,' Pádraig said readily.

They made their way back to the house, parting company at the same part of the garden where they had come together. After carrying on into the living room, Devlin poured himself a large whiskey and sat down in the corner next to John McSherry, immersing himself in the old local tunes that Clancy and Maloney were playing, reassured by the connection he felt with the music. He would have to mingle again soon, he knew, but he wanted to spend half an hour or so listening while he ruminated on the most important thing: he had carried his only brother from this room that very morning.

Evening came over the household and as the majority of guests began to take their leave, Devlin went out to pick up glasses that been left in the garden. The sound of a rookery down the lane caught his attention and he was wondering why he'd not noticed its clamour before when Liam came out to join him.

'Well, cousin, it's been a mighty day,' Liam said, a weariness in his mellow voice. 'I think it will take a long time for me to get used to the idea of Ben's passing.'

'Yes, wasn't it just,' Devlin agreed. 'I can't recall another day quite like it.'

'Tony and I will be off shortly. Your mam seems fine, but I think she'll be glad to have the house back to herself at this stage.'

'You're right there, Liam, and thanks so much again for all you've done today.'

'I see you had the walk with Aoife and Pádraig.'

'I did and it was fine, though I was surprised that they chose today.'

'Oh, I'm not really surprised at all. They will have come here with the intention of planting the seed and giving you time enough to think about it.'

'Ah yes. No doubt my head will be ringing with the politics of it, before I go back. And I was never really intending to get involved over here.'

'None of us ever plan to become involved,' his cousin said gently, with a philosophical tone. 'It just happens.'

After giving a warm farewell to Tony and Liam at the front door, Devlin went inside with the intention of joining Miriam and his mother for a final tidy-up in the kitchen, but as he walked through the living room, he found John McSherry alone in the corner, cradling an empty glass.

'I'm sorry, Michael,' John said, looking up at him with bleary eyes. 'It's the old memories, sometimes they haunt you. But anyway, haven't you got enough on now? I'll be off, so.'

'You most certainly will not, John. I'll join you for one last half-one.'

After replenishing his neighbour's glass, Devlin poured one for himself and sat down. A familiar silence had descended over the house in the minutes since the guests had gone, with the ticking of the old clock once again asserting itself from its position on top of the large dresser containing his mother's fine crockery display.

John was a year older than Devlin and had always been around while he was growing up, so they fell easily into a conversation about their shared childhood and adolescence years, including many memories of Ben.

'I was thinking, Michael,' John said, 'there was a young woman who was very ill a few years ago, just beyond Roaches Rock. She hadn't been the best for a while, a kind of a strange thing it was and no one knew what was wrong with her – doctors, priests, no one. Anyway, she took it really bad and her mother knew that the time had come, so the family gathered and that night there were terrible sounds of fighting and arguing that seemed to be all around the house, as if the forces of the angels and evil were fighting over her soul. Well, the forces of good must have won out, for in the middle of the night, a quietness came down over the house, except for an angelic voice singing. The young woman died with a beautiful smile on her face.'

Just then, Miriam's voice could be plainly heard lilting a tune in the kitchen and John became flustered.

'Oh Michael,' he blurted out, 'I didn't mean anything by it. It's just the old ways. I was only saying that there was only ever a peace around Ben.'

'Don't worry, my old friend,' Devlin spoke softly, putting an arm around him, 'it was grand. I doubt you could ever say the wrong thing.'

He felt a great warmth towards John as they said goodnight and he watched him disappear through a gap in the hedge, as he had often done when they were children. Then, going into the front lounge, he was surprised to find his mother and Miriam sitting together in silence.

'Thanks for taking the time to talk to John,' his mother said appreciatively. 'He spends so much time on his own nowadays, since his father died. The poor crater. Anyway, you two, I am truly exhausted, so I am going to bed.' She stood up and hugged each of her children in turn, a couple of times. 'Though I am heartbroken at this moment, I am also just so grateful that ye are here for the coming days. With the goodness of the land and seasons, there will be a time of healing ahead.'

CHAPTER TEN

'This is becoming a bit of a habit,' Devlin said, stretching his arms slowly as he entered the kitchen.

The table was set and his mother and sister were preparing breakfast; the aromas of food he remembered from his childhood hung tantalisingly in the air and he suddenly realised he was extremely hungry.

'It's sleep you obviously needed, Michael,' his mother said, clapping her hands together, causing a puff of white flour, 'and I'm not surprised you're hungry. I doubt you'll have eaten since yesterday morning.'

The three of them sat down at the deeply grained oak table as Devlin ate a wholesome Irish breakfast with great chunks of homemade soda bread and butter, occasionally smiling at his mam and Miriam between mouthfuls, before finishing with a large mug of tea.

'That was truly wonderful,' he beamed, leaning back in his chair.

'You barely left the pattern on the plate,' Miriam quipped.

'Don't be listening to her,' his mother shook her head. 'There's nothing better than an appetite truly satisfied. Are you set up for the day, then?'

'I am indeed, Mam.'

'Good. Now that it's quiet and I have both of you here, it's time to talk about this house. We have an official meeting with Mr Doran and the councillors before you go back, Michael, and we need to have decided on what will be done.'

'You're right, Mam,' Miriam agreed and then, looking at Devlin, added, 'The time will pass quickly enough, what with the wedding and the match against Curraghcorn this week as well.'

'I would not miss either of those events for sure,' Devlin said with a deep relish in his voice. 'Liam didn't mention the match. Is he still as keen on the football?'

'Keen isn't the word at all,' Miriam replied. 'He finally retired from playing a few years ago and now both he and Tony are on the selection panel for Mullnamorran.'

'I suppose the rivalry with Curraghcorn is still as intense as ever. I remember those encounters alright.' Then, looking at his mother, he said, 'Oh I'm sorry, Mam, here's me starting to reminisce and we should be talking about the house.'

'Oh, it's lovely to hear you talk about those days, Michael, back here in our kitchen, and I do want us to enjoy this time we have together. I have no doubt that Ben is in a good place, so my sadness is bearable now.' His mother paused before continuing. 'As you both know, the house and land is in the ownership of the Devlin family, which is still a wondrous thing to me. When I told Ben, even though he was very ill, he smiled and gripped my hand so enthusiastically. I understand that the meeting with Mr Doran next week is to agree the precise terms.'

'I'm rather late to all of this and I'm sure ye have a good idea of what should happen, so I'm happy to be guided by you,' Devlin responded easily.

'Michael, as the eldest son, the property would automatically be appropriated by you in the event of me dying,' his mother said very practically.

'Mam, I wouldn't be happy about that. It's Miriam who has

been supporting you all these years and it's her who should have the rights of ownership. Wouldn't it be great for Finn, to be raising a family and carrying on the family name here?'

'I was never thinking of it that way,' Miriam responded quickly.

'But it's you who will be here when I've gone back. It definitely seems the right thing to me.'

Smiling at both her children in turn, it was obvious that his mother had an idea in mind as she ran her finger slowly along the grain of the wood in the kitchen table, a mannerism that Devlin remembered well, indicating that she was ruminating on a situation.

Eventually, she spoke with great deliberation. 'There is something about this house that Mr Doran informed me of, something I had not known before. The meadow behind the garden and also Clancy's old cottage do in fact belong to this estate, which means we have more matters to decide upon.'

'That's amazing,' Miriam uttered breathlessly, stunned by this revelation. 'I had no idea.'

'And neither did I,' Mrs Devlin continued. 'Apparently it was always that way, but of course as Dexter's never let us see the deeds, we never knew. Anyway, it's a horse of good fortune that I am not going to let pass by.'

'Amazing indeed,' Devlin said, smiling roundly. 'And didn't old Mr Clancy pass away a few years back? And am I right in thinking that the meadow has always been rented out to the McSherrys?'

'That's right, Michael, and John has always kept an eye on the old cottage up there.'

Devlin and Miriam looked at their mother, each knowing that she would have already thought the matter through and that ultimately they would accept her decision on this matter.

'At the end of the day,' she spoke slowly, 'this is what I would want to happen. Miriam, I would like you to have the house. Michael, I would like you to have Clancy's cottage and the meadow.'

A few moments elapsed with the two siblings looking at one another and it was Miriam who finally broke the silence.

'Mam, I had never thought about owning the house. Michael, what do you think? It would seem like I'm disinheriting you.'

'Miriam, I think it's a wonderful outcome,' Devlin spoke unstintingly, a glow in his blue eyes. 'You deserve it. In your heart you never really left this place. Though I do have one thought… Should the meadow not be linked to the house, as the cottage has its own patch of land up there?'

'So be it,' Mrs Devlin gave her assent. 'I'm happy with that, as the rent from the meadow will help maintain this old house.'

'That's great,' Devlin agreed, 'and at the end of the day, the only outcome should be the one you want, Mam.'

'Thank you both,' she said. 'I am deeply satisfied – really and truly.'

The conversation drifted on to things that were happening in the neighbourhood, until Mrs Devlin stood and excused herself.

'Mrs Hennessey has not been well,' she said, 'and I'm due to visit her. The day looks good again and I've got some pickles, boxty and bread made, so I will take a walk down to see her.'

'Michael, shall we take a stroll and look at Clancy's cottage?' Miriam suggested. 'Or should I say, Michael Devlin's cottage?'

'That sounds a fine idea.'

Leaving by the side gate, they went up the lane lined by thick hedgerows, with Bran trotting along beside them. It was a fine day, with bright sunlight and the constant sound of birdsong, as Devlin and Miriam passed the lush green meadow dotted with wildflowers that bordered the back garden of the house and started their assent towards the cottage.

'I had forgotten how steep a climb this was,' Devlin said, pointing up ahead, 'and look at the orchard there inside the gates – it's gone to rack and ruin alright! Do you remember playing there and sometimes picking the apples for Mr Clancy? We used to rub them until their green and rosy skins shone… He was an eccentric character, but he had great time for us kids, didn't he? Do you remember he kept chocolate bars that he gave to us? He said not to tell Dad and Mam, though I'm sure they knew.'

'They did for sure, but thinking back, he probably just wanted us to think it was our little secret… and here's the cottage. Just look at the stunning red of those roses, aren't they a great mass of blooms? I think John must have pruned them at some stage. They look so well.'

'He must have been looking after it all these years,' he observed, eyeing the old building. 'Fair play to him. Look at the roof and everything; it all looks tidy enough, despite it being empty for so long.'

'Those patterned curtains should be familiar, Michael. They're as old as you are, I bet.'

'They may be even older.' He grinned.

Reaching the gable end of the cottage, they automatically turned to take in the fine view of Mullnamorran and the surrounding plains that Clancy's old home offered, while the sharp cries of the swallows resounded around them as they swooped in to feed their chicks in the nests underneath the eaves.

'They are the most amazing birds. Can you imagine how far they have migrated?' Miriam uttered appreciatively, as she turned towards the remnants of a bench rotting in the garden. 'Mr Clancy used to sit here with his pipe on the fine evenings – you could see the puffs of bluish smoke from our back meadow. He always seemed to know the vessels coming in and out of port. Mam said one of the coastguards would come to see him, to keep him informed.' She paused a moment before adding, 'Do you know, Michael, that Mr Clancy never strayed more than thirty miles from this spot in his whole life – and that was for a county football final. Can you imagine that?'

Devlin did not respond but just smiled and moved his head up and down, as if savouring a pleasant taste.

'Mam always said he was from an older time,' she went on, 'and that he didn't even believe the Regime existed, never mind that it held power. He saw it all as just fanciful thinking.'

'Maybe this bachelor from another time was the lucky one, if he could go through life without having to confront this bizarre modern reality. Talking of the Regime, could you tell me how it works locally, between Mr Doran, the councillors, the law and Erringal? I must admit, I haven't managed to work it out.'

'Well, it isn't that easy to explain, but I can tell you how I think it works. The councillors meet at the old Customs and Harbour Building and I understand that they are all Regime employees, though some of them are never seen in public. Mr Doran is by far the most visible of them and they have jurisdiction over land, fisheries, births, deaths and marriages, along with all other civil contracts, and any disputes or cases requiring decisions at a higher level are settled by a virtual court system. Sweeney, the guard who has a policing role, is based there as well and he can request back-up at any time. Erringal, as you know, is a priest of the oldest tradition and besides his spiritual role in the community, he is also allowed to arbitrate in local disputes. He and Mr Doran have recently started to meet and coordinate affairs locally. This is a new situation and so long as it proves uncontentious, it is thought that it will continue. It's all part of a Regime initiative to acknowledge and legitimise the ancient ways. Fergal and Eimear are two other recognised priests, both of whom are well respected throughout the community. So, in effect, you have a strange marriage of convenience between the Regime and the ancient Celtic spiritual priests, who govern these communities, on the implicit understanding that civil disorder and political defiance will not be tolerated. Many years ago, there was a political rally in Curraghcorn that was quelled in under an hour. The message was swift and clear. Having said that, there *has* been an acceptance of a certain level of autonomy in the regions and so the CMA has been able to operate fairly openly. The Regime's presence has been very low-key in this area, with only a very discreet level of surveillance, including the ubiquitous drones, observation pick-up points and, of course, the usual informers.' She glanced at her brother briefly before asking, 'Is that how you thought it would be?'

'I suppose it is, though the spiritual side of it has pleasantly surprised me. On a completely different note, I was wondering if there are still any bicycles in the shed at home.'

'There are. John has always kept an eye on them. Why, are you going for a ride?'

'I thought I might.'

Ambling back, they stopped once to regard a flock of sheep and lambs in a field above the back meadow; their bright white fleeces caught the eye against the deeply verdant pastures where they grazed and the sound of constant baaing travelling across the countryside provided an uplifting soundscape that sang of new life. Devlin let his eyes wander over the flock while breathing in deeply at the same time, luxuriating in the feeling of being back at home. He turned and, clicking his tongue, he gave his sister a slow wink of appreciation. Miriam knew that words were unnecessary, so she simply smiled at him.

On getting home, Devlin went out to the shed and was delighted to see two bikes that, despite being of a considerable age, looked to be in good working order. He picked the largest one and wheeled it around to the front of the house, where Miriam appeared with sandwiches that she placed in the saddle bag, along with a canteen of water. Meanwhile, Bran, who had been paying close attention to Devlin's preparations for the ride, stood in the driveway and yelped excitedly.

'It looks like you won't be on your own,' Miriam said contentedly.

Devlin set off at a leisurely pace and turned onto the road with Bran trotting easily beside him. Once he had reached the rise in the road, he freewheeled most of the way down towards town, using the brakes to keep his speed in check until he reached the crossroads, where a man called out to him, 'I'm sorry for your loss.'

'Thank you,' Devlin replied, trying to recognise this angular person with greying brown hair while slowing to a stop. 'He will be missed by many.'

'Ah, struggling to get the old memory to work, I see. But I suppose you've done a lot in your life, Michael, and isn't it easy to forget people?'

There was an edge to this man's voice that was confirmed by Bran's stance, which had become hunched and defensive, but Devlin responded as lightly as he could.

'Oh, I've done nothing,' he said. 'Some of us had to travel away, as there was never enough work to go around in those days.'

'And you found some particular work alright.' The man paused before adding coolly, 'You might have known me as Paul Grogan – our family was sometimes known as the Blacks as well, from down beyond the town. Ah, but what's in a name. I remember you alright, what with Liam and the football.'

'I'm sorry, Paul,' Devlin said and, even though he was starting to recall a boy who had similar features to this man, he continued, 'I'm really struggling with the memory, but you look familiar alright. The football you say… There were some good days for sure.'

'There were good days for some,' Paul said sourly, but said nothing more, as if challenging his old acquaintance to go on recalling their younger days.

There was clearly more to Paul's disapproval than simply not being remembered, but Devlin was not prepared to further prolong this encounter, which, even if you were to observe the two men and the wary dog at the crossroads from a distance, you would be able to tell was a tense moment.

'You're looking well anyway,' Devlin said, remounting his bike, 'and maybe our paths will cross again, who knows?'

Paul did not respond initially, standing motionless with a sliced pan loaf under his arm, but as Devlin was cycling away, he called loudly after him, 'We may indeed, we may indeed – who knows?'

Heading north on the old coast road, Devlin put the uncomfortable encounter to the back of his mind, concentrating instead on getting a good rhythm to his cycling after initially finding the old three-speed gear mechanism tricky to operate. They passed two derelict cottages by the roadside and shortly after came to O'Hagan's stores; the former shop cutting a forlorn figure, being half submerged in sand, its front door lying askance across the pathway. He freewheeled to a halt and, leaning the bike against the perimeter wall, drank from his water canteen. There was something about the exterior of the building that struck him as incredibly sad, with its main sign hanging lopsidedly from one remaining screw. He remembered when it was first erected, sporting an optimistically-coloured font that had seemed so modern to the locals back then. As children, he and his friends had stopped here for ice creams and pop, the rotund and jovial Mrs O'Hagan coming out to welcome the group of young cyclists before ushering them inside as though they were her most important customers.

And maybe we were, he reflected, considering that the idea of running a successful shop on this remote road must have been a fanciful venture, even in that era.

Looking at the outline of the front yard, where their bicycles would have been haphazardly laid down, his mind was drawn back to one particular day. The sound of the freshening wind, the creaking sign and a rapid lapping sound mingled and it was as if he could hear the children inside chattering excitedly around the ice cream counter. He did not resist this lapse into reminiscence, as his attention was drawn to a discarded bike, its wheel revolving slowly, ticking. A tall lad stood by the gate with a haughty look on his face and Devlin recognised him straightaway as the same boy who had declared loudly that he didn't like ice cream. It was Paul Grogan. The rest of the children came out with their cones and

Paul looked away, his expression having changed from haughtiness to anger.

Devlin was surprised by the vividness of this memory and shook his head to bring his attention back to the here and now, where the sound of the wind and the creaking of the sign continued, but the lapping had slowed considerably. He waded through the drifted sand that was banked up against the front wall and, clambering across the dislodged front door, he peered inside the shop, where the advertisement on the side of the ice cream cabinet, showing a woman in a swimsuit holding an ice lolly, had faded to the extent that it was barely discernible.

He decided not to cross the threshold, but went around the corner of the building as the lapping sound stopped and Bran lifted his head out of the water butt, looking up at Devlin with his tongue lolling to one side.

'You must have been thirsty, boy.'

He trudged back through the sandbanks and, replacing his water canteen, remounted the bicycle once more. Bran was close to his legs and he stroked him vigorously a few times before saying in an enquiring tone, as if seeking the dog's approval, 'Are you ready to travel a bit further, fella? I want to go to the Crying Cliffs.'

Yelping enthusiastically, Bran led the way and the duo set off again. Turning left at the crossroads, Devlin was confident that it was the right route as the deep sound of the ocean was increasing in its intensity, as was the freshness of the briny wind. The road was becoming more uneven than he remembered, with the tarmac surface becoming virtually non-existent in places, which made ascending the hills a real struggle, but he was determined to keep riding until he reached the bottom of the Crying Hill. The final swooping descent onto the bridge below was very dramatic, as a local dog appeared out of the hedgerow to bark her disapproval at their incursion into her territory. Bran continued to run, looking straight ahead as if he hadn't noticed the collie on the other side of the wheels and in the end, the protesting dog gave up the chase before they had reached the bridge, preferring to air her grievances from the road above.

'Atta boy, Bran!' Devlin shouted approvingly.

Crossing the bridge, he dismounted and wheeled the bike through a gap in the hedge before leaning it against the gable end of a ruined cottage that he reasoned must have dated back to the eighteen hundreds – before the Great Famine. Surveying the remaining walls and imagining the three tiny, damp rooms of the dwelling, a coldness came over Devlin when he considered how harsh a family's life must have been in this hollow, for despite the land's rough beauty and the sparkling river that cascaded close by, a level of suffering and uncertainty would doubtless have been part of their everyday existence. He was feeling a level of inherent sadness in this place that he could not help dwelling on, until the sound of the sea birds, along with Bran's sharp yelping, broke the spell. He then removed the lunch parcel and canteen from the saddle bag, placing them in a knapsack that he slipped over his shoulder, and they took the rough track that wound its way up the hill, cutting a path through the deep banks of gorse bushes alive with full yellow blooms. Devlin stopped a few times on the way up to appreciate the view that was unfolding behind them and as he neared the summit, he heard the constant crying out of the nesting guillemots, an eerie sound from his childhood that had somehow remained with him through the intervening years spent deep in the heart of the city.

After crossing a narrow, rutted field, they reached a barbed wire fence that was the last barrier before the cliffs and the dramatic three hundred-foot drop to the sea. Bending down the top wire, Devlin stepped over onto a secure tuft of grass where he sat down and got his first sighting of the guillemots nesting precariously on ledges in the rock face, while all around, gulls and other sea birds called relentlessly, soaring and swooping on the lively gusts of a bracing westerly wind. He had a momentary feeling of acrophobia when he gazed down at the ocean so far below, but this soon subsided. Bran wandered the length of the clifftop as if he was carrying out an inspection before returning to lie beside him.

Devlin opened the lunch parcel that Miriam had prepared and was amused to see two packages: one labelled *Bran* and the other unmarked. 'Well, someone's certainly looking after you, boy,' he said, unfolding the greaseproof paper containing the dog's dinner and laying it on the ground.

Bran inspected his meal of scraps of grizzle, cheese rinds and stale bread soaked in tea before slowly starting to eat. For his part, Devlin consumed his sandwiches in a distracted manner, his gaze never leaving the guillemots, such was his fascination with the birds' activity. After he'd finished eating, he checked his footing and then stood to take in the panoramic vistas. The expanse and deep aqua colour of the ocean was an awe-inspiring view he had not seen in over twenty-five years and as he looked along the coast, he could plainly see Mullross Pier and beyond that the Shimmering Sands, the most northerly point of the territory they'd cycled to as teenagers. He then let his eye wander inland, reacquainting himself with the wider topography and landmarks. There were a few figures on the Shimmering Sands and in the adjacent sand hills he saw what seemed to be an upended jaunting car, with a horse grazing close by. He made a mental note of its location and the surrounding lanes before taking a moment to savour the cacophony of bird noise, followed by one last look at the Crying Cliffs, and then he headed back down the hill, retrieving his bike from behind the ruined cottage and walking out on to the road where Bran was stood waiting, aware of their intended direction.

'Well, well, well,' Devlin spoke knowingly to the dog, 'I'm beginning to wonder who is leading who here.'

The ride downhill to the harbour was an easy one as he freewheeled most of the way on the recently tarmacked surface and when he reached Mullross Pier, he was intrigued to see how well it was maintained, having once been a neglected facility used only by local fishermen and smugglers. The boats out in the bay reflected this change in fortune as there were luxury yachts and cabin cruisers; their sleek white designs seemed incongruous moored alongside the dourly coloured local craft, which all had defining collision scars and a generous showing of rust. Devlin smiled at the contrast and inhaled deeply once more the pungent smell of seaweed and brine, as if he was appreciating the bouquet of a fine red wine, before riding on.

Going inland, he turned just beyond Burn's Bar into a lane whose surface was initially rough tarmac but soon gave way to a sandy track, so he dismounted and pushed the bike. In the growing heat of the day, he was sweating freely now, with the sand radiating a pleasant, glowing warmth underfoot, and after passing a small cottage on the right, he looked through the gap between two large sand hills and spotted the upended jaunting car. Bran led the way through this opening into the secluded enclosure. The piebald stallion Devlin had espied from the Crying Cliffs was over sixteen hands and lifting his head slowly to observe their approach; he was clearly unperturbed. Tail wagging, the dog ran over and yelped at the horse, who lowered his nose, first sniffing then nuzzling Bran in an affectionate gesture.

A campfire crackled easily in the sunshine and on a chequered blanket close by were two large wooden boxes, clothes and various other items. The encampment was surrounded by golden sand hills on three sides, with a dense copse of silver birch on the other, and it offered a stunning view of the Crying Cliffs; the dramatic detail of the sharply descending rocks, with all their ledges and crevices, could be clearly seen from here.

Laying the bicycle down to give his full attention to the view, Devlin spotted an easel at the far side of the clearing. Walking towards it, he saw it held a large unfinished painting and after initially admiring the perfect perspective, he was stopped in his tracks upon recognising the amazing abstract style that he knew could only be the work of Gráinne. He felt privileged to see the work at this stage of its development and as he knelt down on one knee to study the canvas, he became so engrossed that he did not notice someone coming through the trees until Bran started yelping excitedly, and he turned to see the fine figure of a woman in a swimming costume with a beach towel slung casually across her shoulder, calmly regarding him.

'Well, Bran, I see you're on your travels again,' she said, leaning down and stroking the dog, before addressing the man in front of her. 'Devlin, I assume?'

He felt for a moment like a child who had been caught red-handed stealing apples from an orchard and consequently he just about managed to say, 'You could say that, Gráinne.'

Going over to the open chest, she picked up a long grandfather shirt and slipped it over her shoulders. 'The sun is great, but a redhead like me has to be careful at this time of year. I'm making a drink of tea, would you fancy one?'

'I'd love one for sure. I'm parched,' he said with a clear lift in his voice.

She took a kettle out of another of the large storage boxes and hung it from the apex of the triangular stand that stood over the fire pit. 'Well, you looked like you were venerating that picture,' she spoke with a distinct lilt, 'but it has still got some way to go, and who knows how it will turn out?'

'Your work is great,' he replied a little awkwardly, 'and it's fascinating to see it at this stage, in its natural surroundings.'

'Oh, it isn't me who paints them,' she said, with a shocked expression on her face, 'it's Cuchulainn over there.' She gestured to the horse, who looked back at her blankly. 'The strange thing is, he won't paint when anyone is watching him, so I have to go for a walk or a swim whenever he's feeling inspired. I must admit, he's got a fine technique for a stallion.'

Delighted by her surreal explanation, Devlin burst out laughing and she smiled as she unfolded two chairs that had been leaning beside the car.

'You may as well sit down,' she said. 'I tend to do a lot of work in the mornings, particularly on the composition. When I'm capturing the light, it can be different times of day. I'd say I'm surprised that you found your way here, but as you've the bold Bran with you, maybe I'm not.'

'We were up at the Crying Cliffs and from there I saw the car. I wondered if I could find my way here.'

'Oh, just follow Bran in future. He always seems to know where we'll be camped. It was seeing him that confirmed who you were.'

The sounds of the twig-fire crackling and the low ocean roar played easily on his ears; wood smoke combined with the fresh, salty seaside aromas to form an intoxicating odour that he recognised so well from his childhood. Gráinne lilted a tune as the kettle came to the boil and Devlin looked around the encampment, at Cuchulainn grazing, at the jaunting car and Bran reclining on the blanket, and he was struck by the timelessness of the scene.

It could be a campsite from another age altogether, from centuries ago, he thought.

She looked directly at him with an amused expression and, tilting her head playfully to one side, she asked, 'How do you take your tea?'

For a moment, he savoured the beauty of her face set amongst the tousled auburn hair, before answering jauntily, 'Why, it's milk with no sugar.'

Handing him a steaming mug, she became more earnest in her tone. 'I spent some lovely time around Knockbrack,' she said, 'and got to know your family. Ben's passing is a great loss, but I admire the way he lived his life. Mrs D is great and I have to say that Miriam has become a good friend of mine. And while I'm talking about relationships, Erringal is my uncle and though I wasn't brought up in this area, he has influenced me positively with his enduring spirituality.'

'I didn't know about Erringal being your uncle. He is indeed a man of deep spirituality and our family is indebted to him.'

'There are no debts here when it comes to matters of the spirit or the soul,' she countered lightly. 'Despite your long absence, there is more known about you than you might suspect. It's just the way of it. But don't worry, Devlin. You are safe to talk here and as you said recently to a friend of yours, "In the end, it comes down to trust."'

'Well, well, well.' He could not hide his surprise. 'I have travelled to the Shimmering Sands, the furthest reaches of my childhood world, and it is here I meet the artist whose work bewitched me in the Rawlins – the very building where the course of my destiny was defined. There's a strange symmetry to all of this.'

'I don't mean to make a habit of this,' she said, her bright hazel eyes regarding him closely, 'but I'm going to have to correct you again. The course of your destiny is not defined. You still have many potentially interesting options and you can still be the one shaping that future.'

'You might well be right in what you're saying, as you seem to have a great understanding of my life and situation. Now that in itself is something that I find very intriguing.'

The talk continued to flow and he enjoyed the interplay of ideas that seemed to occur very naturally between them. Gráinne spoke unguardedly about her own spirituality and how her role as an artist drew on the supernatural qualities that the ancient ways possessed. These were ideas that fascinated him and he found talking openly about his own beliefs exhilarating, particularly after all the years of having to be so cautious in conversation.

When there was a lull in their discourse, she stood up and, stretching, said to him, 'That's a mighty amount of talking for two people who have barely met. Now, you mentioned the Shimmering Sands before, Devlin, but by my reckoning, you've not walked along them for nigh on thirty years. So shall we take a stroll there and leave these two to it?'

Devlin was intrigued, for as Gráinne had suggested, Bran was content to stay at the camp with Cuchulainn. The horse lay down on his side and the dog watched idly as a blackbird and robin kept returning to hop around the blanket, looking for any remnants of food. The only real intrusion came later, when two gulls swooped down squawking noisily, but Bran soon chased them away. The heat of the day continued to grow and the sweet, lazy sounds of the seaside afternoon lulled both dog and horse into a drowsy state.

The sun had passed its zenith when Devlin and Gráinne walked away together, taking the path that led through the coppice of trees, once again engrossed in conversation. The ocean, the sands and the western skyway lay before them, as onwards they went towards the Atlantic shore where the waters brightly sparkled. By the time they returned, there was a greater intimacy to their exchanges and if you were to observe them, even from up on the sand hills, the attraction between the two of them was plain to see. Cuchulainn reared up to an upright position and Bran wandered over to meet them, as Devlin took in the scene once more.

'It's an amazing afternoon,' he said. 'These are days that I thought I was destined to just dream about.'

'Maybe you are dreaming,' Gráinne reflected, brushing her hair back vigorously with her hand, 'but don't worry, there's no need for grand farewells. You've another week here and I'm sure we're not finished with each other just yet.'

'And maybe I could stand some more of this treatment, it has to be said. Particularly in a setting like this. Why, a masterpiece could even be painted here,' he responded impishly.

'We shall see about the masterpiece. But beware such talk as it could jinx it.'

'My lips are sealed,' he said dramatically, before turning to face the painting. 'Are you here for a while, then?'

'I am going to work in the evening light for a couple of days as the Crying Cliffs are amazing and I'm planning another painting in this area. I may move on, but I'm not sure yet. It depends if I can find another view that is as inspirational. I camp out when the weather's good and I use Barney's old cottage sometimes, seeing as its empty. You passed it on your way in.' She paused before adding, 'Erringal lives in the cottage with the green door, set back beyond O'Hagan's. He always knows where I am.'

'We will go and leave the artist to it, Bran,' he said brightly, the full gaze of his blue eyes resting easily on her, 'be it the noble Cuchulainn or the grand Gráinne. Either way, I do want to see this painting finished.'

'So be it.' She took his hands in hers. 'This picture will be painted and we will meet again. Feel free to call – if you can manage to find the time.'

His answer was to pull her to him in a full embrace. He was aware of the great naturalness that Gráinne possessed and, dropping his face into her soft and aromatic hair, he had a momentary wish that he could just stay there indefinitely. Then, after reluctantly lifting his head, he saw that Bran was standing in the gap waiting to go, watching them very closely. They kissed and she regarded him with a slow certainty in her bright hazel eyes, before she deliberately shattered the mood of the moment by letting out a merry peel of laughter.

'Away with ye,' she cried, voice alive with mock indignation, 'you're nothing but a blaggard, Devlin. Away on your old bike and take the bold Bran with you.'

The dog yelped at the mention of his name and Devlin grinned at the unexpected humour, saying, 'I suppose I should have known you'd see through me.'

There was one last kiss and after regarding her finely balanced features once more, he reluctantly stood the bike up and pushed it to the gap, where he turned and waved. Gráinne responded by smiling widely and leaning her head to one side, causing her abundant hair to tumble down and completely cover her shoulder in a gesture that years later, Devlin would be able to effortlessly recall.

Walking back down the sandy lane, Devlin regarded the condition of Barney's cottage much more scrupulously that he had earlier in the day.

It's in reasonable order, he thought. *The walls, windows and roof look pretty sound, but it would be a tough enough old outpost in the winter.*

When he reached Burn's Bar, he turned east on the more direct road to Mullnamorran and as he cycled along the well-surfaced road thinking about his time with the captivating artist around the Shimmering Sands, he felt a sense of elation that he was determined to hold on to for as long as he could. The thought occurred to Devlin that it might be useful to know exactly where Erringal lived, given what Gráinne had said earlier, and therefore when he came to a side road that he calculated would bring them out at the crossroads near O'Hagan's, he took it.

Reaching the derelict stores, he saw the small cottage with a green door set back off the road and he wondered why he had not noticed it earlier, not least because of the magnificent oak tree that stood in the garden, providing an excellent leafy canopy for a noisy duck pond below. He had not planned to visit Erringal on this occasion, but as he was trimming the front hedgerow and Bran had stopped at the driveway, he knew that it would be impolite not to call.

'It's lovely to get the chance to talk to you,' Erringal greeted Devlin, seeming genuinely delighted to see him. 'You are most welcome home, Michael.'

Explaining that he'd just seen Gráinne, Devlin spoke with enthusiasm about both her painting and her way of life. The holy man listened intently to this account of his niece and her work with a glow of pleasure radiating from his eyes and a deep smile etched into his face. The two men then had a lengthy discussion about the route he'd taken that day and the flora and fauna that flourished along the coastline, with Devlin marvelling at the old man's knowledge and warmth.

Pleased with his decision to stop, he was remounting his

bike to ride on when Erringal put a hand on his arm and looked scarchingly into his eyes.

'It is a great thing that you came home, even in such sad circumstances.' The old man spoke in warm tones, which were also infused with gravitas. 'But beware, because the politics are hard on your heels. I have heard that there was an explosion last night near Curraghcorn. I mention this because whatever pressures were upon you, they will be increased now. Be sure of who you're talking to and of what you're saying.'

'I will.' Devlin nodded formally to acknowledge the seriousness of Erringal's words, before adding, 'Thank you so much.'

'Call any time you're passing, there's no need to be a stranger. And as you'll know by now, you never really left this land behind.'

Cycling off slowly in the late-afternoon sunshine, with Erringal's final words resonating with him and the sound of the tyres purring on the road, Devlin let his mind dwell lazily on the encounters of the day. When he was nearly home, making the final climb up the rise in the road at Knockbrack, he found the image of Gráinne was foremost in his mind, her encampment having already attained a kind of dreamlike, magical quality for him, and as they swept into the driveway of the home place, Bran barked excitedly to announce their arrival.

CHAPTER ELEVEN

It was an evening that Devlin would remember with great affection. The three of them had a wonderful meal, with John McSherry's sumptuous chicken the centre-piece of the table, surrounded by freshly grown Knockback vegetables, and while they were still eating their neighbour called in with some eggs.

'It looks like you're keeping the Devlin household going for food single-handed at the moment,' Devlin said, pointing to table. 'This chicken is absolutely fantastic.'

'She's fresh enough,' John said, winking. 'She'd have been running around until the other day.'

'Now, you didn't have a name for her, did you?' Miriam asked mischievously. 'We're not eating one of your pets, I hope.'

'Oh no, not at all,' John answered earnestly. 'I never name the beasts.'

'Will you leave the poor man alone?' Mrs Devlin said, but there was a merriment in her voice.

'Oh, don't worry about me, Mam. I'll be leaving you now anyway. I've an early meadow to cut.'

'Will you stay a moment, John?' Mrs Devlin said, taking on a more serious tone. 'I have something to tell you. The house here officially belongs to the Devlin family now and that includes the back meadow and Clancy's place, which you have been renting for years.'

'That's grand news,' John beamed. 'Does that mean I'll be paying rent to you from now on, Mam?'

'I suppose it does, but we can work all that out later. I just wanted you to know.'

'That's mighty news, Mam.'

'Ah, he's been great really,' Mrs Devlin's face was a picture of affection as John went off. 'He has become part of the family since his father passed on. Sometimes he'll even eat with us now.'

Spending the rest of the night in the front room, they discussed recent events from around the neighbourhood, instigated in the most part by Devlin's questions until, inevitably, his encounters with Gráinne and Erringal came up and he found he couldn't hide how impressed he was by the artist and her lifestyle.

'So, you have met the intriguing Gráinne on the shores of the golden Shimmering Sands,' Miriam said, raising her voice. 'She is great, isn't she? I number her as a friend nowadays, so you had better behave yourself, Michael.'

'As you know, Miriam, Gráinne's well fit to look after herself,' Devlin replied.

'It's like you're going back to your adolescence now,' Mrs Devlin interjected, clearly amused, 'bickering over relationships.' She paused a moment before adding, 'She's a woman who is not afraid to live her own life and I like her immensely.'

'I don't know if she told you how her work gained a wider recognition, Michael?' Miriam asked.

'No, she didn't.'

'Of course not – she's too modest. Well, it was quite a few years ago and some of the bigwigs from the Regime were visiting the regions,' she said caustically, before continuing in a more even tone. 'They were looking at the local culture and they came across her paintings. Surprisingly, they really struck a positive note with one couple for certain, who – how can I say this? – had a *strangeness* about themselves.'

'Oh, Miriam, there's no need to say that,' Mrs Devlin protested.

'But it's true,' Miriam insisted. 'They seemed not of this world and that's not a criticism. In fact, it could be a compliment. Anyway, I think its gas, particularly given the abstract nature of her work. For a while, she resisted the idea of the paintings being exhibited away from the west of Ireland, but then she figured it might give people an insight into the beauty of the land and, on another level, the importance of its ancient culture.'

'There is something timeless about them,' Devlin said, a faraway look coming into his eyes. 'Even though they are so modern, they definitely reference the ancient Celts. And artwork aside, she makes a great mug of tea over a camp fire.'

'Indeed,' Miriam agreed, 'and as they say around here, "she has the power, but she wears it lightly".'

'I have enjoyed tonight greatly,' Mrs Devlin announced, rising to her feet, 'but I'll leave you to it.' She hesitated before adding, 'Oh, by the way, Michael – talking of people who have the power, Fergal is still living by the Gorge of the Lost Prince and Liam and Tony often go walking up in that area. They are calling up tomorrow afternoon, if you wanted to go along.'

'Is he still going?' Devlin responded enthusiastically, a bright smile coming over his face. 'We thought he was old when we were cubs.'

'He is,' Miriam said, 'and of course, we will have to start thinking about the wedding the day after. It will start with the dawn vigil, so should be a lovely day.'

'I'm looking forward to that,' Devlin said. 'I'm not sure I was ever at one of the old ceremonies, so you will have to tell me what to expect, sis.'

Stopping in the doorway, Mrs Devlin turned and smiled benignly at her children.

'Good night, you two,' she said quietly, as if she didn't want to disturb them, and indeed she hadn't; they were already deeply involved in another conversation.

The customs and rituals of the local area were of great fascination to Devlin and as Miriam was a very willing source, they became engrossed in talk of the ancient ways for many hours until tiredness eventually overcame them and he said goodnight and went to bed. Going up to his room had become a ritual. He tried to avoid places where the floorboards creaked to make his ascent as quiet as possible. It amused him because in the act of trying to avoid a particular point, he often found one that was even noisier. Then, upon reaching his room, he stood looking out at the fast-moving clouds that were being driven inland by strengthening westerly winds, causing the bright moonlight to break through intermittently. It was a dramatic sky, which he could easily have sat and watched, but recognising how tired he was and not wanting to sleep in the chair again, he went straight to bed.

Resting his head on the pillow, he was aware of falling quickly into a deep sleep and he soon found himself dreaming that he had just disembarked from the Connaught Princess. Barleycorn and Dermot were waiting for him at the ferry terminal; they led the way through the waterfront streets with Devlin ambling behind, fascinated by the sailors from different periods of history that were milling around as they delved deeper into the old docklands, passing a gang of disgruntled seamen talking outside a tavern.

'Ahoy, me old shipmates,' one of the sailors called out. 'Beware, there are press gangs on the streets tonight.'

'A warning well made, me hearties!' Barleycorn replied, as they walked on without slowing.

Slow, heroic pipe music began to fill the air and it was at this point that Barleycorn and Dermot came to a stop, but urged Devlin to keep going. Leaving them behind, he turned a corner and arrived on a familiar street lined with Victorian streetlamps, albeit from a totally different perspective than he'd seen before. He saw James encased in red and yellow beams of light, in the act of trying to resist being lifted, as a full moon shone above the far end of the street.

'Would you leave your friend in a place like this?' James gazed at him, speaking in time with the pulsing of the beams. 'When will you return?'

Then, in time with the flashing lights, Ceridwen's voice emanated weakly from the moon.

'You have gone too far,' she said, 'you'll be out of reach. There'll be no way back.'

The effect was hypnotic and Devlin at once became immersed in this strange pageant, which was playing out before him like a movie. The pipe music was getting louder as the image started to compress horizontally, while the rolling darkness of the top and bottom of the screen grew, as if it was the end of a film and the credits were about to roll. The scene containing his friends continued to be condensed until it formed a beam of churning gold and ruddy moonlight laid across the ocean, forming a pathway to the setting sun. The texture became like one of Gráinne's impasto paintings; all the beautiful fragments of colour alive with the call of discontented voices.

He woke up with a shudder, the final image of the sunset clear in his mind. This was the first time he had dreamed in such a vivid fashion since returning home and it was not a welcome development. Knowing how unsettled he was and that he would not go straight back to sleep, Devlin went downstairs to make a cup of tea.

Entering the dimly lit kitchen, he was surprised to find Miriam sitting at the table.

'You look like you could do with a cup of something.' She gestured towards the teapot. 'There's plenty left.'

'It's as though you were expecting me,' he said, meeting her penetrating gaze.

'You could say that.' Her face softened as she spoke. 'There was an uneasiness in the house that woke me and it seemed to be coming from your room.'

'That well might be the case,' Devlin said, regarding her warmly. 'The powers of insight definitely seem to run deeper in this land than the one I left all those years ago.'

'Maybe we were not as aware back then,' Miriam suggested and they started to talk about Devlin's dream.

The discussion moved on effortlessly, drawing in a range of related matters, as had become the way of their conversation, and the dawn was breaking when they went to bed.

Only his mother was in the kitchen when Devlin went down the next morning and sat at the table. She had obviously been very busy as she placed down a large plateful of breakfast before him.

'You know, I could get used to this,' he said with relish, inhaling the fine aromas. 'The flavour in the food here in Knockbrack is so wonderful, you have no idea.'

He started to eat and she stood beside him, running her fingers through his thick dark curls, saying, 'Are you wearing your hair longer these days, Michael?'

'Oh, it's the way-out-west look,' he responded jovially, impaling potato cake and egg on his fork, 'and the not-had-time-to-get-it-cut style, Mam.'

'You know, it could suit you,' she responded brightly before striking a more moderate tone. 'Miriam is having a lie-in. God knows she deserves it, after all she's done. We are going to the grave later, while you're away up in the hills.'

'That's great. I'm going to clip that hedge at the front before Liam and Tony come.'

'You don't have to be doing that. John will be getting around to it anytime now and you've so little—'

'Mam, I just want to do something for you while I'm here,' he interjected firmly.

'As you wish,' she nodded, the warmth radiating from her eyes. 'Thank you.'

Following breakfast he went into the shed and after some

searching emerged with the shears, spade, rake and brush, all packed into a wheelbarrow, and with Bran padding alongside he walked down the driveway. The day was fine and he clipped away at a leisurely pace, pausing regularly to take in the stunning countryside and its abundance of colour: the richness of the many greens in the landscape, the great variety of bloom scattered throughout the hedgerows and verges, the startling aqua and white of the rolling ocean and the bright cobalt blue of the sky contrasting the fulsome white clouds.

He was raking up the cuttings when Miriam came out.

'Now that's a good job, Michael,' she said, nodding. 'You could be mistaken for a farmer yet.'

'I could be mistaken for many things around here,' he responded jovially.

Miriam laughed and they both turned at the sound of Liam's vehicle coming into view over the rise of the hill. When their cousin pulled up at the gate, he let down his window to inspect Devlin's handiwork.

'You've not lost it, Michael,' he remarked. 'Not a bad job at all.'

'I say a good job,' Tony chipped in, 'and I believe we have a few hedges that need attention ourselves. How are you fixed?'

'Oh, I don't think you boys could afford my prices.'

This very natural interaction by the front gate had a resonance with Devlin as it reminded him of a scene from their adolescence many years before. After tidying up and putting the tools away, he went back into the house to get changed and ready for the jaunt up to the gorge. Miriam was handing over a parcel of sandwiches to Liam when he re-entered the kitchen.

'Now, I don't want you young cubs to be getting hungry,' she said. 'And I don't want you being carried off by the fairies, either.'

'We'll try not to,' Tony responded to the light-hearted hectoring, 'but you never know…'

Miriam and her mother waved the three men off as they

departed in the old vehicle, with Liam driving, Tony in the front passenger seat and Devlin in the back. They turned left, going in the opposite direction from the town and then took a lane that commenced the climb into the hills that reared sharply to the east above Knockbrack. They made their way through the tall and cool firs of the forestry plantation and emerged on higher, uncultivated ground where the wild, native trees formed a very different habitat for another world of insects and plants altogether, which was given an otherworldly feel by the mosses and fern that entirely covered its base and the thicket of interlocking branches that grew overhead. Devlin smiled, remembering that when they were children they would have called such places "fairy glens" and they would have been associated with ancient legends and supernatural occurrences. He also wondered at such an environment being this high up the mountain and if there were underground springs nearby, or other water sources. The glistening tarmac road had given way to a rougher track and while Tony gazed out of the window Liam was very focused on his driving, as the engine laboured noisily through the many gear changes required to ascend the winding route.

The partners were very at ease in each other's company, so much so that they did not feel the need to keep a conversation going and this suited Devlin, as he was intent on enjoying the drive.

'That is truly some view,' he eventually said, looking out the back window when they had cleared the woodlands. 'It's funny, I keep wondering how I could have forgot about this place for all those years.'

'We are nearly up at the gorge now,' Liam said. 'We can park up there. Do you fancy a walk before we go see Fergal?'

'That would be great.'

Liam parked in the shade underneath an overhanging tree and they took a steep footpath that led up through the gorge, whose vegetation was alive with rustic tones and bright verdant shades. The sound of their heavy breathing would remain in Devlin's memory afterwards, along with the constant noise of boots finding their footing on the challenging path until he looked up to see first Tony and then Liam disappear between two large rocks that marked the summit.

Clambering through the opening, Devlin's automatic reaction was to turn around and take in the full sweep of the countryside and coastline.

Tony carried on up the narrow ravine that rose from the viewing point and watching his partner's figure disappear into the dense greenery, Liam said in a voice tinged with both humour and pride, 'He's in his element now; he should have been a mountain goat.'

'He should indeed,' Devlin agreed readily.

'You can see three counties from here,' Liam said, turning, a slow smile lifting his broad features.

'Ah, of course,' Devlin answered, as though the secrets of a mystery had just been revealed to him. 'It all comes back to me.'

The two cousins stood quietly, each taking in the vast planes stretching majestically north and south and the unceasing tidal activity of the Atlantic to the west. It was Liam who eventually broke the silence.

'Well, Michael, if you don't mind, I'd like to finish that conversation I started when you first arrived.'

Devlin turned slightly to look at him as Liam began in a slow, unhurried voice.

'Even though you have only been here a few days, I am sure you will have been picking up on the politics that are starting to consume this place. You'll know of the divide in the organisation and growing militancy of part of the CMA. The explosion yesterday, along with the sporadic drone attacks that have happened here and there, may only be the start of it. There is no doubt in my mind that the organisation will officially separate and there are some things that I want you to consider. The idea of an armed rebellion undoubtedly has its place in our proud history, but given our current position, it would be of the upmost folly to pursue that option at this point. Back in the day, when the battle was against the old British forces, explosions and direct military action received great publicity. This was what made that course of action work – it played on the wider national psyche – but it's a different world now and I will give you an example… A few years ago, in an area of Munster, there was a spate of rebellious actions that included explosions and other attacks. However, nothing was reported. In fact, it was weeks before we in the organisation even heard as, publicly, the Regime did not recognise that anything had happened. Meanwhile, on the ground, there was a mass infiltration of the area. Many people were lifted and many more tampered with, to the extent that no one knew who was a double agent and who wasn't. The surveillance put in place was overwhelming and the area has not completely recovered yet, neither psychologically nor financially.

'I take you at your word, cousin,' Devlin said thoughtfully, after a moment's contemplation, 'and my knowing nothing of this shows how effective the clampdown was. But are you really suggesting a course of non-action?'

'You see that outcrop,' Liam said fervently, turning and pointing up the mountain to the path Tony had taken. 'In a few minutes, you will see Tony appear at its summit, I'll wager. It is, of course, the great burial chamber that we once used to climb to and signifies everything that is ancient and sacred in this land. Its very presence tells me that as well as great creativity and belief, we Celts are endowed with an amazing endurance. Nothing has outlasted us on this land and nothing ever will. It is ours.'

As if on cue, Tony appeared above them, standing proudly on the worn limestone boulder that marked the top of the burial chamber. The cousins both waved to him and he roared down in response, his voice carrying with a startling clarity.

'I remember us doing that as gossoons. It feels like you're shouting from the top of the world.' He paused, then added, 'In answer to your question, Michael, it is not a course of non-action. Our aims include the infiltration of the Regime and the subsequent influencing of its policy. You will notice there has been a relaxing of restrictions around our culture and language. Well, this has not happened totally by chance, or because of the benevolence of the Regime. It's true that some senior Regime members have a fascination for Celtic culture, which is not without irony, since they have systematically eradicated so many others at this stage, but I have to say that plenty of influence has also been wielded for the cause. We have people involved in covert roles, monitoring the Regime's direction of policy and applying pressure, and I now believe it is realistic to start planning for the re-establishment of local-level political structures and for the CMA becoming a mainstream party. So, not non-action, but a long-term strategy that has borne real fruit over the last couple of decades.'

'You know what Pádraig and Aoife would say,' Devlin said, having listened intently to his cousin's words, 'that all this would have happened anyway and the Regime will go no further. The road to autonomy stops here and this great Celtic nation will remain a plaything, a theme park, completely subjugated.'

Liam seemed unsure if Devlin was playing devil's advocate, but whatever the case, his response was passionate.

'That is an opinion I have bitterly contested,' his eyes glistened as he continued, 'but what is not merely an opinion is that any military campaign at this stage would not only be short-lived, but would also result in frightening repercussions for the people we love.'

There followed a silence lasting over thirty seconds, before Liam asked very deliberately, 'Are you of a mind with them?'

'I have only just walked into all this,' Devlin responded, 'though I admit, there does seem to be an inevitability about my eventual involvement. If that's the case, I need to understand as much as possible. I am not of mind with anyone, but it seems time is running out for me to decide.' He took a slow, deep breath. 'So, you have brought me to this high place, Liam, and it reminds me of an old story from the Bible. The devil took the lord to a high place and offered him all the lands that he could see if he did his bidding or worshipped him. I can't remember which.'

'No such grandiose offers here, Michael.' Liam laughed ruefully. 'You will not be offered all the lands that you can see, though you may receive Clancy's meadow. We want you to return over the water, to serve the people of this land, as it is within your nature to pursue the autonomy agenda. I know your deep love of this land will guide you and that you can still rise to a position of some influence. There may even be a pathway laid out before you already.'

'You seem to know more than I do, cousin.'

'That may well be the case.'

'And what of Niall?'

'I'm not sure of the path you are going to take, Michael, so that is all I am prepared to say for now. I have probably gone further than I should have, because of our strong family bond and your history with the CRP – and therefore with the Regime.'

Taking stock for a few moments, Devlin knew that ultimately, this time and place were of great significance to him, even if Liam was not prepared to expand any further. He had been feeling the pull of this old relationship with his cousin and had easily become accustomed to his reasoned tones once more. But there was still something gnawing away at him – something as yet unresolved.

They could hear Tony making his final descent down the path behind them, but neither man turned around.

'You will know my mind in due course,' Devlin uttered quietly. 'What remains of my life will depend on what is decided in the next few weeks, of that I'm sure.'

'That's fine, so,' Liam nodded, as though he wasn't in the slightest bit surprised. 'We will know where we stand then.' Brightening, he turned to greet Tony. 'And how's the mountain goat?'

Exhilarated by both the exertion and his surroundings, Tony alternated between taking in large gulps of air and smiling, and once he had caught his breath the three men started making their way back towards the car, with Devlin bringing up the rear, pausing here and there to take in the different views. When he caught up with his companions again, Liam had the parcel of sandwiches in his hand.

'We shall go and see Fergal,' he said. 'We'd never hear the last of it if we didn't call in for a cup of tea.'

'Are you up here often?' Devlin asked.

'Oh, fairly often. Don't I have to keep the goat exercised?'

'Come on, old timers,' Tony responded with a definite touch of mockery. 'I'll lead the way for ye.'

Imposing fir trees surrounded Fergal's cottage, which was set above a small lake, the dark rippling surface of which was catching the sunlight from over the mountain. Wisps of turf smoke rose lazily from the chimney and yellow climbing roses were clustered around the entrance, with the top half of the door open.

'What a sight,' Devlin couldn't help but smile as he looked at the traditional thatched residence, 'with the door open in welcome. And isn't he the hardy old buck, to be here all-year round.'

'He is for sure,' Tony agreed. 'Oh, Michael – there is one thing. Don't be eating the sandwiches, as they're a great treat for Fergal. We always leave them behind us.'

Recognising the merits of the plan for the food, Devlin nodded, saying with a smile, 'I'll stick to the tea, so.'

They entered the cottage and a lively conversation ensued between Liam, Tony and Fergal, about the neighbourhood, the seasons, the wedding and the weekend football match against Curraghcorn. Devlin was content to listen and stare into the turf fire, over which a large black kettle burbled steadily as the old man prepared incredibly strong tea that was served in brown pot mugs. Devlin felt like a child in the corner of the room whose presence had been forgotten, and with nothing being expected of him, his mind was free to wander, so he thought about what had happened since he had returned home, only occasionally taking note of the talk going on around him.

'It's been a great visit,' he eventually heard Liam say. 'I hope the seasons are with you and the mountain is kind.'

'Why wouldn't they be?' Fergal replied in his deep guttural voice, smiling at each of them in turn. 'Aren't I here and looking after the mountain all these years?' His deep brown eyes came to rest on Devlin. 'It was good to see you, Michael. It's been a long time and even though the cat's got your tongue, I won't count you as a stranger.'

'Thank you, Fergal. I'm sure my tongue will be looser next time.'

The three men left with the sandwiches unopened on the old man's table and headed for Liam's vehicle. The drive back was stunning, with the broadening sun starting to drop slowly towards the sea that was glowing below. What conversation there was focused on the evening landscape.

'We'll not come in,' Tony said as they dropped Devlin off at his mother's front gate. 'The dawn wedding will come soon enough. We'll see you all then.'

Devlin petted an excited Bran as he walked towards the house and when he entered the kitchen he was once more engulfed by the wonderful aromas of home-cooked food, suddenly aware of how hungry he was.

'Well, now that you're finally here, you may as well sit down,' his mother said, turning from the range with a contented smile playing on her lips. 'Miriam will be down in a minute. Did you have a good day?'

'We did indeed – it was stunning up there, Mam. You won't believe the appetite I've got now though.'

Miriam took her place at the table and after a hearty meal the three of them spent the evening in the kitchen, talking in detail about the impending wedding. After saying a few prayers for Ben in the living room, they all went to bed early that evening and Miriam assured Devlin she would give him a wake-up call.

This would not be necessary, however, as he woke from a deep, dreamless sleep in plenty of time and after getting ready, went downstairs to find his mother and sister drinking tea at the old oak table.

'Do you get up for a while every day, Michael?' Miriam asked, smiling sweetly.

'Oh, leave him alone,' Mrs Devlin said with a warm weariness. Behind her back, Devlin pulled a childish face at his sister.

Sitting down, he ate thick chunks of soda bread with butter, cheese and pickle, his last slice being covered in a thick layer of his mother's blackberry and apple jam. Then, after finishing his mug of tea, he pushed his chair back from the table with a contented sigh and the sound of Liam's vehicle reaching the rise in the Mullnamorran road could be plainly heard, signalling his imminent arrival.

The family went out into the darkness, which seemed total except for a faint brightness along the horizon. Liam drove up the driveway and swung around, lighting up the three figures standing at the front of the house.

'Will you keep an eye on this place for me?' Mrs Devlin asked Bran, who responded by growling and slowly wagging his tail a couple of times.

The dog sat down on the step and watched as they all climbed into the back of the vehicle.

'We have a lovely morning for the happy couple,' Tony declared cheerily. 'All aboard and away we go.'

They drove through the dark, silent town, down the harbour road and past the entrance to the graveyard. There was an assortment of vehicles already parked at random intervals along the roadside and there was the familiar jaunting car with Cuchulainn. The noble horse looked up at them briefly as they pulled up, then continued chomping away at the grass verge. The freshness of the morning was striking. They went by the old red boat and took the right fork in the path, following behind a couple that Devlin did not recognise, but who kept turning around to talk to Miriam and his mother.

At the clearing beside the Sailor's Eye, people were gathering as the dark, rolling waves below started to become visible in the slowly dawning light. There was a murmuring of conversation among the assembly and the cockerel's call from nearby MacMurrough's yard was startling in its clarity, when out on the ocean, the bobbing light of an approaching boat caught Devlin's attention. The crowd fell silent as Erringal's voice rose certainly.

'The legends of the lands out to the west will never leave us,' he proclaimed, spreading his arms out wide. 'The gods of old have always been there in the substance of everything and their call is as clear as the cockerel's, if we have the senses to hear. So we humbly wait, for the confirmation that all is well.'

The boat had a ghostly appearance, with its dark red sails raised and a lantern swaying slowly from the prow. The creaking of the aged vessel was heard over the rise and fall of the sea, as the sailor continued to navigate the approach to the jetty, while his companion held up a mirror that reflected the dawning light to the people on the shore.

'Bernadette and Thomas, you are being signalled to go down,' Erringal called out. 'Bring us word from the harbingers of our holy and bountiful sea. Can we proceed upon this union?'

Some of the congregation gently repeated the words, 'Can we proceed upon this union?' until it grew into a babble of reassuring sound.

The couple went down to the small jetty and received a rolled parchment from the messenger, who hugged them both before getting back aboard the vessel. Bernadette and Thomas then climbed back up the narrow path and the boat put out to sea once more.

'You need not fear the sea or seasons,' the messenger cried, 'while you believe and are in their sway. So it's always been – let it be that way.'

Erringal, who had moved forward to the head of the crowd, took the parchment from the couple and read its contents. 'All is indeed well,' he said, smiling. 'We may surely proceed.'

The crowd cheered and the couple were embraced by relatives, friends and neighbours. Devlin had been aware of Miriam breathing more deeply beside him and when she started to sing, her beautiful voice soared high above the chatter of the mingling people. The song was in native Irish, thanking the messengers, who were now returning across the sea, and as he looked around the crowd in the growing brightness of the day, Devlin spotted Gráinne standing behind Erringal.

'So, being thankful for all the sea has given us,' the old man proclaimed, spreading his arms out wide, 'we must still be mindful of ancient voyages and ways. And especially on this day, we should give and receive such blessings warmly, for our hearts are anchored in these days.'

He led the way back along the path to the small clearing by the old boat, where the people gathered closely together. Devlin examined the spine of the old vessel, which seemed just the same as it had been in his childhood, when they'd ran past it with scant regard.

'The strange thing is, it doesn't seem to have rotted any further in our lifetimes,' Miriam said gently, having followed his gaze. 'What is also mysterious is that no one actually knows who the boat belongs to. The only sure thing is that whoever did own it, they are long gone now. It has become a venerated spot – a symbol of our links with the sea.'

'So, we gather in this place of aging,' Erringal's eyes were bright, as his voice was resounding, 'where the spine and skeleton return to prominence in all the seasons. Where the redness of the paint is blood and yet it lives. For all that we might age, we shall endure. For all that we endure, so shall we love. For Thomas and Bernadette, the simple wish: may you live long together and your love outlive us all.'

The crowd cheered, the couple kissed and Erringal brought this part of the ceremony to a close.

'Let us all depart and allow this young couple to spend sweet time together,' he declared, prompting a more earthy acclaim from some in the assembly. 'We shall meet at the hall later to complete this union, sealed securely by the elements and the land – to sing, dance and socialise for all we are worth.'

After another bout of cheering, the crowd started to disperse and Gráinne strolled over to Devlin and his family.

'My respects, Mrs Devlin, Miriam and Michael,' she said in a voice that was both rich and affectionate.

'Thank you, Gráinne,' Mrs Devlin replied. 'We're hearing great things about your latest work.'

'Indeed we are,' Miriam cut in, grinning mischievously. 'Why, even Michael here thinks you're finally getting the hang of this painting lark.'

'Take no notice of her.' Mrs Devlin shook her head. 'She's getting worse with age, I swear she is.'

Gráinne smiled broadly at the remark, a response that confirmed what Devlin had already been told, that his sister and the artist were now indeed good friends.

'Have you finished the Crying Cliffs?' he asked, recovering himself after feeling momentarily embarrassed by Miriam's teasing. 'That's a great perspective you've got there.'

'I have indeed,' she answered, cocking her head slightly and regarding him closely. 'I'm now doing a larger canvas, from a slightly different position. Though the camp hasn't moved on yet.'

'That's great,' Devlin nodded his head firmly, as if that was all he was needing to hear.

'Well, well, well,' Miriam said, turning towards her mother.

'You're terrible, Miriam.' Mrs Devlin rolled her eyes. 'One moment, you will charm the very birds with your singing voice and deeds, and the next, you'll be full of devilment.'

'Oh, isn't it the way of it, Mam,' Miriam countered breezily, 'the sweetness and the spice of life. Anyway, Michael is well able to take it and I need to get my digs in while he's here.' She looked to Gráinne. 'Are you going to the hall later?'

'I probably won't. I've taken to working in the evenings, when the light is as good as this. A good morning to you all and I'll see you soon enough, no doubt.'

Gráinne walked away towards the grazing Cuchulainn and, despite his mother and sister's obvious amusement, Devlin could not help appreciating the way her long, dark green and blue dress moved freely in time with her stride and the sway of her auburn hair.

The family met up with Liam and Tony along the roadside and got a lift back to Knockbrack. Devlin was very pleased to have the opportunity to spend the afternoon gardening with his mother, while Miriam came out to read on the bench, occasionally joining in with their conversation. The sea breeze blew gently though the border plants, which were attracting many butterflies and bees in the warm sunshine, and he thought how well everything looked and smelt. But then a cool tinge of sadness came over him, considering how little time in reality he had back at the home place and how quickly that time was passing.

CHAPTER TWELVE

'The afternoon turned out so well and it looks like it will stay fine,' Mrs Devlin said, looking up at the sky and closing the front door. 'I will enjoy the walk down to the hall. Have you got the flowers there, Miriam?'

'I have, Mam,' Miriam replied, 'and Michael's got the hamper. Did you say John was walking down with us?'

'He is. He's waiting on the road for us.'

A fresh wind blew in off the sea as the four of them walked down the road into town, chatting in the early evening sunshine, and when they reached the hall, a group of townspeople greeted them heartily at the door and also offered their condolences for Ben's passing. This type of interaction would happen many times throughout the evening, with Devlin finding the mingling of sadness over Ben and joy at the couple's union a very natural and reassuring process.

They exchanged well wishes with Bernadette's and Thomas's families, who were situated beside the door, before seating themselves at a table beyond the dance floor. The babble of the growing crowd continued to increase in its intensity, until Erringal stood up and addressed them.

'We will soon welcome Bernadette and Thomas back to this

gathering,' he proclaimed with great passion, 'and we sincerely hope that it is a place they will always feel they can return to. It is from this place that they came and it is this community that will duly give its blessing, but before we bid them enter and the couple take their glorious benediction from the day, will you show your appreciation for their families, who must accept our deep and heartfelt thanks. From the sacred dawn to the closing of the night, we will recognise their nurturing and hold it dear.'

Both the bride and groom's families stood and waved in response to the loud applause and cheering from those assembled, many of whom came forward to embrace and kiss the smiling parents as positive remarks rained down. The musicians on stage played a selection of hornpipes to accompany the lengthy ovation, until Erringal eventually stepped forward again.

'You have shown your appreciation for the families.' He paused and, standing very erect, turned towards the entrance, saying, 'Would you now welcome back these young people, who come into our gaze now as a fully-fledged partnership – Bernadette and Thomas.'

The couple entered the Hall, passing between two large candles, and Erringal went to meet them. Clasping both Bernadette's hands, his expression was tinged with wonderment as he savoured the significance of the occasion. After repeating the same gesture with Thomas, he turned to address the crowd once more.

'You are very welcome before us and with all the generations who have passed before, we welcome you. You have passed between the candles of fertility and friendship, so may your partnership be bountiful. You are proof of our community's enduring presence. May you find you own way and walk a path that is of your own making. The sea and seasons have smiled upon your union and we can only show our gratitude to them. May the westerlies still drive you onwards, or lift you when you travel. Tonight you shall sit with us and remain as long as you wish, for while the future is a prayer yet to be uttered, with uncertainty the way of it, know you have safe harbour here.' Parting his hands, he added, 'Come, sit you down within our midst.'

A powerful ovation followed and the band was already playing as the couple took their place at the elevated table by the stage, which was richly decorated. When the commotion had died down, a quieter period ensued, with people conversing in their own companies while consuming their own food, after which Erringal announced the next stage in the proceedings.

'We have eaten now and before the onset of the fullest celebrations, it would be good to dwell upon the path that led us here – to hear once more the oratory for which we're renowned – and to that end, I call upon the bards.' He gestured towards the table where Fergal and Eimear sat. 'After our repast, some stories of the deeds and doings from bygone times would serve us well, engaging the mind before we sing and dance.'

'Well spoken, Erringal.' Fergal rose, wearing an ornate jacket of great age, and continued in his deep, guttural voice, 'Your words hold us together well. I will indeed tell a story that you might guess is from another time altogether. A time that may seem strange, but that nonetheless can shine a light on who we are. Long ago, there was a young, naïve chief, who had strayed far from his homelands in Mayo. He was chasing a golden stag that had taken refuge in the high gorge above Knockbrack and in chasing the stag up there, he had lost his men, who wondered where he'd gone. A mist came down and a beautiful maiden appeared to him and said, "You have lost yourself in your pursuit and the darkness will soon descend. You have wandered into a land of much danger, where evil spirits are often known. We must be of the sharpest senses." The young chief was entranced by the maiden, who said to him, "Put your hand upon my shoulder and I will lead you to safety in this darkness." Whether because of her enchantment or the night he knew not, but his sight failed him, so he followed her meekly as a lamb into a cave. He sat down and she told him, "Now open your eyes," whereupon he did, but could make out nothing.

"I fear your sight has been taken," she said. "You must stay here, as you would be easy prey for those who wander these steep rocks. It's lucky I chanced by your way. Wait here until tomorrow, when hopefully you shall see the light again."

'She returned the next day to find that the young chief could still see only darkness in the cave. "I will have to go and seek the assistance of spirits greater than I," she said. "Your golden bow and staff will be needed to ward off any tyrants I might meet on such a quest. Give them to me and rest you easy here." She took his bow and staff, and returning some days later, said, "I have managed to meet the Ancient King and he can cure your blindness, but he demands the gold you hold within your purse." The young chief was truly troubled and gave her all his gold. "Stay within the depths of this cave," she said, as she went again, "for its only here true sanctuary can be found from passing tyrants."

'A week passed, but she did not return. Then a shepherd from Knockbrack came to the cave looking for a stray ewe and hearing sighs of anguish from within, called out, "Are you ill within the cave?" The young chief explained what had happened, in response to which the shepherd said, "I'll wager now that your senses are all intact. Come out and see the humble magician who has restored your sight with daylight." The young chief made his way uncertainly to the cave entrance and was overjoyed to see the shepherd smiling in the morning sunlight. Having finally realised the trick that had been played on him, he left the mountain and was glad to accept the shepherd's kind offer of bread and cheese by his humble fire. And that is why, to this day, the rocks up there are known as the Gorge of the Lost Prince.'

Even after Fergal had retaken his seat, the crowd continued to express their approval for the ancient tale and the way it had been told. When finally the comments had subsided, Eimear rose, wearing a long red gown adorned by a sapphire brooch, and spoke in a sweet, lyrical voice.

'There was a terrible time, long after the days that Fergal

brought to life so magically just now. These were days of famine and evictions across the land, which led to mass emigrations. The ordinary people were under the severest of oppression and maybe this is something we can understand now, even all these years later.'

There were loud affirmative remarks from around the hall and she waited for them to die down before continuing.

'Anyway, for those poor souls there was no food and the idea of emigration seemed the only option that they had, so with what little strength they still possessed, they started to walk. Over time, various routes developed and where they could, these starving people made their way to the main coastal ports. As you'll know, the nearest major port to here is Sligo and it's hard to imagine now that in eighteen forty-seven, between April and October, more than thirteen thousand souls would climb aboard one hundred and sixty sailing ships or more, to go to lands that we can only now dream of.' She paused at this moment, in response to an outbreak of appreciative conversation within the crowd.

'Now, there was a family called the Durkans,' she went on, 'who had walked a long way from Cavan and made it to Mullnamorran. The party was fifteen in number and they were in a poorly state, with six of them very ill. They entered the town and stopped in the square, fearing that they could go no further, when people from the town rallied round and gave the Durkans whatever support they could, even though they had little enough themselves, as they were surviving just on fish by this stage. The family rested up for a few days before continuing on their journey to Sligo. One of them, Eamon, was a great musician and he would later say that while the scraps of food and bandages they received were important, it was the spiritual support that nourished their souls when they were at their lowest ebb. In the end, the Durkans made it to Sligo and emigrated on a small ship. The gods smiled on them in the new land and they often reflected on the kindness of the people of this area, inspiring Eamon to write a song chronicling their salvation, *The Stars above Mullnamorran*, which takes us back to those days with its heartfelt moods expressed in the native tongue. Miriam, will you sing it for us now?'

Miriam stood and after steadying herself, rendered the song unaccompanied, receiving a great ovation for her interpretation. When the last notes had subsided, Eimear got back to her feet.

'There are many tales that could be told of this place,' she raised her voice, emphasising every phrase, 'which has withstood so much and given so often. Is it not how we would have it? Why, so many of you have relatives who not that many years ago rescued the forlorn mariners of the Norse Maiden, taking to the sea in a terrible gale and going out to where the stricken craft was floundering on the Dark Rocks. On a night where all the sailors were saved, but we lost Hughie Gillespie and Sean Nolan in the swell. It was not that long ago, my friends. Who knows when we will be called upon again? Whenever that time comes, we shall be prepared for action. Now that the memories have been stirred and we have remembered who we are, it is time for life and joy to hold sway, for as that old Mullnamorran song says…

'For there's always time for living,
When sweet comrades meet by chance,
So comrades, friends and neighbours,
Will you join the merry dance?'

She waved to the musicians, who duly started to play, and the crowd responded immediately, with many taking to the dance floor.

'That was tremendous,' Devlin said, looking to his mother and sister.

'It was,' Mrs Devlin replied, adding thoughtfully, 'and to think that I was worried you'd forgot where you came from, like many a poor crater who never returned again.'

'It is no slight encounter with the home place for sure, Michael,' Miriam said, her voice bristling with spirit. 'By the time we've finished with you, you will be a Mullnamorran man once more. But never mind resting so easy there, you'll never get away without dancing.'

She led her brother to the dance floor, where he remained for the next hour, dancing with neighbours, family members and old acquaintances. When he finally made his way back to the table, he was approached by Aoife.

'Well, now you're nicely warmed up,' she said, 'you'll have a dance with me as well.'

The band, who had for the most part been playing jigs and reels at a fast pace, played a waltz and Devlin and Aoife danced well together while she spoke calmly to him.

'I hope you have been giving our conversation at the wake some thought, Michael.'

'I have indeed,' he said, leaning back to look her in the eye, 'though while the career options are not certain, or even non-existent, I am not in a position to decide on my own direction, if that makes sense – or potential usefulness to any cause.'

'Ah… I suppose that makes sense,' she pulled him close, talking directly into his ear. 'By the way, we're going for a jaunt up to Burn's on Monday night. There's a great session that me and Pádraig go to.' Then, leaning back, she smiled widely. 'And shouldn't you be spending time with the family while you're home?'

'Well, I seem to be doing that for sure.'

She walked him back to his table, where she spoke warmly for a few minutes with his mother and sister.

'You danced very well together, Michael,' Miriam said thoughtfully, as Aoife returned to the dance floor. 'Very much in step, I would say.'

'Ah, but if only the steps of life were as easy to learn as the dances,' he replied, a playfulness in his voice.

'There are some who take the steps of life even more lightly.'

'You two amaze me,' Mrs Devlin said, having previously appeared to be taking no notice of her children's conversation, 'thick as thieves again. If I understand half of what you're saying, I'm doing well.'

A feeling of wellbeing came over Devlin as he took in the

hall, colourfully bedecked in fuchsias, golden rod and mallow, with Clancy's quintet playing at full tilt and the dancers moving in perfect unison. He loved the uninhibited exchanges of the neighbours around him and the way they used language so freely. These times were undoubtedly bizarre and troubling; if you walked into this occasion and felt the joy, exuberance and earthiness of this community in celebration, you could be forgiven for thinking it was another world altogether – and Devlin reflected that maybe it was. He had been lost in his own thoughts for a few minutes, with the prospect of another bicycle ride to the Shimmering Sands coming to the forefront of his mind, when Miriam tugged playfully at his sleeve.

'Penny for your thoughts,' she said.

'Oh, just the usual. Besides, I thought you'd be able to read my thoughts by now.'

'Of course, I could do,' she smiled, opening her eyes very wide, 'but I wouldn't like to intrude.'

She was then called upon to sing and she chose a song that told of a young couple who wandered through the country before finding shelter by the Golden Strand. The assembled company cheered her heartily when the last notes died away and the evening continued to evolve in an improvised manner that included poetic renditions and speeches as well as song and dance.

Mrs Devlin, who had been paying very close attention to everything that had been going on in the hall, turned to her children, saying, 'I must admit to being very tired by this stage. I think I will head home to my bed.'

'Do you know what, Mam, I'll join you,' Miriam responded with a relieved air. 'I'd love the walk.'

'I will join you as well,' Devlin said.

They said goodnight to Bernadette and Thomas, leaving John McSherry in deep conversation with some of the neighbours and Liam and Tony in the company of a group from the Mullnamorran Gaelic Athletic Association in the corner. They set off with the moon shining brightly on the road back home and with a strong, fragrant smell from the fields and hedgerows in the cooling air. Miriam lilted a haunting tune and her mother and brother walked silently either side of her.

'I don't suppose Michael told you, Mam,' she said, as she finished the song reaching the rise of the hill, 'that I beat him in a race to the gatepost the other day?'

'She was cheating, Mam,' Devlin cried out dramatically. 'It wasn't a fair race at all.'

'It's worse the pair of ye are getting.' Mrs Devlin shook her head, smiling.

Going into the house, they went straight to the living room, where Mrs Devlin said two prayers for Ben. Devlin was really taken with the second one and years later would be able to recite its concluding lines:

I'm glad that you're not gone, for that would truly break my heart.

For all that you have known and loved, is held in place by mighty stars.

Mrs Devlin said goodnight and went to bed, while her two children moved to the front room, where Devlin poured himself a whiskey and a glass of wine for his sister.

'I am expecting the full Michael Devlin story now,' Miriam said. 'I don't want an edited version, with all the interesting bits left out.'

They took their drinks out into the back garden and sat on the bench, facing each other. With an owl's deep call resounding through the nearby woods, Devlin proceeded to tell the promised story. He did not withhold anything, covering everything up to and including the past few days, and once he'd started to speak, Miriam focused intently on every word, only stopping him a few times to seek clarification on certain points.

He had gone all the way up to dancing with Aoife at the wedding when Miriam reflected ruefully, 'If you had not come home to your brother's funeral, you would not have come under such pressure to become politically involved. It doesn't seem right. You don't have to engage in this, Michael.'

'We shall see. Maybe it was heading that way already,' he shrugged. 'I don't know. I will have to talk to the Regime and who knows where that will lead. I have been trying to get a true gauge of the situation so that if a decision is required, it will be the best one. It's been brilliant seeing you and Mam again, despite it being brought about by Ben's sad parting, but you were both right in saying I have been marked out by this journey home – it's just I didn't realise to what extent. Anyway, that's enough of that, sis. Do you agree that I've said nothing in the last hour?'

'Indeed,' she gave a knowing smile, 'and even if you did, I wasn't listening. Now, would you give me a push on that old swing before going to bed?'

The memory of pushing Miriam on the swing that night would never leave Devlin. Gaining height, she lilted a tune in time with the pendulum motion and the sound of the rope chafing on the great oak bough above. The wind was blowing through her coppery-coloured hair that streamed behind her and they were transported back in time to their childhood; his mother's garden had once again become a magical place of nocturnal nooks and crannies. When Miriam reached the high point on the swing's trajectory, the rope buckled slightly and he stopped pushing. She swung her long pale legs to keep the momentum going for a while and then gradually let the swing slow down, singing quietly as she rocked back and forth. For a few moments before it came to a standstill, the sound and motion reminded Devlin of the thurible in the act of blessing, and in those moments, the garden was indeed a sacred place.

Miriam got off the swing and they walked across the garden in the moonlight, their silhouettes moving effortlessly across the lawn, leaving the empty whiskey and wine glasses behind on the bench.

The weather was changeable the next day and after breakfast

Devlin sat at the kitchen table, anticipating the match against Curraghcorn.

'It should be a feisty encounter alright,' he said, 'and it looks like there could be rain.'

'I'd take a coat, that's for sure,' his mother replied. 'Are you going with John?'

'Indeed. He said he'd call and we'd go down there handy. A big crowd is expected, I hear.'

'You'd better believe it.' Miriam looked up from her book. 'Strange as it seems, there's great interest from further afield in these tribal encounters. The match is being beamed far and wide.'

'And it's still played out at the crossroads ground.' Devlin shook his head gently. 'I can't believe that – it was falling apart when I was a cub.'

'It all adds to the old Oirish charm, don't you know,' Miriam said sarcastically. 'The tourists and Regimers love it – an old Hooley at the crossroads.'

'Now come on, Miriam,' Mrs Devlin said, 'don't be so cynical. It means a lot to the locals as well, especially with it being Curraghcorn.'

Devlin couldn't help but smile as Miriam beamed angelically at their mother, saying, 'Why, of course, Mama.'

John McSherry appeared at the back door and Mrs Devlin gladly changed the conversation.

'Why, you're in good time, John. Do you fancy a wee drop of tea?'

'I'm fine, thanks, Mam,' John answered. 'Oh, Michael, I was wondering if you fancy looking at the fences on the far side of Clancy's meadow before we go to the match? There are some short-horned cattle beyond there and they'd not think twice about breaking through.'

'You're right there, John, they're spirited alright. We'd better see if it needs reinforcing.'

A conversation regarding the meadow ensued between the two

men while Devlin was putting on his coat and Miriam watched them go with an amused look on her face.

'This farming is a very involving thing indeed, isn't it, Mam?'

Leaving by the back door, the two men did not even notice her remark. After a lengthy inspection of the fences, they set off towards Mullnamorran, with the discussion about the land continuing until they got into town. There was a substantial crowd in the square and music was blurring loudly from the bars, whose windows were decked out with scarves and banners in the Mullnamorran colours of maroon and white.

'This is a mighty crowd,' John observed, looking around appreciatively, 'as busy as I've ever seen it. Would you fancy a drink, Michael?'

'You'll not find me objecting too strongly,' Devlin smiled.

There was a lively atmosphere, with regular banter between the opposing sets of fans, and the two friends made their way through the crowds towards the Bamboo Lounge. On their way inside, they were approached by Paul Grogan.

'They are even coming in all the way from Knockbrack,' he said. 'It must be an important match, boys.'

'Oh, Paul, will you just keep an eye on us poor old culchies,' Devlin spoke with an exaggerated tone of appreciation, 'in case we get lost and never get home.'

'Ah, boys, don't you fret,' came Paul's sharp reply. 'We town lads will take care of ye.'

He made it obvious that he was addressing his own companions, as much as the two men who were entering the premises.

'Well, that's great to know,' Devlin said over his shoulder, going into the bar. 'We can proceed with confidence, so.'

John went to get the drinks and as Devlin glanced across the bustling crowd that was alive with noise and the colours maroon and green, he noticed that Liam and Tony were engaged in conversation with a group in the corner.

Returning with two pints, John was plainly a bit flustered.

'That Paul is a right feckin' dose,' he said. 'He'd put years on you.'

This took Devlin by surprise, as he had rarely heard his neighbour speak ill of anyone before, never mind so vehemently.

'It's just the old townies stuff – we used to rib them years ago,' he said, keen to brush off the encounter as being of little consequence.

'Oh, it's more than that. There are some who would sow divisions all over the place nowadays. Anyway, take no heed, Michael. You haven't time for that sort of thing.'

'Well, isn't this a great day for handing out a bit of a hiding to Curraghcorn?' Liam spoke enthusiastically, as he and Tony appeared beside Devlin and John.

'It is indeed,' John replied and the four men began chatting excitedly about the possible outcomes, which all focused on a Mullnamorran victory, though there was recognition that it would be a close encounter. They were so engrossed in their pre-match discussion that they did not notice Aoife and Pádraig's approach.

'Do you want a drink with us, lads?' Pádraig asked in an overly amiable way. 'Or do you want to save it for drowning your sorrows afterwards?'

'Oh, we seem to be fine here,' Liam said, looking around before adding, 'We will have to save some capacity for the celebratory drinks afterwards.'

'Devil the much celebration you'll be doing,' Aoife countered. 'Mind you, I'll admit there's not much between these teams on the field, though the politics of them seems to be diverging, if you don't mind me saying. Or have you not heard about that over here in the sticks?'

'We have indeed, but it's not so clear-cut,' Tony responded sharply. Having everyone's attention, he continued, 'But talking of diverging, you're from Curraghcorn, Aoife, and that's fair enough, but Pádraig here, I seem to remember him from being around

Mullnamorran, yet now he's wearing the green. He seems to have diverged down the coast.'

This caused much amusement, with even Aoife unable to suppress a smile.

'You could say it's where I'm coming from now,' Pádraig countered abruptly. 'The greater vision will outshine the local viewpoint.'

It was John, having said nothing up to this point, who interjected decisively. 'It's a football match – will you not leave the feckin' politics out of it, lads?'

For a moment the company fell silent, but secretly they were all grateful to him for bringing this exchange to an end, while it was still amiable enough, as they all knew this was not the place for an acrimonious dispute.

'I'm with you there, John,' Devlin raised his glass. 'Here's to a great game and may the best team win.'

They all raised their glasses and, leaning over, Aoife said quietly in Devlin's ear, 'I'm sure we will.'

He did not respond but on finishing his drink followed John outside, where they joined the general movement heading towards the ground. The crowd was good-humoured and the two Knockbrack men became involved in some light-hearted banter with a group of Curraghcorn supporters. Passing the large temporary car park, they then approached the main stand with its impressively refurbished maroon and cream frontage, whereas the rest of the ground looked rundown, with rust showing regularly on the old corrugated structure.

'Wow, some money has been spent here,' Devlin commented. 'To keep the bigwigs and tourists happy, I suppose.'

'There has indeed,' John nodded, 'but don't worry, Michael. They have made no improvements to the Northside Terrace, where we're going. I'd say the byre where I milk has greater creature comforts.'

Smiling at John's remark, Devlin continued to watch the

people mingling in front of the main stand. He spotted Conor and Catherine from the Connaught Princess in the company of Mr Doran and other dignitaries, who he presumed were Regime officials, and he was intrigued by the various parties that were waiting to enter the main stand. He was wondering where they had all come from as, judging by their stylish dress, they were not from the local area, when a nearby conversation amused him.

'Well, which team are you going to shout for?' she was saying.

'Oh, definitely Curraghcorn,' came her partner's assured reply.

'And why is that?'

'Isn't it obvious? They play in green and what could be more Irish that that!'

Devlin did not look at the couple engaging in this exchange, but rather at the strong security and police presence around the entrances. He saw Mr Doran and Conor preparing to go through the gates and was caught off guard as Catherine suddenly turned her gaze in his direction. He looked away immediately, not waiting to see if she had recognised him, and moved towards the corner of the ground, where two programme sellers were projecting their voices to great effect.

'Get your programmes here! Get your programs here! As you can't get them anywhere else, why don't you get them here?'

'Indeed, isn't my old Saxon friend exactly right?' his colleague cried out. 'You wouldn't want to be left short of information about the encounter between the mighty Mullnamorran and the crusading Curraghcorn!'

'He's only right! From the land of saints and scholars, we give you the ancient contest!'

Devlin did not look directly at the sellers as John paused to buy a programme and it was after going around the corner on their way to the Northside Terrace that his friend winced, saying, 'Jaysus, you wouldn't know what thon fellas are trying to say and where at all they came from – I'm sure they're not from around here, anyhow.'

'I'm sure you're right there,' Devlin replied, a faint smile on his lips.

Entering the ground, they decided to have another drink before going up on to the terraces. A boisterous crowd surrounded the small, corrugated iron bar that was painted a bright ochre colour interspersed with rust, a structure held together by rough-sawn timbers, and there was a tremendous atmosphere in the enclosed space as competing fans chanted for their team and hurled derisory comments at their opponent's supporters. John was not deterred by the hubbub going on around him and went through the line-ups of the teams in the programme, pointing out where various players came from and what they did for a living. Devlin would later remember this chaotic scene underneath the stand very fondly, as it was just John and him, the two boys out to enjoy the match.

They went up onto the terrace when the teams were completing their pre-match routines on the pitch. As the ground was virtually full, they had to go along and down many steps, through a sea of fluttering banners and flags being held aloft, to find a place where they'd have a decent view. Devlin carefully surveyed the old ground and besides the modernisation of the main stand, the only major change that he could see was the installation of large screens around the ground, which were currently showing action from past matches.

The throw-in was greeted with an almighty roar and the game started at a furious pace, with both sides trying to wrest the initiative in the opening exchanges. Mullnamorran scored the first point and as the ball sailed between the posts, Devlin found he was roaring his approval. The home side took an early three-point lead, until one of the Curraghcorn forwards drilled the ball into the net to equalise the score, much to the delight of the travelling supporters. There were some feisty physical encounters throughout, most notably one on the twenty-five-minute mark involving six players, which threatened to draw in everyone on the pitch. When these exchanges were replayed on the screen in slow motion, it triggered a tirade of conflicting comments from the crowd and as the teams left the field at half-time, it was Curraghcorn who now led by a single point. The break was twenty minutes long, featuring action replays interspersed with analysis and comments, which for the most part were relayed from other venues. The second half began with both teams having short periods of ascendency, keeping the whole crowd fully engaged until, with only a few minutes remaining, Curraghcorn scored a point that put them two ahead, and the mood of the home supporters on the Northside Terrace slumped. Devlin and John exchanged a flurry of concerned remarks, reassuring each other that it wasn't over yet, while at the same time fearing the worst. The game was on a knife's edge when Kielty, the nimble Mullnamorran forward, ran expertly through the away defence, but just as he seemed to have the goal at his mercy, he sliced the shot horrendously wide. This was a signal for jeers and celebrations from the travelling supporters, as the officials hoisted a notice saying that there would be three minutes of added time.

'It's got to be the goal,' John said pluckily.

Curraghcorn's forwards attacked again in an effort to finally kill the game off, but the move broke down. Mullnamorran picked up the ball and, inter-passing quickly between the half-forwards, they moved into the opposition's half. The sense of drama in the crowd was palpable as this was undoubtedly going to be the last chance to launch an attack. A long ball was played into the goal mouth and it dropped between the defenders into the only unoccupied space to be seen in the goal area. Quickest to react to this unexpected situation was Kielty, who darted through the ranks of green and white into the opening, grasping the ball. He bounced it once, taking a synchronised step to the left and the supporters around Devlin gasped as he drew back his foot and connected perfectly. The crowd erupted. In all the pandemonium, Devlin didn't see the actual shot cross the line, but knew by its trajectory that this one was a goal. The net bulged, the players celebrated wildly and he was amazed to see John doing the steps of a triumphant jig in the ensuing mayhem. There were only a few seconds left in the match, with barely enough time to kick off again before the referee blew for full-time, bringing a mighty roar from the terraces, as the Mullnamorran team secured a famous victory.

Once the celebrations had died down, they started to make their way towards the exit. Replays of the goal were being shown on screens and in the main stand, people were still cheering every time Kielty's shot was shown rocketing into the net. After taking in the scene one more time, Devlin moved to the exiting gangway, where all the supporters seemed to be leaving the Northside Terrace at the same time. The tightly-packed crowd swayed out of the ground as excited comments were yelled back and forth and a steady chant of 'Mull-na-morran' filled the late-afternoon air.

Outside, supporters from the Northside Terrace converged with those from the rest of the ground. There was a swirling motion and Devlin turned to see an unexpected scuffle breaking out, causing a further surge in the crowd. He felt something catch his leg and he was starting to lose his footing when a sharp crack landed on the side of his head. He lost consciousness for a few moments, during which time John and others in the immediate vicinity instinctively supported him to stay upright. There was pandemonium all around them and frustrated remarks being shouted to no avail, as whoever was responsible for the attack had managed to disappear into the sea of bodies streaming away from the ground.

Two blue and red drones swooped low and circled briefly, agitating some of the supporters, before flying off towards the town. Devlin ambled along unsteadily for a few yards, but soon felt surer of his footing, realising that it was the shock rather that the severity of the attack that had momentarily stunned his senses. By the time they got down to the main road, he had recovered sufficiently to walk confidently and began to disperse the group of well-meaning fans who'd gathered around him.

'Go on ahead, lads,' he urged them, 'I'm grand. You go ahead to town, there's celebrating to be done.'

One of the supporters lingered after the others had gone on, a grave look on his pale features as he handed Devlin a bottle of water.

'You've got a few splashes of blood on you there,' he said, hesitating before adding, 'I've never seen the likes of that… well, not for years. That was a hurly stick you were done with and it looked to me like it was planned.' After pausing again, he then asked, 'Have you got any enemies?'

'Ah, we'll get to the bottom of it. I'm fine for sure. Now, you get on your way to town.'

The man stood pensively for a moment before handing Devlin his Mullnamorran scarf and walking away.

'He's right about the blood,' John said.

'I'm grand, John. Honestly. If we can just lay low for a few moments…'

They avoided any further interest by turning onto the pathway that the wedding party had taken the morning before. Reaching the upturned boat, Devlin sat down to examine the wound gingerly with both hands, finding a lump above his ear that was crowned by a cut.

'It's not a bad one,' he said, feeling around, 'barely a nick.'

John produced a handkerchief, which he doused with water from the bottle to wipe away the blood. He then produced a hip flask from the inside pocket of his jacket and unscrewed the top saying, 'I brought this along in case we had some celebrating to be done.'

'Well, you are a wonder indeed,' Devlin accepted the drink gratefully, continuing in a bright and breezy way, 'and the bleeding has stopped as well. This whiskey obviously has miraculous powers.'

'Your man there was right.' John gazed at him doubtfully. 'That was no accident and I've a few ideas who it might have been.'

'I've got a few ideas myself,' Devlin acknowledged, 'but as you said earlier, John, I really haven't the time now and there are more important things to worry about.' Looking down, he ran his hand slowly along the grain of the aged timber with its obdurate red paint, reflecting for a few moments on the diverging forces involved in the struggle for independence and how that might play out locally, before whispering involuntarily, 'The blood's been spilt so many times before – must it be spilt again?'

'What's that, Michael?' John asked urgently. 'What's that you said? Are you sure you're OK?'

'Never surer.' Devlin looked up, smiling, and took another swig of whiskey. 'Though I'd better not drink all of this, had I? I would be in real trouble then.'

Walking back through the graveyard, they took the back lane home and, looking down on Mullnamorran in the throes of a great celebration, Devlin could not help but smile at the cheering, music, song and spontaneous bouts of cheering that were emanating from town. *It is indeed a famous day,* he thought, *and even more so for me, who never thought I'd know such days again.*

The rain that had been forecast for earlier finally came as they were on the homeward stretch to Knockbrack, only adding to the dishevelled look of the two returning football fans. The maroon and white Mullnamorran scarf proved very useful to Devlin as he wrapped it around his neck to cover the blood on his shirt and John's hip flask was emptied before they got to the rise in the road, ensuring that the boys were in good spirits by the time they got back to the home place. Mrs Devlin was putting her gardening tools away as they arrived at the front gate.

Not wanting to worry his mother, Devlin went straight into the kitchen to give Miriam a brief summary of what had happened.

'You go upstairs and clean up,' she said, 'and I'll be up in a minute.' Then, upon inspecting the wound more closely, she smiled, tapping it lightly. 'I may put a wee stitch in that. It's a good job you haven't been to the barbers in a while.'

John was still in the kitchen when Mrs Devlin came in from the garden.

'Wasn't it great about the match,' she said, her face uplifted by a full smile. 'You could hear the roars from here, John.'

'It was great, Mam,' John agreed. 'I've never seen a bigger crowd and when young Kielty fired that one in…'

'Where's Michael?' she asked quickly, having noticed Devlin's absence.

'Would you believe this pair of boyos?' Miriam said, appearing in the doorway. 'They're not fit to be let out at all. They go to the match and get drinking and then Michael does no more than trip on the Northside terracing and gives his head a crack on that old corrugated sheeting. He's fine, though, and just gone up to change.'

'I'm sorry, Mam,' John said solemnly. 'We maybe had a good few.'

'Well, as long as he's alright.' Mrs Devlin's expression softened slightly.

'Oh, don't you know how hard-headed our Michael is?' Miriam spoke in a very matter-of-fact way. 'I'll just check on him and we'll be down for tea shortly, Mam.'

He was still in the bathroom when his sister came up and, after a further inspection, instructed him to sit on the edge of the bath while she administered a spirit solution.

'I'm going to enjoy this,' she said, a distinct sparkle in her eyes. 'I could say it won't hurt, but I'd be lying.'

Devlin was still feeling a stinging sensation to the wound when she took a small first aid box from the old metal cabinet and inserted a couple of stitches that, contrary to her warning, he found sharp but very bearable.

'Oh, I do enjoy inflicting a bit of pain,' she whispered theatrically, holding his hair back to admire her handiwork.

'Don't I know it,' he grimaced slightly, while wondering how his sister had become so proficient at such a procedure.

Resisting the urge to ask her, he gave some thought to the resilience and ability that he had observed within his own community since coming back. He had resigned himself to the fact that there was a limit to what he would be able to learn during a single trip, though this did nothing to suppress the smile that came to his lips as he changed for tea. It had been a great day at the football and he was anticipating his healthy appetite being satisfied – the aromas of his mother's food were rising from the kitchen once more.

After the meal, Devlin spent a quiet evening around the home place, walking the land and doing chores. Later, he relaxed in the front room, talking easily with his mother and sister before heading upstairs where, despite the wound still being a little sore, he slept soundly in his old bed.

CHAPTER THIRTEEN

Devlin woke early and even though he had a dull headache that was not unlike a hangover, he did not anticipate it affecting his plans for the day. It had rained heavily overnight, which had cleared the air to set up a fine morning. After going down to the kitchen and finding that for once he was the earliest riser, he made tea and cut four lumps of soda bread with cheese; two for breakfast and two for later, with Bran watching his every move expectedly, much to Devlin's amusement.

'Whenever I see you, you're always a few steps ahead of me,' he said, moving in a sprightly way.

After breakfast he went into the back garden, wheeling the bike out of the shed and to the front of the house. Devlin was loading the saddle bag with the picnic and canteen when his mother appeared at the front door.

'Well, Michael, you seem determined to get another cycle in,' she smiled, her hair hanging loose over her shoulders. 'How is the head this morning?'

'The head's fine. And I imagine the Shimmering Sands will be lovely on a morning like this,' he answered playfully.

'I'm sure they will be, particularly if the artist is in residence.'

'Talking of the artist, I didn't know that she'd spent time

around Knockbrack and painted here. Now, those paintings would be worth seeing for sure.'

'I never saw any of them finished myself… By the way, Michael, we need to sign some documentation regarding the house and Clancy's down at the Harbour Office. Mr Doran has suggested we go in tomorrow afternoon, if that would suit you?'

'That would be great. I'll be back later, Mam.'

He cycled away in good spirits, with Bran in close attendance, and in no time at all, they had reached the crossroads outside Mullnamorran. At the next junction, where they took the more direct road to Mullross, Devlin was surprised to see a green camouflaged drone that was obviously taking an interest in their progress as it swooped down low, flying only a few yards overhead. So, slowing to a stop he dismounted and leaned the bike against the remnants of a dry-stone wall. Drinking from his canteen, he watched as Bran barked vehemently at the mechanical intruder, which was still poised above the road, and as it came down even lower, hovering only five feet off the ground, the dog took a run at it, attempting to seize it in mid-air, which sent the small craft veering off towards the hedgerows, where it whizzed back and forth attempting to avoid its indignant canine pursuer. There was something very comical about this performance and it suddenly occurred to Devlin that it must have happened many times before. He started to laugh, causing the drone to stop in mid-air and Bran to turn around and face him, panting, with his tongue lolling out the side of his mouth.

'I would have thought you'd have more sense, Bran,' Devlin spoke as if reprimanding the dog, but there was a clear sparkle in his eyes.

Bran gave him a quizzical look and then turned back to confront his nemesis once more, as, in a gesture that was truly comical, the drone tilted its wings while rocking on its floating axis, appearing to mimic the movements of an animal shaking itself. Bran barked in protest and the craft did a final sweep of the area before ascending and disappearing in the direction of the town, which Devlin took as their cue to get moving again.

They kept a steady pace on the undulating road to Mullross and the rest of the journey was uneventful. The day was really starting to heat up as they approached Burn's Bar. Turning down the sandy track that led to Barney's cottage, Devlin did not hesitate when entering the encampment and laid his bike down beside the jaunting car. Seeing no sign of Gráinne, he set off in search of her new painting location, unsurprised to find Bran opting to stay behind with Cuchulainn.

Climbing a high sand hill through the knee-length spiky grasses to gain a better vantage point, Devlin saw her in a mid-distance clearing. He felt a surge of admiration as he considered the solitary nature of her lifestyle and the dedication she had to her art. After a quick walk along the sandy tracks that wove their way through the pale yellow dunes, he arrived at the small enclosure where the artist was working on a large canvas. Seeing her in action at close quarters for the first time, he was immediately struck by how physical she was while painting, making very definite movements with the brush, viewing the image from different perspectives and relentlessly scrutinising the landscape. Rather than announce himself, he carried on watching her quietly for a few minutes, wanting to commit the image to memory. Her face was completely covered by a broad-brimmed sage hat, but the red hair was clearly visible against the lilac smock she was wearing. He had a momentary sense of being caught in the act again by Gráinne when she turned on her heels in one swift, sudden movement and, eyeing him mischievously, said, 'Well, Mr Devlin, have you taken to stalking the sand hills now, annoying poor artists at their work?'

'Did you know I was coming?' he asked, surprised. 'That I was here?'

'Now, what do you think?' She laughed. 'Still, it's lovely to see you.'

She put the palette and brush down on the stool and he

instinctively took her in his arms as they exchanged a number of very natural kisses.

'And it's lovely to see you,' he said. 'I hadn't planned to—'

'I'm not sure we have a lot of time for planning,' she interrupted him, before bursting into a spontaneous peel of laughter.

He was mesmerised by what she had found so amusing until he looked down at his shirt, which had been imprinted by with blue, cadmium yellow and a range of grey oil paints from her smock. They were both consumed by the merriment of the situation, as she pointed to the detail on the newly redesigned T-shirt.

'You have your own masterpiece there,' she said, 'a totally original work.'

They were still laughing when a drone came over the sand hills from the direction of Mullross Pier, causing the marram grass to sway in an agitated way and an abrupt change in Gráinne's demeanour. Her hazel eyes came into sharp focus and she stared intently at the approaching craft, which stopped in mid-flight, then veered over the largest sand hill before heading back towards town.

'That was amazing,' Devlin said, genuinely impressed. 'It was almost as if there was a change or blockage in the signals it was receiving.'

'I didn't want to get too deeply into the detail of what's going on,' she said, seemingly sizing him up as she spoke, 'with your stay being so short, but your explanation was not that far out.' She paused before continuing. 'While we are talking of such things, there's another ancient power that has been effectively adapted for these strange days.' She pointed to a set of caves that were prominent in the image on her canvas. 'You will know that people of insight once found openings to the otherworld through these places and I want you to know that if you should find or dream of them yourself and focus your attention there, you can call for safe passage or find succour.'

He looked directly at her, taking more than ten seconds to consider what had happened and the information she'd given him.

'I'm glad that I have made an impression,' she said, an impish smile coming across her features as she looked again at his shirt.

'Believe me, you have,' he said with warmth and conviction. 'There are things that have happened and been said here that I won't forget.'

'That's lovely, and who knows what lies ahead? Anyway, returning to your earlier question, when you asked if I knew that you were coming... Now that would be telling, wouldn't it, but let's just say that I put a costume on under my smock, in case we got the chance to swim.'

'Great minds do indeed think alike,' Devlin smiled broadly, lowering his trousers to reveal a pair of swimming trunks.

'And if fools seldom differ, let us be merry ones.'

She picked up a towel that had been hanging from the back of her easel and they walked off towards the broad golden expanse of the Shimmering Sands. The sun had risen to its zenith, the ocean's waves sparkled with millions of individual shards of light and the couple swam and played as children would, with the cool, glistening Atlantic yielding to their every movement, simply enjoying the beauty of the day and the growing contentment they both felt, realising it was a rare opportunity that had come their way.

Returning to the encampment, Gráinne gathered together some nearby kindling and lit a fire, over which she hung the large blackened kettle.

'You mind the brew,' she said, her voice lingering over the words. 'I've filled some water butts from Barney's cottage, which will serve us well indeed.'

Listening to the dual sounds of the water coming to the boil and Gráinne rinsing the sea water from her body on the other side of the jaunting car, Devlin's mind and senses were alive with possibilities. More than anything else though, the notion came to him that this was a ceremony and rite of passage – one that they were destined to go through together.

'I'll take over now,' she said, appearing at his side wearing a green and golden beach dress. 'You go wash that brine away as you'll have to be cycling back soon.'

As he stood naked behind the car, letting the clear water run down his body, it occurred to him that this was no ordinary situation, and was one he was determined to savour. He let his gaze wander along the craggy outline of the Crying Cliffs and the severe limestone ridges that fell dramatically down hundreds of feet to the dark entrance of the caves below, until he was pulled from his reverie by the sound of tea being poured.

'Have you taken root there, Devlin?' Gráinne called out, no shortage of amusement in her voice. 'I'll have to send Bran around there to chase you out of it.'

'Can a man not take his time showering and enjoying the view?' came the leisurely reply.

After drying off and dressing, he returned to the fire and sat opposite her. They drank their tea and for the first time, an awkward silence came over them, with Gráinne appearing to study the landscape and Devlin just looking deep into the fire, until eventually he looked at her with a sad smile, saying, 'I'm not sure where to start…'

'Well, maybe you shouldn't,' she cut him off gently. 'We are neither of us youngsters and we have come to know how the greatest things can happen by chance, or at least they may seem to. What's happened here is lovely, but it is too early for this conversation, so let's leave the dramatic words to others. Can't we just say we've not finished with each other yet?'

'We've not indeed,' he answered enthusiastically, a strong reaffirming smile lifting his features. 'And who knows what lies ahead?'

'Indeed. Now ride away with your faithful Bran and I'll call to see the Devlins tomorrow. No doubt Miriam will know the best time.'

'That would be great.'

They parted with a long hug and two kisses and he walked away through the gap to where Bran was waiting. Mounting the bike, he slowly waved to her three times before cycling away and for her part, she stood smiling with her arms folded and head inclined, a position she would maintain long after he had gone from view.

Devlin had expected to feel a bit down on this homeward journey as he had set off that morning in the belief that this would be his last meeting with Gráinne, but tomorrow's prospective visit had significantly lifted his spirits. Whistling as he cycled along, it seemed no time until they were nearing Mullnamorran and Devlin turned at the crossroads and started the steady climb to the home place.

Mrs Devlin was in the garden when he returned and he went out to join her. Miriam had gone visiting neighbours and he was pleased to have some time alone with his mother in her favoured environment, for she was always at her most relaxed while gardening. Weeding side by side, they talked about the home place and when they were finished and were clearing away the tools she said to him, 'Michael, I know that you and Miriam are close. Maybe that's why I haven't spoken to you about things that are going on and what you are doing. I have been so delighted to have you here, particularly with Ben's passing, and I just never got around to asking about what your plans were.'

'Mam, its fine,' he said reassuringly, 'you've had more than enough to worry about. In answer to your question, I can say with honesty that I don't know what I'm going to do. I'm still like the teenager who left here all those years ago – you'd wonder had I grown up at all.'

'Oh, you've grown up OK,' she smiled warmly, 'and there are a lot of people that seem to be interested in what you'll do next. I hear Aoife and Pádraig are calling later and you're going to a session.' She paused before adding, 'I would never interfere,

Michael, but you need to tread as carefully as you possibly can.'

'You never said a truer word.' He put an arm around her shoulder and hugged her. 'I will tread carefully, Mam.'

The family had a late tea and were just clearing away when Aoife and Pádraig's arrival provoked some good-humoured banter around the kitchen table, mostly about the match.

'I don't suppose you'd fancy coming to the session, Miriam?' Pádraig asked. 'It would be great to hear that voice of yours raised in the bar.'

'Oh, I'm not as suited with those old rebel songs nowadays,' Miriam answered. 'They're just not in the right key for me.'

'It isn't just the old songs,' Aoife said enthusiastically. 'The music is great.'

'I'll pass, if it's all the same. I hope you have a great night.'

Pádraig drove and while Devlin was looking forward to the music, part of him did wonder what else the night might hold. They chatted easily about some of the characters from the locality and were nearly at Mullross when Aoife changed the course of the conversation.

'I suppose it's fair to say that besides the music, there will also be a few who have a similar political agenda to ourselves,' she remarked.

'I don't suppose I'm that surprised,' Devlin said in a guarded way, 'but I'm not here to have my arm twisted; I'm here for the music. I'll make my own decisions in my own time.'

'That's understood,' she nodded, causing her bobbed hair to move back and forth. 'Honestly, it will be grand.'

Arriving at Burn's, they passed through the lounge, where two family groups were seated, and went into the back bar, following the sound of the musicians who were already in full flow. Pádraig talked to the barman while getting the drinks and Aoife led Devlin to a table in the corner. There was a great lift in the tunes being played and Devlin was soon immersed in the music; both he and Pádraig were drinking pints and Aoife was on lime and soda. The stout was exceptionally good and he found he was drinking at a faster rate than he normally would have, but he did not feel out of place in this as the majority of the clientele was consuming alcohol at a brisk pace. A man sitting beside him sang the first song in a throaty, raucous voice, causing the table to vibrate with the power of his rendition.

'And a thousand pikes were flashing by the rising of the moon…'

The atmosphere became charged as the tunes were interspersed with more patriotic songs, which Devlin found uplifting, reminding him of sessions years ago, so he decided to just enjoy the night for what it was. He had some interesting interactions and since no one asked for his name, he got the impression that they already knew.

A burly man who was called Killoran sat down next to him, talking in a high, passionate voice about the Regime and the changes that were coming. He spoke about the glory of the rising that was underway and its power to galvanise the people into action, as well as overseas cells that lay dormant, just awaiting the order. He took obvious pleasure in singling out Devlin's own area of the city, referencing the Rainbow by name, and while Devlin nodded his head throughout this narrative, he had the strangest feeling that they were playing out a scene from some historic film, though despite this great familiarity with much that Killoran said, his final words did make an impression.

'Don't worry, we're not just living in the past,' he said. 'The explosions and the old shenanigans are just a way of prodding the dinosaur to let him know we're here, while we make further incursions into the organisation. The strategies are everything nowadays, Devlin – but of course, Aoife and Pádraig know well about all that stuff. Anyway, I'll be seeing you, no doubt.'

When the music stopped, a consultation ensued as the players started to put their instruments away and Aoife went over to talk to them. Devlin was struck by how comfortable she was in their presence.

'They are going to Mangan's to carry on,' she informed them, returning to the table. 'They're great musicians, but contrary as be dammed. I thought they'd be here for the night.'

'Well, we might as well go along for a nightcap,' Pádraig said with fervour, 'it's nearly on the way home. What do you think, Michael?'

Devlin had found the drink wonderful that night and the thought of a couple more was appealing, but sensing a tension between the couple, he answered diplomatically. 'It's down to the driver, unless you fancy a long walk home, Pádraig.'

Aoife's eyes were exceptionally alive when she scrutinised the two men.

'I have to admit, Michael, you look OK,' she said, 'and I've seen you look worse, Pádraig… Go on, we'll call in at Mangan's, but only for a couple. It's a rarity for the old shebeen to be open nowadays.'

After the session broke up, they left Burn's with a fresh westerly wind blowing inland and drove two miles towards Mullnamorran, turning off at an inconspicuous side road. Devlin vaguely remembered Mangan's from his teenage years, but he would not have been able to find his way there, so he found himself instinctively looking out for landmarks as the headlights shone down a succession of narrow lanes that cut through heath and wild woodlands that showed little sign of human habitation. Meanwhile, in the front seat, Pádraig was singing away.

'In Boolavogue, as the sun was setting on the bright May meadows of Shelmalier… a rebel hand set the heather blazing and brought the neighbours from far and near…'

'You're a long way from Boolavogue, boy,' Aoife commented in a mocking tone.

'Aren't I there in spirit, though?' he said bullishly. 'And aren't you lucky to be regaled along the way?'

'Aren't I just,' she responded dryly.

He carried on with the song. *'Then Father Murphy from old Kilcormack spurred up the rocks with a warning cry…'*

'The balladeer doesn't need much spurring on tonight, aye, Devlin,' Aoife said over her shoulder.

Looking at the rear-view mirror, Devlin could see there was now an amusement in her facial expression, so he decided to just relax and enjoy the drive.

Many of those who had been at Burn's had made their way to the remote, unlicensed establishment. Its frontage, with its cracked rendering and boarded over front window, gave the impression of being derelict. If by any chance you were to visit Mangan's on such a night, it would not be until you went around back of the building and opened the weather-beaten tongue and groove door that its function would become clear. The very basic interior comprised of an assortment of tables and chairs strewn about in no discernible order and Devlin noticed that even though it was summer, a dank chill hung in the air, reasoning that was why the portraits of old republican patriots hanging on the wall were so badly discoloured.

Pádraig returned from the makeshift bar that was in a side-room with pints of beer as there was no stout and a glass of water instead of soda. The mood of this session was low-key in comparison to Burn's and Devlin sensed that in addition to a lack of vibrancy in the tunes, there was also a palpable uneasiness among the clientele. Even Aoife, whose mood had been relaxed to the point of playfulness when they entered, had now became distinctly edgy and by the second pint, Devlin could feel his own mood dipping as he struggled to grasp what was happening around him; the music was changing pitch jarringly and people seemed to be coming in and out of focus. A dispute erupted on a table at the other side of the room, but he was more concerned with trying to work out why things had taken such a nightmarish turn, going far beyond the effects that could be expected from the amount of alcohol he'd consumed.

'There's real trouble brewing here,' Aoife spoke quietly, but there was an unmistakable tension in her voice. 'I know those people. They should not be here and you certainly shouldn't be here, Michael. We need to get you out.'

He had barely been taking in what she was saying, but the last sentence resonated and, accompanied by his cousin, he made a lurching movement for the door. The rapidly sobering Pádraig supported him as they crossed the yard to where the empty barrels stood.

'Sit here a minute,' he said sharply, 'and breathe in deeply. I don't know what happened with them pints, but I must get Aoife. There could be ructions here tonight.'

Watching the blurred outline of Pádraig's figure re-entering the pub, he tried to calculate what would happen next, but his thoughts were totally incoherent. Then, a few moments after his cousin had left him, he was possessed by an incredibly strong urge to move, having become acutely aware of his present vulnerability. He knew that in such a charged and dangerous atmosphere he was more or less a sitting duck and as he staggered towards the back corner of the building, he made out a group of men standing in heated conversation beside Aoife's car. Instinctively, he turned away just in time to avoid being noticed and after colliding with a beer barrel, he stumbled into the woodlands behind the pub, making a concerted effort to walk in a straight line, when to walk at all was challenging enough with the trees and bushes seeming to be in motion around him. In an effort to centre himself, he looked up at the heavens, staring at the moon and the misshapen clouds that were tumbling across the sky, but this only disorientated him further.

Refocusing his attention on avoiding the trees that were in his path, he did not know how much ground he had covered and he did wonder if he was in fact progressing at all, as he could hear acrimonious voices not too far away. Their terse words became more audible and having realised that he could not run without giving away his position, he sank to his knees behind a tree. Grasping the rough oak bark, his primary aim was concealment, but he could not stop himself watching what was happening in the nearby clearing. The image was pulsing in and out, but he could make out a man being dragged by three others and then thrown against a tree. The first blows landed and though he averted his gaze, the sound of their impact was inordinately loud, seeming to echo through the woods, while he remained kneeling with his forehead pressed against the tree, trying to control his breathing as repeated blows rained down. Later, he would wonder what made him look again, as he saw a hurling stick being raised so high that the whiteness of its ash wood caught in the moonlight and the head of the club itself looked like a half-moon against the clear sky before it came down towards its victim, who emitted a puppy-like yelp.

'Let's be done with it,' a high voice that seemed vaguely familiar said decisively. 'There's only one way to sort him out.'

Devlin put his head against the rough bark again, hearing a shuffling noise before a single shot rang out. There was mumbling and then the sound of dragging accompanied by heavy breathing, which he imagined was the body being taken away. That was when instinct kicked in and, after waiting for the group to leave the clearing, he started to move cautiously in a crouched position, resisting the urge to try to run. His progress was slow and awkward and though he could still hear the sounds of activity in the woods, they were increasingly distorted and beginning to recede. Eventually, feeling that the wind and the moonlight were somehow leading him clear of the danger, he stood upright and stumbled on until he came to a glade and his attention was caught by a branch that did not appear to be attached to any tree.

Beautiful music, the likes of which he had never heard before, was emanating from the severed limb, leaving him totally entranced by sweet refrains from distant lands, inviting him to journey there, though he knew somehow that it wasn't yet the time. What he did not know, however, was if the glade was a dream or some sort of hallucination, but whatever the case, something told him that he needed to keep moving, as danger could still be lurking in the woods. He became aware of the sound of the ocean on the wind and noticed that the trees were getting smaller. Devlin looked through a clearing westward and saw the moonlit Atlantic, breaking spectacularly by the caves at the base of the Crying Cliffs, and felt a great sense of relief. It was a scene that Gráinne might have painted, and recalling what she had said about entrances to other worlds, he gazed intently at the base of the caves and called for safe passage. The echo of his own voice reverberated in his ears and without hesitation he took a track that led from the furthest edge of the glade – one that he had not noticed before.

The path led downwards and he followed it blindly until he heard the unmistakeable sound of a horse's hooves trotting. His heart lifted and without a second thought, he walked resolutely in that direction, only to stagger through a hedgerow and fall headlong onto a sandy track, landing directly in the path of the oncoming Cuchulainn. The horse came to a halt before lowering its head and snuffling Devlin in much in the same way he greeted Bran, and then moments later, Gráinne appeared at his side, stooping down to help him to his feet. Groggy though he was, the way her hair cascaded around his face would remain with him, as would her priceless quip.

'Well, fair play to you, Devlin. You do like to get as much as you can from your days out.'

His ascent on to the jaunting car was very much a joint effort and no sooner had she manoeuvred him into the right position than he collapsed into the seat. He would later remember the great sense of relief that he felt when passing out alongside her and the soft clucking sound of her tongue, as throughout the journey she urged Cuchulainn on. The rhythm of the car going to Barney's

Cottage was incessant, to the extent that when she put him to bed, he was still rocking backward and forward with that gentle motion. He went straight back to sleep, but was soon woken by a sharp tugging of the shoulder.

'Come on, you must drink this,' she spoke urgently, then added, 'there will be time enough for sleep.'

He swallowed the sharp-tasting liquid and after taking in the glowing familiarity of her features, drifted off again. Devlin had no idea how many times he slipped in and out of consciousness after that, but on each occasion, the image came to him of Gráinne bent over, working diligently on his clothes. When he finally came around fully, she softened her lips into a slight smile and nodded her head slowly in affirmation, reassuring him that all was well. He looked around the part-lit room, which was obviously a functioning bedsit, with a bow-legged pine table by the window, a white enamel cooker in the corner and a glowing fire, which Gráinne sat beside on a straight-backed oak chair.

'Are you alright?' she asked him plainly.

'I am,' he answered. 'And is this your bed?'

'Sometimes,' she answered, a playfulness coming back into her voice. 'But it appears in use at the moment.'

She looked naturally at him and with the fire crackling away behind her, he was captivated by her beauty. He motioned for her to come over and she sat down next to him on the bed, holding both his hands in hers. Moments passed with them just looking at each other as the sound of the ocean stirred on the wind. He let out a sigh.

'Gráinne, will you join me?' he asked, in a warm, easy voice.

'Why, Mr Devlin,' she smiled, cocking her head in a coy manner, 'you have shocked me altogether with that suggestion.' Saying nothing else, she then undressed slowly and, standing over him, looked closely at him once more. 'Seriously, are you sure you're alright?'

'Have no doubt,' he said, gazing appreciatively at her fine body, 'I certainly am.'

She climbed into bed and they fell immediately into a deep embrace. When he opened his eyes, he looked above the fireplace and saw the Sacred Heart looking down on them, right hand raised in the act of blessing.

'Do you think he would bless us?' he asked, running a hand gently down her cheek.

'Oh, he surely would,' she answered, her hazel eyes animated as she ran a hand through his tangled, curly hair. 'He was a proper priest in the old days, before they dressed him up like that. He knew the value of the ancient ways.'

Neither she nor Devlin would forget the consummation of their union beneath the old sacred image that Barney had venerated. For over an hour and a half, they were totally given over to each other, making love that was both intense and playful, while engaging in sweet talk spiced with humour.

The fire had long gone out when a deeply contented Devlin dozed off and Gráinne turned over on her side, gazing out of the window as she spoke inwardly.

After sadness for poor Ben brought you home, she began, *you made your way out here to the Shimmering Sands and me. There are many things that I could have planned for, but not this. My pictures being placed in that dark building to entice you was the work of a greater force than me and as I lie here with your breath gently on my back, I know the time is so very short and we must use it well. Rest easy now, love, for your way was never going to be easy and it's a contentious crossroads that you've reached. For you, those politics; for me, my art. Our time was never meant to be entirely our own. We cannot be greedy, it can't be our way, so we must take a bite and a sup and make light of it.*

It is strange, the agonising you must face as you enter your Gethsemane. I know well the way you will go but I must watch as the course of it is run, and restless I shall be, but as you've somehow found your way to me, so you shall find your way again. It's not a path that must be walked alone – there is so much that could and even should be said, but I fear the information will at best weigh you down, at worst be a magnet to the evil forces, so I'll spare my tongue for you and just smile. I shall paint my pictures and dream for you. I will watch over you and never say how long I have been waiting for these moments. Your time of sleep is almost over, so let's hope the dark scenes are diminishing in your mind and you can move freely now. It's time to wake. I'll spare my tongue for you and just smile. I shall paint my pictures and dream for you.

Devlin came to and facing Gráinne said, 'I suppose it's time – I must away.' There was an uncertain smile on his face as he went on. 'I have no words for the night I spent under old Barney's roof, I really haven't. And what was the draft you gave me? Whatever it was, it was truly magical.'

'Rest easy,' she placed a finger lightly on his lips, 'there's a danger in knowing too much.'

'Yesterday, we started to talk about ourselves and our coming together and you said it was too early.'

Caught in the full gaze of his deep blue eyes, she put a finger to his lips again, saying, 'I did indeed – but you must now realise. It is too late.'

'We're committed so,' he said, 'under Barney's Sacred Heart.'

'We are, and to seal this pact,' she paused before lightening the mood, 'why, I'll even give you a lift home.'

They washed at the old Belfast sink in the back room and dressed for the journey back to Knockbrack. Devlin made the bed and while Gráinne was checking that the fire was out, he wondered when they might have the opportunity to share such domestic tasks again. She went to a row of pictures that were underneath the table and after looking through them, she picked one out and wrapped it in newspaper, without letting him see what it was.

'You've got a very nosey streak in you, Devlin,' she said teasingly. 'You will just have to wait.'

Leading him out of the cottage, she locked the back door and after showing him the key, placed it underneath a stone by the water butt. Then there was one more lingering kiss and caress, with the canvas resting easily between them, before they walked down the path, where numerous golden rod speared out of the overgrown margins.

Gráinne did not urge her faithful horse to go beyond walking pace, for which Devlin was thankful, as this prolonged their time together. He talked in vague terms about what his recollections of the night before were, while she nodded her head in acknowledgement, making only the one comment.

'Don't try to hang on to the brutal memories,' she advised. 'There are dark days upon us and I am just glad that they had the presence of mind to get you out of there.'

A look of concern came over his face as he realised that he hadn't made contact with anyone since leaving the bar. 'I wonder if they know that—'

'Don't worry,' she interjected, 'they know that you are safe and so do Miriam and your Mam.'

'Thank you.' He leaned back in his seat and relaxed. 'Maybe you're right, Gráinne. There are too many things for me to know right now, though I am thinking the future might change all that.'

'I'm sure you are right,' she smiled to herself, 'but one thing I find remarkable is the appearance of the singing branch. That's an ancient tale, you know.'

'No, I didn't know that.'

'Oh yes, the severed bough sang a magical tune from another land altogether – an otherworldly place, as I remember. The tune was to entice the pilgrim to travel to a place of wonderful delights and true knowledge, so that when they returned to their own people, they could guide them with great wisdom. Such a journey would indeed be a spiritual one, so perhaps it's because of a growing insight that you were being called upon to travel. It could have been a message relating to your future.'

'It's incredible on one level, yet on another level it seems so relevant.' He exhaled slowly and, taking her hand in his, said, 'I can feel a shifting in me, if that makes sense. It's been an amazing few days.'

A period of silence followed this remark and then for the rest of the journey they conversed sporadically about the countryside they were passing through. Bran joined them when they got to the rise at Knockbrack and Gráinne urged Cuchulainn to pick up speed as they neared Devlin's home place, making a dramatic sweeping entry into the driveway, where Miriam and Mrs Devlin stood waiting outside the front door, having been alerted by the dog's excited yelps.

'Are you alright, Michael?' Mrs Devlin asked, her face etched in concern.

'I am, Mam,' he answered positively. 'It was a bit of an unruly night, but there was salvation at hand. I'm fine. Honestly.'

'Well, I suppose you don't look too much the worse for it,' she said, looking him up and down.

'Mam, this fella could make a drama out of anything,' Miriam laughed, as Gráinne walked forward and presented the painting she'd brought to Mrs Devlin.

'I hope you like the bohemian wrapping paper, Mrs D.'

'Oh, I do.' Mrs Devlin smiled with a deep appreciation, unfolding the newspaper and holding the canvas of Mullnamorran Harbour at an arm's length. 'It's really wonderful, but you can't just give it to us. I mean, it will be worth—'

'It belongs here now,' Gráinne said decisively, 'and that's final.'

'Thank you so much for the painting and thank you for...' Mrs Devlin began, but trailed off without finishing her sentence.

Miriam pulled the artist in close for a deep hug.

'Thanks for getting him out of it, sister,' she whispered in her ear. 'You're a star.'

An awkward few moments followed, with everyone looking at Gráinne, who inclined her head and smiled, saying, 'So all's well. I know you have things to do and time is short for ye all, so I'll be off.'

Devlin moved towards her and with one defining gesture, took her in his arms and kissed her, while his mother and sister watched on.

'It would be lovely if you could join us for tea,' Mrs Devlin said as the couple parted. 'We'll be having it about seven o'clock, if that suits?'

'I will, of course,' Gráinne replied enthusiastically, climbing up on to the jaunting car and taking the reins. 'It would be a pleasure.'

CHAPTER FOURTEEN

After a showery day, the evening was going to be a glorious one. The shrubs and hedges in the front garden were drying out in the late afternoon sunshine and Mrs Devlin, who had been sitting at the kitchen table with her children, went over to the window.

'Tony will be here soon,' she said. 'It's so good of him, but I said he needn't have bothered. We could have walked down to the Harbour Office. Look how lovely it is now.'

Devlin joined her. 'Oh, he wanted to, Mam.' He wrapped an arm around her. 'Listen, won't it be great to get those papers signed and for the family to officially have the house, meadow and Clancy's?'

'Of course, dear,' she said distantly, nuzzling her face into his sleeve.

'Here he is,' Devlin announced, and as the vehicle entered the driveway he unclasped his arm from round his mother and, turning to Miriam, said, 'Come on, haven't we got important things to be doing?'

Tony and Miriam chatted away in the front on the drive down, while Devlin and his mother remained silent in the back. The function of the Harbour Building had changed greatly over the years; it had originally been single-storeyed and used merely to weigh-in fish, but its current extended structure was developed to house the activities of the Regime and was much larger than the one Devlin recalled. Tony left them outside, saying it would be a good opportunity for him to explore the waterfront, and as they entered through the front door, Mr Doran was waiting for them in the hallway.

'Welcome, welcome,' he said, 'will you come through?' He pointed to a meeting room just off the main corridor and carried on talking as they entered. 'Oh, I was forgetting, there is an old acquaintance of yours here today, Michael, who would like to see you for a few minutes. Is that OK, Mrs Devlin?'

Before anyone could answer, a tall man with thinning dark hair appeared at the bottom of the corridor. 'Great to see you again, Devlin,' he said, stepping forward, hand extended. 'I was in the area and when Mr Doran said you were coming in, I couldn't miss the chance of a quick catch-up.'

'Why, it has been years, hasn't it?' Devlin said lightly, as his mother and sister watched on warily. 'And fancy you being in this area.' He looked around at his family. 'It's fine, Mam, we won't be long.'

Mr Doran ushered the women into the meeting room as Devlin followed the man, whose name suddenly came to him as they progressed along a dimly lit corridor that led into the heart of the building.

'Well, McGee, you're wearing very well,' he said quite casually, as if he was a regular acquaintance.

'It's great that you remember me, Devlin.' McGee sounded genuinely pleased. 'I won't detain you too long.'

Stepping into a small office, he indicated two chairs arranged around a low table and they both sat down.

'You of all people know what a wonderful culture has been allowed to flourish out here in the West,' he began, becoming rather officious, as he started what was obviously a prepared speech. 'Unfortunately, however, there are unsavoury, rebellious elements that readily appear on the fringes. They need to be rooted out and we *will* root them out.' He paused, as if waiting for a reaction, but Devlin remained silent and McGee continued. 'Talking of culture, as you know, things are well observed in the locality, right down to where the hurling stick comes down. I mean, I could show you footage, but it really is unnecessary.'

'Indeed.' Devlin gave a slight nod of recognition.

'The thing is, my friend – and you might well have already considered this – the old corporation of Dexter's had been failing for many, many years and in recent times it has only survived as a result of support provided by the Regime. Not overtly, but in essence it has been the case. So, in reality, the home place and Clancy's could be seen as a gift from the organisation and you won't be surprised to hear that there are some expectations that would come with the ownership of the property. Obviously, we wouldn't want to enter into such an agreement with someone who had hostile intent towards the organisation and just on that point, if such a situation arose, the organisation would always assume the right of repossession.' McGee smiled, unable to hide his pleasure at issuing this threat. 'I am sorry if this sounds a little crude, Devlin, or an affront to the loyalty you demonstrated while working for the CRP.'

'It is my mother who the offer was made to,' Devlin replied calmly, 'not me. My father served Dexter's in good faith throughout the best years of his life, having been offered the property as part of his initial contract discussions, and that cannot be changed, even in this world of smoke and mirrors. That is still the nub of it, so thank you for your observations and warning, all of which I will heed. I will join my family now and beyond that, I have an appointment at the Rawlins when I return across the water. No doubt my relationship with the Regime will be discussed in greater detail then.'

Both men stood and as Devlin was walking out of the office, McGee called after him, 'That was some match, wasn't it? I thought Mullnamorran were dead and buried.'

'I thought the same myself.' Devlin paused in the doorway, the trace of a smile on his face. 'It was some contest alright.'

By the time Devlin had re-joined his family, the papers were ready and duly signed, with Mr Doran being thanked warmly for facilitating the formal transfer of ownership. Once this was done, they did not delay leaving the building afterwards and were pleased to see Tony walking briskly towards them on his way back from the harbour.

'Are you in need of a lift to Knockbrack?' he asked with a flourish.

'We are indeed, my good man,' Miriam answered, waving her hand airily.

On the way home, they discussed the strange layout of the Harbour Building, with Tony being particularly interested to hear how it had changed since his last visit there as a teenager, and once they were back in the kitchen, he asked brightly, 'What are the chances of a cuppa, Mrs D?'

'Oh, you won't be waiting long on that score,' Miriam said, as her mother placed the brewing pot on the table, along with some treacle bread and butter.

'Now, could you manage to pour me one?' Mrs Devlin asked. 'Oh, and Tony, are you of a mind to stay for dinner? Gráinne and John will be joining us, so another guest would not be a problem.'

'I will be getting off after this,' Tony said, smiling cheerfully and raising his brimming cup. 'Liam will be back now and he's threatening to cut back the verges by the side of the house – they're like a jungle at the moment – to the point of threatening the view and that would never do.' He paused and, looking at Devlin, said, 'Though I am tempted, as Gráinne is such good company.'

'Oh, whatever could you mean by that?' Miriam responded, her voice dramatically raised. 'Surely you're not trying to embarrass my big brother?'

'I wouldn't do that. I just heard a story about a romantic bicycle journey to the Shimmering Sands, that's all.'

'Is there nothing secret around here?' Devlin protested, but with a mirthful expression.

'You should know the answer to that by now, Michael,' Miriam said, winking at her brother. 'Nothing is off the table and everyone is fair game.'

After a lively conversation around the table, Tony got up and changed the mood totally by saying, 'Liam is giving you a lift to Ben Bulben tomorrow, so I won't see you before you leave, Michael. It has been great meeting you, even in such sad circumstances, and I hope you travel well.'

The words seemed to hang in the air until Devlin's chair grated on the flag floor and, going over to Tony, he put an arm around his shoulder and walked him out the door.

'Would you ever shell some of those peas for me?' Mrs Devlin asked Miriam, a look of resignation on her face.

After a lengthy chat with Tony outside, Devlin came back in and said, 'I just want to have a look at that fence at the front. I noticed a few suspect places when I was doing the hedge.'

He was inspecting the cracked timber laths under the watchful eye of a robin, who was observing his progress from the top of the gate post, when Aoife's vehicle came slowly down the road and pulled up on the grass verge. Pádraig hopped out and walked quickly through the gate.

'Are you OK?' he asked, his voice animated and his blue-grey eyes focused hard on Devlin. 'That was a fierce night altogether – we had no idea it would turn out that way. Did you know your drink was spiked?'

'I gathered that, though not a lot else. I'm fine. And by the way, thanks for helping me out of that situation,' Devlin replied, by which time Aoife had joined them.

'The thing is, Michael,' Pádraig continued, 'I went to the toilet after I'd ordered the drinks, so whoever did it must have done it then, but as we were both on pints, it could have been meant for either of us.'

'That's true, I suppose.' Devlin sounded unconvinced. 'As for me, I instinctively wanted to get away and when I saw people in heated discussion beside your vehicle, I just bolted into the woods.'

'We tried to find you, but it was like you'd disappeared altogether.'

Aoife, who had been silent up to this point, asked Devlin, 'I just wondered if you saw anything during your wanderings in the woods?'

'No,' he answered, their gazes locking for a good few moments. 'I was in a rare old state and hallucinating. There's little I can remember, even now. It must have been some potion.' He paused before adding, 'Why, did something else happen?'

'No, nothing of note, I'm sure,' she assured him. 'The main thing is that you're fine, and wasn't it a great coincidence that Gráinne was in the area for a moonlight jaunt in her car?'

'Wasn't it just,' he agreed whimsically, 'and isn't it great how people know exactly what's going on out here in Connaught, even without those fancy ways of communicating?'

'Isn't it just,' Aoife nodded her head, smiling broadly now.

'What will you do when you go back over yonder?' Pádraig interjected, a sudden sharpness in his voice.

'I really am not sure, as I don't know what the Regime's intentions are in the West. If I did get involved with them again, that's if they'd want me, then they would have a specific role for me. For sure. So how much use I'd be, who knows?'

'But are you with us?' his cousin persisted.

At this point, a large drone came over the rise, heading directly towards them, and they all turned round. Aoife reacted immediately by staring at it intently and it veered off course before heading back towards Mullnamorran.

'That's very impressive,' Devlin said, regarding her closely. 'It really is.'

There was a long pause as they watched the retreating craft

disappear into the distance and then Devlin took the opportunity to address his cousin's unanswered question.

'There is no point in me being with anyone, if I am not involved. So therefore I reserve the right to find out what is possible before that decision is made. I am a pragmatist. I am discounting nothing, but I really think you are overplaying my importance in this. I am not that important.'

'Maybe at this moment you're not.' Aoife's eyes were sparkling when she said with great precision, 'But what matters, is that you are saying if you do get involved with the Regime again and our agenda looks to be the right one to achieve autonomy, or even independence, in the west of Ireland, you would seriously consider joining us?'

Taking a deep breath, he gazed very directly firstly at Aoife and then Pádraig, before looking intently at the town of Mullnamorran, whereupon a distant recollection came to mind of him setting sail with friends from the harbour, to fish for mackerel. Many seconds passed in silence, as if they were all taking stock.

The smile that had been inspired by this childhood memory of putting to sea was already starting to fade from Devlin's lips and a sombreness had infused his deep blue eyes, when he responded in slow, mellow tones, 'If I do again get involved in the politics over there, then your offer will be under serious consideration. I know enough about the history of the struggle to know that it is not always the most obvious or even the safest course of action that is best. So thank you, your offer is appreciated and we shall see what fate holds for us all and if indeed our fates are going to be aligned. But in the midst of all this I will make my own decisions, with my family in mind.'

'There is a sense and brilliance in the shimmering words you are using, Michael. And maybe it has to be that way. For that's your trade. But you do know that you are dancing on the head of a very sharp pin?' As Aoife made these observations, her eyes were fixed on Devlin, whose face glowed with the radiance of the broad sun that was dropping lower in the sky.

Turning, he smiled at them and there was a touch of mischief in his expression as he emitted a low laugh, saying, 'And don't I know it.'

Devlin's attention was drawn to the sound of his sister marching down the stone driveway towards them and, looking in her direction, he said in a playful tone, 'Ah, we'll all have to keep dancing. For a while, anyway.'

'Well, this has developed into a fine fence inspection team,' Miriam said, a real edge to her voice. 'What are the findings of the report, Pádraig?'

'The fence will be grand for a few years yet, cousin.'

'Let's hope so. Now, are you coming in? Mam wants to know.'

'No, Michael's time here is short, so we'll get off. You can see us anytime. We were just checking this man was OK after last night.' Aoife's voice and demeanour were calm.

'He even seems to have enjoyed it, this strange brother of mine. He's not the brightest but I must admit, his ability to bounce back is impressive.'

Devlin just smiled and then offered Padraig his hand. 'It's been good getting to know you again,' he said, 'and thanks for last night.'

Aoife moved forward and Devlin was about to shake her hand when she leant forward and seized him in a firm hug. The words she whispered quickly in his ear, with her fragrant blonde hair brushing against his face, would resonate with him later.

'Have faith. It can be done – really and truly.'

Pádraig and Aoife drove away and the siblings linked arms as they walked slowly back towards the house.

'Michael, Gráinne and yourself getting together is great and Mam thinks so as well,' Miriam said, 'but I honestly never saw it coming.'

'Believe me,' Devlin replied, with a look of contentment playing on his lips, 'like so many other things around here, neither did I.'

The kitchen was a bustle of activity for the next half an hour as the family prepared for dinner.

'This looks very promising, Mam,' Devlin said, setting the table with wine glasses, 'but I'm feeling a bit guilty about having all my meals cooked for me. If I was around for longer, I would cook for you.'

'Will you listen to him, Mam, he's threatening us now,' Miriam responded tartly.

'Don't be listening to her.' Mrs Devlin stopped mashing the potatoes and turned to look approvingly upon her son. 'That's a lovely thought, Michael.'

'In all honesty,' he said, 'that's what I'd like to plan for.'

A slow smile appeared on his mother's face, while Miriam gazed at him without comment; the sound of vegetables slowly bubbling was the dominant noise in the kitchen as John entered though the back door.

'Am I alright for time, Mam?' he asked.

'You're grand, John,' Mrs Devlin answered. 'Just sit yourself down. Michael, will you get him a beer? There are some in the cabinet there.'

Bran yelped excitedly, signalling that Gráinne's arrival was imminent and after pouring John a beer Devlin went outside to watch her approaching the house. They had a few minutes together in the driveway and as soon as they entered, Mrs Devlin greeted the artist warmly.

'Will you sit down there,' she indicated a space at the table, 'and you will have to take us as you find us. Michael, are you going to open the wine?'

'I'm sorry about the wine waiter,' Miriam said primly. 'He's very new and a little… uncultured.'

This was a meal that Devlin would remember vividly years later, with John and Gráinne joining the family at the table. Everything was as he would have wanted it to be, save for the absence of his younger brother, but even that momentous event did not cast a shadow over the mood of the company. The conversation didn't waver and John had never seemed more relaxed in the house, even drinking some wine and telling tales about Devlin and him when they were cubs. Gráinne sparkled throughout, giving Devlin the notion that after all that had happened between them in the last few days, this was their wedding meal. He chided himself for having such fanciful thoughts, until he noticed her smiling knowingly at him across the table.

At the end of the meal, everyone got up to clear away and wash up and when the table was cleared, Mrs Devlin addressed the couple. 'There's not enough work for all of us here,' she said. 'Miriam and I will soon polish these bits off, so why don't you take a stroll? It's such a lovely evening.'

With that, Devlin and Gráinne moved towards the back door, with John following close behind.

'Michael, I meant to show you the roof of the byre up at Clancy's,' John said. 'I think it may need some attention.'

The three of them went out into the garden and Miriam smiled at her mother.

'I don't know if Gráinne wanted a chaperone,' she said, 'but it looks like she's got one.'

'Knowing Michael, he'll see the fun in the situation,' Mrs Devlin replied with a twinkle in her eye, scrubbing the inside of the potato pan with wire wool.

Meanwhile, as the exiting trio made their way up the back lane, the two men discussed how much growth there was on the meadow and the state of the fences. Throughout the conversation, Devlin and Gráinne exchanged the occasional wry smile, unseen by their companion, who was totally engrossed in countryside affairs, until they reached the cottage and John pointed to the roof of the byre in question.

'You see the way that galvanised sheet is badly rusted at the corner?' he said. 'It will soon be leaking if it's not replaced.'

John turned to find Devlin standing with his arm around

Gráinne's waist as he replied, 'You are surely right, John. Will you ever be able to get it done before the winter?'

'Sweet Jesus, I had no idea you two had got together,' John cried, his face reddening. 'And me wittering on about the roof, ye must think me a right eejit! You should have said something, Michael.' He stopped his talking for a moment to regard them properly before adding, 'though, that's great news altogether.'

'I'm sorry, there just didn't seem to be the right moment somehow,' Devlin said.

'And I thought you were concerned about my honour.' A highly amused Gráinne stepped forward and gave John a big hug.

'Its great news altogether,' he repeated with sincerity and the couple were still smiling as he went round the gable of the cottage muttering to himself. 'Jesus, man, have you no eyes in your head, or any cop on at all?' He then set off down the lane, turning once to declare emphatically, 'It's great news and I wish you all the luck in the world.'

These departing words rang in their ears. Sitting down on the top step of Clancy's porch they looked out at the view over Mullnamorran, the sunset gilding the buildings of the town as a fishing boat made its slow entry into the harbour, its prow jerking up and down against the ebbing tide.

'We have John's blessing,' Gráinne eventually broke the silence, her hazel eyes infused by the sunset, 'and that is well enough for me.'

'We have Miriam's and me mam's as well,' Devlin said, his cheeks pronounced as he smiled, 'so alongside Barney's Sacred Heart, aren't we in great shape altogether. Now, should I not be carrying you over the threshold?'

'I'm not sure it's advisable for a man of your age.' She spoke softly, brushing her auburn locks against his face.

'You could be right there. And as it's you who's taken to rescuing me, maybe you should be doing the lifting?'

'Maybe,' she smiled lazily.

The sun was sinking low in the sky, catching the fields, trees and hedgerows in a deep mystical light with the two of them silently entwined and, as Gráinne would remember fondly years later, the keen sound of the swallows scissoring across the front of the cottage, as if to underscore the beauty of the evening. Over a quarter of an hour passed without a word being said as they observed the ending of a truly momentous day.

'I'll have to be going now,' she finally spoke, a reluctance in her voice. 'You'll have to be spending some time with that lovely family of yours.'

'I will,' he said, turning to face her.

'I hate to break this sweet spell with serious talk but…' She hesitated a moment. 'We were talking about powers that are emerging in you, Devlin, and I'm sure you will work to cultivate them, as they will serve you well in the days ahead.'

'You're right, I'm sure. I don't know if it is being home again, but I seem to have been picking up on people's thoughts. I knew for certain that I had connected with you the night that you came to my rescue, even though I was in such a bad state.'

'You spoke of the severed branch,' she said slowly and deliberately, 'and besides the music calling you to another land, it is also a call to higher things. I suppose it could be seen as your calling at this moment in time. You saw something earlier that night in the woods that is inherently dangerous to you. You can deaden a memory by focusing on it and, in effect, blanking it out, so it won't show up in your thoughts. That is if you have developed the power and I'm sure you have. Some people have expunged memories altogether, but beware, that can leave you vulnerable because you lose the full recall of what has happened to you.'

'I was thinking the same thing about the branch, to be honest. And in my dealings with the Regime, I learnt early on the value of observing without trying to analyse at the time. By doing that, my own thoughts and intentions remained hidden, which has served me well. Maybe I have been developing my own mental powers without thinking too much about it, if that makes sense.'

'I'm sure you are right and I am not in any way telling you what to do.' She gave his arm a squeeze. 'It's just that things are changing for you, Devlin, and you may need different skills in the days ahead.'

'It's well appreciated, believe me. Is there anything else you need to tell me before you go?'

'No, I'm sure you will manage to figure it all out. Just know that whatever happens, there is always help and succour close by.'

'In that case, I have one last thing to say to you.' He paused and, gazing at her, he said with a slow deliberation. 'The cottage here is now officially owned by the family and has been signed over to me personally. I'd love it if you would use it while I'm away.'

Gráinne's lips parted and she smiled broadly at him for a few seconds, before opening her eyes wide and saying slowly, 'And what about when you are here?'

'Oh, I'm sure we'll figure something out.' He ran his hand slowly through her hair.

'Seriously, it would be lovely to have a base here. As much as I love Barney's Sacred Heart, it is a little on the damp side down there, particularly from autumn onwards.'

'Then it's settled.'

'It feels like I'm being taken into the family.'

'You are,' he said definitely.

They went back to the home place, down the stony lane resounding with lyrical blackbird song, and entered by the back door, where Mrs Devlin and her daughter were drinking tea at the kitchen table, the setting sun glowing low through the window, giving a fiery effect to Miriam's coppery-coloured hair.

'Will you have a cup of tea before you go?' Mrs Devlin asked.

'No, thank you, Mrs D,' Gráinne answered, 'I'll have to be off. I've got the noble Cuchulainn waiting and he'll be restless to be getting home.'

'Well, maybe he'd find the pastures around Clancy's to his liking.' Miriam's bright blue eyes shone as she made this remark.

'I'm certainly hoping so,' Devlin said and, looking at his mother, added, 'Gráinne is going to be using Clancy's, Mam.'

Mrs Devlin got smartly to her feet and clasped both of the artist's hands in hers. 'I'm delighted,' she said. 'May good fortune be before you both.'

Outside, the couple shared one last hug before Gráinne drove away with the lantern of the car rocking gently; the vision-like image of her disappearing over the rise, her silhouette surrounded by the dying embers of the setting sun, was one that would be burnt into his memory.

He had been so preoccupied with the sunset that he hadn't noticed the multiple stars appearing across the sky and as he suddenly became aware of their presence, it seemed a miraculous moment, as if he hadn't seen it happen before. Another thing he hadn't noticed was that Miriam was now standing by his shoulder.

'Are you OK, brother?' she asked, cupping his elbow snuggly in her hand.

'I'm fine,' he answered, 'and feeling alive to everything. I was just thinking about these mysterious lands that we come from and the strange times into which we are heading. To think that after all these years, I came home for Ben's funeral to find a world that was even more diverse and fascinating than the one I had cultivated in my own imagination.'

'It's a different place to the one you left for sure, more spiritually and politically vigorous, and you're more alive to it now, I'd say. Are you ready for tomorrow?'

He considered the question carefully before answering, 'If you had asked me a few days ago, I would have said I'm not sure, but now I am. For years, memories of the west of Ireland have sustained me, but now it is the reality of these lands today and their spiritual certainty that have revived me. Why would I not be ready?'

A silence followed, which he knew was leading to a further question.

'Am I to believe that you have decided on a certain course of action when you return?' she asked.

'I have not,' he said, 'as I do not know yet what the options are.'

'I just thought that old colleague turning up at the Harbour Office might have thrown some light on the matter,' she nudged him gently in the ribs.

'CRP tittle-tattle, that's all. No, that changed nothing and you know what, sis, I may not do anything at all.'

'I'll repeat what I said before,' she said, looking unconvinced by his answer. 'Your involvement in the past does not make you responsible for what happens in the future, even though many would like you to feel that way.'

He turned and led her back towards the house. 'Don't worry, sis,' he gave her a reassuring hug, 'I won't be blackmailed into doing anyone else's bidding. Now, will you have a drink with me?'

They went back inside and joined their mother, who was sitting at the kitchen table. When asked if she wanted a drink, she responded positively.

'I will, Michael,' she nodded. 'There is still some wine left. Miriam, will you have one?'

'I will, Mam, and no doubt your Prodigal Son here will have a whiskey.'

Mrs Devlin smiled at both of them, but her eyes no longer carried the same sparkle, as the melancholy of the coming days was starting to play on her mind; days when she was bound to be missing Ben and when concerns for Michael's progress would also be prominent in her mind.

Staying at the kitchen table, they drank convivially, managing to talk in an upbeat way about possible renovations to both the family home and Clancy's cottage until the conversation reached a natural conclusion and Mrs Devlin finished the last of her wine.

'Will you come to the living room with me?' she said, looking fervently at them both in turn. 'I feel it will help us be closer to Ben tonight. For while there can be sadness on many levels, there is no room for regret.'

They gathered together as if Ben's wicker coffin was still there and after a period of quiet reflection, Mrs Devlin spoke out loud.

'Well, the days are longer without you, Ben,' she began, 'even though I know you are not far away. All these things that would have made you smile or saddened you have happened and life goes on, but knowing you are in a nearby place gives us comfort, even on this night when Michael is leaving us once more. Of course, there's the big gossip – your big brother has hitched himself to the magical Gráinne and I know you would be ribbing him if you had half a chance, but then again, you're probably doing that right now… Your presence is still with us, clear as daylight, bright as a star and twice as welcome. Now, as a family, we bid a farewell to Michael and, like the ancient pilgrims, we are unsure when we will see him again, but a large part of him will remain here with us and as the old blessing says, "For while the light is sometimes distant, while you hold your faith, it won't be lost." This is all building to the future, a tapestry that holds our many threads together, woven into the complex picture that we can only glimpse now and again but you can see it all, so please watch over your brother, whose headstrong nature is a friend and foe, for he may need a guardian angel in the times ahead. Your presence is still with us, clear as daylight, bright as a star and twice as welcome.'

She turned to embrace her son, clasping both of her hands around his chin. 'Well, I'm off to bed, Michael, as tomorrow will come soon enough. Don't you two be lingering too long.'

'Goodnight, Mam,' they both said in unison, watching her steady step on the stairs.

'She's amazing,' Miriam said, 'using prayer rather than talking to you directly. You can be sure that whatever you do next will be at the forefront of her mind.'

'I know,' Devlin replied thoughtfully, for once gazing downwards. 'Do you know, Miriam, it's been brilliant spending this time with you, and if we went and sat down in the front room, we'd fall into one of those crazy, deep conversations about the politics and spirituality of it all.'

'Then let us leave it here and go to bed,' she said, looking calmly at him. 'Your spirituality has grown before my eyes, brother, and hopefully your way is long. So let us tread the stairs to bed.'

'For the stars are shining over our heads,' he completed the couplet. 'I've not heard that since we were children. Where did it come from? Is it a poem?'

'I've no idea, but Dad used to say it,' she said, hugging her brother. 'You're right, we've reconnected famously. So, goodnight, Michael. The morning will be on us soon and I don't want to be giving you the cold flannel treatment to be getting you out of bed.'

'No, that would never do,' he laughed softly. 'Goodnight, Miriam.'

Going straight up the stairs, not bothering to avoid any creaking floorboards, he made a brief stop in the bathroom and after undressing, lay down in his bed. There were many thoughts that could have been playing on his mind, including the prospect of tomorrow's journey back to the distant city and his future contact with the Regime, but Devlin was feeling remarkably calm and slept dreamlessly.

The front door was open when Devlin came down the stairs the next morning and he noticed a blackbird darting urgently out from under the hedge, a worm wriggling in its beak, and overhead the rooks cawed noisily, flying out from their nests, making for open countryside. He paused for a few moments to take in the scene and a slow smile crossed his features as he watched the departing crows while appreciating the sounds and smells of the fresh summer morning that were filling the hallway.

'You get up for a while every day, then,' Miriam greeted him cheerily, as he appeared in the kitchen doorway. 'We were thinking you had changed your mind about going back.'

Devlin had his breakfast while his mother made sandwiches and a steady flow of conversation filled the room. After he'd finished eating, he went back upstairs to complete his packing and heard no words being spoken between his mother and sister until Liam arrived. Then, for the last time, he surveyed every detail of the garden below, where so much had happened, and he realised that he was indeed ready to go.

He descended the stairs briskly, determined that his leaving would not be too drawn out, as he knew that emotions were very close to the surface. 'The lift is really appreciated,' he said to his cousin, 'I don't know how I'd go on without it.'

'It's only down the road,' Liam smiled, 'and a grand drive. Just make sure it's not as long until the next time I give you a lift.'

Devlin led the way to the front door, where the four of them stood silently, waiting for Mrs Devlin to speak.

'John wishes you safe travelling,' she eventually said, 'and says that he hates the goodbyes – as do I.' Taking her son in her arms, he was deeply moved, for looking into her familiar blue eyes, he felt the full glow of the love that she had for him. She loosened her caress and her greying brown hair hung very naturally as she spoke again. 'I'm sure more than enough has been said, so wherever that travelling might take you, I wish you luck and may we see you again – soon.'

'Your words are ringing in my ears now,' Devlin said, 'and so they will remain, I'm sure. I will return as soon as the times and the seasons permit.'

'Never mind the fancy words, Michael.' Miriam gave him a searching look, before pulling him in tight for one last hug. 'Just remember where your home is.'

'Don't worry sis. I will.'

Bran yelped at his feet and reaching down, he gave him three firm strokes, saying, 'Now, boy. You need to be watching over things here.'

Without further delay, he was out and getting into Liam's vehicle, as the sharp, yapping tone of Bran's barking echoed in the still morning air. For a moment, he didn't look back at the house, as he could sense the tears forming in Miriam's eyes, matching his own, but when the engine started, he turned to wave slowly at his mother and sister, even managing a smile. The vehicle turned slowly in the driveway, tyres crunching on the rough stone, and then they were off. Going over the rise in the road, he had a momentary wish that his departure had not been so perfunctory, but as they headed down towards Mullnamorran, he knew it was for the best.

The two cousins talked in a fairly light-hearted manner about football and the various goings-on in the locality during the journey. Devlin was glad of the distraction; he did not want to think too deeply about his leaving or what the future might hold.

They were not far from Ben Bulben when Liam said, 'You're sounding like a local once again, Michael.'

'I'm feeling like a local once again.'

'Yet you will soon be in another place and having decisions to make. Do you remember our conversation at the gorge?'

'I do. I will meet the Regime when I return and find out what they have in mind for me and for Connaught. I will make a decision when I know what their intentions are and if it makes sense for me to enlist again. If I can influence the course of events favourably for our people, then I will be getting involved – if I can't, then I won't.'

'That all makes perfect sense, but there are many who would say you are just sitting on the fence, and you know that can be a dangerous place to be when there are snipers about.' He paused before continuing. 'Your trip up to Mangan's was noted the other night. Are you aware what happened up there?'

'Oh, someone spiked my drink and I made a hasty exit, so if

something did happen, I missed it. As for me being visible, hasn't that always been the way of it?'

'Still able to glide through those situations. Still as laidback as ever.' His cousin turned, smiling at him.

'Not laidback, but your political interest in me is based on my being able to operate in precisely that way – moving and operating between parties with differing interests – so you shouldn't be too surprised.'

'Fair enough,' Liam laughed, 'we'll let it roll and I'll take you at your word, though God knows where that leads us. By the way, I was amazed to hear about yourself and Gráinne.'

'Believe me, I am amazed myself, though the gods will have to be on our side if we are to stand a chance.'

'I can only imagine that means we will be seeing you more often, so I for one will be wishing you both well.' His broad features set in an easy expression, staring ahead.

'Thanks, cousin. Your wishes are well received.' Looking at Liam, he was thinking how he had become well used to his calm and reasoned tones again.

Arriving at the pick-up point, Liam pulled up on the main road and, looking up at Ben Bulben, said thoughtfully, 'Now there's a mountain that has seen it all. The legendary Fianna warriors roamed those slopes in the third century and there are so many amazing legends associated with it. Did you ever hear of the Noble Six, Michael?'

'I seem to remember it was during the civil war in the nineteen-twenties,' Devlin answered.

'That's right. They were surrounded in Sligo Town and their armoured car was blown up by pro-treaty forces. The six of them went up Ben Bulben and they weren't armed at this stage – they were executed after surrendering. It's hard to imagine such a terrible thing in such a beautiful place, so let's hope we never see such days again.' The words hung in the air for a few moments before he added, 'I'm sorry for getting serious, and just when you are leaving.'

'Ah, it can't be helped sometimes,' Devlin said. Getting out of the vehicle, they shook hands. 'And the message is clear enough for us both to hear.'

'Well, it's a great place for parting,' Liam spoke positively, 'but I won't prolong this. You know these shuttles are the only thing that run on time in this country and I'm not keen on being around them.' He checked his watch. 'By my reckoning, it will be here in seven minutes, so I hope all goes well and if by any chance someone wants to talk about Clancy's cottage, you will know they are friendly.'

Devlin nodded his head in recognition of this potential arrangement. 'So, the old ways are still the best. I will mind out for what you've told me. Travel well yourself, cousin, and it might be an idea to watch your own back. It's not only me who's very visible at the moment.'

'You could have a point there, Michael.' He smiled and walked away and Devlin thought again how perfectly his cousin's rugged features, warm brown hair and worn tweed jacket blended in with the Sligo landscape.

Liam's battered vehicle drove away down the road and Devlin turned towards the immense flat-topped mountain, whose sheer limestone cliffs gave way to the lower verdant slopes that ran naturally down to the Ocean. He was struck again by the majesty of the landscape and thought, *Well, Ben Bulben, you are indeed a sight for sore eyes, especially for those of us who have spent too long in the mundane greyness of the city. You are shrouded in mystery and legend and over the centuries you have seen it all, including many of the likes of us, plying our political trade. So maybe it's you who knows who'll succeed and who will fail, but I know you're also a great one for withholding a secret, so I'm not likely to be finding out any time too soon. Anyway, whatever the outcome, here's hoping it won't be so long before I stand before you again.*

CHAPTER FIFTEEN

After boarding the shuttle, Devlin inspected the bundle of sandwiches that his mother had provided. He smiled at the quantity of them – easily enough to sustain him throughout the journey back to the city. Settling back in his seat and closing his eyes, he allowed his mind to go blank, not thinking about anything in particular and deliberately suppressing any details of his memorable trip.

Arriving at the port, he stood before the Connaught Princess, surrounded by the familiar buzz of activity that had accompanied his outward departure: the bustling crowds, the luggage in transit and the portside staff organising and barking out orders. He stopped for a moment to take in the scene, deeply inhaling the briny air, when the ship's horn sounded loudly and a familiar face approached him from the side.

'Well, fancy meeting you here,' Paul Grogan said. 'On your way back so soon?'

Devlin had to look twice to confirm that the tall figure in a long coat was really him; he was one person he would not have expected to meet at the Dublin terminal.

'I am surprised to see you travelling yourself,' he answered. 'I didn't know you had business over yonder.'

'No, I don't suppose you did, did you?' Paul said, a confident tone to his voice. 'Not an old culchie like myself. My business won't be as high-flying as yours, but there's still some seasonal harvesting work and I have people over there it would be good to see.'

The two men weighed each other up, with Devlin thinking that there was something different about this Paul to the edgy man he had met at the crossroads and then it suddenly came to him that it was that he was assured and totally at home in this setting.

'I hope you have a good trip,' Devlin said wholeheartedly.

Paul prolonged the encounter by saying quietly, 'Oh, don't worry. You could say I know the ropes at this stage.' He paused and there was a fervour in his slate blue eyes as he continued. 'It's funny, isn't it? We could be enemies, or even on the same side, but that's not the main point. The main point is that the people shouldn't be put to the lions for the entertainment of it, to use an old biblical reference. You may be sure that I'm not in the habit of pulling thorns from the lion's paw.'

Devlin was puzzled by Paul's words, but he responded brightly nevertheless. 'I'm sure you're not,' he said. 'I hope the work goes well and you meet the people you want to.'

'I'm sure I will, much like yourself,' Paul moved slightly closer and continued. 'I've got ten days on a stretch and then I'm meeting some folk I know the weekend after next for a notable day. We may even get to an old hunting ground in your neck of the woods, the Rainbow. If all goes well, that is.'

'You really do surprise me,' Devlin said in a measured tone. 'It sounds like there's a good chance we will meet again.'

'A very good chance, I'm sure. See you around, Devlin.'

Paul turned into the crowd, quickly becoming indistinguishable from all the others making their way along the dockside. Realising that he had been lingering and prolonging his own departure, Devlin joined the general shuffling movement towards the gangway, where he boarded the ship and made his way to the main reception area to check on the cabin he had been allocated, as he intended to rest up during the voyage. Making his way across the floor, he came face to face with Conor and Catherine again.

'We have had a fantastic time,' Conor said, grasping Devlin's hand in his, 'we really have.'

'Wonderful!' Catherine continued the praise for Ireland. 'Majestic countryside and fantastic people. We had a ball.'

'We went way out west and even went to a football match.' Conor released his grip. 'What an atmosphere, the place was hopping – and you'll never guess what, we bumped into an old colleague of mine who said he knows you. McGee is his name. You're a dark horse, aren't you, Devlin? He said you had a lot to do with the regional programmes and… maybe I shouldn't say this, but…' He hesitated, looking around him before continuing. 'He said you might be getting involved again, if you know what I mean?'

'That was supposed to be a secret,' Catherine said, remonstrating with her husband.

'It's no problem,' Devlin smiled reassuringly, 'as long as it doesn't go any further than the three of us.'

'Oh, believe me, it won't,' Conor insisted. 'Of course, it's none of my business, but I'd jump at the chance if I were you, as you're obviously well thought of and you could have a great future.'

'It is *definitely* none of your business, Conor,' Catherine spoke sharply. 'I'm so sorry, Mr Devlin.'

'Don't worry,' Devlin's warm gaze was resting easily on the couple. 'I really am pleased that you had a great time. Now, if you'll excuse me, I'm going to get my head down for a bit. It was lovely to see you both again.'

The couple went to get a drink in the bar, while Devlin walked over to check the cabin allocations information, when Kelly, who had been directing people as they boarded the ship, appeared at his side.

'Have you found yourself yet?' Kelly asked jovially.

'I have,' Devlin answered. 'I'm in number seventeen again.'

'A lovely cabin indeed, nice and quiet. I hope you're travelling has gone well.'

'I was at my mother's place, far out in the west, a little place called Mullnamorran. She has a lovely garden there.'

Kelly's demeanour changed momentarily, a puzzled look passing over his face before he recovered his poise.

'That sounds wonderful,' he said. 'It's a lovely part of the world, I believe.'

'It is indeed,' Devlin said, as he walked off towards his cabin.

It was a spur of the moment idea to mention the home place, but he was fascinated by the reaction it caused and there was a wry smile on his face as he went to catch up on some of the sleep he had missed out on during the trip, knowing that challenging days lay ahead.

Entering the cabin, he took off his clothes, climbed onto the bunk, stretched out under a single sheet and soon slipped into a gentle doze. He did not venture outside again during the course of the crossing and was already showered and dressed by the time a crew member came along the corridor announcing that they would be landing shortly. When he threw his bag on his shoulder and opened the door, he saw Paul leaving his cabin and decided to pause until his fellow countryman had turned the corner and was out of sight before stepping out into the corridor. He was not in the mood for company, so he took the passageway to a side deck, where he watched the ship make its final approach. Dockers were waiting below with hawsers in hand and there were a significant number of people outside the terminal building, including Barleycorn and Dermot, waving energetically at the Connaught Princess. Looking along the line of this welcoming assembly, his gaze came to a halt at a man of medium build with brown hair, wearing a blue corded jacket and flat cap. Something had drawn Devlin's eye to this man of unremarkable appearance and it was not until he moved his head to look up at the ship that he realised why – it was, without doubt, Carr.

Passing through the ship's main reception area, Devlin pulled up the collar of his jacket and donned a cap that was not unlike Carr's before making his descent down the gangway. Twenty yards in front of him, in among the throng of passengers bustling noisily along the dockside, he saw Paul scanning the waiting people in an understated way, until he located the man in the blue corded jacket, who nodded slowly in his direction. Then, after glancing up at the ship once more, Carr disappeared out of view into the terminal building.

Devlin was fascinated by his old colleague's presence at the dockside, but having no desire to meet him at this time, he immersed himself within a party that was ambling across the concourse. Glancing from underneath the peak of his cap, he observed Paul standing near the departure notices board, where Carr reappeared alongside him. They had a short conversation, which seemed casual in its nature, and then Paul picked up his bag and walking away briskly, boarded a shuttle that set off immediately. The group that Devlin had latched on to stopped by the general store and he continued to watch Carr, who spoke to a staff member in uniform before going into the Customs and Immigration Offices. After perusing an Irish travel portal for a few minutes, Devlin went to the shuttle departure area to begin the last leg of his journey back to the Village.

The shuttle dropped Devlin off outside the Colosseum, where he noticed a poster and made a mental note of the football match the weekend after next that it was advertising. Walking briskly away from the Village, avoiding the Leanings District, he went directly to his apartment block. Once home, he went straight into his work room and switched on his machine, to find a notification from the Regime, saying that they hoped his trip had not been too arduous and that his presence was expected at the Rawlins Building at twelve-thirty p.m. the following day. Devlin's next stop was the living room and while the kettle was boiling, he was struck by the realisation that he was very hungry. He had only eaten one of his mother's sandwiches on the journey back, so after making a large pot of tea, he sat down at the table to have the remainder, savouring the familiar flavours as he figured that this would be the last real taste of the home place he would get in a good while.

After eating, he rang home to let them know that the journey had been fine and all was well. He and his sister had a brief conversation that felt very stilted, particularly as they had been communicating so naturally face-to-face less that twenty-four hours before.

Towards the end of the call, as if it was an afterthought, Devlin said lightly, 'Oh, Miriam, I saw someone from the other side of Mullnamorran at the port who was travelling. He recognised me, in fact. He said his name was Paul.'

She paused a moment before responding. 'Oh, did you? You do surprise me. There are not too many travelling, even now.'

'He still does some of the seasonal work, apparently. Maybe you'll mention it to Liam as he played football at one stage, I think. You know how they all knocked round together.'

'It's a small world alright. Anyway, you look after yourself and I'll be in touch soon.'

Lowering his device from his ear, he noticed a message on it from Ceridwen:

Have you heard anything? I've only official contacts. Need to know how he is.

Speak soon. C x.

Over the next few hours, Devlin spent most of his time looking out at the city, listening to traditional Irish music. He was feeling unsettled after his trip and the old tunes reflected this homesickness. Before going to bed, he unpacked his clothes and, after going to the bathroom, retired for the night.

He was restless in bed for a good while before dropping off to sleep, whereupon he seemed to enter a dreamlike ancient land, where he was tied to a stake in the water, with waves crashing in and swirling round his chest. Engulfed in the motion of the tide, the leather straps were chafing harshly against his wrists, but while he was undoubtedly scared that the end was nigh, he also felt a great curiosity about the surrounding elements. He could hear pipe music playing and soon recognised that the waves were not ordinary seawater, but had been infused by slithers and strands of James's lifting and Ceridwen's moonlight calls. These were waves he'd known before, he realised, and although the water was rising, his empathy with his friend's plight meant that he was not attempting to escape.

The music became louder and he looked directly at the setting sun casting its fiery glow on the tide. He was transfixed until the sound of a sweet, familiar voice urged him to resist his inertia and to strike out boldly for the west, at which point his hands became frenzied and tore free of the straps, and he swam directly towards the sunset.

I have returned but cannot drown in this tide, he thought, projecting the same mantra over and over as he freestyled through the waves: *I cannot drown in this tide.*

Once he was clear of danger, he eased into a steady breaststroke and looking at the sinking orb; he knew his direction was sound and reaching home was only a matter of time.

The next day he was up early, but still feeling a little groggy from the travel and a very disturbed night's sleep, so he decided that an early morning run would dispel the lethargy and sharpen him up for the day ahead. Thus, maintaining a brisk pace along the streets of the Village, he crossed the square and completed four laps of the Colosseum before heading back through the Leanings District, where he stopped at the stores for provisions, before strolling back to his apartment block to have a leisurely breakfast.

Having allowed himself plenty of time for his journey to the Rawlins Building, Devlin was in good spirits as he rode briskly past the allotments. Reaching the Village outskirts, he saw a

Transkill transporter and he dismounted. Walking the length of the vehicle, he almost bumped into the worker with the spiky silver hair he'd interacted with before; their paths crossed when she was disembarking.

'Are you OK?' he asked, looking in her dark eyes.

'You shouldn't talk to me,' she replied. 'It's not right.'

'Do you like your job?' he continued, not wanting to let this opportunity pass.

'Do you think that because we're not human, we haven't got feelings?' she said, suddenly becoming upset and bolting back onto the transporter.

He had thought his questions might cause a level of confusion, but even he was surprised by the vehemence of her reaction. Knowing that he would not be able to pursue the matter any further, he jumped on his bike and sped away.

The rest of the journey was unremarkable and after securing his bike, he stood for a few minutes looking at the exterior of the old building. Upon entering, he went into the gallery to be greeted by Smith, who said with enthusiasm, 'It's good to see you again. I was sure you'd be back to view this exhibition.'

'You're right, I've found it very interesting on many levels.' Devlin smiled and immediately started to view the paintings that had taken on an even greater significance for him.

He was very glad that he had allowed for half an hour in the gallery before his meeting and he did not try to analyse the scenes in any great depth as he had before, preferring simply to relax, feeling he was in Gráinne's company while viewing landscapes of his childhood. Time passed very quickly and when he did eventually check his device, he found it was time to leave.

Walking away from the gallery, he took the now-familiar route and entered the large hall, where he followed the pulsing ochre light along the picture rail until he arrived at the third door, which he did not hesitate to walk through.

In the viewing room, the lighting was dimmed in preparation

for a showing and the voice of Don, his old mentor, announced over the sound system, 'Now please take your seat for a short film.'

Sniffing the odour of popcorn once more, Devlin looked around the empty auditorium and sat down. Don's voice spoke more confidentially as the images started to appear.

'There is no commentary,' he explained, 'as we didn't think it was needed.'

The film showed James being lifted, followed by a close-up of him sitting on an outdoor bench, looking confused.

'I don't know what I was doing in the old days,' he was saying. 'Real folly, if you ask me. Very strange company to be taking up with indeed, but maybe if you want some information on Devlin, I could help you there. I've told you some little gems already, but maybe there's more.'

The next clip was of the recent match between Mullnamorran and Curraghcorn being shown at a venue similar to the Rainbow, complete with betting odds and replayed highlights of the action. The gambling activity covered both the match and the subplot, as punters tried to identify *Interlopers* and *Subversives* among the crowd. Devlin noticed that the match commentary was in a language he had not heard before.

With the final whistle, the scene shifted to show the fans streaming away from the ground, where a descending hurling stick could be plainly seen above the sea of people. These short clips were followed by grainy shots from outside Burn's Bar as patrons came and went, including Aoife, Pádraig and himself. The film then came to an abrupt end, leaving Devlin looking intently at the edge of the screen, thinking about James, and the footage of his former ally was replayed. Once this had finished, he got up and walked through a door to the left of the screen, entering a small, darkly lit room that reminded him of the one where he'd had supervision when working for the CRP. He sat down in front of another screen, on which a blurred image of Don appeared, wearing a dark green top that complimented his sandy hair and brown eyes.

'Well, isn't this like the old days?' Devlin said brightly. 'Good to see you, Don. You don't seem to have aged a bit.'

'Still using the humorous remarks,' Don responded and, staring straight ahead with a benign expression on his face, added, 'I was impressed by your manipulation of the screen. Where did you learn that?'

'I'm not sure I should be telling you such things – at least until I know why I'm here.'

'What did you think of the footage? Have you any comments?'

Devlin was listening closely to his mentor's voice, which had the same mellow intonation, though he fancied it was of a marginally lower pitch.

'I'm pretty outraged, I have to say.'

'Outraged? Is that because it was intrusive?'

'No, not at all,' Devlin's voice became very theatrical. 'It's the fact that none of the shots caught my best profile.'

There was a delay, during which Don's face froze in a smile, before he replied.

'I've missed that sense of fun,' he said. 'You want to know why you are here. The reason is that I have been asked to screen you for suitability, before interview. The screening is being observed and I may seek guidance and clarification during the process. So I will start that process. For many years since you left the CRP, you have lived here in the city. Your involvement with the Allotments Association has been observed. The political policies of the Regime in Ireland have changed since you left the organisation. You will see by the gambling on the football match that there is an interest in the west of Ireland and its customs and heritage. The Irish culture has survived and there is a growing recognition of its uniqueness. It is one of the very few places governed by the Regime where such a spiritual richness exists. There is an intention that it will carry on. We understand that such a culture is a complex thing, comprising many facets such as spirituality, the sport, the music, and of course, the politics of autonomy.'

'I suppose this much I knew, having observed the way many influential people from the organisation are heading there for their holidays. There is something I would like you to clarify for me before we go any further, though. It could be said that to a large extent, the Regime, particularly in its early days, has overseen the demise of various cultures, having seemingly seen little value in them. So, with that in mind, are you saying that the culture of the Regime has changed? I would like to know what you and the organisation above you feel about these things. If "feel" is the right word.'

This brought a long pause, with Don's image again becoming blurred.

'Yes, "feel" is the right word for it,' he eventually said. 'When I managed you, our sessions stirred certain emotions within me that I would later realise were feelings of envy. It was an envy for your pure humanity. You were responding to situations from your own perspective, not giving the programmed responses of a set of protocols.

'The Regime has not got a set culture and it is in fact changing. Though, from outside the organisation, this is not that obvious. There is a recent recognition of the particular benefits that the Irish culture gives to its people. It seems to improve their health, wellbeing and outlook on life. But there are many different levels to this cultural exploration and its impact. It is an evolving situation. Things don't stay the same.'

'There is one thing I always wanted to ask you and now seems the right time. Don, what are you?'

There was yet another long pause, before the screen came into focus again and Don spoke.

'I am not sure it is the right time. But I am allowed to tell you that I'm not totally of human origin,' he said, 'though I have assimilated many of the mannerisms. I have been affected by people like you, Devlin. I have said as much as I can at this stage about the organisation and the background of staff members.

Before we proceed, can you state your position in relation to the organisation and the west of Ireland? This is important if we're to progress to the next stage.'

After taking two deep breaths and running a hand through his long curly hair, Devlin gave his answer. 'I have always identified strongly with my homelands in the west of Ireland and the culture of my family, so I have a love for the music, song and sport of my people and a deep interest in Celtic spirituality. I would say that I identify more strongly with these things now than I did when I worked for the CRP, and the interest in a greater autonomy for the region is still very much part of me. As for the organisation, I have always known its immense power and efficiency and while I recognise the good it has done, I have also had misgivings about some of its past actions. The intentions of the Regime in the west of Ireland really interest me, but without knowing what they are, I can't really comment further. That's the vital part for me. If I know what the proposals are, I will be able to say what I feel about that direction of travel. I hope that is all clear enough for you.'

'Thank you for your statement,' Don said, 'very humanly put. I will check if it is clear enough and if it is acceptable. Can I just ask you to wait a moment?' The screen went blank for a couple of minutes before he returned with a smile on his face. 'I am pleased to say that everything is satisfactory. We have an offer that we want to put to you. Will you return for a more formal interview tomorrow, at the same time?'

'I will indeed,' Devlin responded in an upbeat manner, before leaning forward in his chair and saying in a lower voice. 'Now, could you tell me how James is, and can he be visited?'

'I have been kept fully informed of this situation. I expected you to bring it up. He is in recuperation. Did you know he was a Survaid?' Don hesitated here and then corrected himself. 'I meant to say surveillance aid. The strange incident down by the docks was a malfunction on his part. Part of his role was to observe you and this he did willingly. Nothing of importance was revealed. Were you aware that he was betraying you?'

'I thought he could be, but it didn't really affect my behaviour. I had nothing to hide, as you will know,' Devlin answered coolly. 'Betrayal is a strong word, Don. The changing of sides and deceitful actions can be very human attributes. Did James volunteer?'

'I have not got that information. Does that matter now?'

'I don't know if his sister suspects any of this. It's hard to say. I do know she's a very intuitive woman and may have her suspicions by now. What I do know is that she's extremely worried.'

'Tell her to contact our security department and to give his details. He will be released soon. I understand that he won't be operational again. What is that saying you use? He's being put out to grass.'

'Will she be told that he was a Survaid?'

'There is no reason she should be.'

'That's good. I'll be back at the same time tomorrow.'

Standing up decisively, he turned away from the screen where Don's image was fading and went back through the viewing room. His demeanour appeared bright and his movements were sure as he retraced his steps back to the gallery and, without stopping, walked past each painting on his way to the reception desk, where Smith was looking at him expectantly.

'I will be catching the exhibition again before it finishes,' he said, in a relaxed manner, 'all being well.'

'That's good to hear,' came the invigilator's approving reply.

Cycling back to the Village, he was drawn to the poster for the coming football match at the Colosseum and the sudden realisation came to him that it all fitted together with Paul's rather obscure words at the port; the Christians and lions would be meeting in the Colosseum and the notable date was the same day as the match. He pondered this momentarily before walking his bike across the square to the produce hall, where Jenkins was stood on the steps.

'That's going to be a lovely evening, Jenkins,' Devlin called out heartily.

'It is indeed,' Jenkins agreed. 'I hope your trip was not too emotionally taxing. Such a difficult thing altogether and him being so young as well.'

'The trip was fine, considering, and your thoughts are appreciated.'

'You look different, Devlin,' Jenkins looked at him closely, 'and it's not just the longer hair.'

'Don't you worry yourself, my produce-haggling adversary,' Devlin said lightly. 'It's probably just that I'm ageing at last.'

'We all have to change in this life, in the face of what it has become,' Jenkins looked at him again, a glint in his eye. 'In the end, even the best of us have to.'

'I will leave you with your deep reflections on life, the expanding universe, the cabbages and the kings.'

Devlin mounted his bike and cycled into the Leanings District, reflecting upon the certainty these humdrum streets of character had afforded him through some very strange and volatile times. He stopped outside the Rainbow, where Quinn was stood on a stepladder, watering the hanging baskets.

'They must be the best looked-after hanging baskets in the city,' Devlin remarked.

'I love the flowers,' Quinn said conspiratorially, as if divulging a great secret, 'but I'm no enthusiast for the painting, Devlin.' He leaned back on his ladder, assessing the worn exterior of the pub. 'Mind you, I'd say the faded look gives a mystique to the old place. If you think about it, the colours of a rainbow are often faded and only occasionally really strong.'

'Well, fair play to you, Quinn. I never knew you'd put so much thought into that faded exterior.'

'Isn't life like that?' Quinn smiled, raising one eyebrow particularly high. 'It's not what you do or don't do – it's what you say about it afterwards.'

'You're a walking wonder.'

'Isn't that the truth? There's a great group here tomorrow, if you're in the mood for music.'

Devlin regarded him and was struck by the alertness in his eyes and the spontaneity of his thinking.

'I might be able to fit that into my busy schedule,' he said jovially.

'Did everything go alright over yonder? You seem in good enough form.' Quinn lowered his tone enquiring about the funeral.

'Oh, it was a sad occasion for sure, but uplifting as well. I'll see you tomorrow.'

Calling in at the stores again on his way back to the flat, Devlin was coming out with some food supplies when his device alerted. It was another message from Ceridwen.

Have you heard anything? Do you want to meet up later? C

Devlin didn't give it a second thought before replying.

Yes, that's fine. Where and when?

Shall we say 8-00, at the park where we spoke before? C

That's great. See you then.

Devlin was putting his device away again when it started to ring. Seeing it was Amir's unregistered number, he answered straight away.

'How are you doing, my friend?'

'We have had a change of plans and are back in the city for a few days,' Amir said, somewhat mysteriously. 'I have discovered a cousin of mine and will be staying with him for a few nights. I will explain… Would you like to meet up? Would the day after tomorrow be a good time?'

Devlin hesitated a moment before saying. 'Tomorrow would be better for me.'

'Why, of course,' Amir said, after a brief pause. 'Shall I come to you?'

'Yes, say seven-thirty, if that's OK with you?'

'That would be fine.'

Returning to the apartments, Devlin was surprised to see a man wearing a blazer, shirt and tie on the desk, as it was not usually occupied at that time of day. Looking up from his machine, the receptionist was very eager in his manner.

'There have been no communications,' he announced, 'and all is quiet on this fine afternoon.'

'We seem to be experiencing a heightened state of security,' Devlin said, noticing the extra monitors that had been fitted in the office. 'It's good to know that you're looking after us all so well.'

'You can never be too careful, sir.'

Devlin took the lift up to his flat and prepared a meal, which he ate slowly. Then, going into his work room, he spent two hours tidying up the tools that had been haphazardly stored away, at the same time reviewing his various unfinished projects, including a very old table with barley sugar legs, which he planned to strip down and polish. It was time well spent for he managed to establish a sense of order and decide what was worth keeping and what could be thrown out.

Leaving by the front entrance, Devlin said goodbye to the man on reception and even volunteered the information that he was going to meet a friend. He walked briskly through the old streets in his raincoat, for even though it wasn't raining when he left, there was a distinct possibility of showers. As he passed through the old sandstone columns that stood at the park's entrance, he briefly wondered how the encounter might go before making his way through the overgrown trees that lay beyond.

As he approached the meeting place, he knew that Ceridwen was already there, as the brightness of her blonde hair showed strongly through the copse of trees.

'Now that you're here,' she said, looking intently at him and getting straight to the point, 'tell me what you know about James.'

'From what I can gather, he has undergone intense

interrogation,' he said, sitting down and looking out at the rolling countryside, 'and I am assuming that some things have been taken from his memory. He is in a period of recuperation and will be released soon. If you contact the Regime's internal security line, you will be able to arrange to see him.'

'From what you can gather? You have suddenly become indistinct in your powers of observation, Devlin. Have you seen him yourself?' Ceridwen's voice had become harsh in its tone.

'I was directed to go to the Regime's offices when I returned from Ireland,' he turned to face her. 'I made enquiries about James when I was there and I was shown some footage of him. He was confused, but that's to be expected.'

'To be expected? Are you sure you know which side of this dispute you're on? Was he already a mole when he was lifted? Was he watching you? If so, what was that trip to the docks all about?' She had become very upright issuing these questions and he was aware of how impressive a figure she cut when stirred.

The intensity of this encounter took him by surprise and Devlin was feeling distinctly uncomfortable as he knew that, while his answers were, strictly speaking truthful, there were things that he was omitting.

'I had no reason to suspect that. As for the docks, who knows what he was doing? Listen, Ceridwen, you will be able to talk to him yourself in the next few days, I'm sure.'

'That's as maybe, but I'm talking to you now, Devlin. You seem to have shifted your position and I have to admit that I'm not totally reading this.' She looked at him closely, running her hand along the side of his head where the hurling stick wound was still healing. 'Your trip home for Ben's funeral has left its mark on you. You seem to have changed on an emotional level, Devlin – could it be you have fallen in love?'

'You are certainly tuned in when it comes to feelings and you are right in what you say,' Devlin responded, somewhat uneasily, 'but beyond that, the journey has re-engaged me with my home place and all of its political complexities, which I am determined not to embroil you in.'

'It sounds like you're going to be lost to us again, then. Are you about to disappear once more into the devil's kitchen?'

'That is not my intention, Ceridwen.'

'It may not be your intention, but there is no way of knowing the outcome of such actions. This was always on the cards, I suppose, and I can see that your love has powerful and persuasive charms – but you are changing. It seems that the spiritual enlightenment you were experiencing is gathering pace as well.'

'As always, you have a good insight into what is going on. I knew beforehand that this meeting could leave you underwhelmed and I apologise for that. You gave me such support and there is no doubting my affection. If events hadn't taken a totally different direction—'

'You don't need to say this.' She raised a hand to cut him off. 'You are speaking in half-truths now and I suspect it's with a mistaken motive of softening the perceived blow. We are not lovers, Devlin. We were never an item. You owe me nothing, but I will take your words as proof of how close we nearly were… How close we nearly were.'

They both looked silently at the distant clouds rolling in from the mountains, with Ceridwen's charged words still hovering between them. Their closeness had taken them to a place where their union had seemed very probable, but all that had changed now and he had been so consumed by recent events that he had not realised that, on some level at least, they would be saying goodbye to each other this evening. She knew that he was keeping things from her and he knew that this did not bode well for their future, but there was no alternative in his mind. The withholding of potentially dangerous information from close ones for their own good and his safety was a strategy that he was already resolved to employing.

'I will see James and hopefully he will recover to a good extent,' she eventually broke the silence, a conciliatory tone in her voice. 'I am assuming he will be of no use to them now and thus will be left in peace.'

'I am sure that will be the case.'

'Is that all you know?' She looked at him inquiringly.

'That is all I will say,' he said definitely.

'If you are to become involved with the Regime again, I am sure he will not take it well, given all that has happened. You never know how he will come out of this,' she sighed deeply. 'Remember our conversations about the ancient ways and combating the forces of the oppression so reliant on logic – how our instinct could win out in the end? I know you can't go into details, but did your trip throw further light on this quest? Is there cause for hope out in the West?'

'There is,' he said, a sparkle in his eyes for the first time that evening, 'and though you're right that I can't be specific, the dream does indeed live on – and should live on.'

'Another thing we talked about was how, at the end of the day, sometimes you just have to trust. Well, I have to say, Devlin that mine is shaken now, but that is enough of these words. I have James's welfare to concern me now. Hopefully you won't become a casualty of the cause you're going to take up and James will find true healing. Then, who knows? The future is a long time and we must still hope for different days ahead.'

'Thank you, Ceridwen,' he said, caressing her.

They didn't speak as they walked back through the park along the broken path under the dark, imposing trees, until she stopped abruptly at the gates.

'I think our paths go in different directions from here,' she said. 'I have made arrangements for tonight.'

'Are you sure you are alright?'

'I am. I know the way I'm going and what I have to do,' she replied resolutely.

They embraced lightly and exchanged kisses on each other's

cheeks, and if you were to come upon them there, it would be easy to think that they were brother and sister.

'I believe that your fiery queen's heart is in the right place.' She spoke with a generosity of spirit. 'Go as easily as you can and I'm sure news of your progress won't be hard to come by. For me, besides James, I feel the call of the Cambrian Mountains and the deep, murmuring valleys. There are other days ahead.'

Smiling fully for the first time that evening, she turned and walked away; not once did she look back as her footsteps echoed confidently on the old sandstone pavement, and he watched her until she reached the large Victorian lamp post at the corner and disappeared from view.

CHAPTER SIXTEEN

When Devlin got back to the flat, he made himself a sandwich and a large mug of tea, which he was just finishing when he received a call from his sister. Miriam was positive in her tone, talking about what had been happening at home, but he sensed she was building up to something.

'Our new lodger has moved into Clancy's cottage,' she eventually said, 'and she's settling in famously. It'll be great to have Gráinne about the place.'

The news gave him a great boost and he said very warmly, 'That's really good news. A real friend about the place for you to talk to, sis.'

'It will be for sure, so all is fine here. How are you getting on?'

'I'm fine, just getting a few things sorted out around the flat. I've got some new work coming up.'

Miriam did not enquire about the details of this work, instead saying lightly, 'Oh, I almost forgot, you said you met a Paul from beyond the town. Well, I mentioned it to Liam and he said he only vaguely remembered him from the football and couldn't be sure. He did say he was surprised he was over there. Anyway, that's all the news from here. Mam sends her love as well. We'll speak soon.'

The last rays of light from the setting sun were penetrating through dark clouds on the horizon and as he looked closely at the surrounding city streets, Devlin could not help reflecting morosely on how narrow and congested they seemed, particularly in comparison to the expansive skylines and stunning landscapes of Connaught that he'd recently left behind.

An hour and a half passed with him sitting by the window, alternating between reading, listening to music and occasionally looking from the window, before he took himself wearily to bed. As he had intended, sleep came virtually instantaneously. He lost consciousness as soon as his head nestled into the pillow, experiencing nothing beyond a deep darkness until, in the distance, he observed a warm glowing scene that attracted him. Moving forward, he realised he was entering the sand dunes of his youth and, standing on top of the largest hill, he looked down at his family camped on the beach. Miriam and Ben were playing by the edge of the sea and his father was watching them while playing his harmonica. The strong green colour of his mother's swimsuit was plainly visible and she waved to him as she called out, 'Don't be too long, lunch will soon be ready. Just explore one more land.'

'Don't worry, Mam,' he shouted back, 'I'll be with you soon.'

Carrying a branch that he had been brushing against the marram grass, he raised it up and hurled it at a copse of nearby trees. The severed limb made a wondrous singing sound as it whirled through the air and the trees obligingly parted, letting it sail on through. Mesmerised, he followed its trajectory into a bright glade, where the branch hovered in front of him with no visible means of support and he realised that he was no longer a child, but a grown man.

'Why, you have come a long way, Devlin,' a sweet, husky voice spoke to him. 'There must be things that you want to know.'

'I have followed the severed singing branch,' he said, after a few moments of consideration, 'and I want to know, if I immerse myself in the heart of that strange, harsh organisation, is there hope for its banishment? Can this branch and its way help clear the path to a golden Celtic dawn?'

He heard a sigh and then the wind blew through the trees, causing the leaves to rustle energetically around him, before the voice came again in slow measured tones. 'We are of this land and will be here when these latest intruders have been seen off. Nothing is surer. The path and duration of the struggle depend on the decisions that you and others make.'

'What of the ancient skills and powers? Are they enough to do this job?'

'You have gained some powers that have led you here, Devlin, and you have people around you who can support your effort to go further, but if you are asking if you yourself can see the job through, that is the wrong question. This is no task for a glory hunter; you should banish such thoughts from your mind. The ancient skills and powers, when allied with bravery and guile, will take you well along the way, but it may not be your destiny to finish the story – the detail of that scenario is not yet known. As you yourself have kept saying, it is for our people we must act, and their children's children. Choose wisely and go surely, my friend.'

The branch disappeared and Devlin was suddenly overcome by a great tiredness. The wind blew again through the leaves and he understood that there was nothing else to say, so he sat down and, leaning against a tree, fell asleep.

He woke early the next day and after breakfast went down to the allotments, where he found that in the short space of time he had been away, his plot seemed to have become very overgrown, so he set about weeding and tidying. He was in a kneeling position when a familiar face appeared above the fence.

'Do you know, Devlin,' Denis spoke in his lilting way, 'with your long hair and all, you look just like a picture of the Lord I once saw, kneeling in the Garden of Gethsemane.'

'In that case, you must be Peter, my disciple,' Devlin responded, lifting his hand as if to bless his friend. 'Will you not come and watch a while with me.'

'I haven't got time for that malarkey, I've got potatoes to harvest,' Denis laughed, but then, lowering his tone, said, 'But tell me, how did the trip go? Are you OK?'

'It went well really. Ben's funeral was a sad occasion, of course, but also a very uplifting experience.'

The conversation between the two friends inevitably moved on to the allotments and produce, with Denis explaining that a formal proposal had been put to the Regime about the reorganisation of the AA and that the response had been encouraging. As a result, Kirsty and the rest of the committee were feeling very positive and the good news had quickly filtered through the allotments. Denis was elated, talking at length about how the changes would improve things, and Devlin listened intently at first, but by and by his mind started to drift on to possible implications of the meeting he had that afternoon.

'Are you alright?' Denis asked, noticing Devlin's absence. 'It's just that you seem a bit distracted, whereas I thought you'd be delighted.' He hesitated, looking closely at him before adding, 'I don't know, but maybe there's a sadness in you that wasn't there before.'

'No, it is great news,' Devlin said, walking over to the fence and clasping his friend's hand. 'I'm sorry, but don't you worry about me. I'll soon be firing on all cylinders again. It's just the effect of the trip – the funeral and seeing my family again.'

On his way back to the flat, Devlin realised that he barely had time to change, so after a quick turnaround, he was once more cycling to the Business District. Securing his bike outside the Rawlins Building, it occurred to him that he could go through the main door at this stage, but he decided to continue entering through the gallery, at least until there was a conclusion to this phase of meetings with the Regime. At the reception, Smith greeted him.

'Good to see you again.'

Devlin smiled as he swept past, walking quickly through the gallery and corridor that led to the main building. He stopped at the toilets and after relieving himself, washed his hands and face and then peered deep into the mirror, searching for the changes in appearance that both Jenkins and Denis had remarked upon, but seeing nothing different except maybe a tiredness round the eyes. He did, however, notice how long his hair had grown and thought how a visit to the barber was definitely called for, particularly since his wound had now virtually healed.

Following the same route as always, he entered the hall with the pulsing amber lights in the picture rail, which accompanied him to the third door on the right. He remembered that the first time he had encountered this system, he had playfully said "open sesame" before entering, but on this occasion, to his surprise, McGee came walking briskly towards him from the other side.

'Oh, it's great to see you again, Devlin,' McGee said, fixing him with his dark piercing eyes, 'and so soon. I'm just back myself – what a trip.'

'And it's good to see you,' Devlin said, smiling magnanimously and moving aside to allow McGee to pass.

Entering the viewing room, he made his way to the open door on the far side of the screen, where he found an open-plan area encased in beams of different-coloured light, like the one where he had met the CRP team, but the dimensions of this space were smaller, with various monitors surrounding a single chair and just the one prominent screen at the front. He stood in the doorway until Don's voice announced, 'Welcome Devlin. Would you sit down?'

He sat down in the chair and was immediately aware of impulses bouncing back and forth between the monitors, as if in conversation. The effect was like being in the midst of an electronic river of communication and in addition to this activity, he had the sense that his own thought patterns were being observed. This did not unduly bother him as he had expected it as part of the interview.

Eventually, the monitors became dormant and Don's face appeared on the large screen.

'We will now start the interview,' he said. 'You are surrounded by individuals who will remain visually anonymous. Designated representatives will conduct the interview by questions and comments relayed through the monitors. There will be a delay between each question and response. This allows for the processing of information by all members of the panel.'

'That's fine,' Devlin smiled easily.

'Do not try to address each individual monitor,' Don added. 'That will be trying for everyone. You can gaze ahead at this screen, which will remain blank throughout this stage of the interview.'

Devlin nodded his assent and a slow melodic voice to his left said, 'It is recorded that you left the CRP after some very positive contributions. You cited personal reasons, but you also felt a sense of frustration that the work was not leading to greater autonomy for the Celtic regions. Is this accurate?'

'It is accurate,' Devlin replied simply, looking straight ahead.

'Could you explain what happened after you left the CRP?'

'I suppose I was disillusioned with politics then and I needed time to make sense of my situation. Because of my involvement with the CRP, some of my community and family were suspicious of me, figuring I had betrayed my people by working so closely with the Regime. Others felt some good work had been done, but even so, you could say that my position was ambiguous and had divided opinion.' Devlin paused, as there were impulses coming through and obviously comments being passed between the monitors. He continued once they had subsided. 'So, for a period I laid low in the city and, to use an old saying, I licked my wounds. Eventually I got involved in the allotments and genuinely enjoyed the gardening, so when the opportunity came to develop some new ways of working in the Allotments Association, I readily got involved.'

'When you heard of your mother's predicament with the Dexter Foundation and the family home, was that a surprise to you?' a different voiced piped up, sharper than the last.

'It was.'

'Did you realise that the Regime had taken over that failing organisation?'

'No.'

'Family members of yours are involved in the movement for greater independence in the west of Ireland. Some are moderates, while others would try to shoot and bomb the Regime out of existence, given the chance. Where do you stand on this?'

'Bombing seems a futile course of action, particularly as the Regime has shown a commitment to allowing the culture of the west of Ireland to flourish. The mainstream arm of the CMA doesn't seem all that far away from the position that the organisation is adopting now and though not a total consensus, I see reasons for hope. However, I reiterate that my family and my culture are my ultimate concerns.'

Devlin's blue eyes looked serenely ahead at the screen and he spoke calmly. If you were to observe him at this point of the interview, you would assume that these questions had been envisioned beforehand, so easily had the answers come to him.

'Devlin, you are remarkably cool under pressure. You use words very easily. This is a particular skill of yours, as is your ability to moderate the thoughts that you receive and emit.' A woman with a strong Scottish accent continued to develop her observation. 'I am not paying you a compliment here, but rather highlighting a potential issue. You have the skills to use words well and conceal your thoughts. Some of us are concerned that you will not be totally open with the Regime.'

'The skills that you refer to were developed through my involvement with the CRP, based on an initial instinct to keep my desire for greater independence concealed.' Devlin paused, aware that he was speaking with a slight Mullnamorran accent. 'I was young then and a certain level of subterfuge was needed in order to stay involved with my family and community, given their largely nationalistic political feelings. Since leaving college and joining the CRP, there has been a paradoxical quality to my existence, which you could say has become second nature to me. I can understand why you have asked the question but at the end of the day, I was honest about my thoughts with Don, which is the main thing.'

There were many impulses passing across the floor and this interaction lasted for many minutes, until the woman who had asked the last question spoke again.

'As I said, you are very good with words,' she said. 'You also have an interest in Celtic spirituality. Would you say that is an overriding religious belief that guides your actions?'

'My understanding of Celtic spirituality is that it provides a framework for living that aligns closely with the seasons and the land. It has existed for thousands of years and is a vital part of the culture that we are trying to protect. When you ask if it guides my actions – it does not specify any set of rules or dogma that must be followed and instead offers underpinning values for living in harmony with the elements and the planet.'

'Also linked to Celtic spirituality are specific skills and powers,' a particularly enthusiastic voice spoke up, 'ones that have been maintained by the priests and the so-called "gifted ones". You are aware of these powers?'

'I am aware of such ancient powers, yes,' he responded with a trace of hesitancy in his voice.

'These powers that your people possess operate on a different level to the ones scientifically established by the Regime and its allies. Would you say that is accurate?'

'There does appear to be a difference in the origin of these powers, but as I don't have an in-depth understanding of how either of them came about, I find it hard to comment specifically,' Devlin said, speaking in a slow, measured tone.

'Do you think these powers pose a direct threat to the Regime?'

'From what I know – and I stress that it's not a lot – no.'

'But given that they originate from a different source, you must see why they are of great interest? Would you be involved in investigating such ancient Celtic powers?'

'I hardly seem qualified.' He paused again, before saying positively, 'But yes, I would be very interested to be involved in such an investigation.'

There was another hubbub of activity between the screens, before the sharp voice said, 'James, who visited your apartment, was a Survaid and part of his purpose in this was to observe you as you were being considered for another role within the organisation. Were you aware of this? You are aware of the crackdowns, or purges, as they are called. There are also other methods employed by the Regime to counter revolutionary forces and maintain order. How would you feel about working within an organisation that employs such strategies?'

'I suppose that deep down, I was suspicious of James, but as I liked both him and his sister, I just went along with it. I wasn't involved in anything covert, so I had nothing to hide from him. I thought that she had no notion of his possible involvement, so it wasn't really a problem for me. The purges and liftings of individuals is something that I have always struggled with and I would want them to be avoided wherever possible. I am assuming that this interview is for some sort of political role, in which case, I am also assuming that part of the role would be to negate the need for such tactics, although I realise that I may be getting ahead of things in coming to that conclusion.'

This provoked an intense bout of interactions between the monitors, as Don's voice returned and said, 'Could you give us a few minutes please? There are matters that we have to consider at this point.'

Sitting back in his chair, Devlin waited for a lengthy period of time until the activity died down and his mentor appeared on the screen again.

'We are ready to move on, Devlin,' Don said. 'Your assumption that the role you are being interviewed for is a political one is correct. After considering some of the things you have said, there are a couple of points that need to be stressed.'

'Your impression of the way the purges are used is interesting,' a woman spoke very slowly, in a distinct accent Devlin could not identify. 'You are being considered for a political role. Can you foresee situations where you would authorise such actions?'

'If serious bloodshed was envisaged,' Devlin answered sombrely, 'or a heinous revolution planned, I could see myself authorising such an action, yes. But I go back to my original point: I would like to think that my role would be to make such actions unnecessary.'

'This point needs to be made plain,' the sharp man's voice came through once more. 'The Regime will not be forced from power. It is also the case that actions such as purges are often part of a strategic plan that is authorised at a higher level and therefore something that we have no control over. We just need to be clear about that. With that in mind, do you want to go ahead with the rest of the interview? By continuing, you are expressing a firm commitment to the organisation?'

Devlin nodded slowly. 'I agree, but I still need to know what it is I'm being considered for if I'm to accept a position.'

'That is understood,' the Scottish woman responded, speaking with great clarity. 'I can tell you that the organisation wants to put a new political structure in place in Ireland, which will obviously require governance. The role you are being considered for is central to its implementation. To establish a model for governing in this way, we are going to start in the old province of your origin, Connaught. We need people who have diplomatic skills and a deep understanding of the country. This has become a necessity as we have been encouraging the Irish culture to thrive, but there is presently no platform for political aspirations – and in that void, there is the potential for revolutionaries to flourish.'

Devlin nodded his head again as he looked around at all the monitors that were surrounding him and he was about to speak when Don interjected.

'We would like you to take twenty-four hours to consider this offer. We are prepared to answer more questions about the organisation once you have fully committed to this role. First, we require you to consider your position. You will be entering into a role that will require a far higher level of commitment than previously. You will come under a greater level of scrutiny and ultimately pressure. You can call this twenty-four hours a cooling off period. Will you return at two o'clock tomorrow afternoon?'

'Yes.'

The monitors started to emit signals gently back and forth as Devlin left the room, giving him the distinct impression that they were chatting among themselves. He passed through the viewing room and entered the hall, which was now very busy, as if some particular activity or event had just finished. Glad of the hubbub of interaction, he made his way quickly towards the doors and went briskly along the corridors that led to the gallery, where he approached the reception desk.

'I know the exhibition received an extension, but do you know when it actually finishes?' he asked.

'It will finish next Wednesday,' Smith answered. 'Such a popular exhibition. Who would have thought that abstract paintings of the west coast of Ireland would arouse so much interest in a city over here?'

'Who indeed?' Devlin replied, before walking out of the gallery, but he was stopped in his tracks in the foyer by the sight of a heavy downpour outside.

Content to wait for the rain to stop, he watched the people who were caught in the deluge as they hurried frantically to their destinations, as the large droplets drummed on the pavements and the sheer volume of water made a distinct gurgling sound entering the drains. He looked out across the square, reflecting on the position he was in – neither inside nor outside the Rawlins, in a no-man's land that he knew he couldn't occupy much longer.

The rain stopped very suddenly and Devlin took the opportunity to retrieve his bicycle from beside the confectionary stand, sharing a rueful smile with the ice cream seller, then mounted his bike and cycled away, whistling a tune and making no effort to avoid the many puddles on the sodden streets. As he entered the Village, he cycled through the square, passing the Colosseum before entering the Leanings District. He had already made the decision to go to the music session at the Rainbow and, arriving at the pub, he walked his bike in and leaned it against the door of the old grocery shop before entering the bar.

While waiting to be served, Devlin looked around and saw a few vaguely familiar faces, but none that were of his acquaintance.

'What will it be?' Quinn asked, coming over to serve him.

'A pint would be great,' he responded, acknowledging the musicians. 'They sound in good form.'

'They are for sure. Oh, by the way, Niall was in before and asking after you. I expect he will be back later, but you never know. He's a great one for keeping on the move.'

'He is indeed,' Devlin agreed, adding impulsively, 'Listen, Quinn, if any stranger should ask for me tonight, could you say you haven't seen me?'

'Oh, I can do that alright,' Quinn raised an eyebrow. 'Things must be on the move so.'

'You could say that, yes. I'll go over to one of the far alcoves, beyond the musicians. I just fancy a quiet drink listening to the tunes.'

'It's not a problem, Devlin. Deidre will keep an eye on you for the drink.'

'It's a strange thing, travelling, Quinn,' Devlin said, taking hold of his pint. 'It's funny how it can unsettle you. Have you travelled away from this place in the last few years at all?'

'Now, why would I be travelling away from here?' he replied, giving a questioning look. 'I've no reason to, and isn't it a strange thing for you to be asking?'

'You're right,' Devlin smiled, concluding, 'isn't it strange, indeed.'

He found an alcove at the far side of the room, where he could remain concealed or, alternatively, by leaning forward, get a clear view of the bar if he was so inclined. The session was in full swing, so he leant back in his seat, giving his full attention to the music, and the time passed easily.

'Do want another one of them?' Deirdre asked, having spotted that his glass was almost empty.

'That I would.'

'I like the longer hair, Devlin,' she said, returning from the bar with his drink. 'You have the look of the Lord about you.'

'That's good. Are you in need of salvation?'

'Oh no,' she smiled at him, saying jauntily, 'I think it's going to hell in a hand cart I'll be. If it's all the same…' she lingered a moment after putting down the pint, adding in a gentler tone, 'there is a stranger who has been asking for you at the bar just now.'

'Thanks, Deirdre,' Devlin said brightly. 'You're a star.'

Peering around the column, he saw Paul Grogan in deep conversation with two men who looked familiar beside the bar. The musicians played another set of lively reels before taking a break, at which point Paul went over to talk to the fiddler, who appeared to look over in the direction of the alcove where Devlin was sitting, but his gaze continued moving on round the bar without pausing.

When the music started once more, Deirdre brought him another pint.

'I suppose you would rather be at Clancy's cottage,' she said, setting the glass down on the table.

'Well, I am genuinely surprised,' he responded, his brow furrowing slightly.

'There is a house down the road that has a picture of Dublin in the window,' she went on, ignoring his remark, 'if for any reason you should need to go sightseeing. And if you have a mind to call – feel free.'

'Will you let me know when there is more space up by the bar?' he said, as she was turning to go. 'Oh, and would you ever get me half a bottle of the Special Label whiskey?'

'Right you are.' Deirdre swept up the empty glass nonchalantly and went to the bar.

The session recommenced with a set of jigs that were well known to him. They originated in Sligo and were made famous by the legendary fiddle master Michael Coleman. The memory came back to him of the tall, willowy Mr Devlin, his head cocked to one side appreciatively, his dark wavy hair very prominent while he listened to the music, pointing out the subtleties to his young son, a reverence in his voice and a bright sparkle in his eye. These were memories that he had overlooked, or maybe even blocked out, during the times when their relationship was in a more acrimonious state, but they came back to him that evening, as he listened appreciatively to the fiddler's ornamentations, giving him a feeling of warmth and connection with his father that he had not experienced in many a year.

When the set of tunes finished, there was a tear in his eye as he applauded loudly for the performance, his father and the culture of the west of Ireland. He was considering it an appropriate time to leave when Deirdre reappeared at his table.

'The people you referred to have left, so it may be a good time for you to go – if you're of the mind. Still no sign of your Niall, though. Oh, and here's your half bottle.'

'Thanks, Deirdre,' he slipped the bottle into his inside pocket. 'If I don't see you through the week, I'll see you through the window.'

'Right you are, and who knows where and when that will be?' she responded, with a distinct brightness in her brown eyes.

'Who indeed.' He smiled fully at her and then she moved away collecting glasses, merging with the rest of the clientele.

He sent a message to Amir on his device and then got up and made his way across the room, waving casually to Quinn, who responded by inclining his head to one side.

Devlin walked out of the bar and was taking hold of the handlebars on his bike when he heard the muffled sounds of two shots being fired in quick succession. He looked behind him, but as there was no reaction from the people inside the Rainbow, he reasoned that the bar was too far from the street for them to hear. Pushing his bike cautiously out onto the pavement, he saw the tall Marcel standing transfixed outside Café Jordan, staring intently down the street, and when he followed his gaze to the next corner, there was a large bloodstain on the pavement and fresh splashes on the wall. Above the scene lingered the residue of bluey green lights, hovering in mid-air, and for a moment he was struck by how pretty the disappearing radiance was, reminding him of crib illuminations he had seen in his childhood, during times of peace and joy.

Marcel was still stationary, his purple-rimmed glasses seeming to emphasise the anxiety in his eyes, as Devlin called over to him, 'I'll be seeing you.'

The owner of the café waved by way of reply, but his expression did not change. Devlin briskly cycled off, wondering how much longer he could keep riding out his luck, feeling that fate was surely closing in on him.

Approaching the allotments, he spotted Amir standing near the gates, a carrier bike leaning against the railings next to him, with Presto the cat sitting in the front basket.

'Well, it's good to see the two of you,' Devlin spoke with an affable air.

'It's good to see you.' Amir sounded concerned. 'But I was surprised by this late change in arrangements. Is everything alright?'

'I'm not totally sure if things are alright or not,' Devlin said, gesturing towards the vegetable plots and then leading the way along the path to his shed, 'but I thought we could meet in a place closer to nature this evening.'

Unlocking the door, he turned to his friend and said brightly, 'Welcome to my potting emporium.'

'The crows are amazing tonight, aren't they?' Amir paused in the open doorway, with Presto in his arms. 'And such a sky, too. The weather has been impossible to predict recently. Look at those clearing clouds, and there will even be a fine sunset.'

'Indeed, these are great days for sky watchers. Now, come in and make yourselves at home,' Devlin said with a sweep of his arm.

Amir took a seat near the door and put down Presto, who moved stealthily through the cluttered interior, obviously detecting many scents that interested her.

'You will find all kinds of things in here, Presto. You may even root out some rodents for me,' Devlin said, unscrewing the top of the bottle of Special Label that he produced from his inside pocket and pouring a good measure for himself into an enamel mug before offering the bottle to his guest. 'I don't suppose I can tempt you?'

'No, I will remain sober tonight, for a change,' Amir replied, a touch of amusement in his voice.

Devlin looked around the earthy interior of the shed, noticing the haphazard way that tools and supplies appeared to be stowed.

'You wouldn't think that everything has its place and purpose, would you?' he said and paused to take a drink. 'But in the midst of chaos, there is really order. I mean, look at this humble work bench. It is my altar and you, my chosen priest. The cleric I would confide in and even confess to.'

'You are in a strange mood tonight, Devlin,' Amir said, peering closely at him. 'I am very interested to hear what you will say next.'

'Well, these are strange and chaotic days, but maybe we'll find some clarity, particularly in regard to my role in this confusion.'

A short time elapsed where both men appeared to be listening to the rooks outside and then Devlin spoke again.

'We have talked about Celtic spirituality before,' he began, 'and I have since observed my people embracing it again, which greatly warms my heart. In the shorter term, however, the politics of nationalism dominate the picture and I find myself at the centre of a storm, a tempest that is threatening both in Ireland and also over here. I now know that by intervening in this struggle, I could alleviate the situation, even though it would put me at odds with others; whereas if I do nothing, it will put me in alignment with another group. So, it appears that I am required to commit myself either way.'

'As I said before, some people are capable of doing weighty things, Devlin, and you will therefore be called upon. You are both blessed and cursed in that sense.'

Devlin looked at the cat, who had settled herself on a pile of sacks by the door.

'You rest easy, Presto,' he said. 'I think it is you who is blessed, while I am simply cursed. You know, Amir, the closer I get to the Regime now, the more I see cracks of vulnerability that weren't there before – or at least, I couldn't see them. I have seen androids and other beings seeming to experience very human emotions, such as envy, amusement and irrational anger. There is no doubt in my mind that things are changing and perhaps the Regime and its allies are not as impenetrable as we once thought.'

'If I can be your priest then I can also be your devil's advocate,' Amir spoke with clarity. 'If things are changing now, why not let them change? And you just stand back and state your neutrality?'

'I could stand back, but what would I do now that I have been energised and inspired? I dream of setting out on the long-term quest to find that spiritual certainty and seeing my family again has brought me closer to achieving it. Experiencing so much of Ireland again has deeply affected me.'

'There is also a serious emotional change. Have you found someone particularly special, Devlin?'

'Is it so obvious?'

'Not exactly, but it would make sense… Is this love drawing you in a certain direction?'

Devlin considered this question carefully before answering. 'Not exactly, as it was already my direction of travel. The potential of the bombs and the subsequent purges have weighed heavily on my mind, but so has my inactivity in this situation – a situation that seems to have gathered me into its midst. It is not clear to me yet, but there has to be a better way to navigate these times – a less lethal way.'

'That is why they have come to you. They know you will search for their answers.'

'This is my culture. *They* are my answers.'

'You are claiming your heritage, my friend,' Amir said slowly, his dark eyes glistening as he considered every word before he spoke. 'Whatever the weight of this yoke, you are preparing yourself to bear it. You have already decided that your course is set. It seems it is now only a case of who you are on board with.'

'I knew I could rely on you,' Devlin laughed, raising the enamel mug to his friend. 'I know you were surprised when I asked to meet you tonight instead and particularly here. So, be assured that all is as it should be. I hope you escape attention in the days ahead.'

'Oh, don't worry. The Regime has interviewed me before. They consider me an eccentric religious character of no threat and I will endeavour to keep it that way.'

Amir then went on to outline how he had made contact with his cousin and what they planned to do in the coming days and weeks, before a silence descended over the shed as Devlin became immersed in his own dark thoughts again.

'I think it's time we were going,' Amir said, reaching over and lifting Presto gently. 'We don't want to be arriving at my cousin's too late. I'll look forward to seeing you in the future, wherever that might be.'

'Thanks again my friend, and here's to the future.'

'May we get there safely.' A mysterious smile on his lips, he placed the cat back in the front basket.

After watching his visitors leave, Devlin looked across the dense vegetation of the allotments that was becoming etched in darkness and locked up his shed. The rookery was quiet and his mood was lifting as he made his way slowly back to the apartment block.

Walking in through the main doors, the new receptionist smiled warmly at Devlin, as if they were colleagues of many years.

'Everything is in order here,' he reported. 'All ship-shape, one might say, if one was a nautical person.' He allowed himself a chuckle at his little joke and Devlin responded in kind.

'Very good, Number One,' he gave a mock salute. 'Carry on, then.'

Inspecting the paintwork of his bicycle on the way up in the lift, Devlin was considering the amount of work a good renovation job would involve as there were many patches where it was worn and rusty, and by the time he'd reached his floor, he was coming to the conclusion that it was probably not worth it, given the age and condition of the bike.

After preparing a meal by boiling potatoes from the bottom of the cupboard and adding them to tinned fish, pickle and tomato, he checked the machine in his work room and found no new messages other than a reminder about tomorrow's meeting at the Rawlins. The term used to describe the encounter – a 'final review of position' – amused him, but after looking at the words again, he thought that maybe they were entirely accurate. He returned to the living room and as he consumed his supper, he felt curiously relaxed even though he knew significant changes were at hand.

Another interesting nocturnal skyline was forming over the city as he settled in a chair by the window, but his eye was drawn to an area of the Village where lights were pulsing, signifying a level of unrest. Having another drink of whiskey, he rolled the spirit around his tongue, appreciating the cool, fiery flavour as he watched the airspace over the Village, feeling a sense of relief when the normal patchwork of nuanced light and shade returned again. Before long, a great tiredness started to come over him, yet something told him to check his device, which he did, finding a message that he had missed earlier. It was from Ceridwen, conveying a simple statement that required no answer.

I have made arrangements to pick up James. The healing must start here.

We all have our journeys to take. Good luck. C x

CHAPTER SEVENTEEN

Dropping off to sleep that night, Devlin felt a sense of relief as he was whisked away from the tribulations of a strange and demanding day, slowly entering a dream in which he had just woken up and was listening to the comforting sound of the wind blowing through the trees. He had no inclination to look up until the husky golden voice spoke to him again.

'You have slept long enough, Devlin. It is time you were going.'

He looked around him and saw that he was in the same glade where he had been the night before. His attention was drawn to a group of people in the surrounding woodland dressed in ancient garb, checking sailing tackle as if in preparation for a voyage. Beside him lay a long tunic, sandals and kit bag.

'You must change now,' the voice said.

Putting on the tunic, he marvelled at how comfortable it felt – very much belying its coarse appearance – and after stepping into the sandals, he found two bronze bangles by the tree, which he slipped onto his right arm. Regarding himself, he felt like a hero from one of the ancient song cycles, about to set off on an epic quest. As he faced the far side of the glade, the voice told him, 'Take the branch with you. You'll have need of that again. It showed you the way here, but you have much farther to go.' He picked up the branch and the voice continued, 'You are not simply setting off to find some land of milk and honey. Your quest is more complex than that. The long battle to re-establish the ancient ways has begun and hopefully you have a significant part to play.'

A fresh wind blew through the glade and Gráinne's voice whispered urgently, 'There are some powers that should help you on your way. Interventions using the ancient ways for surveillance or disruption are not traceable by the Regime since they instantly dissolve, as you saw with the drone interventions. This is a major advantage as they cannot locate the source, but you must be aware that if they're used repeatedly, the pattern will show up.'

'Don't worry if you cannot see the way ahead,' the golden voice interjected, 'as there is no set plan laid out before you. We are creatures of instinct and we can combat the grinding forces of logic much more effectively with instinctive thrusts. If you find you are in a position of apparent isolation, this can also be a shield that will help to protect you. No doubt you have found its shelter before.'

Then a voice that for all the world sounded like Miriam's spoke to him gently. 'As your heart is so deeply believing in this venture, you cannot help but further the cause,' she said. 'If your feelings change, I for one will certainly know it, so fear not on that front; and if you are, or the cause is, in peril, you will know the way back.'

Devlin had stood transfixed throughout all this and only relaxed when the husky voice said, 'It is time for you to go. The tide will soon be full.'

Picking up his kit bag, he walked to the edge of the glade and was approached by a tall woman carrying a long oar, which she placed in his right hand.

'It's time to take your place,' she said with authority. 'We are going down to the boat.'

The crew assembled in two lines of six on a path that led through the towering pines. Devlin stood alongside the last man, his kit bag slung over one shoulder and his oar balanced on the other, as an order to march was issued and the company started its descent on the broad, sandy track that took them through the woods. They were met by a magnificent view of the bay; the rugged rock formations, the deep golden sand colour of the beach and the sharply descending slopes were all so well known to Devlin, but not this particular scene. Nearing the coastline he was breathing heavily, and when the order came to halt they stopped on a plateau of rock above the glistening sea. The tunics that the sailors wore had a bluey green hue in the sunlight, which glowed in a way that was oddly familiar to him. He considered this for a moment before he noticed his family on the beach across the harbour. His mother was folding up the chequered blanket, his father was packing a bag and Miriam and Ben were returning from paddling in the sea.

Waving her hand enthusiastically, his mother appeared to be the only one who had noticed Devlin's party, which was boarding a single-masted rowing vessel moored by the jetty. One by one, the crew climbed down a creaking wooden ladder and he was starting his own descent when he heard his mother call, 'Have you not finished exploring yet, Michael? It's getting very late.'

'Don't worry, Mam,' he shouted a little awkwardly back. 'The exploring's nearly done.'

When he was in place, the boat cast off and from the outset, the whole crew were stroking in unison. Devlin noticed a familiar-looking old man at the tiller who he had not seen while boarding. He said, with a distinctive Mullnamorran lilt to his voice, 'Rest easy now, Michael. We have a long way to go yet.'

Passing the cliffs on the port side, they rounded the headland and the old man pulled hard on the tiller, setting course for the shadowy outline of a set of islands on the horizon. They continued to row until the boat started to be taken out by the prevailing currents, at which point the pull became amazing and the crew cheered as the tiller man declared, 'Ship oar, my mates. We're in the hands of destiny now.'

The next morning, Devlin woke up feeling disorientated; his dream of the voyage seemed to have lasted all of the night. After feeling the need for a long shower to sharpen his senses, followed by a substantial breakfast, he decided that he wanted to finish tidying up his plot, since the weather looked relatively settled that morning.

He had just brought his tools out in the barrow, ready to start work, when Denis came over, saying, 'It's good to see you back in the routine, Devlin. I was wondering if I'd have to show you how to dig again.'

'Is this how you use it?' he asked, smiling at his friend while holding the spade the wrong way around.

'I'm glad to see you haven't lost your sense of humour,' Denis chuckled.

'I'm hoping it'll be one of the last senses I'm left with.'

'Amen to that. The same would go for me, my friend,' Denis agreed, before pausing to give Devlin a searching look and then completely changing the subject. 'There was a lot of trouble in the Village yesterday evening. It's been building up and the word is it's something to do with your compatriots. I was just wondering if the old Devlin, who had his finger on the political pulse, knew what was going on – or maybe it's just a storm in the old teacup?'

A sad smile came over Devlin's face and it was a true reflection of how he was feeling, for in all his years on the allotments, Irish politics had never been brought up in such a direct way before. Having a genuine respect and affection for Denis, he did not want to patronise him, so he took a moment to consider his words before answering.

'The hope is that things will settle down soon,' he said, 'and though I have no control over what is going on right now, my instinct tells me that this will be the case. There have always been Irish political factions ready for rebellion and if you add to that the inevitable reaction of the Regime, it's an explosive cocktail. If things follow a pattern then hopefully, after a few days—'

'I hope you're right,' Denis interrupted, looking Devlin directly in the eye, 'but some people fear that something worse will happen.'

Devlin suddenly felt strangely cornered by this situation, as he could not work out if his friend thought he could change the course of events, or if he was just looking for reassurance. In the end, he said positively, 'I think things will die down soon enough.'

'So, we're hoping for the storm in a teacup option.' Denis winked slowly, then said, 'Isn't this a sombre conversation for two old cabbage cultivators to be having?'

'Isn't it just. By the way, let me know if you've got any spare produce for the Exchange next week.'

'I will, but there seems little chance of my family's appetite diminishing in any way by then,' Denis said, laughing as he went off to continue his work.

It took Devlin two hours to finish the jobs he had intended to do and when he had completed them and was putting his tools away in the shed, it occurred to him that Rachel had still not put in an appearance that morning, which he found a little strange. Nevertheless, he started on the walk back to his flat, waving to Denis as he went. A strange misty drizzle was starting to fall as he entered the building.

'I hope you're alright,' the receptionist said, sounding concerned. 'It's not good to be walking in the rain. You could catch a chill.'

'Oh, I'm fine,' Devlin smiled. 'It does us Celts good to be close to the seasons.'

A momentary look of puzzlement came over the man's face, which he soon corrected before saying, 'Oh, of course. That is good. I'll have to remember that one.'

Devlin glanced at the office behind reception and noted that the furthest screen was showing the immediate streets outside, with the faint babble of an unfamiliar language emanating from the surrounding monitors.

'I know it must seem very intrusive,' the receptionist said, appearing uncomfortable at Devlin's interest in the surveillance set-up, 'but it helps to keep us all safe.'

'Oh, I'm sure you're right. Keep the good work going, Number One.'

Rather than use the lift, he went up the fire escape stairs with the rationale that it was because he still had his gardening clothes and working boots on, but he knew that this didn't make any logical sense as he'd already entered the building in that attire. The truth was that, deep down, he liked to change his routines and the way he did things, as this was seen as predominately a human trait.

An hour later, he came out of the lift wheeling his bike, dressed smartly in his tweed jacket and good clothes. An elderly couple who lived two floors beneath him were waiting to ascend and he acknowledged them graciously before walking through the reception area, where the receptionist was talking earnestly into his device. Outside, Devlin gazed up at the changeable skies and slipped his rucksack on his shoulders before cycling away.

Just as Devlin was approaching the Village, a heavy shower started and he stopped the bike to take out his waterproof gear. A Transkill vehicle was parked on the street and a team of workers were making their way along the pavement, sheltering under a moving umbrella, and among them was the tall worker with spiky silver hair he had spoken to the day before. She was looking in his direction as he fumbled with his cycling cape and dropped his rucksack on the wet floor, provoking a mirthful expression to flicker across her face, which he at once reciprocated. It was a very brief and natural interaction, but one that he instantly committed to his memory. The work group then disappeared around a corner and after finally getting his weatherproof layer on, he cycled off briskly along the rain-soaked streets.

At the Rawlins Building, a weak sun was peeking uncertainly through the clouds as he secured his bike before removing the cycling cape. He was early again and looking up at the building, he made a snap decision to take another walk round the adjacent streets. The Business District was its usual mix of office workers, residents and tourists and he enjoyed the stroll, as he found some side streets that he had not been down before, coming across some very interesting buildings. It was exactly one fifty-five when he entered the gallery.

'What a day that is,' Smith greeted him very naturally. 'It looks like you have been out in the weather.'

'I have for sure,' Devlin replied cheerily and after walking past the toilets, he was admitted into the main part of the building.

He followed the same sequence of events as usual on his way to the viewing room. The door on the far side of the screen was open and Don's voice said, 'Would you please come through.'

Entering the space where he'd been interviewed the day before, the beams of light that formed its perimeter were pulsing slowly. There were intermittent interactions between the surrounding monitors and the main screen showed Don's hazy image. Devlin sat in the centrally situated chair and his old mentor commenced proceedings.

'I will repeat some things that were said yesterday,' he began formally, 'as there are additional members and observers on the interview panel who need to be brought up to speed. The organisation is going to put a new political structure in place in Ireland, which will need governance. You are being considered for a significant role in developing and implementing this strategy. The initial pilot project will be based in the Connaught region. If you consent to your application for this role going ahead, I will outline the next stage of the process. Do you want to proceed?'

'I do.'

'Then we will progress. You understand that from this point, you are committing yourself? This means that you can be brought in for interview at any time, to check that you are pursuing the agreed strategy. We need to be reassured of your commitment to the aims of the Regime at all times. If a problem occurred in this area, you would be withdrawn from service and investigated. Do you accept these terms?'

'I do.'

Don's image had already started to fade on the screen when he said, 'That is all in order, then. Look ahead during the interactions. You don't have to address anyone in particular.'

The woman with a Scottish accent, who had addressed him last time, spoke up first.

'Devlin, this is a large step you are taking. You are committing yourself to the organisation, so it makes sense for you to find out more about how it is operating now. It has certainly changed significantly over the last twenty-five years.'

'You are a naturally inquisitive person,' the man with the sharp voice said, 'and I am sure you have some questions about the current organisation. Can you consider what you would like to ask? Could you keep it concise?'

'Of course, just give me a few moments.'

The space settled into a gentle buzz of activity around Devlin, who was pleased to find that he could think coherently in this situation. He decided on his questions and cleared his throat before commencing.

'When I was a youngster, there were regular bulletins about the great progressions made, particularly in the fields of science and space exploration. My question is, have intelligences from other planets been contacted, and if so, have these links had an effect on the Regime?'

'You have asked a very far-reaching question,' the woman answered at once. 'Let me start by stating one fundamental point, which is crucial to understanding the way the organisation works. It is compartmentalised in its structure and this guarantees the security and efficiency of each department operating below the Higher Command Board. We are in the Geopolitical Department

– or Geo-Part, as we are known – and we only have access to the information that is fed down to us by the HCB.'

'The answer to your question is that other intelligences have been reached,' a man with a gentle voice added, 'and through now-established lines of communication, exchanges of information have taken place, as well as personal appearances being facilitated. This has been a gateway to other worlds – a two-way street, you might say – and a very exciting development. Now, if I am reading your thoughts accurately, you want to know how this has changed the Regime.'

'You are aware that artificial intelligence was developed on Earth long ago,' the woman came back in, 'and there are fine specimens of androids that you have no doubt encountered. As my colleague has said, there are representations from other worlds inputting into the organisation and they have a great interest in humanity in the broadest sense, and the Irish culture has very definitely caught their attention. Within the Geo-Part and even on this interview panel, in fact, there is a participation from other planets and I can say with certainty that it has greatly improved the diversity of thought available to us.'

There was a prolonged hubbub between the screens and Devlin was content to let it wash over him, as he could tell it was one of approval.

'I believe your first question has been answered,' the man with the sharp voice said. 'That is all the information we can release at this time. What is your next question?'

'Some human emotions and instincts were not replicated in early androids and I wondered if this was because such aspects were not desired, or merely a result of the technological limitations of the time. I have recently met some individuals who appear to be starting to feel in a more human way and I wanted to know if that's an intentional strategy. In conclusion to this question, if these observations are correct, might this lead to a return to more traditional political systems, such as localised democracy?'

'I will respond to your observations about the qualities of androids,' the woman said, 'and the AI that has been created. As you know, the technology was initially quite basic, with the aim being simply to produce beings to complete certain tasks, but that has changed considerably and the creatures we see nowadays are far more sophisticated – far more aligned with the human model. The ability to experience emotions such as frustration and anger is wired into them, though they have not always been activated.'

'There have been cases of malfunctions,' a man with a strong Irish accent picked up the theme, 'resulting in rogue emotions being triggered and even violent reactions. It has been acknowledged that the more sophisticated we get in developing AI and pursuing emotional creativity, the more danger there is of this happening. I would say that human qualities per se are not undesirable, but as you know, the end result of thousands of years of so-called civilisation was total chaos, evidenced by the unworkable extremes of the internet and social media – which, as you know, had to be withdrawn from general service. So we are understandably moving cautiously in this area. There is also something else worth noting at this time. There is a perception circulating that the Regime is run by AI and other intelligences, but that is not the case. There is still a massive amount of human input driving the planet's development.'

'It is a field of development under constant review,' the woman said very slowly. 'To give you some idea of the issues faced, I will pose an ethical question. Are other beings entitled to the same emotional freedom that humans have traditionally had? If not, would it be right to change that?' She paused before adding, 'Many people would say we are playing God, to use a human phrase, and in answer to that, I would say, increasingly we have no other option, because God's rules seemed to be directed solely at humans, whereas we are interacting in worlds outside of that scope.'

'Democracy as a political system has been discredited,' the

sharp man said. 'Hopefully, the work you are commencing will result in a higher level of autonomy for your home region and we will see how that goes – if it can be maintained in an acceptable manner. You have seen the growing interest there is in activities such as sport and even gambling. There is a recognition of the amazing ability humans have to enjoy life, which is something that other beings aspire to. As that old expression says, "What are we doing this for at the end of the day?"'

'That is true. I would also like to say something,' a new voice interjected in a particularly sweet tone. 'AI and androids have been brought into the organisation and played a key role in the development of the Regime. It is only fair that we have the capacity to experience life fully. It is only by such experience we can understand the dilemmas faced by humans, and contribute in a meaningful way to a process like this interview.'

There followed a general interaction between the screens, after which the woman said brightly, 'As we expected, you have asked some very perceptive questions that have provoked great discussion on the panel. Is there anything else before we move on to the next phase?'

'What are the Regime's political intentions when it comes to Ireland?' Devlin's response was plainly put.

'There are no pre-set intentions,' the Irishman fielded this one very definitely. 'The beauty of its culture is now recognised and its ongoing survival is desired, but the violent political history of the nation will not be repeated. This needs to be clearly understood. The proposed political structures are a way of keeping control while allowing a level of autonomy that this distinct society seems to need. That is all that can be said at this time. It is the first province of Ireland where this will be tried, so it will be watched closely.'

This sparked another prolonged bout of murmuring between the screens before the woman spoke again.

'The process has reached its conclusion,' she announced.

'We are prepared to offer you this prominent position within the coordination arm of a new political structure in Connaught. The exact role will be defined after initial negotiations and the setting up of the political structures required. Do you accept?'

Devlin made a point of looking towards each monitor in turn and then at the screen, before answering definitively, 'I accept.'

'Congratulations, Mr Devlin,' the man with the sharp voice said. 'We will now zone out and leave you to your mentor, Don. He will set out the details of what happens next.'

'Congratulations, Devlin,' Don said cheerily, reappearing on the main screen. 'I was sure you would succeed.'

'Thank you, Don, but it remains to be seen if I'll have success or not.'

'I have to inform you of your arrangements, but first there is some other business. You messaged earlier about a potential plot in the Village. I need to clarify some points. Do you know the name of the man who spoke to you at the Dublin dockside? Who was the man he met at the port when he arrived?'

'I'm not really sure; he is someone from my childhood, who was not from our area, who I didn't recognise – it was him who claimed to recognise me. And I don't know his name. He introduced himself as Paul, but there is a good chance that isn't his name, as I would imagine he would have wanted to conceal his identity. I am sorry it's all a bit confusing, but it was an encounter that came right out of the blue. The man he met at the port was particularly inconspicuous, being of medium height, with dark hair, I think, and wearing an informal dark jacket. I'm sorry, I only got a brief glimpse of him when I was moving across the concourse.'

'And what did the man at the dockside in Dublin say to you?'

'He spoke in an allegorical way about the Christians and the lions and said he was meaning to come to the Village. He mentioned a special date, which coincides with a football match at the Colosseum this Saturday. I initially thought he was just talking nonsense, but then after the disturbances last night, I decided it would be best to report it.'

'Did you speak to him on board the Connaught Princess?'

'No.'

'You were in the Rainbow last night. Did you see anything else?'

'No, nothing. I was laying low, just staying out of the way and listening to the music. When I left, it looked like there had been a disturbance outside, but I did not know what that was about.'

'So, that is all you know relevant to this matter?' Don asked, speaking very slowly.

'It is. I put what I could accurately recall in the report,' Devlin said, gazing steadily at his mentor.

'This information will be passed on, but as I understand it, the organisation was aware of this threat and it has been dealt with. Thank you. Now, you are to be immediately transitioned into your new role. If you go back to your flat and pack your personal belongings, a vehicle will call at twenty-one hundred hours to take you to a secure hotel. The rest of your belongings will go into storage for the time being and you will be able to access them later. The receptionist at your apartments is aware of the arrangements, so you can liaise with him. We will contact the company you have been working with to inform them of your change in role. Your flat will remain vacant for now. I'm sure the Allotments Association will make arrangements for someone to maintain your plot.'

'I must admit, I am surprised by the speed of all this. Is it absolutely necessary?'

'You will be based in Ireland. The reason you are being moved straightaway into secure accommodation is because of the political sensitivity. There is a strong possibility of you becoming a target.'

'I understand,' Devlin said in a resigned tone.

'There is one last thing, Devlin. I have enjoyed being your mentor once again, but you are moving into a job which is more political in its nature, so therefore you will be working with both the Geo-Part and the Ascension Party. As a result of this, your supervision arrangements will change. You will liaise with Boyle. He will contact you at the hotel.'

'Oh, that's a shame. I was looking forward to resuming our regular one-to-ones. I'd hoped that you would still be involved.'

'Yes, I would have liked that also, if it's not too human a thing to say,' Don said, smiling sadly at his own remark. 'Still, I hope all goes well in this new initiative and I will be watching your progress with interest. Transport has been arranged to take you home directly from here.'

Devlin had been quite compliant so far, seeing the sense in what was being proposed, but at this point he said defiantly, 'I'll be fine cycling.'

'Are you sure?' Don frowned. 'If so, I propose that you go straight home. There is no point in any unnecessary interactions at this point, as this could put you in a difficult or even dangerous position.'

'I am hearing you loud and clear, Don. But I will be fine cycling.'

Leaving the now-familiar interview space, Devlin retraced his route through the building and, stopping besides the painting entitled the *Ainspiorad Glór na Maidine* (*The Devil's Morning Glory*), he recognised the symbolic importance of this wonderful image of the west of Ireland being set in the heart of Rawlins. After briefly acknowledging this, he marched towards the reception, where Smith sat up expectantly and said, 'Good afternoon. I hope everything is well with you.'

Knowing there was nothing that he needed to say, Devlin smiled at the invigilator and carried on into the street. He was glad to see that rain had stopped, so he wouldn't need to take the wet cape out of his rucksack. If you were to watch the relaxed cyclist mount his bike and whistle a tune as he rode away, you would be left in no doubt that he had a plan for the day and knew where he was going. This was indeed the case, as he felt a swell of pure pleasure at the thought of going back to Ireland; the fact that many difficult issues would need to be faced up to as a result of that return was something he was prepared to deal with in the days ahead.

A drone seemed to be following his progress out of the Business District and he felt a reassurance in this, as it meant things were happening in the way he would have expected. By the time he had reached the Village, the rain was starting to fall incessantly again and he felt the dampness seeping through his tweed jacket. The drone seemed to have lost interest in him by this point. He entered the Leanings and surged on through the familiar twisting lanes, and when he neared the Rainbow he was surprised to see Quinn standing in the doorway, regarding his approach.

'Well, you look like a man whose thrown caution to the wind,' Quinn remarked as Devlin pulled up.

'Oh no, nothing so dramatic,' Devlin said, sweeping water off the arm of his jacket, 'though I may have some travelling to do.'

'So I can't tempt you with some good music or fine stout?' The publican's eyebrow raised in expectation.

'No, not tonight, but there'll be other days, my friend. Oh, and have you seen Niall?'

'No, I've not seen him. Anyway, travel well, Devlin, and good luck.'

'Good luck,' Devlin responded, moving off once again.

He was watching the windows of the small terraced houses as he rode along and, reaching the next to last one, he saw a small postcard of Dublin subtly displayed behind the glass. The door was ajar and he could plainly hear the refrain of an old street song being played:

Alive, alive-oh,
Alive, alive-oh,
Crying cockles and mussels,
Alive, alive-oh…

The rain became heavier still and as he was already wet to the skin, there was no point in stopping to put waterproofs on. Meanwhile, the refrain of the song had become lodged in his mind and he found he was singing the words in time to the rhythm of his pedalling. He passed the allotments, which were deserted due to the downpour, and as he arrived at his apartment block, the receptionist stood up with a sharp intake of breath.

'You are drenched,' he said, alarm in his voice. 'Is there anything I can do?'

'Try not to worry yourself,' Devlin said and, amused by his concern, he ran his hand through his wavy hair, causing a shower of water droplets. 'I will not melt. I am sorry about bringing the weather in with me.'

'Oh, don't worry about that. I'll have it wiped up in a minute. Now, you go upstairs and get your packing done.'

'Thanks,' Devlin said, striding towards the lift, 'I will call down if I need anything.'

'I am aware of your departure arrangements and have put some packaging products outside your flat. If there is anything else you need, please let me know.'

'Don't worry, Number One, I will.'

He found a stack of collapsed boxes next to the door of his flat, which he took inside with him. He then showered, dressed and set about packing his possessions for storage. Using all of the boxes provided, he became totally immersed in the task and was surprised when he eventually looked at his device and saw it would soon be time to go. Moving to the work room and turning on the old machine, there was a confirmation of his new assignment, as well as a message from Don saying that he hoped all went well. Next, he made a sandwich and threw out the few stale bits of food that were left in the fridge and cupboards. He was just finishing washing down the kitchen area when the call came from reception to remind him that his transport was due in ten minutes.

'I will be down shortly,' he said, wringing out the dishcloth.

Going through each room of the flat, he re-checked their contents and confirmed that everything was in order, before going into the bedroom and completing his packing by placing the carefully folded jumper, which contained a branch, in the top of his old leather suitcase, clicking it shut and then placing it by the door. Now ready to go, he walked over to the window for a last look at the familiar panorama of the city and happened to spot his copy of Dante's *Divine Comedy* behind the chair. The image of the taut figure in a foetal position caught his attention, as he thought about how the strange story of pilgrimage seemed much more relevant to him now than it had when he was struggling through the early chapters. Picking up the book and placing it firmly on the table, he felt certain that this was not the last he would hear of this ancient tale.

Leaving the flat with his wet tweed jacket in one hand and his suitcase in the other, he slammed the door shut behind him and, on the way down in the lift, listened to the sound of the mechanism that he had become so accustomed to hearing.

'Well, that's the way life is, my old war horse,' he said cheerily. 'One moment you're up and the next you're coming down. You never know what's going to happen next.'

He thanked the receptionist warmly on the way out. Devlin then boarded the waiting vehicle, which was parked directly outside the building, and took the first seat he came to, as a formal voice informed him that it would be twenty-five minutes before they reached their destination so perhaps he should take the opportunity to relax. The shuttle set off immediately and he settled back, closing his eyes, maintaining that position for the duration of the journey.

Arriving at the hotel, the shuttle announcer said that his room number was fourteen-thirteen and he should take the far entrance, which was exclusively for Regime business representatives. Devlin gave his thanks and without looking back, picked up his suitcase and stepped onto the street, where he was immediately struck by the liveliness of the crowds thronging the pavement. They were manifestly in a high state of excitement, with many calling boisterously to one another and many singing. He allowed himself to be drawn along in the general flow and as he entered the grand foyer, the scene and atmosphere reminded him of the lounge bar on board the Connaught Princess. The group he had come in with drifted over towards the area where tinsel streamers hung from the chandeliers and drinks were being served, while he split off and approached the reception desk and gave his name and room number to the two on-duty staff members, who wore black blazers with a blue trim.

'Why, Mr Devlin, you've come in through the wrong entrance,' one of the men behind the desk informed him in a sing-song voice.

'Oh, now, Mr Green, it's an easy mistake to make,' his colleague joined in jovially.

'Indeed it is, Mr Walsh. It could happen to anyone if they were to be swept along with the crowd.'

'You're very right there, it's easy to get swept along with the crowd.'

Devlin smiled at the repartee between the two men.

'Now, if you take that doorway,' Green pointed to an exit on the far side of the room, 'it leads directly to the business reception area. It will save you going out into the street again. We don't want you going out of your way.'

'No, it's more than our job's worth, letting people go out of their way.'

'You're right, Mr Walsh. We don't want Mr Devlin going too far out of his way.'

Leaving the two men chuckling in cahoots with each other, Devlin headed for the exit. Pausing when he reached the doorway, he looked back at a catering crew that had just entered the foyer, dressed all in black. The military precision of their movements caught his attention and as he inspected their line, his gaze stopped at the last one, whose features bore a striking resemblance to someone he'd seen occasionally with Niall in the Rainbow.

After one more glance across the scene of social merriment, he pushed open the door and walked decisively into the business reception area.

CHAPTER EIGHTEEN

'It's so good to see you, Mr Devlin,' a receptionist with short dark hair and a bright smile greeted him. 'Your room is fourteen-thirteen. For your information, all floors above the twelfth are reserved for Regime members on official business, while the lower ones are used by patrons for recreational and leisure purposes. I have a message to say that Mr Boyle will meet you at your room shortly and I think that's everything... Oh, do you need a hand with that rather large case?'

'No, I'll be fine,' Devlin smiled, nodding slowly. 'Thank you.'

He entered the lift, which was of a very contemporary design and very spacious, particularly compared to the cramped and noisy one in his block of flats. Ascending to the fourteenth floor, he made his way to his room and was immediately attracted to the view out of the window, with the dark, rolling river flowing below and on the opposite bank, the old Parliament Buildings. It was a perspective of the city that was unfamiliar to him and he stood for many minutes taking in the nuances of the scene.

He had not contacted the home place since the interview and decided now was a perfect opportunity to make the call, so he sat on the bed and entered the number into his device. His mother answered and there followed a lovely exchange, during which he informed her briefly about the job and thus his imminent return to Ireland. His mother was delighted and excitedly relayed the information to his sister and Gráinne, who happened to be visiting.

'We have been listening to some of Dad's old recordings this evening,' Miriam came on the line in high spirits, 'and it's been great craic. It was the mad artist's idea. Do you want a word with her? I'd say she's not too bad an addition to the neighbourhood.'

'That would be great,' Devlin spoke warmly.

A good few moments elapsed and he could hear the familiar old song *Of Connaught Shores* playing in the background. He found the lyrics strangely poignant:

I'm restless now and sleep it is not coming,

My thoughts rest on those distant Connaught shores.

If I could return – but now I know that I am dreaming,

Destined to wander, here forevermore...

'Well, that's a fine song to be playing when an old man rings home from a distant shore,' Gráinne said brightly. 'I'm wondering if you are still a dreamer, Devlin.'

'You can be sure of that,' he said, picking up on her chirpy mood. 'I hope you're settling into the majestic Clancy's cottage.'

'It's majestic enough for me, for sure. Miriam has been a great help in getting me settled in and John has taken me under his wing. Not to mention, I get the best tea in Mullnamorran from Mrs D... I believe you could be heading back in this direction and everything has been going so well here, too.'

'Aren't all you artists supposed to be tortured anyway?' Devlin responded to her off-handed remark and continued by saying humorously, 'You seem far too happy altogether to me.'

The call ended with Devlin saying goodbye to everyone and then he allowed himself a few quiet moments to reflect on how well things were working out at the home place.

He was just taking his wash bag out of the suitcase when a rhythmic knocking sounded and when Devlin opened the door, there stood a smartly dressed man, who was smiling widely and carrying a bottle in one hand and two glasses in the other.

'Good to meet you,' he said with a flourish as he walked into the room, needing no invitation. His dark hair was tinged with grey. 'It's Boyle here and I thought you could maybe do with a little spiritual sustenance at this stage.'

Devlin was very pleasantly surprised by the manner of his appearance, in particular by the gifts he was bearing, and he gestured to a small table near the window.

'You're as welcome as the flowers in May,' Devlin said jauntily, 'especially when you bring such a fine Irish whiskey.'

The two men sat down on either side of the table and after pouring two generous measures, Boyle raised his glass.

'Sláinte,' he toasted. 'I do enjoy drinking with a man who appreciates a good whiskey.'

'You can be sure of that,' Devlin returned the gesture. 'Well, fair play to you, Boyle. That was quite some entrance.'

'It would be fair to say that I am likely to be a very different mentor to Don. A different animal altogether, you might say. By the way, this room is clear of surveillance, a new initiative for accommodation used by higher-level operatives – the rationale being that it promotes greater trust all round.' He laughed and took a swig of his drink. 'I watched your interviews and I must say, I liked your questions. Yes, you managed to wring as much information out of the situation as you could. That's a talent alright. I'm looking forward to working with you.'

Devlin, who had been weighing up his drinking partner, smiled broadly at this.

'We should get on famously,' he said, 'if this initial encounter is anything to go by. Do I detect a Kerry accent?'

'You do indeed,' Boyle confirmed, appreciating the observation, before his voice suddenly took on a more serious tone. 'I need to level with you, Devlin. I was given permission to have a short one-on-one with you ahead of the inaugural board meeting, which will take place in an hour's time. Because of the political sensitivity, it was decided that a bona fide human who understands the subtleties of the Irish situation would be a better option for mentoring you. My own interest in the Irish situation has never waned and as I am a realist when it comes to the role of the Regime, I was seen as an ideal candidate. The Higher Command Board are understandably very cautious about this piece of work, as it is the first time they have entered into a process that could lead to greater autonomy for a region. It is an unfamiliar direction of travel for them, should we say. Therefore, they want to be informed every step of the way and, more importantly, to fully understand the process. They will no doubt be all over us like a rash, but there's one great consolation – won't I be right by your side.'

Both men drained their glasses and Boyle immediately moved to refill them.

'It could be said that a part of your role will be keeping an eye on me,' Devlin spoke softly, 'which I would totally understand, but from the way you are talking, it sounds like you are also planning to be proactive in the job yourself.'

'Indeed, I will keep a watchful eye on you,' Boyle admitted, 'but as you are accountable to the board, you will therefore be feeding back to them about me, too. So, we will both be under severe scrutiny, my friend. I am also impressed that you picked up on my role, including the option of becoming involved directly in the work myself. That will become clearer when the working party is operational, but we shall come to that later. It's what we have both signed up for and a greater level of autonomy for the west of Ireland is well worth the hair shirt that both of us are going to have to wear.'

'I will wear that hair shirt willingly, Boyle,' Devlin said resolutely, 'if it takes our people forward.'

'Why, if we succeed in Connaught, we may move down to Munster province and Kerry. Now, there's a thought that gladdens my heart.' Boyle paused, looking intently at Devlin before carrying on in a more subdued tone. 'However, there is always the danger of sudden, destabilising revolutionary activity – the kind that some of our people have always had a penchant for – so we must beware. Your nationalistic contacts in the Village and at home are known, Devlin, but good enough, you informed us of that one particular threat. There will be others for sure, though.'

'Were you aware of that particular threat before I submitted the information?'

'I am not avoiding the question when I say that I don't know. The Counter-Intelligence Department dealt with it and because of the compartmentalised nature of the organisation, I wasn't informed. In any case, they are watching subversive activity all the time. In fact, the Regime realised that the CID is an ideal training ground for their top operatives, as the work requires a high level of understanding of complex situations, a great resourcefulness and, of course, the ability to be ruthless.'

'Why, from what you're saying, you must have been trained there yourself,' Devlin said playfully.

'There's a big "no comment" on that, for now at least – but there you go again, Devlin, always trying to extract that extra bit of information. It can be a dangerous pastime.'

'Oh come now, Boyle, you're not suggesting I should rein in my curiosity, are you?'

'Sometimes it can be a wise move. Also, you need to limit your contact with people who are known to be pursuing a rebel agenda, including your family. I shouldn't need to spell this out, but if either you or I were to be caught passing on sensitive information to these people, then the work would be doomed. It's a high wire we're going to be walking, my friend, and a long way down.'

'It is indeed. It's a good job I don't have acrophobia.'

'I really do believe that our compatriots issuing the tired cry of freedom have outlived their usefulness.' Boyle cradled his drink. 'This endless arm-wrestle between the factions and the conflicting ideologies, the unending threat of violence and the impending chaos that we've seen so often before – the recipe always ends up too toxic. There are different days coming, though, and we have the opportunity to make them better ones.'

'It is ironic that we are so close to those old buildings,' Devlin glanced out of the window at Parliament, 'which, for most of our people, symbolise centuries of oppression. I know there is truth in what you say, but our people have never been cowed for long and the Celtic spirit will endure beyond any days that we can visualise.'

'You're right in what you're saying, Devlin, and that is why you can afford to tread easily, my friend. Maybe we will be judged by history as playing the longer game – and besides, we both know that any violent action will be effortlessly crushed.'

'There is a good level of understanding here, Boyle, but while we have the bottle open and an empty room, let me be clear. You have spoken of the longer game, but I will extract as much as I can for my people from the coming situations. With all due respect to the Regime, they headhunted me for this role knowing my autonomous leanings and my family connections, all this was in plain sight – so we're all going forward with our eyes wide open.'

'Then we have an understanding of each other but I, too, must be clear. If in your striving you covertly involve forces that are outside this project, I will bring you down. I know exactly where I stand on that front.' Boyle drained his glass again and, smiling widely, said, 'That said, I am truly looking forward to the days ahead. We have an unparalleled opportunity and having now come to grips with each other for the first time, I am confident we can take it forward. If you come to the Celtic Retreat, located in the Turquoise Lounge, in half an hour, a bit more flesh will be put on the bones. I shall leave the whiskey with you. No doubt you will find some use for it.'

'I will for sure,' Devlin replied, raising his glass once more. 'I hope all our sessions will be accompanied by such a fine spirit.'

'If only,' Boyle said over his shoulder, laughing on his way out of the room.

After the door had closed, Devlin felt a curious mix of

emotions as he reflected on his first meeting with his new mentor – if mentor was what he was, as he realised that the closeness of this relationship and the Regime's great interest in the project pointed to exceedingly intense days ahead. He felt that the metaphor of a hair shirt might prove to be very accurate.

He went into the bathroom and, after checking that his head wound was sufficiently healed, he extracted Miriam's stitches and said wryly to his reflection, 'Here's looking at you, sis.' He then had a long shower, luxuriating in both the pressure and heat of the water's flow. When he was drying off, Devlin smiled to himself, as he found he was gently singing *Of Connaught Shores*. Dressing quickly, he poured a large glass of water and went over to the window, where the darkness and power of the old river in the moonlight really struck him, as did the ornate fragility of the Parliament buildings. An old man in a wheelchair was being pushed along the riverbank by a younger woman who could have been his daughter, and as she pointed across the river in movements that were vital and energetic, her flowing blonde hair was highlighted by the moonlight. The old man appeared to be nodding his head in agreement with whatever she was saying and after watching them for a few more minutes, Devlin finished his water and left the room ready for his meeting in the Turquoise Lounge.

As he walked down the corridor, the lift doors opened and a woman in a bright yellow cocktail dress stepped out with her black sling back shoes casually dangling from her right hand. She locked eyes with Devlin and after a slight hesitation said, 'Well, fancy meeting you here.'

Stopping mid-stride, he regarded her tastefully made-up facial features and sharp green eyes for a few seconds and then the realisation dawned that this was Elenora.

'I am sorry for not recognising you at first,' he said, 'but you look so different from the last time I saw you.'

'We do manage to have some fun here sometimes,' she

replied, moving a step closer to him. 'I think it's a good thing, don't you?'

'It's a good idea, I'm sure. I have to thank you once again for guiding me through the screened intelligence that time.'

'I always seem to be helping people, but I found helping you and your mother particularly pleasurable.'

She looked at him for a few seconds, during which time her pleased expression did not alter.

'Anyway, it is great to see you,' he said, 'but I do have a meeting scheduled in the Turquoise Lounge and I'm due there shortly.'

'That's good. I am going that way also, so as you have just arrived, I can show you the way.'

Devlin did not comment on her knowledge of his whereabouts as she placed her hand on his arm for balance and, leaning her fine blonde hair close, slipped on her shoes.

'I am in the pool of experienced operatives that the organisation maintains on standby,' she said confidingly as they started walking. 'I have heard about the project in Ireland and it sounds really interesting. I am sure you will be hiring soon and I would like to be considered.'

'You are slightly ahead of me there, Elenora,' Devlin said, as they arrived at their destination. 'I don't know how things will work just yet, but when the project is set up and ready to go, I am sure you will be considered.'

She gazed up at him and he seemed to be drawn into her eyes, where an image of them slowly embracing moved fleetingly, like a flickering candle flame. He was momentarily transfixed by this apparition that she had been able to conjure up between them and she gave him a knowing smile.

'Well, there you are – we are here,' she said, gesturing towards the *Turquoise Lounge* sign on the doorway. 'I hope your meeting goes well.'

'Thank you,' he said, recovering himself. 'You seem to specialise in coming to my rescue.'

Not responding, she watched as he opened the door, obviously not intending to accompany him into the lounge. Devlin thought momentarily about the different personas of Elenora he'd encountered, logging the details of this latest meeting in his mind, knowing it was something he would reflect on at some later date.

He entered a very large area, where the main illuminations had a strong turquoise tint hovering above multiple areas, where various groups of individuals gathered around tables. The brilliant lighting of these individual spaces impressed him, as did the fact that, as far as he could see, different activities were happening in each one. Walking forward, he focused his attention on a green vase table where a card game was in progress. Standing beside the man who had just dealt the cards, he was fascinated by how the game was being played in total silence; the surrounding activities not impinging in any way on the players. On the far side of the table, Chilton gave him a flinty grin, picking up his hand, and the two men exchanged a lengthy look before his old colleague placed his cards down slowly and, forming his right hand into the shape of a gun, pointed across the room. Looking in the direction indicated, Devlin saw a sign for the Celtic Retreat and turning to walk towards it, he heard Chilton call after him, 'Don't forget that you owe me one, my old rebel friend.'

Devlin turned to reply but the card players had re-immersed themselves in their game and he took that as his cue to walk briskly across the floor and into the Celtic Retreat, which had no door as such, but rather an opening that led into a passageway. As he progressed, he could feel a cool breeze upon his face and a fragrance in his nostrils and he realised that he was entering a garden. Looking around him, he saw large trees, flowers in bloom and a cultivated lawn bathed in moonlight. Ahead of him, set up on the grass, was a table with two chairs, one of which was occupied by Boyle.

'Well, you managed to find your way here.' His mentor stood to greet him. 'Please, take a seat.'

The two men sat down and Devlin noticed a large screen situated on the other side of the immaculate lawn.

'It's a very impressive setting,' he said, 'and I am more than a little interested to see what will happen next.'

'I'm sure you won't be disappointed,' Boyle said. 'There has been a lot of work done in recent years with set locations and image transfers and obviously, the innovations around screen intelligence have pushed this on tremendously. I believe you have had some experience of these technologies recently at the Rawlins.'

'I have indeed.'

'Well, what has been discovered is that apart from making experiences more pleasurable, these advancements have also changed the bounds of consciousness. There will be plenty of time to explore all that stuff later, though. I only mention it now because it is the means by which the next part of our journey will be facilitated.'

The screen came to life and a man whose sharp, piping voice Devlin recognised from his interview spoke. 'Welcome to you, Boyle and Devlin,' he said. 'Welcome to the start of this journey, which we hope will be a fruitful one for us all. My name is Sage and I shall introduce you to my colleagues on the board in due course. We are aware it has been a long day for you, so we intend to keep this session short.'

Thumbnail images bearing different symbols appeared on the outer edges of the screen. The one in the top left, which had an owl on a green background, started pulsing and Devlin realised that this green was actually the colour sage.

'Ah, that is very good, Devlin,' Sage said. 'You are quick to pick up on things. You will probably realise that Boyle is aware of what is going to happen and this short session is very much for your benefit. I will take the lead for this evening and there will be fuller introductions at the next stage. That is when you will get to meet the various members of this board, who all witnessed your interview.' There were murmurings of approval from the screen, before he cleared his throat and continued in a more powerful voice. 'I have to say, I am looking forward to working on these new governance structures in Connaught. Boyle and Devlin, I am sure you will be excellent facilitators, as you are both certainly custodians of this intriguing Celtic culture and your specialist knowledge will help us all to understand its intricacies. There is a recognition of the spontaneous and creative abilities you will bring to the table, if that is the correct phrase?'

'"Bring to the table" is exactly the right phrase to use,' Boyle answered approvingly.

'There are members of this board who have not had the chance to work directly with such creative human facilitators such as yourselves,' Sage went on, 'and they are looking forward to that opportunity. It feels like we're starting off on a great adventure together and this board will be part of your progress, as in addition to our supervisory capacity, we will be an excellent and diverse resource to you both. We will also be part of the political structures that will ultimately be put in place. Now, after that brief introduction, we come to the point where your main work location will be revealed. It is a place you will be entering in reality soon enough and if I may use an Irish expression, *good luck*.'

The thumbnail symbols pulsed and there was a rippling noise as, having been blurred up until this point, the main part of the screen came into focus, showing a large room with a long table, dresser and sideboards. Kneeling by an impressive open fireplace was a man wearing a long apron over a country shirt and tweed trousers, lighting a stack of kindling. The flames seemed to catch straightaway and getting to his feet, he turned around and looked directly at them, clearly expecting them to be there.

'Good evening,' he said a genial smile on his aged features as he wiped his hands on the long, dark apron, 'my name is Eamon and may I welcome you to Mullross Lodge. I am very happy to say that this will be your base and the venue where many of your meetings and negotiations will take place – a fine old place that has been recently renovated to great effect, as you will see. I understand that this is not that far from your home of Mullnamorran, Mr Devlin, so I am hoping you will feel particularly settled here. I am sure that the lodge will be perfect for your purposes, with its rugged country feel, excellent food and, of course, superb security features, being set within dense woodlands. Besides these practical aspects, the Lodge has access to some wonderful beaches and we have leisure craft ready to explore the spectacular Atlantic coastline. So all in all, I would say we are rightly proud of what we can offer.'

Eamon had been undoing his apron strings while speaking, then, after pausing to slip it off, he continued. 'A new era of Irish politics may well be born here, which I find to be a wonderful prospect, and if I may be so bold as to venture an opinion, the idea of it being conceived out here in the West, which many consider the spiritual home of Ireland, is a truly brilliant one. Anyway, you don't need my observations. Just be assured that the team and I will make sure all your needs are catered for, while I'm sure the great landscapes and skies of County Sligo will help provide ongoing inspiration, as an old song from these parts says: *"When the darkness falls and candles sway, when fireside embers fade and die, Sligo moon beams will show the way"*. Now, I must be getting on, but feel free to come and explore for yourselves.'

With that, Eamon looked slowly around the expansive lounge again and after checking that everything was in order, he walked out of the room.

'Shall we take a closer look?' Boyle asked. As Devlin turned to look at him he was struck by the youthfulness of his features. 'I've not been in yet myself. It must be a strange feeling for you, to be so close to home. Do you remember this place from your childhood?'

'It was somewhere that we never got close to, back then,' Devlin spoke distractedly, as he was recalling sightings of the lodge long ago and the strange feelings that it had evoked. 'Hidden away in the woods and with guard dogs, as I remember. We made up bizarre stories about the people who might have lived here. As children do.' He paused before asking, 'So, do I just focus on the left-hand side of the screen, then?'

'You do indeed. I'll see you there,' Boyle said brightly.

Repeating the same procedure as when he'd entered his mother's garden from the Rawlins, Devlin appeared in the lounge of Mullross Lodge. After taking a moment to feel the pleasing effect of gravity when materialising, he walked the length of the room and back, taking note of the many items of grand oak furniture and the two rustic chandeliers, illuminated by candles. It was not the type of venue he was attracted to, but its proximity to the home place definitely felt an advantage. As he approached the bay window, he became aware that they were on the first floor of the building, with far reaching views of the surrounding countryside, magically lit by a full moon shining brightly over the Atlantic. He also noted a path leading through the woods that meandered on until it reached a steep hill, where he thought he saw the figure of a fox, staring with an otherworldly gaze back at the lodge, but before he could focus accurately on the animal it had bolted out of sight and when he considered it's retreating movements, he realised that it was more likely to have been a dog. Devlin did not dwell on this strange sighting, but found himself beginning to warm to the situation.

It was a good five minutes before Boyle made his appearance.

'I'm sorry about that,' his mentor apologised. 'Sage had some other matters he wanted to discuss – but don't worry, they were unrelated to our work.'

Devlin did not respond as he was captivated by the nocturnal landscape, being particularly pleased by such a good sighting of the Crying Cliffs by moonlight, even though they were a good distance away to the south.

'I sensed that you were not exactly enamoured by this choice of venue and in particular its location,' Boyle said, joining him at the window. 'And I am aware that there are locals who won't exactly be putting out the flags of welcome, but you should know that there was no intention to cause you any discomfort. All things considered, I'd say it's a great option that will more than meet our needs.'

'Listen, I don't suppose we'd win a popularity contest in any part of Ireland at the moment,' Devlin responded, continuing in a way that was both amiable and considered, 'but maybe that will change. We shall see. This lodge is set in a part of the country that you could not stumble across by chance, so if remoteness was a crucial factor, you couldn't have picked a much better spot. And I have to admit, the whole idea and setting is growing on me.'

'Well, I do have a really good feeling about this place, Devlin, and in particular the venture we are about to embark on. The view out there is tremendous and that's only by night. It must be some sight when the sun is shining.'

'It truly is and you will be able to see it all for yourself soon enough. And I'm sure these momentous days ahead will be anything but boring.'

Up to this point, Devlin had been fully engaged in the conversation with his colleague, but his attention was beginning to waver, as he had just spotted the darkness of the caves at the base of the Crying Cliffs.

'There could be some great days ahead, Devlin, if we play our cards right,' Boyle said enthusiastically. 'And looking out at this scene – and I can't believe I'm saying this as a Kerry man – I'm really drawn to this country.'

Gazing into the distant shadowy caves, a primary instinct was stirring within Devlin and he felt the familiar pull.

'Why wouldn't you be drawn, Boyle?' he said, his blue eyes burning fervently. 'Why wouldn't you be drawn?'

BIBLIOGRAPHY AND ACKNOWLEDGEMENTS

The ancient story that Ceridwen relates on page 55 is taken from *The Mabinogion*, a book compiled in Middle Welsh in the 12th–13th centuries, taken from earlier oral traditions.

The lyrics of *The Rising of the Moon* on page 137 were written by John Keegan Casey (1846–70) and included in a collection of his songs and poems in 1866, *A Wreath of Shamrocks*. The melody was taken from an earlier ballad called *The Wearing of the Green*.

The lyrics of *Boolavogue*, which feature on page 138, were written by Patrick Joseph McCall in 1898. He set them to the air of an older tune, *Eocaill (Youghal Habour)*.

The lyrics of *Alive, alive–oh*, which feature on page 190, were taken from the song *Molly Malone*. This is believed to be a Dublin street song and there have been many versions published and recorded over the years.

All other poetry, prayers and song lyrics that feature in this book were written by Ray Rooney.